Driven to the borders of an unfamiliar forest by an ever-expanding drought, two rival brothers find their fortunes and that of their tribe entwined in a long-forgotten conflict between the old gods of the world. Clay's fervent belief in devotion to the gods does nothing to prepare him for their true natures, while Laughing Dog's self-assured insistence that his destiny is his own leads him on a very different journey. As battle lines are drawn, each brother must decide where his allegiance truly lies—a decision that will change each of them forever.

GOD OF CLAY

THE FIRE BEARERS:
BOOK ONE

by Ryan Campbell

SOFAWOLF

SAINT PAUL, MN

This book is a work of fiction. The characters, incidents, and dialogue are drawn from the authors' imaginations and are not to be construed as real. Any resemblance to actual events, persons or Gods, living or dead, is entirely coincidental.

God of Clay

Printed in the United States of America

Second Edition: First POD Printing, October 2021

ISBN 978-1-936689-31-6

Sofawolf Press, Inc.
PO Box 11868
Saint Paul, MN 55111-0868
www.sofawolf.com

Cover and Interior art Copyright © 2013 by Zhivago

CHAPTERS & ILLUSTRATIONS

This book is for my husband,
and the love of stories that brought us together.

Acknowledgements

My thanks go out to:

My readers: Matthew Charles, Kevin Frane, Kevin Kane, Watts Martin, Trendane Sparks, and Tim Susman. Without them, this book would not exist.

The editors at Sofawolf who took a chance on my story and the thorough work they did to help turn it into a polished book.

My artist, Zhivago, who was patient through every nitpick, suggestion, correction, and complete change of mind as she spun purely imagined concepts into visual works of art.

Most of all, thanks to my husband, David, who put up with me dragging him out on long walks to rant about all the story problems, and who has been a constant source of loving support through the whole process. His unwavering belief in me is something I will spend a lifetime laboring to deserve.

—Ryan

Black Clouds

Doto crouched in the forest, his clawed fingers pressing down beneath the grasses and bed of fallen leaves to touch the earth below. He went out, out, into the soil, into the trunks of the trees, the branches and leaves, the grasses and ferns. He felt the air swaying branches, the sunlight on the leaves. He felt rodents skittering across the forest floor. He felt the air thrum under millions of beating insect wings. He wormed through the earth and crawled under bark. He leapt from branch to branch and winged over the canopy. He spread himself out, farther and farther. Through the keen eyes of the birds and the considering gaze of a monkey clinging to a branch above, he could see himself, crouched on the ground far below, so still that he was nearly undetectable. The sun shafts floated across his rosettes, making his spotted frame melt into the patterns of leaves and earth.

He breathed the breeze. He dug his fingers deeper into the earth, and the trees stretched their roots outward. All the surrounding life lived through him. But all was not right. There was an uneasiness in the forest, somewhere around the edges. Could great Atekye have risen herself up in the south of the forest, swelling her swamps to flood the forest floor once again? No, he thought. That was too far away for him to sense. And the uneasiness felt as though it were coming from the north. He had not felt the forest respond like this before. The signs were subtle, but pressing: trees and stems felt tense, stiff against the tug of the wind. Blossoms folded inward, and the lianas that climbed to the canopy gripped their branches more tightly. The forest was uneasy.

His fur prickled with the confirmation of what he had been noticing for some time. He ought to hear cicadas croaking their mating calls, drowning out the crickets in the grass, but they were quieter than usual. Birds sang territorial cries, betraying their discomfort, warning the rest of the forest to keep away from their nests and thickets. Baboons screamed their claim of the entire forest in hostile, challenging shrieks.

Doto withdrew his senses from the forest, lifted his fingers from the soil, brushed them lightly across the fronds of nearby ferns. Rather than curling gracefully around his touch, they simply bent aside like dead things. No, something was certainly wrong. And if something was wrong in the forest, that meant something would be wrong with Kwaee. Doto's heart sank. He had been hoping to convince his father to travel with him, to visit the mountains in the east, or the shores in the west. They had made such trips long ago, when Doto had been only a cub, and he longed for them again. But for a very long time now, Kwaee had kept himself shut away in his temple. Even on the best days, he could be irascible and mean-tempered. On the worst...Doto pulled his mind away from such thoughts. There would be no journey to the mountains.

Perhaps if he could determine the nature of the trouble in the forest, he could solve it. It would be no good asking his father: sitting in his temple with his ears and nose closed to the outside world, Kwaee was seldom aware of the happenings in the forest. Doto attended them for him, whether the problem was blight on the eastern ebonies or a drought in the north. These things could trouble Kwaee without him being aware of them, like an itch from a biting fly, and he could be unpleasant as long as they persisted. Resolving them was a matter of practicality as much as duty. If Doto were ever to have a chance of persuading his father to venture outside his temple, he would first need to resolve whatever disturbed him.

He stood again, breathing deeply, tasting the mid-afternoon. Here below the canopy, the air was hot and damp and still, and it smelled of all the usual things: earth, the recent passing of duikers, the scuttle of beetles around the rocks, the coming rain. He could smell the baboons even from this distance. There was something else on the wind, too, a trace scent, familiar and yet strange, too faint to place. It plucked at his memory.

Two grey parrots sidled along the branches above him. "Parrots," he said to them, looking up. They regarded him with impudent gazes. "The forest stirs. Kwaee does not sleep. Tell me what is wrong."

"What is wrong?" one parrot repeated, sounding incredulous. "What is wrong?" He turned to his mate. "What is wrong," he muttered.

Doto snorted. He ought to have known better than to ask a parrot. He let his senses flow outward again, through the roots of trees and along the hum of gnat wings. Everything was tense, but the trees and gnats provided no clues. When the forest was uneasy, Kwaee was uneasy, and when Kwaee was uneasy, the forest was uneasy. Trouble a god, and you troubled your whole world.

He twitched his ears backward toward the sounds of thousands of tiny feet moving over the loam. His fur lifted and stood on end with the familiar energy in the air that told him a god was nearby—a lesser god, perhaps, but a god nonetheless. Behind him, a parade of ants was approaching, winding their way around roots and fallen leaves, carrying assorted bits of food and earth. A very large ant led them, his head half as high as Doto's knee, and he walked upright, in the manner of the gods. He was munching a pear, his mandibles clicking in a rhythmic pattern. He wore an expression of deep focus, but looked up when Doto's shadow fell over him. "Brother Doto." He grinned between bites of fruit. He did not stop marching forward, nor did his subjects stop moving behind him.

"Good day, Brother Atetea," Doto said, dipping his head. "Where are you headed today?"

The god shrugged his four shoulders. "We are building a new palace," he said around his mouthful. "This one bigger than the last. There will be so much more room for our larders! Rooms upon rooms of sticky, tasty fruit. I would invite you to come inside, but as usual, you are so terribly oversized."

"Yes," Doto agreed. "I am." He considered. Atetea might be only god of ants, but there were ants throughout the forest. If they had noticed anything unusual, Atetea would know of it. "Tell me, Brother, have you noticed the stillness in the forest today?"

"Stillness?" Atetea led his train in spiraling patterns around Doto, maintaining the same vigilant march, keeping his followers always on the move. "It is busy as always for us. Much food to collect, more rooms to dig. One day our palace shall spread beneath the entire forest—the grandest you have ever seen!"

Doto shrugged. He did not understand Atetea's endless compulsion to dig and burrow. But a god guided the laws of nature, and so Atetea must lead the ants in their endless harvesting and tunneling. They carried away dead material and served as food for many creatures, and thus, in his way, Atetea served Kwaee. Though he never seemed to see it that way. "Yes, build your palace below the forest. And then Father Wem will send the rain and flood you out, and you will have to begin again."

"Not this time! No, this time we shall make our walls so strong that even water will not get in! It will be not just a palace, but a fortress, a mighty stronghold!" He thrust out his tiny, armored chest and sunk his mandibles deep into the pear once more, antennae bobbing up and down in ambitious optimism.

"If you collapse part of my forest, I will be annoyed with you," Doto advised him.

"Your forest?" Atetea regarded him with a beady gaze. "I thought it was Kwaee's forest."

"I will inherit it one day. It is as good as mine," Doto said stiffly. "And I care for it now. But there is something wrong, and it has Kwaee very upset."

"Upset? That would explain why he was surlier than usual. I saw him this morning." Atetea marched up one side of a tree, his train dutifully carrying their loads behind him. "He was very grouchy. Rude, even."

"Did he say why?"

"He wasn't very communicative. I don't think he actually knew what was bothering him. You know how he's been. Never goes looking any more. Perhaps you might take a look for him." His black eyes glittered. "Might please him a bit, hmm?"

"I think so," Doto said. "That's why I am trying to find out." He stood. "Thank you, Brother Atetea. Happy building."

"And good hunting to you, Brother Doto. Take care not to step on my subjects." Atetea buried his face into his pear once more, resuming his cadence toward, Doto assumed, one of the many portals to his underground realm.

So even Kwaee did not know what troubled the forest. Doto carefully stepped over the line of ants as it obediently followed the winding twists and spirals Atetea had wandered during their conversation. He followed the valley to a nearby hill. A treetop would at least give him a good view; perhaps he could see what was happening. He moved swiftly, darting back and forth among the trees, his feet making no sound in the grass as he traveled, and the forest bowed before him, stalks graciously bending aside so as not to trip him, roots of trees flattening into the soil, rocks reverently nudging themselves deep into the earth below his toes.

Awarenesses moved in and out of his own as he passed near them: the sharp, keen thoughts of birds, the tiny, confused whirls of insects, the purposeful, hungry patience of moles in the soil, the lazy readiness of snakes. They sensed him moving near them too, and paused in obeisance, careful to move out of his path.

At the top of the hill he found a tree suitable for climbing. It was tall and its branches were large, thick, and numerous, extending out far above the forest floor, some reaching higher and higher until they jutted up above the canopy. Its limbs were mossy, sprouting with smaller shrubs reaching urgently toward the blocked sunlight above. His claws slid out, and he sank them into the bark, feeling the comfortable, stretching tug against his fingers and toes as he climbed out onto one of the lower-hanging branches.

A thudding sound resonated through the ground, and he could feel the approaching awareness of something much larger than birds or moles. Elephants.

He crouched on the branch of the tree, gazing down at the dusky hides of the elephants as their herd approached from the east, their gaits slow and unworried. Whatever uneasiness was affecting the forest did not seem to be bothering them, but then, elephants tended not to pay attention to birds or baboons or the stiffness of plants. They trundled beneath him, tails snapping to brush away flies. His claws dug into the bark as the tree swayed, but his balance had always been excellent, and he had little fear of falling. Twelve cows and three calves. It was a large herd, their footsteps heavy. He held still, preferring they pass unaware of him. Elephants were impossible to get rid of once they'd taken an interest, and they took it quite easily, so he guarded his presence and stilled himself, letting what little sunlight filtered through the canopy play entrancingly across his rosettes. He became invisible.

He need not have made the effort. The herd was far too garrulous to notice him, yammering to each other about what some stupid bull had done this morning, and how muddy the water had been. Because they'd stirred it up themselves, most likely. Once they had passed, he stood upright again, sank claws into the trunk of the tree, and climbed higher. Eighty feet from the ground now, and still he could hear the elephant footsteps—but no, the sound was too regular, too fast. His ears twitched toward it. Gorillas beating, perhaps? He sniffed the air again. Here too, he could pick up that peculiar odor, a sour tickle in his nostrils.

He climbed higher, a hundred feet, a hundred and twenty. Near the top branches of the trees, he lifted his head and peered around, trying to catch the sound. It was clear, steady, regular, like his heartbeat, and yet far away.

The tree he had chosen was taller than most, and so he clung to its trunk and turned, peering out across the canopy. Outward the forest sprawled, far outward, more than a million steps in any direction but north. To the east it thickened and climbed into high, shaggy green mountains; to the south it sheltered the great river, Asubonten, and spread it out into vast swamps. Follow it to the western edge, and it met the sea. But to the north, not far away at all, the forest trailed out into the savanna, and it was from here that the sound thudded and rattled.

Above the canopy, the eagles soared in lazy, idyllic spirals, scanning the trees below for monkeys. He sank his claws more deeply into the tree trunk and called the forest to him, sending his sight upward, higher and higher, until he could gaze through the eagles' keen and hungry eyes. Through their vision the forest was clear and crisp, and movement blazed sharply. He turned their heads, commanded them to look north. Of course, the eagles would not obey him as well as they would his father, but for small tasks, they would be compliant. North there was indeed movement to catch his attention: a cloud, rising above the savanna. A black cloud. His fur stood on end. *Ogya.*

The scent in his nostrils, so faint that he could barely identify it, was so easy to place now, he could rake himself for not knowing it before: the foul reek of the blazing god, the scorch of lightning. Now, too, he recognized that regular thud and rattle, though he had never before heard it himself. It was the dread rhythm in the old tales his father used to tell, a knell from old and terrible histories: the Cry of the Dead. He tore his gaze from the eagles' eyes in abrupt fear. Across the northern sky seven eagles screamed simultaneously, folded their wings, and dropped, seven dark spots plummeting toward the canopy. They caught themselves before striking the trees, recovering from their disorientation and dizziness, broad wings unfolding. Even from here he could feel their resentment toward him. He regretted it, but he had no time to lose: he had to alert his father.

Pushing out from the top of the tree, Doto let himself fall toward the ground. He caught his weight on one branch, legs bunching, and leapt forward to grapple another, careful not to rend the bark with his claws too severely. He let himself fall the final eighty feet, landing lightly on all fours, a cloud of leaves rising around him. Then he ran. He ran like no mortal creature could, faster than the duiker or the okapi, faster than the eagles could fly, even faster than the leopards—honored with his shape and that of his father—could move. He bounded from rock to tree trunk to gully to hill, a golden blur moving through the forest, which bent aside to permit him, leaving no trace of his passing. The Cry of the Dead pulsed behind him, still sounding in his ears.

The forest was darkening by the time he reached Kwaee's temple, but still the crickets were quieter than normal, the night birds calling seldom. His father's house was huge and cavernous and green, a monstrous, mossy hollow in the forest, sheltered by trees that extended their heavy branches out farther than trees should, bending around the space Kwaee had made for himself. It was the heart of the jungle; not always where it was deepest, nor the farthest from the savanna, but always the heart. From here the forest's life pulsed outward to its furthest reaches. The air was thick and heavy with it, buzzing with potential. Doto always felt intoxicated here, drunk on the heady rush of power that surrounded his father. Here he dared not run, but set his feet down reverently between the fronds of ferns and sprouting mushrooms, stepping lightly down rocks that had grown shaggy with verdant mosses. Brooks ran down into the hollow and pooled in a pond at the center of the temple, dark and murky green, blooming with purple lilies. Above the pond was a massive moabi tree, the tallest in the entire forest, its limbs reaching high, spreading outward like the embracing arms of Mother Fam. This was Kwaee's throne, and in the gnarled crooks of its roots he sprawled, leaning back and to one side.

He was a large leopard, greater in size than Doto, and across his rosettes the sun played even at night, granting him its brilliance and yet leaving him—when he wished to be—unseeable. The end of his tail twitched in impatience. He had apparently been consuming a flamingo, one gnawed pink leg clutched between his clawed fingers, and he did not look pleased at all to see Doto. The brightly colored feathers that sprouted from his brow and temples were raised high and imperious.

Doto crouched at the foot of the moabi tree on all fours, like the animals. "Great Kwaee," he said.

"Yes," his father agreed. He did not look at Doto, but slouched lower in his throne. His voice was filled with weariness. "What is it you want,

Doto? I do not care to hear more of your incessant wheedling today. I have told you over and over, the forest cares for itself. A god does not meddle with the course of nature. He oversees it; he never becomes *involved* with it." He gave his meal a considering expression, and tore a bite away from it. Doto looked up, and just as he was about to speak, Kwaee continued, talking through a full mouth. "So if you're looking for me to help you feed some poor starving hippopotamuses or think up a new kind of fruiting vine, you are wasting my time as well as yours. The forest will look after itself."

"I look after the forest," Doto protested, before he could stop himself. It was the wrong thing to say.

Kwaee swallowed and turned to gaze at him, his eyes gone round and furious. "Do you."

"I mean…" Doto scrambled for the words that would calm his father. "I mean that I look after these troubling issues that arise. I do my best to resolve them so that you may be at peace."

"Peace," Kwaee repeated, as if the word disgusted him. "I have had none of that today. My body chafes against itself."

"Yes, that is why I have come to you. I have seen what disturbs you."

"And you have come to help me out, is that it? So fawning. So gracious. Like your mother." Kwaee pointed at him with the flamingo leg.

Doto tried to keep the flinch from his face. It had not been a compliment. Kwaee only mentioned her when he was feeling especially nasty. "Yes," he answered. "I've come to help."

"I know what it is you've come to do. Why you *help*. You don't have the strength to simply take what you want from me."

Doto spread his arms in astonishment. "Father—Great Kwaee, I want nothing from you."

"Nothing?" Kwaee asked casually. He turned his attention to the flamingo leg, plucking out feathers as though they were obscuring something enormously interesting. "Not for the beasts and plants you look after to one day recognize you as their god? To win my forest over from me bit by bit? You don't want these things from me? You should. If you were a true god, you would."

"But I only look after those things because you shelter yourself in here!" Doto protested. "If you would only look outside your temple walls once in a while, you would see."

"See what?" his father demanded. "The forest cares for itself. So what will I see? Whatever incipient trouble has you anxious and fretting this day? Squabbling baboons? A new spreading fungus? A beetle with a wounded foot?"

"No, father!"

"Then what? What worthless nonsense is bothering you now?"

"Fire bearers!" Doto shouted. He was gratified to see his father freeze with a look of shock, his divine plumage flattening back against his forehead and ears.

"What did you say?" Kwaee asked him in a hoarse whisper.

"Fire bearers, father. They have returned to the forest."

Kwaee shook his head. "No. No, that is impossible. The fire bearers are gone, long gone. They were destroyed. You have seen something else and mistaken them. Apes, perhaps. They can be very like apes."

Doto bristled. "I know an ape. I am a forest god too."

"Then you saw them? The fire bearers, you witnessed them with your own eyes?"

"Not directly, no," Doto admitted, and before his father could dismiss him further, he hastily added, "But I saw the black clouds. And I heard the Cry of the Dead."

"The Cry of the Dead," Kwaee repeated. "This sound you heard, what was it like?"

"Like a giant's heartbeat in a deep hole."

Kwaee slumped back into the cradle of the moabi, an odd expression written across his face. Doto could not discern it, and did not like it. "So it may be," Kwaee murmured to himself. "And yet it may not. They were never to return. Sarmu swore it." His gaze slid back toward Doto. "You say you did not see these fire bearers."

"No, father. As soon as I was certain it was them, I came straight here."

Kwaee sat up taller, gazing down his muzzle. "And how would you be so certain, hmm? They have not been near the forest since you were a cub. Did you stop and ask yourself if these were truly the black clouds, if the sounds were truly the Cry of the Dead?"

Astonished, Doto stammered, "But—but what else could they be?"

"Did you go to find out? Did you find their nest? See how they made the clouds and Cry? No, of course you did not. You scampered straight here." Kwaee sneered, exposing predatory fangs. "How dutiful. How conscientious."

Doto could not understand how the conversation had turned against him. Hadn't he done everything he was supposed to do? "Father, if you would just open your eyes and look outside the walls of your own temple for once, you could see for yourself that they—"

"Impudence!" Kwaee roared, leaping to his feet, his plumage raised high. He drew back his paw, claws bared, and Doto flinched back, raising his own paws in front of his face. Then Kwaee paused, lowered his arm, and settled back into the tree. "I have warned you in the past not to speak to me of this. If you are not begging me to take meaningless trips with you, you are asking me to intervene with problems, or pestering me about visiting your own temple, as if I could wish to have anything to do with that." A vine curled around the ankle of Kwaee's dropped meal and elevated it back up to his outstretched paw. "Why should I believe these supposed fire bearers aren't merely some sort of childish prank?"

"A prank?" Doto repeated in disbelief. "You think I would invent tales of Ogya just to rile you? I know better than that. And you've felt them coming too—that's why you've been so upset today. That's why the forest has been so tense. You must know I wouldn't lie to you about this."

"No, I suppose you would not. All the same, you may be deceived about what you have seen. We must be certain that they are, in fact, fire bearers. And we must learn what their intentions are. If Ogya indeed advances upon the forest, then we must know of it." He licked his teeth in thought. "You must go to them. Seek out their nest. Learn why they are there, and what their intentions are."

Doto gaped. He could find no words of response to what Kwaee had asked of him. The god might as well have demanded Doto change the savanna into forest, or spit in the eye of Father Wem. "Father—"

"Go," Kwaee cut him off firmly. "And when you have learned all you can, capture one of them. Bring it back to me alive. I will have questions for it."

"Questions?" Doto asked. His heart was pounding faster, tail beginning to switch. Why would his father request this? How could he? "But—but how am I to approach them safely? Are they not the ancient enemy? Did they not nearly destroy the forest once? And you want me to capture one of them? How?"

"Enough of your sniveling." Kwaee's plumage spread across his brow, red, blue and gold feathers cresting high and proud. "Are you a god, or are you not? They are only animals, after all. You want to increase your dominion over the forest beyond your tiny little grove? Then prove to me you are not a weakling."

Doto's ears burned hot. "I am not a weakling," he said, unconsciously flexing his claws. *I'm not the one hiding away in his temple.*

"Good." His father smiled then, and there was a trace of his old kindness in it—the pride he'd shown when Doto had hunted successfully, or sprouted thorns beneath his footprints. "I know you still have it in you to be my son. Show me that you can take on our old enemies. Show me that you're worthy to sit at my side."

"At your side?" Doto's breath caught in his throat. He glanced at the gnarled trunk that formed the forest god's throne. He could grow his own, smaller moabi tree there, if Kwaee let him. No more wandering the forest in empty isolation. No more sitting in his temple watching the days flicker by in endless progression. He looked hopefully back at his father's face, but the warm expression had passed like the sun gone back behind clouds.

Kwaee hesitated before speaking again. "Yes. At my side. *If* you can bring me back a full report and a fire bearer, alive and able to answer any questions. If you can prove to me that you are no longer the mewling whelp your mother made you."

Doto nodded, trying to keep his sudden rush of enthusiasm from showing. "Of course, father. Somehow I will find a way to do this."

"And if you cannot," Kwaee added, "then I see little reason why you would ever need to disturb me again." He leaned back into the tree, turning his gaze from Doto. "Do you understand?"

As quickly as the enthusiasm had arisen, it fell. Doto stared at his toes and felt the numbing shock wash over him. Ever again? "Yes, Great Kwaee," he said.

"Good." Kwaee tore another bite from the flamingo leg. He did not look back.

⁓

Doto's emotions boiled within him as he stalked through the forest, and all around him, the world reflected his confusion and frustration back at him. Vines with thick, poisonous thorns and delicate flowers sprouted in his footsteps, their stalks prostrating themselves beneath his switching tail. Insects buzzed in sudden, furious swarms or dropped in exhaustion to the forest floor; mated birds shrieked territorial challenges at each other and then nestled close again; bush vipers dangled from their branches and hissed at the ground.

How could his father have asked him to do this? Mere animals they might be, but the bearers were dangerous—everyone knew it. They served Ogya, and Ogya was the enemy. They were the demons of the old tales, the scourge of the forest. They heralded the advance of the Firelands. And his father feared them. Of that, Doto was certain. Why else would Kwaee refuse to leave his temple, even to peer outside of it?

Doto had not met many of the other greater gods. He had met Asubonten in her river several times, and Atekye would venture into the forest when the swamps grew heavy. The lesser gods, who ruled their animals, could travel wherever their charges moved, but the greater gods seldom left their domains—to do so would render them vulnerable. But Atekye was aware of every larva that stirred in her swamp, and Asubonten, when she did not lie dreaming, felt her river from raindrop to delta. Only Kwaee remained huddled inside his temple, his eyes shut to his domains. And it seemed he would rather risk his son's safety than open them for even a moment.

Doto snarled aloud in frustration, and behind him two small trees felled themselves, cracking and groaning as they crashed to the forest floor. His hopes of persuading Kwaee to venture out on a journey to the forest borders had been ill-founded. Even had the fire bearers not chosen this moment to return, it was plain that Kwaee would never brook any such suggestion. Instead Doto would make that journey alone, into the claws of peril, and if he failed, his father might never allow him into the temple again. That was unimaginable. Cruel Kwaee might be at times, but only because he needed Doto to learn to be strong, to be ready to inherit his part of the forest. And when Kwaee smiled, when he said, "Well done," Doto knew he had earned it. Considering the possibility of never seeing that smile again made his blood slow in his veins, and the plants around him drooped and wilted. If Kwaee shut him out, he would be alone in the vast forest, with no one to talk to but the busy and distracted lesser gods, or the beasts who venerated him, but could not truly understand him. He shuddered at the thought of it.

But then, if he succeeded, if he captured one of Ogya's minions and brought it before his father, everything could be different. Doto stretched his paws, feeling his claws slide out of the sheaths at his fingertips. Kwaee would not have set an impossible task before him. If he could not face down a single fire bearer, then Kwaee would be right to disown him: he would be no god at all. He thought of how he had cringed at the order and felt ashamed. No wonder his father had been disgusted with him.

He flexed his claws again. He would do this. He would prove that he was a true forest god, a son to be proud of. He would bring a fire bearer to Kwaee, and then finally take his place at his side. And then, day by day, he would bring his father steadily out of his temple, open his eyes, and show him the world once more.

But there was no reason to hurry, he decided. Using his divine speed might somehow alert the fire bearers or their god of his approach. Better to keep things steady and quiet. Rain came in the middle of the night, pouring down heavily, matting his fur, but he ignored it, continuing on toward the northern edge of the forest where he had seen the black clouds. The farther north he went, the more nervous he grew, his tail switching behind him. The fire bearers stole power from the forest. Would they steal his as well, somehow? Would he dry up when he grew close, like the Firelands had? Surely there was no danger of that; Kwaee would have warned him were there that sort of risk. Unless, he worried, as a god, this was something he was supposed to figure out on his own. The closer he drew to the northern border of the forest, the more the worry ate at him.

The rain ended toward early morning, and in the still-dark sky the moon glinted above the treetops. Had Doto hastened, he could easily have found the bearers by now. Perhaps his father was wondering now if he'd succeeded; perhaps he was even worried. There was no point to hurrying, though. It would do the old god good to feel a little concern for his son. It would make the moment all the more fulfilling when Doto presented his catch.

Near the edge of the forest, the trees did not grow quite as high, so the brush was thicker. Giant bushes and brambles choked each other for the sunlight allowed through gaps in the branches above, and the lianas grew so thick that they threatened to break the tree limbs from which they dangled. The plants moved aside for Doto, parting obediently around him as he stalked through the underbrush. There were different animals here: forest hogs moved through the thickets, and occasionally he felt the glint of a civet's eyes from behind a tree.

The edge of the forest was near, but he did not sense the bearers. He could climb a tree and attempt to find them again, but he thought perhaps he had seen the black clouds farther west, so he went in that direction, occasionally testing the air. The cool morning heated as the sun rose higher in the sky. Now almost a full day had passed since he had first seen trace of the bearers.

The reek of fire was fainter than before, but still present in the air, and it grew stronger the farther west he traveled, so he knew he was moving in the right direction.

A god knows no fear, he told himself, but all the same, the stronger the scent of char in his nostrils, the slower his pace went. The forest grew even thinner; to his left, through the tree trunks and underbrush, he could sometimes glimpse open spaces and grass, and he could feel something: a dulling of his power, and farther to the north, an edge where it stopped, a numbing blindness. The end of the forest and his father's domain. Whenever he sensed it, he turned his mind away from it. The air here was dryer, too, its arid touch raw in his nose. He slunk stealthily now through the forest; if the bearers could threaten a god, then it would be wise for him to avoid their detection, and if Ogya himself were among them... He shuddered. Best not even to think about that possibility.

That evening, he began to notice traces in the forest: shallow prints like a chimpanzee's, bushes that had been rent apart as if by savage claws, places where leaves had been crushed. His ears twitched. There was pain nearby. Normally he would have ignored it; pain was part of life, part of the forest, but this felt strange. He crept toward it. The scent of blood was in his nostrils, reminding him that he was hungry. His ears perked toward the direction of the scent, detecting the labored breathing of a dying animal.

On all fours he crept through the brush, moving with absolute silence, until he came upon the source of the pain. On its side, breathing in slowing gasps, lay a forest hog, slumped against the base of a tree. Its eyes rolled toward him, recognizing him as a god, its back hooves scuffling feebly in the dirt.

Doto regarded it warily; it was stinking with heat and exhaustion, having seemingly run some distance. There was a deep wound in its side, dark with blood. He stepped toward the hog and leaned close, placing his paw on its side. It did not resist, of course. Animals did not resist gods. Except, he reminded himself, for the fire bearers. Pain flared up in the hog as he nudged at the wound, investigating it, and it gave a faint squeal. The wound was strange, not a crushing wound as if it had been beaten, nor a slash like the rake of claws. It was deep, like a bite, but the tooth would have to belong to something larger than a crocodile, and the land here was too dry for those. Doto sent himself into the hog's mind and quelled its pain so that it would not struggle, then slipped two fingers into the wound to test its depth. It was a deep gash indeed, and no tooth he knew of could make such a bite. His fingers reached in nearly to the paw before nudging against something strange and hard inside. He latched onto it with his claws and drew it out. The thing was covered with dark blood, and slippery, but it was unmistakably a bit of stone that had somehow become lodged deep within the hog.

Doto's fur stood up again along his spine. The fire bearers bit with teeth of stone. What manner of monsters were they? The hog's eyes closed as its breaths grew shorter and shorter, and then ceased altogether. Doto was hungry, but he did not like the thought of consuming a beast killed by stone teeth. The fear was irrational, surely. A god did not fear illness or curses. All the same, he did not trust it. Almost he turned around and headed back into the depths of the forest, where there were no bearers nor black clouds nor stone teeth, where it was familiar and safe. But there it would be empty.

His father would not speak to him, would be ashamed. He had faced the bearers and lived. So, too, would Doto.

But it would not hurt to move even more slowly than before. He crept, now, foot by foot, through the forest, pausing when he heard noise or smelled anything unusual, letting his rosettes disguise him as part of the forest. Each time, though, the alarm proved unwarranted. The sun sank down below the trees before him, and as night filled the forest, so too did the stench of fire, sharper and more acrid than Doto had ever known it, which meant that it was close, and recent. He steeled himself and moved toward the scent, and it was soon joined by the scent of animals, smelling a bit like chimpanzee and a bit like hog. Before him, he could see lights like the burn of the sun on the horizon, but that had already set. This was fire.

He froze, remaining perfectly still, his whiskers quivering, ears focused toward the lights. There were sounds coming from ahead, from what could only be the nest of the fire bearers. They had an odd, chattering language unlike any he had heard before. Though gods knew the speeches of all the animals in their domains, these chatters were from outside the forest, and too distant and mingled for him to learn easily.

He needed a better view. He could borrow the eyes of birds, but not without alerting anything else that might be sensitive to the presence of gods. Ogya might have granted the bearers that ability somehow, or worse, he might be keeping a watch himself through all their burning flames scattered about their nest. Besides, most birds' eyes were all but useless at night. Looking left and right, Doto selected a suitable tree and quietly climbed it, keeping the trunk between himself and the lights of the nest to the west. He dared not think what might happen to him if he were seen. Surely as a god he would have little to fear, he told himself, but it was best to be cautious. He reached a high limb and climbed out along it; it was thick enough to conceal him from the ground. From here he drew himself up into a crouch and peered out at the bearers' nest.

They were yet some distance away, perched on the edge of the forest, in the open grasses where the savanna began. It was an uncomfortable area for a forest god, where the power of the forest weakened and ended.

Doto had once ventured up to the fringes of the forest, peering out into the savanna, and there his senses had been muted, the light dimming, the sounds seeming to come from underwater. There on the fringe, his great speed had slowed, his limbs weakened, and his awareness of the world around him—the sunlight on the leaves, the sway of branches in the trees—had been stripped away from him. He had ventured as far as he could tolerate it, and then, frightened and exhausted, had darted back into the safe comfort of his forest once more. He did not think that the bearers kept their nest—or at least not all of it—so close to the forest's edge that he would suffer, but approaching it would be unpleasant, and he could be vulnerable as well. It was not the place he wanted to meet the ancient enemy.

The light of their fire was bright and intense, but through Ogya's power they controlled it, and it did not spread. The nest itself was odd, filled with what seemed to be strange plants, like giant mushrooms. There were many felled trees and branches lying about, arranged in little piles, and from some of these, the fire burned. Here and there Doto could see the flesh of animals, eerily torn away from their bodies and lying along the ground or atop the odd plants. But it was the sight of the bearers themselves that froze his breath and sent his mind into a dizzying spin.

His whole life, he had been lied to about the fire bearers, the animals who had allied themselves with Ogya against all the other gods in exchange for his power, the animals who shared his hunger for the power of all those other gods, who at Ogya's behest sought to destroy the land and obliterate the power of the gods. The lie was walking plainly before him, in defiance of all the old stories.

The fire bearers were not animals. They stood upright, on two legs, like Doto and Kwaee, like Atetea and Atekye and even Asubonten when she emerged from her river. They stood like gods.

Gaps in the Wall

"You're going to fall," Clay told Laughing Dog, standing at the bottom of the palm and peering up at him, eyes shaded from the sun.

"I never fall." His brother was hanging near the top of the tree, strong brown legs linked around the trunk. He dangled from the stalk of one broad fan and sawed with his knife at the stem of a pendulous bunch of yellow dates. "When have you ever known me to lose my footing in a tree?"

"You fell once," Clay reminded him. "Three times the height of a man, remember? And father whipped me for letting you climb it in the first place."

"That was different. I was eight. Careful, here it comes." Laughing Dog's knife cut through the stalk, and the heavy bunch dropped toward Clay, who caught it in both hands. The sweet smell of the fresh dates made his mouth water.

"You were eight, and I told you not to climb it, and you did anyway. And you fell. And I got whipped for it."

Laughing Dog sighed. "I'm not going to fall. I've done this many times. What's got you so worked up?" He shifted around the tree to another dangling cluster of dates.

Clay looked over his shoulder. He could barely make out the village wall from here. "I just don't know if it's a good idea to be this far into the forest. We don't know the gods here. Nor the beasts. There could be dangers."

"We know Kwaee," Laughing Dog said. "Say a prayer to him if you're uncomfortable. You like praying."

"That's not the point," Clay objected, but he muttered a prayer to Kwaee under his breath nonetheless, asking that the god send them protection from the dangers of the forest.

"Anyway," Laughing Dog added in between grunts as he worked his knife, "I didn't see any date palms farther out, did you?"

"No, but Father said that no one was to go into the forest. If I'd known that this is where you planned to go, I wouldn't have come."

"So don't tell him," Laughing Dog said. "Anyhow, he won't care. We're not *that* far in. Here comes another."

Clay set down the first bunch of dates to catch another dropping toward him. As he did, he caught the gaze of a black monkey sitting a little ways into the forest. He had never seen its type before. It watched him with seeming interest. He didn't like it. It was proof that they were strangers here. He missed the open grasses of the savanna. That was home. That was where the people were supposed to live. Here under the trees, everything was unfamiliar, alien. Possibly hostile. "I just think we should be more careful," he said. "We should have asked permission before coming out here."

Laughing Dog was already sawing through the third and last ripe bunch of dates on the tree. Other fruited bunches jutted outward, but their dates were small and green. It would be many days before they could be harvested. "Permission from father? Or the gods? You know, if you ask permission for everything, you never get to have any fun." Keeping his legs hooked, he leaned backward to dangle upside down from the bent palm, reaching down toward Clay with the final bunch of dates. Clay took it, and then Laughing Dog let go with his feet, flipping in the air to land upright, albeit heavily, on the ground. Clay rolled his eyes at the showy move, but Laughing Dog just grinned and took two of the date stalks from him, swinging one over each shoulder. "Or do anything worthwhile."

"I'm too busy to do anything worthwhile," Clay said. "Always looking after you."

Laughing Dog gave him a good-natured shove to the shoulder that sent him stumbling. "Jealous, that's what's you are."

Clay snorted. "Jealous? Of you, little brother? What have I got to be jealous of?"

"I'm taller than you," Laughing Dog pointed out.

"Easier to be seen in a hunt."

"Stronger, too." He stretched out his broad shoulders.

"Just makes you slower."

"And more desirable. Or so all the many women have told me."

"Well, there's your mistake," Clay said. "They're all confusing you with our older brother. They think you're going to be king someday. It's disappointing, really, how you believe all this flattery."

Laughing Dog scowled, which in Clay's estimation did nothing for his claims to handsomeness. "Great Ram might be the heir, but I'm twice the hunter he is. And better looking, too. If he weren't going to be King he'd have no prospects at all. He's such a stiff old sheep."

Clay laughed at that. "He is. Though maybe he wouldn't be if he weren't going to be King."

"So what's your reason, then?" Laughing Dog asked. He hopped up onto a log and balanced along it.

Clay stepped up behind him and nearly teetered off. Probably because he was carrying dates on only one shoulder instead of both. "My reason for what?"

"For being so uptight about everything all the time. You're not going to be King."

"I'm not uptight!"

"You are."

The fences of the village weren't far off now, and Clay's mouth watered as he picked up the scent of roasting goat meat. He sighed. "Well, I might be King someday, if, Wem stay it, something should happen to Great Ram. And so might you, you know. If a sickness were to take both of us, or a lion. Anything could happen."

Laughing Dog shrugged. "We left the lions behind in the savanna. And if there were a chance of that, well then, all the more reason why I should enjoy my life now."

The fences had one wide opening, a gate, where a guard would always stand watch. In their old homes, they'd needed to watch against hyenas, but here it was mainly monkeys from the forest, some tiny, some enormous and dangerous-looking. Plus you never knew what else was beneath those dark branches, hungry and waiting.

"Fresh dates? Those will spice up dinner tonight," said Left Rabbit, who was on watch for the day. He was leaning against the fence, shaded beneath a canopy of palm leaves he'd built for himself. Clay liked Left Rabbit. He was a lighthearted fellow with an open expression and a slow, hesitant smile that said he was ready to laugh at the joke just as soon as he understood it. He was a fast runner as well, second in sheer speed only to Clay, and so they often paired up in hunts. But despite that, Rabbit tended to follow closely at Laughing Dog's heels every chance he had.

"What, these?" Laughing Dog hefted up both heavy bunches. "These aren't for you, Rabbit. You'd better go out and find your own."

Left Rabbit grinned uncertainly. "Really? Did you—did you get those from the forest, Dog? Only the King said no one was supposed to be going in without a scouting party."

"We are a scouting party," Laughing Dog said. "We were scouting for dates. And we found some."

"Oh," Left Rabbit said. He looked at the ground, then up at Laughing Dog again, brow furrowed. "That makes sense. Right. But I can't go out now. I'm on watch."

"My brother is teasing you, Rabbit." Clay plucked a yellow date from the bunch and tossed it to the guard. "Of course you can have some."

Left Rabbit's grin reappeared even wider than before. "I knew he was only teasing," he said, leaning back against the fence. "He kids me all the time."

"Course you knew," Laughing Dog said. He strode past Left Rabbit through the gate.

"See you at dinner," Left Rabbit called, waving after him. He crunched down on his date without looking at Clay.

Clay sighed. "See you at dinner, Rabbit," he said, and then hurried after his brother.

"Ugh," Laughing Dog said when Clay caught up to him, "I think his gourd is getting more hollow by the day."

"He's not stupid. He's more coherent when you're not around. He just admires you."

"A little too much. It's strange. *He's* strange."

Clay shrugged. "He looks up to you. He has since he was little."

"Yes, but back then I was little too. I don't know. He bothers me."

"Well, I think you should be nice to him." They walked past the small, domed tents of the hunters, built of stoutly lashed wooden branches and bone, wrapped with stretched hide. Most of their hunters kept their tents near the village gate so that they could easily defend against encroaching animals, as well as be able to rise for the early mornings that hunts demanded without waking others. These were sturdy structures, built to last, not easily dismantled and carried away. "I wish he liked me half as much as he likes you."

"Why in Wem's name would you want that?" Laughing Dog asked. "Then you'd just have him following you everywhere all the time, begging you for attention, asking you endless questions. He's annoying and slow-witted."

And also strong and kind, Clay thought, though he didn't say this out loud. He knew how that conversation would go.

Past the hunter's tents, the village opened up into a wide work area: here rock could be honed into spear and arrow tips, wood could be carved, clay shaped into pottery and fired. Currently, little work was going on, though there were a few men drilling and polishing beads, and women checking over the leaf wall for the hunt tomorrow.

And there was Broken Calabash with his flute, playing a wistful melody that Clay had not heard in many rains. It was a song of home, and it brought back to him, intensely, the memories of their village in the northern savanna, long before the droughts and fires had driven them south. The people had not stayed here for more than a couple of moons, but everyone seemed to sense that this was where they would remain. There was a forest here, so there would be rain. They would not move again. So now they had proper homes to live in, a wall around their tents, and Calabash played his tune of homestead and contentment. Clay was glad to hear it; it chased away his misgivings about the strangeness of the forest.

When they reached the food preparation area, they were spotted by the children, who had gathered around to watch the spitted goat cooking—the one that had made Clay's stomach growl earlier. Laughing Dog gave a good-natured groan as the children rushed over, clustering around him and Clay, hands held up for dates.

"All right, all right," said Laughing Dog. "But I haven't got a free hand. Get Clay to give you some."

Clay plucked dates off of his bunch and began handing them to the children, trying to give only one to each, but it was hard to tell which upward-reaching arm belonged to which child. "Slow down, slow down, one for each of you," he said, trying not to laugh. It seemed not so long ago that he and his brother had been pushing and shoving to get a handful of whatever treats a scout had brought back, but that was just a trick of time, because of course there had not been an abundance of food in a long time, and never, as far as he could remember, with the variety to be found here.

"Did you find date palms in the savanna?" asked Baobab. She was a short, sturdy-limbed girl, the daughter of the Teller, and, people said, most likely to be the next Teller. Anything she heard or saw soon rattled around the village like the shaking of a seed gourd.

Clay cast a cautious glance toward Laughing Dog. Left Rabbit had been right: strictly speaking, they were not supposed to have ventured into the forest.

But whatever misgivings Clay might have had were not shared by Laughing Dog, who only shook his head. "No," he told them in a dramatic tone. "We found them deep, deep in the dark forest."

The children gasped, and they looked at Clay and Laughing Dog with widening eyes. "You went by yourself?" asked Little Elephant. He had seen the rains only six times, and his expression of admiration was glossed by date smears across his mouth.

"We went with each other," Clay told Little Elephant, "and we prayed for the gods to guard us and the forest to welcome us. It is safer for adults than for little children." He emphasized that last part and gave Laughing Dog a meaningful frown.

"Oh yes," Laughing Dog said. "When you're grown and you are strong and wise, you can face all kinds of dangers."

Clay sighed. That hadn't been the point he was trying to make. "But even then," he added, "you must be careful, and look to your people and to the gods for guidance."

"Did you see any demons?" Little Elephant asked. He had stepped halfway behind another child and was peering out at Laughing Dog.

Laughing Dog laughed. "There are no demons in the forest. But there are big, ferocious animals with huge teeth! Clay and I scared them away with our spears!"

"You haven't got your spears," Baobab pointed out in a loud voice. "Did you leave them in the forest?"

"All right, all right, our knives," Laughing Dog said.

Clay wanted to interrupt and tell the children that there had been no ferocious animals, but he decided it would be better for them to foster a healthy fear of the forest than to think it was safe, and perhaps go traipsing into it on their own one day. Who knew what was in there that would be dangerous? Certainly poisonous snakes. Baboons. And leopards, too. No. Much better for them to be afraid.

"Soon I will have a hunting knife," said All The Stars, an older boy who was already beginning to pock with adulthood. "Father says I can have one. I won't be afraid of the forest." Some of the younger children gazed at him in admiration, and he seemed to notice it, for he squared his shoulders.

"You should be afraid of it," Baobab told him. She tilted her head back and fixed Laughing Dog with a challenging gaze. "There *are* demons. The stories say so. And if Kwaee gets mad at you, then they will tear you into pieces."

"That's not exactly how the stories go," Clay began, but Baobab cut him off.

"The Teller's my father, not yours," she said. "I know all the stories. And in the story of Black Bird, he went into Kwaee's sacred lands without being asked to, and Kwaee forgave him, but then he killed Kwaee's favorite deer, and so Kwaee called out his demons, and they pulled his legs until they came off, and they pulled his arms until they came off, and they pulled his head until it came off too, and that is a true story."

"You're not supposed to know that story, Baobab," Clay said sternly. "It's not for children." And for good reason, he thought to himself. Several of them looked really frightened, and even All The Stars was casting nervous glances in the direction of the forest. Clay couldn't even see Little Elephant anymore—either the little boy had run off without being seen, or was hiding behind one of the larger children.

"I know *all* the stories," Baobab informed him. "Probably even ones you haven't heard of."

Laughing Dog chuckled in a loud voice. He had set down his date bunches. "That may be true, Baobab, but they are old stories, aren't they?"

"Of course they're old!" The girl seemed affronted that the question even be considered. "That's what makes them true!"

"It's what makes them stories," said Laughing Dog. "Times change. Things change. Things that were true long ago might be less true now."

Clay had heard him start this sort of conversation before, and it never went well. "Laughing Dog," he said in a warning tone, but his brother ignored him.

"Why should the gods mind if you enter their sacred lands? Maybe *they* are afraid of *us*!"

The blood drained from Clay's face. This was not something Laughing Dog should be saying, especially to children.

"Let me tell you another story," Laughing Dog said. "Once there was a man named Strong Hyena, and he was brave, yes, and mighty. And he went traveling into the gods' lands, and the gods were angry, and they shook their great fists. 'Don't come into our lands, Strong Hyena,' they said! But Strong Hyena was so brave that he did not listen, and he went deeper and deeper into the sacred lands. There he found the gods' special deer. 'Don't you touch our special deer,' the gods said, and they showed their great teeth, and they wagged their great heads. But Strong Hyena was hungry, and he was not afraid, so he killed a deer for himself, and ate it. Then the gods were very angry, and they sent their demons after him. But the meat of the special deer had made Strong Hyena even mightier, so what did he do?"

The children were silent. This story had no answers they knew. They looked uncomfortable. "He ran away?" one ventured.

Baobab answered with furious certainty. "He died," she said. "The demons pulled him apart and he died. That is what happened."

"Not this time!" Laughing Dog said. "Strong Hyena fought the demons. He punched them in their demon faces. He took his knife and cut their throats, and they died. And then they could never pull anyone's arms or legs off again." He grinned broadly at Baobab, whose face had gone dark purple, her lips pressed firmly together.

A couple of the children gave tentative cheers, but most just looked shocked.

"Okay," Clay said. "Okay, children. That was not a true story. You know how the stories are told. That one was just a joke. It's a funny story."

"I didn't think it was funny at all," Baobab declared.

Laughing Dog took Clay's elbow and pulled him aside. "Clay," he muttered through the side of his mouth, "what are you doing?"

"What are *you* doing?" Clay whispered back. "This isn't right."

"What's not right is teaching our children to be afraid. We should be teaching them to be brave and strong!"

"That's not your decision!" Clay hissed the words under his breath. "And it's not about teaching them fear. It's about teaching them reverence and respect."

Laughing Dog shrugged. "Maybe those are just other words for fear," he said.

⌒⌒⌒

The King's tent was larger than any other, so large that five or six men at once might stand upright with comfort. Hides could be drawn back to open it to the night sky and the cooler air, or they could be closed to shelter the tent from rains or the heat of the day. They were open now, propped on poles to let in light and air, but not admitting direct sunlight. Clay sat respectfully on comfortable pelt-draped straw next to Laughing Dog. They had been summoned. Lately, it was the only way they spoke to their father. He was the King, and that came before all else.

There was a little fire pit in the middle of the tent, not big enough for cooking food, but large enough for light, and for burning fragrances and oils to keep insects away. King First Claw sat on his stool across from them. His age-whitened brows were lowered, his mouth pulling down the corners of his grey beard. "You have disappointed me again," he said. He turned his eyes to each of them.

Clay counted down the heartbeats until Laughing Dog spoke: three, two, one...

"Father, I—"

"Be silent!" the King growled. "Your sin is not that you have said too little, Laughing Dog. That has never been your crime." He fixed Clay with a stare. "It is bad enough that the two of you went into the forest without a scouting party, against my express orders. How am I to expect obedience from my people when I cannot even command it from my own sons?"

He looked at each of them again, as if expecting an answer. Clay hoped Laughing Dog was wise enough not to reply, and thanked Wem when he did not.

"You shame me. Your disobedience weakens me, and so it weakens our people. But that, at least, is understandable. That I could forgive. I remember what it is to be a young man, to be fearless. But these stories you told the children…" He rubbed his fingers across his smooth scalp. "Killing demons? Defying the gods? What do you think these stories will teach them? Why would you tell them these things? Tell them that the old stories don't matter?"

He stood abruptly, towering over them as they sat. Fury sparked in his eyes. "How dare you? How dare you so flippantly compromise and challenge the old tales? Do you think yourselves gods? Prophets?" He glared at each of them. "Well?"

"No, Father," Clay said. "Of course not."

The King turned to Laughing Dog. "And you? How about you? Are you a prophet?"

Laughing Dog's jaw set, and Clay knew with dismay that he was about to be stubborn. "They're only stories, Father."

The King's temples bulged. "Only stories. Have I been such an absent father? How could I have raised you so poorly that you could think that? These tales are our history. They are the soul of our people. When you change them—when you dishonor them so, you dishonor us. You rob us of our soul. That is something I cannot allow, even from princes."

He crossed his arms behind his back and turned away. "Tomorrow you will both spend the day mending the wall, from dawn to dusk. The work should give you plenty of time to consider the importance of preserving our people."

A weight of dismay sank in Clay. The task would be grueling, back-breaking work even in the twilight hours, to say nothing of the midday sun. Still, he would have gladly borne the punishment, were it not for the hunt the day after. He had been looking forward to the thrill of it for days now, and could not keep himself from speaking out. "But Father, that will leave us exhausted. We will be of no use in the hunt!"

The King did not turn. "You should be grateful I allow you to participate in the hunt at all! Were we not so dependent on both your skills, you would be laboring for two days instead of one. I will not alter my decision on this. Do you understand?"

"Yes, Father," Clay said, hanging his head.

Laughing Dog echoed the words, but from the corner of his eye, Clay could see that he kept his chin lifted, proud and defiant.

The King nodded. "Laughing Dog, you may go."

"Thank you, Father."

Clay kept still as his brother stood and exited the tent. He wondered why he was not being dismissed. Surely he had not committed some further misdeed for which he was to be punished? His father was silent for a time, his back turned, and Clay began to wonder if he had simply neglected to dismiss him and wasn't aware he was still there. He was about to say something when his father finally spoke.

"I suppose you think me unjust."

He did, but it would have been disrespectful to admit it. "I've never known you to make decisions without reasons, even if I don't always understand them. I do...I do wonder why you punished me equally. Laughing Dog told the story."

"And you could have stopped him." His father turned, finally. The anger was gone from his eyes, and it was replaced with a deep weariness, heavy as the clouds at sunset. "You are his older brother, Clay. He is your responsibility. You cannot stand by and be silent while he flouts our laws. I will not be alive forever, and Great Ram will be King when I am gone. Who will look after Laughing Dog and guide him if not you?"

Clay shook his head. "I try, Father, honestly, but you know how headstrong he is. He doesn't listen to me."

"You must make him listen. Do what you have to." The wrinkles around his eyes deepened. "I'm afraid we are losing him. Right now he flirts with blasphemy, but if he truly begins to defy the gods, the ways of the people, then he will not be part of us for long. One way or another, he must learn to put aside his arrogance. He does not listen to me anymore, nor the Teller, nor any of the other elders. But you are his older brother. He loves you. He will listen to you. You must make him understand." His father reached out a brown, wrinkled hand, and Clay took it, feeling the comforting strength in it as he was helped to his feet.

"I will do my best," he said.

"I know you will. You are a good son." King First Claw clasped Clay's head in his hands, gripping the back of his neck, the side of his face. He smiled. "You boys are everything to me. I would give up all I have for you. I know that we have seen difficult years, but there are better ones to come. I hope that I will be able to be a King less often, and a father more."

He dropped his hands. "Now go and see how your brother has decided to sulk about all this."

"Thank you, Father." Clay turned to go.

As he was exiting, his father added, "And be sure you don't exhaust yourself on that wall tomorrow. We need those feet of yours at their swiftest for the hunt."

Clay had spent his life knowing little but heat. The seasons of dry and rain did not vary much in temperature, though when the rains came, their coolness was exhilarating and joyful. He had known days so hot that the baked earth would kill the insects that crawled on it, so hot that it cooked your tongue into a wooden thing and made your eyes sticky and painful. He had seen days so hot that the grass could catch itself on fire before your eyes. But never had he known heats like those on the edge of the forest.

In the afternoons, the day would grow hotter, but not dry. Instead, the air would turn fat and heavy. It would catch in your throat, and rather than breathe it, you had to swallow it into your lungs, where it would sit like a wet toad. It felt as though Wem had gathered you up in cruel arms and was squeezing you, not so much as to kill you, but just to torment you. There was no escaping the heat. The shade held no relief—heat collected inside the tents and made them nearly as miserable as outdoors. To be forced to labor in such a heat was a harsh punishment indeed.

It was midday, and Clay and Laughing Dog had been working since dawn. Mending the fence was not an easy task. Thick branches had to be cut, trimmed, and shaved down until they were smooth. Holes had to be dug deep to hold the branches, and then filled in and packed tightly. Then twine had to be stripped from palm and twisted into cords that could be used to bind the logs together. If the holes were not dug deep enough, the logs not planted firmly enough, a loose one could bring down a whole section of the wall, and it would need to be rebuilt. The sweat poured from the two of them, draining them, and they had to drink copiously to fend off heat sickness. Fortunately, while food might still be sometimes scarce, water near the forest was never an issue. The rains fell dependably, and today was no exception.

Clay was grateful for the downpour when it came; though the heat in the air did not diminish, the water soothed his skin and provided an excuse to take a break from digging holes. There would be no sense in digging when the water would just fill it in and make mud. In addition, the rain would soften the earth and make their task easier afterward. He sat with Laughing Dog against the fence and twisted twine, watching the great forest nod and shiver in the rain. They let the water soak their hair and clean the dirt from their skin, and they tilted back their heads to catch the raindrops in their mouths.

They had spoken little during the day, silenced by the hard work and the thickness of the air, but now Clay looked up into the cloudy sky, blinking droplets out of his eyes. "We never have to worry about water here," he said. "It still seems strange."

Laughing Dog didn't look up from his work. His fingertips were cracked and bleeding from working with the coarse twine, the rain dissolving his bright blood as soon as it appeared. "People say we'll stay here."

"I hope so," Clay said. "I am so tired of moving our village every time the rains don't come."

"I guess it's harder for you than for me." Laughing Dog cinched his knots tight. "I don't really remember much about before. There are a few things. I remember Uncle Six growing crops. I remember taking trips to the river, when it flowed. But mostly I remember leaving most of what we owned behind. Heading for some new place to live, where, each time, people said it would be better. I guess I got used to it. It's strange to think that we'll be here for the next rains, and the rains after that."

"Rains." Clay snorted. "We'll have to find a new word for time. They come almost every day, here. How will we know how old we are? Or when it is time to plant crops again?"

"The stars are still the same." Laughing Dog squinted up through the rain, as if expecting to see them. "We'll know by the changing of the stars."

Clay nodded. "But you're right. It is strange to think of staying here. Strange and wonderful. No more long walks with children and elders dying. No more searching for water with parched throats, or empty bellies while we scout for game tracks for days." He looked out toward the dark forest. "There's much to grow accustomed to here. It's different. But I'm glad that we've found a place. Not to have to leave again...I thank the gods every night."

"I'm sure you do," Laughing Dog muttered.

Clay glanced up at the comment, remembering his father's caution from the previous day.

"But you're right," his brother said, flashing him that easy grin once again. "It's good to find a place we can keep."

"You know," Clay said, adopting a casual tone, "when so much has changed, it's especially important that we remember who we are and where we come from."

Laughing Dog groaned. "Not you too. Not again. Isn't it enough that we have to kill ourselves digging and stripping wood all day? Does there have to be lectures, too?"

"Well, why do you think we're out here now?" Clay asked.

"I'm out here because I don't obediently repeat everything that falls out of Father's or the Teller's mouth," Laughing Dog said. "I don't really know why you're being punished."

"Because I—" Clay faltered.

"Why didn't you stand up for yourself? Is this what you want to be doing right now?"

"Of course not, but—"

"But what?" Laughing Dog cinched another knot of twine and dropped the log he was holding. "You didn't want to come into the forest yesterday with me, either. But you did."

"Something could have happened to you."

"So you were looking after me."

"Yes!"

"And you're out here being punished for what?"

Clay blinked. "For not—for not looking after you."

Laughing Dog laughed. "And what sense does that make? Don't you see that you'd just be happier if you did what you wanted?"

"It isn't that simple!" Clay pulled a strip of twine away from a palm leaf and it snapped too short to be of use. He bit off a curse before he spoke it. "You're my younger brother."

"That doesn't make it your job to follow me around and make sure I behave," Laughing Dog said, fixing Clay with a steady gaze. Rain poured over his eyebrows and down his cheeks, and he rubbed it out of his eyes with the back of his hand.

"Who else is going to do it? Father and Great Ram are both too busy!" Clay saw lightning rake down somewhere north, and then thunder snarled across the sky.

"I can take care of myself!" Laughing Dog shouted above the boom.

"No, you can't!" The thunder ended just before the words, leaving Clay to shout them into the hiss of the rain, uncomfortably loud. "No, you can't," he said again, quieter. "You don't see what you're doing. People are talking about you."

"Let them talk," Laughing Dog said, scowling.

"You don't understand," Clay said. "Father's worried. These things you say, they're dangerous. You could anger the gods against all of us. And just when we've found a home."

"Anger the gods?" Laughing Dog said. He stood, mouth twisted into a disbelieving grin. "And what will they do to us? Take away the rains? Our food? Our homes? Kill off our children? They've already done all these things to us, Clay. What did we do to anger them then?"

Clay stood to look him in the eyes. "You know we don't know that. Maybe someone cursed us. Or maybe we just failed to please them enough. All we can do is try harder to show them we're worthy." Thunder shook the sky again, and Clay wondered with sudden fear if this very argument could be angering Wem.

"If they were displeased by that, then why didn't they tell us?" Laughing Dog said. "And if the gods are so vain and cruel that they will punish me for not telling the right stories, then maybe the gods just need to grow up."

Clay blinked at him in the rain, dumbfounded. How could he voice such blasphemy? How could he have so little faith? He stepped forward, clamping his hand over his brother's mouth, action preceding his intention. "Listen to me," he said into Laughing Dog's ear. "You can't say these things. Do you understand me? You can't. If you do, something terrible is going to happen. I think Father is going to send you away."

Laughing Dog stepped back, shaking his head and chuckling. "You're making lions of mongooses, Clay. He wouldn't send me away. I'm his son. I'm a prince. I'm one of the best hunters in the village."

"He would," Clay felt dread certainty strengthen his voice. "He would if he had to." The rain was still falling heavily, but to the west, shafts of sunlight were breaking through the clouds. The muggy heat of the afternoon would soon return. Storms here were regular, but often brief. "Laughing Dog, listen. You have to promise. Promise that you won't talk like this anymore. Promise that you'll look to the gods for guidance and wisdom."

His brother blinked, and then put his hand to his forehead and rubbed at his temples. "You really need to relax a little. Maybe it'd be good for you, just once in your life, to defy them."

Clay stared at him, then turned out toward the forest again, gazing into its dark and frightening depths. He said nothing aloud, but felt the prayer on his lips. *Gods of earth and sky, of fire and water, we have been lost for so long. We need to be reminded that we are not alone. Reveal yourselves to us.*

There was no answer, of course. No bolt of lightning striking before them, no divine being wreathed in fire erupting from the ground. Clay had not expected such a reply. The gods did not bend their wills so readily to a prayer from one lowly person, and their answers could be capricious and subtle.

"Just think about what I've said, Laughing Dog."

"I will, as long as you do the same."

The rain was lessening now, and the ground steamed as it began to heat once more. There were knots to tie, holes to dig, posts to set. Clay turned from the forest, and as he did so, he thought he saw the flash of green eyes regarding him, high up on a branch. He looked again, and there, a good way in the forest, but still visible, were the eyes again, and a compact, muscled form, covered with spots, crouching on a limb. Then the clouds cleared, and light shone down between the leafy fingers of the trees, illuminating the branch Clay had been staring at. The spots were not spots at all, merely shadows, and what he had taken for eyes, two small green leaves on a dangling vine. Nothing was there.

"Well then, Clay, was a lesson learned today?"

Clay looked up through his weariness to see Great Ram striding toward him, shoulders back, neck and arms adorned with his fine cloth and jewelry, rings swinging from his ears. He looked a little foolish, dressed so finely on an ordinary evening, but perhaps there had been a meeting of the elders, or perhaps he was going to be with his wife. Probably neither of these were true, though. Ram was taking every chance he got to flaunt his wealth as King-to-be.

"I am too tired to tell right now, Ram," he answered. It was the truth. His shoulders and arms ached with weariness, so much so that he wondered how much use he would be in the hunt tomorrow. The thought chagrined him. He had been looking forward to it for weeks now. He would send a prayer to Wem tonight to ask for strength and energy.

"Well, come, then, let us see your handiwork." Ram waved grandly toward the wall. "Will it keep the baboons out?"

Clay wanted nothing more than to eat a meal and return to his tent to rest, but he could hardly refuse his brother. "Parts of it will. We didn't have time to fix the whole thing, of course."

"Didn't have time?" Great Ram arched an eyebrow, leaning his head toward Clay in an imitation of one of their father's favorite gestures. "I'm surprised to hear that. Do you know why?"

Clay waited for him to explain.

"Would it surprise you to know that I saw you and your brother sitting idle for a long period of time today?"

"We did no such thing," Clay protested. "We worked the whole day. I can hardly stand up because of it."

Great Ram shook his head slowly, his earrings waggling back and forth. "You disappoint me, Clay. You are usually so truthful. But I saw you, in midafternoon, just sitting there in the rain."

For a moment, Clay was dumbfounded. "But—but it was raining!" he finally managed. "What else were we to do? Any holes we dug would have filled in. Poles would have tipped over."

"Your punishment, as I understood it, was to work from dawn to dusk, wasn't it? I didn't hear anything about stopping whenever things got a little wet." Ram peered at the wall as if inspecting it, and then gave firm shoves to a couple of posts—not, Clay noted, even posts that he or Laughing Dog had re-set that day. "Fine work," he said. "Fine work. But the two of you could have accomplished more, had you not idled."

Clay squeezed his hands into fists behind his back, nails digging into his palms.

"But I'm of no mind to extend your punishment this time," Great Ram said with a magnanimous smile.

"Not like you could," Clay muttered.

"What was that?" Ram's smile hardened on his face.

"You don't get to punish me," Clay said, louder. "You're not the King."

"Oh, but I will be." The smile had fled Ram's lips. His eyes narrowed. "I will be King, and you and your little brother had better learn to respect me. The sooner, the better. Because you won't be getting any special favors or treatment just because you're related to the King."

He straightened his back again, recomposing his features into what he probably imagined was a noble expression. Clay thought it just made him look as though he had to relieve himself. "I will be a just King, and a fair one. And I will do whatever I have to do to protect our people." He glowered at Clay again. "Whatever I have to. Do you understand that?"

Clay sighed. "I understand."

"Good." Great Ram pushed on the post again, and then rapped at it with his knuckles. "It's good work here," he said. "Good work."

〰

Clay's tent was finally beginning to cool in the evening. He crouched in the dim light and gripped his spear with both hands. The wood was rough against his fingers, the little yellow feather that was bound to the haft, and identified it as his, tickling at his knee. "Spear," he said low, so only he and the spear could hear, "with your permission I took you from the acacia, and with your permission I carved you into the shape of a spear. Now, with your permission I hunt with you tomorrow. Bend your spirit to my purpose, fly straight and true, and help me to kill meat for our dinner and hides for our homes."

He heard footsteps outside his tent, and then Laughing Dog poked his head inside. "There you are. I was looking for you. You're blessing your spear. Should I come back later?"

"I'm finished," Clay said. "Come in. Have you blessed yours already?" As soon as he asked the question, he feared the answer.

Laughing Dog stooped into the tent and sat down cross-legged on a stuffed hide, resting his own spear across his knees. "I haven't blessed my spears since the last flood," he said. "And I have still killed more eland and boar than you and Great Ram combined."

Clay cast a fearful glance toward the entrance to his tent, half-expecting to see his father or one of the elders standing there and frowning.

"Don't look so nervous!" Laughing Dog chuckled the words, reaching forward to pat Clay on the shoulder. "It's not so terrible a thing as all that. Plenty of the hunters don't bless their spears. Or their knives. Or reeds, or meat, none of it. Only when people are watching. You're the only one who takes it so seriously."

"That's not true, Laughing Dog." Clay rubbed at his face. "You know it's not. I don't understand you lately. Why have you been doing this? Why are you flouting all our traditions?"

"Why do you cling to them so?" Laughing Dog asked. "What have they ever done for you? For us? Did prayer and worship save our people from flame and drought? Did they save our mother? Think, Clay. It was only when we abandoned our ancestor's home that we had a chance to live. It's only now that we're taking up new ways near the forest that things have begun to get better for us."

"You know that we're not supposed to hold the gods accountable for our misfortune," Clay said, exasperated. "They're gods. It's their right to punish us if they want to. Remember the story the Teller says every year, about the—"

"Enough of what the Teller says," Laughing Dog snapped. "Enough of stories, of—of angry gods and prayers and all that sanctimonious pig shit. When I am out on the hunt, what makes the difference between hunger and feasting?" He balled his fist, slapping his tensed arm with the other hand. "This!" he said. He grasped his spear with both hands, the tips of his dark knuckles going white. "This, guided by my arm. The strength in my legs, the swiftness of my feet. Those are what decide. Not gods, somewhere far off, unconcerned with us. Not the will of the wood, nor the spirit of the tree you cut it from. You think if you kill more eland than Left Rabbit, it's because the gods favor you more, or because your prayers are stronger?"

Clay shook his head. "I can't hear any more of this," he said. He felt sick to hear his brother speaking this way, a spiked bur of worry forming in his stomach. "Wasn't a day of punishment enough for you? What started this?"

"I don't know." Laughing Dog leaned back on his hands. "Everything, I guess. Settling here, having to find new ways to do everything. Father seems more irritable with me than ever. And Ram, haven't you seen the way he acts?"

"He has been difficult," Clay admitted.

"Difficult!" Laughing Dog snorted. "He acts as though he's King already. Bossing everyone around—not just us, but everyone, and taking the best of every meal."

"It's his right." Great Ram's behavior had certainly been frustrating lately, even infuriating, but it was not Clay's place to call this into question, and certainly not Laughing Dog's. Their father would rein Ram in if he had to.

"Oh yes, because he had the tremendous good sense to be born before you or me. Look, he's going to be King one day. Fine, good for him, he's lucky. Blessed by the gods, whatever. But you and I have to find our own way. If we are to be great, then we must make ourselves great. Why should we not, if the gods have chosen not to bless us as they did our brother?"

Clay frowned. "What do you mean, make ourselves great? We're important to the people. We're both excellent hunters."

Laughing Dog's eyes glinted in the twilight. "We are, true, but we could be more than that. We could lead our people forward. Show them that they don't need to rely on the gods. Respect them, revere them, certainly," he added hastily, when Clay opened his mouth to protest. "Worship them. But while we're doing this, why should we deny the strength of our own limbs? When you bless your spear, are you not saying to it, 'I submit to your will, wood?' Whose will is stronger? Yours or the wood? Then why should you not command the spear to fly where you will, to dig its point deep into your prey?"

"But we cannot command the spirits of the world," Clay protested.

"Did not Father command *us* to labor in the sun all day?" Laughing Dog seemed to have been expecting the objection. "If a man can command the spirit of another man, why should he not command that of his spear? Why should he go through life on his knees, beseeching and begging everything in the world for permission to live?"

"You know the stories," Clay said, faltering.

Laughing Dog scowled. "Yes, I know the stories. I've heard them all my life. When I am not hearing them from the Teller, I have Great Ram or you reminding me of them. I am sick of the stories. We are slaves to the stories."

Clay felt ill. His father had asked him to look after Laughing Dog, to guide him, and he was failing. But what could he do? What words could he turn to if not the wisdom of their ancestors?

"That is why I have come to you with a proposal," Laughing Dog said. "You've blessed your spear, and I haven't. If you are right about the spirit world, then your spear should fly truer than mine, yes? Because the wood of my spear may turn against me, the stone not pierce my quarry. I bend the spirits of wood and stone to my own will and my own strength, and you beg yours for cooperation."

"That's not exactly what—"

"I know, I know. But it's true all the same, isn't it? If the gods will it, your spear will beat mine tomorrow."

"Yes," Clay said, frowning. "If the gods will it."

"So *pray* for it. Tonight, pray that the gods will prove to me that they command the will of all things. Pray that they humble me before them."

"But that's not right," Clay protested. "Remember the story of Tanager, who tested the gods and was punished? It's wrong!"

"Of course it's wrong," Laughing Dog said, his voice smooth and sweet as honey. "And we would not test the gods. What I propose is to give them an opportunity. Bless your spear, and if you kill more eland than I tomorrow, then I promise that from tomorrow forward, you will hear no more false stories from me. I will bless my spears and knives, and accept the wisdom of the elders."

Clay looked up into his brother's eyes. Laughing Dog had never lied to him, not so far as he could remember, and if there was a lie in his gaze now, Clay could not see it. "Forever?" he asked. "Just like that, you'll agree to dance the stories again and bless your home?"

Laughing Dog reached up to the beads around his neck and twisted them in his fingers. "Perhaps not forever," he said. "But for a time. Let us say, roughly, two rains. If two rains worth of quiet devotion cannot convince me of the gods' power, then perhaps I cannot be convinced. But it is a long time you and the gods will have to work on me." He grinned. "I can't say I'll look forward to that."

"And what if you kill more than I do?" Clay asked. "You'll just go on doing what you're doing?"

Laughing Dog's grin broadened. "Ah. Then that is my opportunity. I want to help our people try new ways—urge them to be strong and confident, to master the world around us instead of wheedling at it to help us. But I'm young, and people don't always listen to me. You, people like. They listen to you. You're well-known as a...thoughtful person. If I win our wager tomorrow, then you must accept that my own ideas have merit. You must help me to convince Father that I am right. And then you and I can work side by side to get our people to try a better way of doing things. And maybe next time tragedy comes to us, instead of praying to the gods to help us, we can help ourselves."

"You can't be serious!" Clay half-shouted the words. Then, in a more hushed tone, mindful that their father and brother could be in their tents nearby, added, "You don't think that I would turn my back on the gods simply because of a wager, do you?"

"I would never ask you to turn your back on the gods. In fact, that is exactly what I am asking you not to do. Listen. If you do not win our wager tomorrow, is that not the gods' will? You will have blessed your spear and prayed for their intervention. So whatever happens during our hunt must be what they wish to happen. Unless you believe that by your own qualities you have defied their power, and the spirits in your spear." Laughing Dog laughed, apparently at his own cleverness. "It's so perfect, Clay. If you pray for this, and you lose tomorrow, that means the gods want you to help me. They will be using us as their instruments to make our people stronger."

Clay frowned. He felt that there was something wrong in his brother's argument, some hole or problem that he could not see. "I don't know..."

"It would be your chance to look after me," Laughing Dog said. His grin took on an impish curl. "I know you're very interested in that right now."

"You—you know about that? You listened in on Father and me yesterday!"

Laughing Dog shrugged. "A tent hide isn't a wall, Clay. I can hardly help it if conversations carry."

"You shouldn't have listened, though." Clay folded his arms.

"Well, anyhow, I heard. And I want to help you." Laughing Dog leaned forward and clapped Clay on the shoulder. "Oh, don't look so angry. It's good for me to know that he's concerned. Look. Will you take the wager?"

"I don't know. I need to think about it."

"Well, you have tonight. You can let me know in the morning." Laughing Dog stood. "Good night. Get your rest. We both need it after today. And you more than I do if you plan on beating me!"

"Good night," Clay said. "Rest well."

Laughing Dog stood and exited the tent, leaving Clay alone in the darkening night with his thoughts.

He sharpened his knife, consumed what was left of his dinner—Red Moth had thoughtfully provided a larger than usual meal to help feed away the exhaustion of the day's work—and then he lay back on his hides, arms crossed behind his head.

Through the opening in the roof of his tent, he could see the stars glittering. There were the jaws of the great crocodile, the plumage of the show-me bird. Laughing Dog had said everything had changed since the people left their old home, but he was wrong. The stars were still the same. The gods had not changed. Father Wem had put the stars up in the sky to guide the people long ago, and it was those stars that had led them here, to the edge of the great forest.

Clay closed his eyes to them, thinking of what Laughing Dog had proposed. There were cautions against testing the gods. There was the story of Aloe Aloe, who had trusted the gods so completely that she had leapt from one of the high places and prayed for Father Wem to catch her. And when she fell and broke her arms and legs on the rocks below, she wailed to the gods, asking, why did you not catch me? Why did you not save me when I trusted in you? And the gods answered back, did we not give you eyes to see the cliff? Did we not give you feet to keep from rolling off the cliff? Did we not give you hands to climb carefully down it?

Laughing Dog had always been fond of that story, Clay recalled. It was a warning against expecting the gods to do whatever you prayed for, of course. They would not stop someone from his own foolishness. Could the wager be a test of the gods? Perhaps. But also, he considered, the story was about not being blind to the gifts in your life, the tools the gods provided to help you make your path and solve problems. Perhaps this wager itself was such a gift: not a test of the gods, but an opportunity for them to work their wonders. It could be, as Laughing Dog suggested, the very chance Clay needed to persuade his brother that the gods did guide his fate, and that they did seek his reverence.

And what did he risk if he lost the wager? Only that he would help his brother find new ways to help their people survive this strange land they now must call home. That was not so terrible. He could manage that without blasphemy.

He sighed, looking up at the stars again. If he spoke of this to his father or the elders, that would only get Laughing Dog in more trouble. It might cost him his inheritance. And Laughing Dog would feel betrayed, and not trust him again. No, he decided. He would put this in the gods' hands. He would accept Laughing Dog's wager.

He closed his eyes, feeling the weariness in his bones pull his limbs down toward the earth. Putting the decision behind him was relieving. As he sank toward sleep, he knew that tomorrow, everything would go according to the will of the gods, and that was enough.

The Turn of the Hunt

It was dark still when Left Rabbit thumped at his tent to wake him. Before sunrise, most of the eland would still be asleep, and those that had risen would be less alert to hunters. Clay rolled to his feet, catching up his spear and knife, and crept out of the entrance. He nodded to Left Rabbit. Neither of them would speak until outside the village. Waking those who were not required to be up so early would be rude.

Laughing Dog already waited near his own tent, and next to him stood Great Ram. Ram wore only his waistcloth; his fine clothes would be an impediment during the hunt. Around his neck, by a leather strap, hung his buffalo horn, white and grey against his dark brown chest. He nodded to Clay, and Clay dipped his head politely, stifling a yawn.

Clay stretched his legs, feeling their stiffness. They were definitely sore, but, he was pleased to note, not half so aching and weary as he had feared. The large meal and early night had gone a long way toward recovering him.

Left Rabbit beckoned, and together the three of them crept through the village, stepping quietly, so as not to disturb any sleepers. Near the village gate, the other hunters milled about sleepily, some leaning on their spears. Clay and his brothers seemed to be the last stragglers; once they arrived, they all filed out of the gate together.

Outside the wall, people felt more free to murmur. The sunrise was barely an ember-glow in the east, but the birds were already singing it up, chirping and whistling in the tree branches. Clay looked out across the savanna to the north and east. It was not true savanna, not like he'd known. There were too many trees here, not enough open field, but it was not forest either. It was a border, something in between the two. The morning light was growing pale and soft, the trees spotting the grassland dark, ambiguous shapes.

Someone gave him a firm nudge to his side, and he turned, startled.

"Have you given thought to my proposal?" Laughing Dog asked. He sounded serious for once, not joking.

"I have," Clay muttered back. He looked to make sure Left Rabbit wasn't tagging along too closely, and then smiled up at Laughing Dog. "They will show you their truth. I know it."

"And I will show you my strength," Laughing Dog returned. He held out his spear, the blue parrot feather that marked it as his fluttering at the end of its leather cord.

Clay hesitated. The Teller would not approve of this wager, he thought. Neither would his father. They would call it testing the gods. At best, it was risky. But what else was he to do? He knocked his own spear firmly against Laughing Dog's. "Agreed," he said.

His brother smiled broadly and squeezed his shoulder. "You won't regret it, I promise you."

"Good morning, brothers," Great Ram said from behind them. His voice was loud and booming, out of place in the quiet morning. "The herders are prepared. Are you ready to run?"

"We are ready!" said Laughing Dog with enthusiasm.

Clay simply nodded, saying another silent prayer to the spirits, asking them to guide the events of the day, to show his brother the value of asking their blessings.

"Then let us hunt. The sun will rise very soon. May earth and sky grant us many kills today."

Clay looked over to Laughing Dog, who flashed him an impudent grin.

The other hunters, some still sleepy, laughed and joked with each other for a while as they walked through the open forest, but as they approached the small herd of eland that grazed a short walk away, they quieted down. One loud word, one wrong movement could startle the herd, and then they would all go home empty-handed. A few of the elands slept, but most stood alert, keeping a watchful eye on the encroaching humans. Elands were skittish animals. Getting close enough to throw a spear with enough strength and accuracy to kill would be next to impossible, and one thrown spear would cause the rest to flee.

Great Ram and Laughing Dog broke away, taking most of the hunters with them. They crept through the grass toward the head of the herd, leaving two hunters flanking the eland there, the rest moving on beyond, leaving only Clay and Left Rabbit to wait behind. They knelt some distance apart, waiting, each next to a tree.

Being the fastest runners in the tribe, he and Left Rabbit were always placed behind the herd. Left Rabbit could nearly keep pace with his namesake, but Clay was faster still. He dug his toes into the dirt again, stretching out the muscles in his thighs and legs. He felt like a bent stalk of bamboo, straining to be loosed.

The sun had not yet risen, but the birds knew it was coming. The loud chuckle of hornbills mingled with the screeches of finches and grenadiers. Clay watched over one shoulder as the sky lightened, a pale yellow brightening over the grass. Then, after a few moments more, the orange eye of the sun winked above the horizon. Great Ram's horn sounded, clear and urgent, from the west.

That was the signal. Clay stood and turned toward the herd before the sun burned into his vision, and he could see Left Rabbit standing too, about a hundred paces to his right. His movement alerted a nearby eland. It grunted and flicked an ear, regarding him distrustfully. He lifted his spear high, watching Left Rabbit do the same.

"Hey hey hey hey hey hey!" He called at the top of his lungs. He clattered his spear loudly against the tree. "Hey hey hey hey hey hey!" The eland started, giving a sudden leap toward the herd. Clay ran toward it, shaking his spear. "Hey hey hey hey hey hey!" To his right, he could see Left Rabbit running as well, and could hear him calling out. A small group of elands had started to jog away from him. The herd was slow to rouse this morning. Some mornings they would be off like startled mice; others, they were tired and unsure of the danger. Clay ran directly toward a small group, shouting again, and this time all four of them sprang forward, kicking up a cloud of dust. The herd was alert now; other members kicked to their feet, bounding forward, and Clay and Left Rabbit raced after them.

Before them the large, tawny group dashed in panic, gaining ground on the runners. They tried to break to the left, but as they did so, the hunter placed near the front of the herd leapt out from behind a tree, clattering his spear against it and shouting. The elands were agile, powerful runners, and banked swiftly to the right, but again a hunter jumped up and shouted. Together, they funneled the herd forward. Clay ran in swift leaps, springing forward like the elands. Almost, he could forget about meat today: the wind was in his hair and face, and speed was in his belly, carrying him forward on the breeze. Running was his joy. He was fast, yes, faster than Left Rabbit, faster than any in his tribe, but the elands were faster still. In the open grassland the hunters would have had no chance, but here, where the forest met the savanna, it was easier. The elands had to weave back and forth to avoid striking each other or running into the trees, and that slowed them down.

Clay was losing ground on the herd, far out of reach of a spear's throw now squinting his eyes to keep out the dust kicked up by the pounding hooves. But the hunt was not over yet, nor the race. He ran. He whooped for the joy of it, and ran. Somewhere behind him he heard Left Rabbit return his whoop.

Ahead, the herd would try to break to the right or left again, and there again would be another pair of hunters to leap out with their spears waving and propel the elands forward. Many times this practice would not work, and the hunters would have to take the chance they were offered, throw their spears and hope for the best. A spear thrown at an animal's flank or haunches would most likely wound, but not kill. He had caught up to the other hunters now: there was Firefly, and there was Great Ram. He did not stop running. Ahead, he could see Laughing Dog, racing too, chasing the elands toward the place in the forest where the trees were thicker. If the hunt were over now, they would go home without meat or hides. But the hunt was not over.

Ahead, in the trees, fifteen more hunters had been waiting in place since the early morning, lying low in the grass and behind trees. Now they got to their feet, standing in a semi-circle, directly in the path of the stampeding elands. As Clay ran, he could see the hunters lifting long poles, each nearly twice the height of a man. With the poles they lifted a tall curtain, tightly woven of coarse grasses and palm fronds, extending from the tops of the poles all the way to the ground. It stretched wide, from man to man, winding between the trees in the shape of a crescent moon, blocking the path of the bounding elands.

Uncertain, the animals faltered, darting back and forth, trying to find a way around the seemingly solid wall that impeded their escape from the hunters racing up behind them, their herd mates caught in between. They cast to and fro, trapped in the dead end, but there was no way out. They bleated in panic, turned about, and bounded in the direction they had come, but now the rising sun shone in their eyes, and they were blinded. Their leaps were chaotic, erratic, and in their frantic attempt to reverse direction, propelled them into the paths of their oncoming herd mates. Clay could hear their panicked bleats, the clatter of horns, and the thumps of heavy bodies as they struck each other in their struggle to turn about.

He was catching up now, the others not far behind him, the elands running back toward them in dazzled confusion. His speed had begun to flag with exhaustion, but new energy surged through him and he flew like an eagle toward them, his toes seeming barely to touch the ground. Ahead a short distance he finally saw Laughing Dog, standing in the path of the blinded elands, which now moved slowly enough to keep up with, to strike with a spear. He saw the blue feather of his brother's spear dart through the air toward an approaching eland, and heard its shriek of alarm and pain. Remembering their wager, he slowed, readying his own spear; if Laughing Dog took down the eland, and Clay could not lance his own, he'd have lost the wager.

The herd bounded toward him. He stopped, lifting his spear as they approached. It was better to hunt eland when they ran toward you; your spear could strike the neck or the forequarters, taking the animal down more easily, but it was more dangerous. Eland were massive, and had deadly horns. To be struck by one almost certainly meant death. Two were running straight at him now. He prepared to throw his spear and then leap to either side should they not break. They bore down on him, lowering their horns, their muscled bodies pounding with frightened leaps, sharp hooves jabbing at the ground. A strange rattling sound came from the two of them. He held for one moment longer, the beat of a bird's wings.

To either side the elands darted; between them bounded a third, leaping through the air. Its eyes were mad with pain and terror, a froth spattering from its open mouth. For a moment, Clay thought it had three horns, but no, there was a flash of blue: the third horn was Laughing Dog's spear. He had thrown high, and its point had embedded itself in the animal's withers. The spear's haft was knocking back and forth between its horns as it leapt. The eland struck the ground and jumped forward again, only five spear lengths away.

Clay pushed backward away from it, and then he was falling, his own spear pointed toward it as if he might somehow catch the animal upon its point. The eland's hooves were drawn up against its chest; it flew toward him, and there was nothing he could do but fall—a slow, dreamy fall. The sunrise burned in its maddened eyes like fire. The air rushed from Clay's lungs as his back hit the ground, and a beat later his head struck the earth. He tried to get up, to roll, but it was taking forever, and then over his head a dark shape flew, the belly and legs of the eland. Pale and tan fur, the tuft at its belly, the hooves pressed against its chest, pointing backward.

Its hooves clattered against the earth and rock behind him, and then he was staring at the pale morning sky and the tops of trees. It had missed him. He was alive. He heard the thunder of the rest of the herd passing him on either side. His chest was still constricted, the air stolen from it. His back bucked against the ground as he tried to breathe, but the air would not come. Then it returned all at once, in a great, rasping gasp.

He sat upright and screamed. His voice rang in his ears. He took another, deeper breath and screamed again. He did not understand why he was screaming. His fingers dug into the earth. The end of his left leg had a foot, but it was not shaped like a foot should be. It was bent, and twisted, and his red blood spilled from it onto the ground. Yellow shards jutted up from it.

His head turned around and around inside itself. He wanted nothing more than to run, to get up and run away from the terrible thing on the end of his leg. Instead, he fell into darkness.

He knew the pain even before he woke, a burning ache in his foot, more terrible than any he had felt before, and so by the time he came back to consciousness, he was already familiar with it. He had hazy memories of waking several times, of being carried, seeing the hot sun above and hearing people speaking anxiously about him.

For a time he did not open his eyes, but lay quietly wrestling with the pain and listening to the sound of the crickets outside and the crackle of a small fire nearby. It was night. He could smell the raw body-scent of a tent, and the air was warm and stuffy. He did not want to think about what had happened. The ache crawled up the bone of his leg, gnawing at it. He blinked his eyes open. As he had guessed, he was lying on a bed of hides in Cloud's tent. Above him, on cords of twine, were strung bundles of various flowers and roots, bones from bird and antelope, all blackened from the smoke of her little fire. Cloud was there, too, her hair a bush of white and grey. She was hunched over a clay pot in which something boiled.

Although he had barely stirred, and she was facing away from him, she turned when his eyes opened. "Good," she said. She was very old and had few teeth left, but those that remained gleamed like ivory in her smile. "You are awake." She dipped a calabash in the pot and carried it over to him in slow, shuffling steps. "Drink," she told him, lifting the gourd to his lips. The liquid steamed and smelled bitter. "But little sips only. It is very hot."

Clay took a tiny taste of the concoction, and then another. It was far bitterer than it smelled, and thick, almost syrupy, but its flavor was familiar and comforting. "What is it?" he asked.

"Willow bark for the pain," said Cloud, "And violet tree root for the healing. Oldupai to keep the rot away. Other things as well."

He remembered his boyhood fevers, the ones that had made him sweat and vomit and see strange things. Cloud had cared for him then, and given him these kinds of potions before, and he had always felt much better afterward. He took a few more sips, and Cloud tilted the cup back for him, nodding in approbation. His gaze drifted over to his legs as he sipped, and the pain throbbed more intensely with his stare. His foot was wrapped in leaves, and there seemed to be some sort of poultice beneath them, green juice running down his leg. He remembered how the foot had looked before he'd blacked out, a pulpy mass with extruded bone, and thought maybe it had just looked worse than it was. He cast a hopeful glance up at Cloud.

She had always had a weariness behind her fierce eyes, for as long as he had known her, but it deepened at his implicit question, and she shook her head. The syrupy mixture in his stomach wanted to come back up. "The bones are shattered. The muscle torn. I cleaned it and set the bones as well as I could do, and I stitched the wound and wrapped it. If we're lucky, you won't lose the whole leg. But you're going to walk with a limp, if you walk at all."

Clay stared at her. He could not make sense of her words. "But I—but I run." His tongue was thick and stupid between his teeth.

Pity darkened Cloud's face. "Not any more, child. The gods have found a different path for you."

The gods. He had forgotten. The wager, the foolish tempting of fate. "No," he slurred. "They didn't choose this for me. I did. I brought it on myself."

Cloud's fingers gripped at her robe, twisting it. It was an old one, green and threadbare, made from some fabric bought from a northern trader. Her husband had given it to her long ago, Clay recalled. Then he'd died of a sickness she hadn't been able to cure. The reminder was not a comforting one right now. "That's despairing talk, that is. And I won't have it from you. You blame yourself for everything, but this? This is just an accident. A terrible misfortune. The eland that ran you down was in pain and terrified. The will of each spirit is strong, and even the gods cannot turn it if it doesn't wish to be turned. You did nothing wrong, you understand? Nothing."

She said it only because she didn't know Clay's foolishness. She thought him blameless, but if she realized the agreement he had made with Laughing Dog, she would not be so kind. The truth throbbed in his chest, his head, his foot. He longed to release it into the air, but if he did, then Laughing Dog would be in far more trouble than he.

Cloud leaned toward him. "Clay," she said. "Tell me you understand."

He stared up at her through pained eyes. He wanted to tell her. Instead he groaned, and turned away from her, curling toward his knees. When his foot grazed the edge of the bed, a searing flame of agony licked around it, and gnawed deep into the bones of his ankle. He knew without looking the expression she would be making, her hard jaw set, lips bunched tight in disapproval. He'd seen it often as a child when she suspected he was up to something but couldn't prove it.

"It's difficult now," she finally said. "But you'll feel better when the pain eases. Life is beating you down hard enough already. You don't have to go helping it out."

He closed his eyes and tried to tear his mind away from the heartbeat of pain in his foot, and then he was far away, back in the grand village they had lived in twelve rains ago. The savanna was golden and shimmering in the heat, and there were lions or large ants crawling over the hills, picking at them with their feet and tearing bits away. The plucking made tiny sounds of terrible importance, sounds that burrowed into his mind and throbbed there. He hated the sounds, the endless mad plucking at the hills that formed squares and diamonds and twisted toward the sky. So he ran away from it, ran faster and faster until his feet barely touched the ground, and there was a joy in it, a joy in the flight. He ran into darkness and the miserable sounds faded with the light. Then there was no need to run at all.

He woke drenched in sweat, his eyes opening to morning light. He was still in Cloud's tent, and Laughing Dog was leaning over him. "Clay? You're awake."

Clay nodded. His tongue was like a hot stone in his throat. "Water," he rasped.

Laughing Dog brought him a gourd of water, and he drank from it greedily. The soothing of his throat was immediate and welcome.

"You were twitching around a lot. Cloud said you had a fever."

"I remember bad dreams." The water knotted in his stomach, so he sipped more slowly.

"Fever dreams are awful," Laughing Dog said. "Remember the time I had a fever, and I told Cloud worms were coming out of her face? And then I reached up and tried to pull them out?" He stood, making pinching motions at the air. He was tall enough that he had to stoop slightly in the tent. Now Clay noticed that Cloud stood behind him, stirring at her pot, her back turned.

"How are you feeling?" Laughing Dog asked, crouching to peer at Clay's leg.

Clay shook his head. He was still woozy from the sleep, and probably the concoctions Cloud had given him. "It hurts. Like nothing I've ever felt before."

"I'm so sorry this happened," Laughing Dog said. "Cloud told us that it was serious, but we all hoped you might recover. Father has been in to see you twice since you fell. I haven't seen him so distraught since Mother died." He gripped Clay's leg above the injured area, lifting up so that he could inspect it. His hands were rough, and when they squeezed, it sent thudding hammers of pain up the bone. Clay clenched his teeth, hissing through them. "Sorry," Laughing Dog said. "I didn't think that would hurt."

"Everything hurts," Clay said.

Cloud floated into view and leaned down. "You are in that much pain?" she asked.

Clay nodded.

"I will go and get you more willow bark," she said, straightening and wiping her hands on her dress. "It will not take the pain away, but it will dull its teeth a little."

"There, you see?" Laughing Dog said as she left. "Cloud will take good care of you. In time, you will feel better."

"In time?" Clay repeated, numb. "Time will not grow me a new foot, will it? It's destroyed. I will not run again. I may not even be able to walk. My days as a hunter are over." Saying the words aloud, admitting them, gave them an awful weight and finality. "My life is over," he said with creeping realization.

"Don't talk that way!" Laughing Dog frowned. "Many hunters have injuries that stop them from hunting anymore."

"When they have seen thirty-five or forty rains! Not scarce more than twenty." Clay slumped back onto the hides, staring up at the roof of the tent. "And they have other skills. Long Neck worked leather after he hurt his shoulder. And when Twig began taking short breaths, he fell back on his carpentry. But I'm not skilled with my hands. And besides, I love running. I love the hunt. What am I to do without that?"

Laughing Dog's frown only deepened. "But you know what you're going to do. You and me, together." He looked back over his shoulder and then leaned in closer to Clay. "We had an agreement," he whispered.

An agreement? Clay blinked up at him, confused. "What agreement?"

The frown on Laughing Dog's face was erased by sudden concern. "Have you forgotten? Our wager that we made, before the hunt. You agreed that you would help me if you lost. And you did."

"Lost the wager? What do you mean I lost?"

"Well, I felled an eland," Laughing Dog said. "The one that ran you down. My spear weakened it enough that I was able to kill it. And you didn't." He brightened. "Ah, but of course you wouldn't remember that because you were injured at the time." He was still keeping his voice low.

Clay, however, was too incensed to keep quiet. He gripped at Laughing Dog's vest with both hands and pulled him close, twisting the leather between his fingers in lieu of twisting his brother's throat. "I lost the wager because I was lying on the ground *without a foot*," he said through his teeth. "You're really going to come to me now when my whole life has been taken away from me and claim you won?"

Laughing Dog pulled away and stood, looking puzzled. Clay could not keep hold in his weakened condition, and he fell to his side, sprawled halfway off the bed. Stone teeth gnawed at the bones of his foot and leg, rolling them back and forth as they chewed.

"You're angry," Laughing Dog said. "I understand. It has been a hard time for you. But you must agree, I won the wager. Surely you must accept that the gods must have wished me to win."

"The gods were angry with me for making the wager in the first place!" Clay exclaimed. "That is why I am lying here now. It's a punishment for testing them."

"You think the gods did this to you? Could it not have been pure chance? Either way, Clay, you have to admit that I won." He squatted again and helped Clay back onto the bed, causing more rolling waves of pain.

"You didn't win," Clay groaned. "You lost. I lost. We both did."

"No. Clay, you're confused. I killed an eland. That was the agreement."

"Yes, and I took it. And what do you think Father will do when you start talking blasphemy to the people?"

Laughing Dog shrugged. "He'll do the same as he always does: give me some minor punishment and forget about it. Besides, people will listen more with you helping me. You're very...spiritual. Everyone knows that. They will say, 'Laughing Dog has some big ideas, but I wasn't sure about them, but now that Clay agrees—'"

"They'll look down their noses," Clay said. "They'll cluck their tongues and say, 'Look at that poor boy cursing the gods for taking his foot. How easily the faith of the young is shattered.' And they won't listen to either of us, and they'll be right not to."

"How can you say that?" Anger burned low in Laughing Dog's eyes now. Clay had seen it before, that stubborn fire that came when he wasn't getting what he wanted. "Clay, I know you think the gods did this to you, but—"

"You did this to me!" Clay shouted. He knew he wasn't right to, but between the pain and the insensate, unfeeling response from his brother he couldn't keep it down any longer. He felt it break forth from inside him, contained for so long and now bursting open like an egg cooking in its shell. Still, he lowered his voice before continuing, lest the sound carry too far from their tent. "You spit in the faces of the gods. You refuse to bless your spears, to honor the spirits of the land. And then Father punishes me for not minding you. And so I try to protect you, and you fight me all the time. And then, *then*, Father tells me that I need to look after you or he will be forced to take drastic measures, and you use that information to goad me into taking your wager, a wager that tests the gods, and so *they* punish me for it. It's your fault, Laughing Dog. Yours. My foot is gone—my life is gone—because of you, and you're too stubborn to understand why I did it."

He tried to sit up, to reach out toward his brother, to beg him to see the plain message the gods had sent, but the movement bit fiercely at his leg and foot, and he collapsed backward, crying out, tears squeezing from the corners of his eyes at the agonizing pain.

"So," Laughing Dog said, his voice stiff with anger, "does that mean you intend to go back on your word after all?"

Clay sighed. As quickly as it had come, his frustration ebbed. He felt too weary to fight Laughing Dog any longer. What arguments did he have against his brother anyway? As always, fate had found him. It was better just to accept it. He would pray for the gods to intervene. All he could do was pray. "No," he said. "I'll do what I said. I'll hold up my end."

Laughing Dog smiled. "You won't be sorry, Clay! Together, we can help people. We can show them a new way, show them that we can be masters of our own worlds. That we no longer have to bow under the tyranny of old gods—"

"And what tyranny would that be?" Cloud asked. Her voice was hard and dangerous.

All other considerations fled Clay's mind as he turned his head to see the elder standing in the doorway to the tent, sunlight filtering through the fluff of her hair. How long had she been standing there? How much had she heard?

Had they been standing outside, Laughing Dog would no doubt have stood and squared his shoulders, but inside, stooped below the low ceiling of the tent, he could only hunch like a startled cat. "They…you know, they make us…pray all the time. And we have to do all these stupid things like waste our best wood on incense dust, and burn the best game instead of eating it. And all these stories make no sense."

"I'm well aware of your sage and experienced opinions on the gods," Cloud said. "But what I don't understand is why your brother would volunteer to help you spread them." Her eyes darted back and forth between them, and when neither answered, she snapped, "Well?"

Laughing Dog rubbed at the back of his head, fingers pushing between the braids. "Clay and I made a wager. If I killed more eland during the hunt, then he was supposed to help me teach people a new way of doing things."

"A new way? What way?"

"A way without the gods." His jaw tightened. "Where we depend upon our own strength and our own abilities. A way where *we* are the gods."

Cloud's dark eyes widened. "A way where—" She looked to Clay. "Why would you make an agreement like that?"

Clay's mind was still reeling from this last audacity of Laughing Dog's. "I—I don't…" he began. "I thought the gods would not let me lose. I thought I could help him."

Laughing Dog snorted. "And I thought you would learn a lesson from it."

"You should keep that fool mouth of yours shut before you fall in it any farther," Cloud said. Laughing Dog kept silent, but his eyes burned with anger. "Clay, you know we don't test the spirits. Not for our gain, not for our amusement. How many times have you heard the stories and the lessons? You know better than to play this kind of game." Her voice softened. "I guess you know too well, now. You're not the one who needs guidance."

She was silent, then, her lips pressed into a hard white line, her gaze distant and measuring. She stared at Laughing Dog and rubbed her chin. "No," she said. "It's got to be done. The King must be told."

"Wait," Clay said. "Please, Cloud, there's no need to talk to our father about this."

Cloud paused by the entry, then shook her head, slow and sad. "No," she said. "The boy is a danger, not just to himself, but to the best of us. You proved that yourself. He must learn." She disappeared.

Laughing Dog sighed. "Don't worry, Clay. It'll be fine. You know Father. He won't do anything. Another day working on the wall, maybe. Or maybe he'll force me to spend some hours with the Teller like he did when we were kids. Remember that? You don't need to worry about me." He crouched down and patted Clay on the shoulder. "Besides, now I have you on my side. I knew you'd keep your word when you lost."

Clay reached up and gripped his brother's arm. "Please, Laughing Dog. Reconsider. It was a stupid wager to make. It's true that I lost, but that doesn't mean you're right about things. If you keep talking this way, things are going to get bad."

Laughing Dog's brow knitted. "Why do you have to be so stubborn, Clay? You never admit you're wrong! How can you help me convince people if you won't even listen to me? You're selfish. That's what you are. Selfish."

Clay said nothing. He closed his eyes and turned away, sending all his weariness and frustration into the hard, hot sphere of pain at the end of his leg. He focused on it until Laughing Dog finally stormed out.

Ant With a Leaf came to see him once while he was recovering. Her eyes were dark and angry. She leaned right over his bed and asked into his face, "What did you tell them about my promised?"

"I didn't say anything," Clay protested. "Laughing Dog said it himself."

"I think you lie." She squinted her eyes into knives. Though she could not run as fast as Clay, she was far better with a bow than he with a spear, and was regarded as one of the village's most capable hunters. She had been promised as Laughing Dog's bride—though in truth, it was more that she had promised herself—but she had declared that she would not wed while the people did not have plenty of food. She had told Laughing Dog that she could hardly hunt for everyone if she were with child, and so their ceremony was delayed and delayed, first through their people's migration across the savanna, and then when they were learning to hunt and forage and grow new foods here on the edge of the forest. Privately, Clay suspected she was simply waiting to find out if her chosen husband was going to grow up.

"You can ask Cloud," Clay told her. "She can tell you what happened. She's the one who went to the King." He felt a little guilty for throwing the blame onto Cloud, who had done nothing but care for him and stand up for him, but he was tired of being confronted over all these problems as if he had been the one to cause them.

"I will talk to her, you can be certain of that," Ant said. "But I think you wanted this to happen."

Clay stared at her, then slumped back into his bed and closed his eyes, too tired to deal with her temper. "You're mad. Why would I want my foot to be hurt?"

"Not the foot. My promised to get in trouble."

"*Is* he in trouble? My father likes to forgive him for everything."

"And you like to tell on him for everything. Always trying to get him in trouble. You are always talking about the gods this, and the gods that, but I think you are just trying to hide something." He saw her shadow fall over him through his closed lids and opened them to see her finger in his face. "Something not right about you. I wanted you first, Clay. I made myself beautiful so you would notice. I ran with you in the hunts and challenged you. I sat next to you at fire after fire, and you did not even look at me. Then I learned that you are a foolish boy. I decided I did not want a fool for a husband, so I chose Laughing Dog instead. And now I think maybe you're trying to stop him from being with me too."

Clay was still lost on her previous comment to consider this latest accusation. Ant With a Leaf had been interested in him? He had had no idea. He had certainly never thought of her that way, but he thought of no women in his village that way. He had regarded his brothers' avid interest in their figures and lascivious comments with continued puzzlement, never really understanding what it was they found so fascinating, what it was that drove them, as they grew taller and became men, to hunger after them.

If he were being honest with himself, he sometimes lay in his tent and imagined Left Rabbit creeping in to meet him in the night—but these desires were forbidden by his people and by the gods, and so he took care not to linger on them any more than he could help it.

"I would never do that, Ant With a Leaf," he said. "I want my brother to be happy with our people. But that's not going to happen if he keeps spiting the gods like this. He could bring down ruin on himself. On all of us." He glanced meaningfully toward his bandaged leg. "Somebody has to talk to him."

There was still anger in her face, but the set of her jaw softened. "It is true that he has been saying unwise things lately," she said. "But that is all the more reason not to make things worse for him. Maybe you do not see how bad things have been getting. You are never really with us. Always off running, staring into the forest or the sky. People talk, you know. Not just about Laughing Dog."

"Do they?"

She grunted an affirmation. "They say, 'That Clay! He wants to be with the gods so badly he has sent one foot to them early.'"

Clay didn't find this very funny, but he swallowed the sour taste in his mouth. "I guess I can come off a little sky-minded."

"Yes. You can." Her dark eyes glittered in satisfaction. "But they say the opposite of my promised. They say he will come to a bad end. They say he is angry at the gods because he will not be King, because it will be Great Ram and maybe someday you. There is to be a council fire in two days. I have spoken to Laughing Dog, and he will apologize to the people for what he has done."

That did not sound like Laughing Dog. "He said that?"

Ant With a Leaf lifted her head high. "I told him he will. He had better listen to his promised or I will make him very sorry."

Clay sat up partway and winced as his throbbing pain transformed into an intense flare. His back was sore from lying down for so long. "Ant, make sure you know what he's going to say. You know how he can be. If he gets upset, he could make things even worse. He could be taken from the hunt. If he manages to say the wrong thing, he could even risk his inheritance."

"I will make certain that he understands," Ant said. She put her hand on Clay's arm. "Everything will be all right. Don't worry."

⌢⌢⌢

The night was dark and cooler than usual, but the council fire burned all the higher. Clay was glad to be out in the evening air after so long in the hot and smoky medicine tent, even though the breeze seemed to make his leg ache more. The night was moonless, and so above them the stars sparkled more brightly than usual.

Sitting around the fire, some leaning back on their hands, some cross-legged, some squatting, was his tribe: to his right, Great Ram, looking serious and stoic; his wife, Hibiscus, at his side; and to the right of them, their father, King First Claw. Laughing Dog stood to Clay's left, staring sullenly into the fire. He had not spoken to Clay since their argument.

It had been a week since the hunt when Clay had fallen, and the searing pain in his foot had faded to a persistent, gnawing ache that sometimes extended all the way up to his knee. He had dared to look at the injury once when Cloud reapplied the poultice, but in the red, sticky mass there was no shape he could recognize. Many had come to visit him and express their sympathies, but none quite knew what to say. Injuries during hunts were not rare, and deaths were not unheard of, but to be crippled so was considered a great disappointment. Some tried to laugh and joke with him, some were sober or terse, and nearly everyone seemed to have some word of advice or wisdom that sounded, to him, false or useless. Some wanted to know the reason Laughing Dog no longer hunted with them, and then Clay would grow quiet and say nothing.

Whispers had been going around the village that tonight would be a special occasion, and indeed, a great feast had been prepared, including spiced boar, palm dates, and crispy fried caterpillars, all of which, Clay couldn't help noticing, were among Laughing Dog's favorite foods. The bonfire burned higher than usual, and many danced with energy. Clay yearned to join in; despite his leg, the drumbeats were in his blood. He wanted to leap and twirl and crouch. But he would never do any of these things again. He wondered if, over time, he would forget what the drums felt like in his bones, or if always he would feel the urge, arresting him, propelling him, calling him to something that was impossible.

Now, though, the dances had died down, and people were heavy and sleepy with food. The Teller stood, his arms raised. The wind lifted, catching the zebra skin tied about his plump shoulders. "Oh People of the Savanna," he called over the sound of the fire, which had begun to pop and roar more loudly in the breeze. "Would you hear the tale of the buffalo horn?"

"We would hear it," the tribe called the answer back.

Clay looked toward Laughing Dog; his brother's lips moved, but Clay could not hear whether he said the words. He knew his brother would not care to hear this particular tale.

"Then listen well," said the Teller. "When the world was young and wet, Wem, the Sky Father, looked down on it and saw all of the creatures that he had made. He saw lion and elephant, alligator and scorpion, stork and monkey, antelope and frog. And all were weak and helpless and could not eat.

"'Come,' said the Sky Father, to the animals, 'so that I may give you gifts that will help you to survive this world.' And so the animals came one by one, and he gave them great powers. So to elephant, he gave tremendous size and a powerful trunk, and to serpent he gave fangs and a wide mouth. To lion he gave mighty claws; to monkey, nimble feet and tail. And so on. And at the last, he came to man, who by bad luck had been at the very end of the line.

"'What can you give me?' asked man. 'For it seems you have nothing left. You have given away the last of your claws to cheetah, and the last of your fangs to baboon. Hippo has taken all the great weight remaining, and giraffe has greedily taken every bit of the height.'

"'It is true,' said Father Wem. 'I have none of these things left to give.' And man was dismayed, and tore at his hair. 'How will I survive?' he asked Father Wem. 'You have not even given me a coat of fur so that I may stay warm at night. With no gifts, I will die.'

"'No,' said Father Wem. 'You will not die. To you I give every single gift I have given to all my creatures. When you need claws, then you shall take claws from cheetah, and when you need fur to keep you warm, you shall take it from zebra. If you need teeth, you may even take them from the very stones. All that I have, and all that I have given to others is yours to use, provided you ask permission of those who owned them first. Request their gifts of them, and they cannot refuse you.'

"Then man was glad, for surely this was the greatest gift of all, to be able to take for himself anything he needed from the Sky Father's creatures. And for a time he grew happy and strong. He thrived and had many children. But after a while, he grew so proud with his great strength that he forgot Father Wem's condition.

"One day man was walking through the savanna and became hungry. Nearby he could see some buffalo, and he thought of meat. He went to a nearby tree, and took his knife, and from the tree he cut a spear. But so proud was he that he did not ask the tree for the spear, but cut it out without permission. 'All gifts of the world are mine,' said man."

Clay looked over at Laughing Dog, who caught his gaze and turned away, staring furiously into the fire.

"And man threw the spear at the buffalo and killed it, and he did not ask forgiveness. With his knife he cut it open and ate its meat, and did not pray for permission from the spirit of the buffalo. And with a stone he cracked its skull and took a horn for himself."

People around the fire spit into the dirt at the selfish pride of the man; Clay watched Laughing Dog, and he did not.

"Then, in the night, the meat in man's stomach grew angry at having been taken from its buffalo without permission, so it turned and soured. Man woke up wet with illness, and the meat left his stomach. 'I will use the horn,' said man, 'and summon my kinsmen to help me and carry me back to camp.' So he lifted the horn to his lips and blew. But the horn was angry at having been taken from the buffalo without permission, so instead of calling the man's kinsmen, it called a mighty lion. When man saw the lion coming, he threw his spear at it, but the spear was angry at having been torn from the tree without permission, so instead of striking the lion, it fell to the earth. Then man grew frightened, and forgetting his illness, he ran from the lion to a tree, and attempted to climb it. But, great pity, my people, this was the very tree from which he had cut his spear without asking permission, and the tree was angry. So when man tried to climb it, it shook and shrugged, and he fell down to the earth, and could not escape the lion.

"Then man prayed to Father Wem. 'Please save me!' he cried, 'for all your gifts have turned against me, and I am helpless, and will die!'

"Then the Sky Father was angry, and made great clouds. 'No,' he said. 'I will not save you, for you have taken all the gifts of my creatures as if they were your own. Only gods may take without asking. Because you have taken without permission, I will let my creatures take something from you.' And then the lion left. Man hurried back to his kinsmen, but when he returned to his village, the lions had killed them, every one."

There was quiet around the fire now. Clay had heard this tale a few times before, and it was always treated as a serious one. The Teller walked around the fire, looking at each of them. Clay looked up at him as he walked by. He knew him well. The man was fat, old, and kind, and knew how to weave fascinating patterns with dyed hair, and when he was not Telling, loved to joke and play games. Now was not a moment of jest.

"Now we are charged by the Sky Father to remember that on this land, everything is ours, and yet nothing is ours but our own bodies. When we are separated from something that is part of us, do we not feel pain? Do we not feel anger?" The Teller looked right at Clay as he said this, and Clay nodded and called, "We do feel it," in response.

"And when one we love is taken from us, do we not feel pain and anger?"

The people around the fire murmured their assent.

"Of course we do. There is a madness that comes when we are torn from ourselves. So too all living things," said the Teller. "Even the earth and stone. We must never forget this." He was staring at Laughing Dog now.

"We will never forget," said the people.

But Laughing Dog looked up at the Teller and did not speak.

"We must never forget this," repeated the Teller more firmly, but with an encouraging tone in his voice.

The people looked at Laughing Dog. Clay felt an uneasy prickle up the back of his neck. This was the part where Laughing Dog was supposed to apologize. Something was about to go badly wrong.

The village was silent, except for the crackle and pop of the fire.

"Oh come on," said Laughing Dog finally, his voice awkwardly loud. "It's only stories."

"Son!" That was their father's voice, sharp with a warning tone that Clay had long ago learned to treat with instant seriousness; often it could be followed by a knock across the back or the head with a spear haft.

Laughing Dog shook his head. "No, Father, you know they're just stories. It's good for the children, but nobody really believes…" He looked at the people around the council fire. He stepped toward them, in front of Clay, a dark silhouette against the high, raging flames of orange and red. "You don't honestly believe that at some point in time the animals were all lining up without teeth and claws, and—and the Sky Father was passing them out like presents, do you?"

Their father got to his feet. Age slowed his movements, but he stood to his usual proud height. Clay thought he could see sadness in his eyes. "Laughing Dog, my son." He reached out his hand. "You are forgetting your youth. Listen to the wisdom of your elders. You need only to say you trust in that wisdom, and that you will not forget it. Promise us all that you will regard the spirits of the world with respect, and we will let this pass."

Laughing Dog looked down at their father's hand as if he had never seen it before. His brow was furrowed, thrown into twisted shadow by the light of the bonfire. "Of course I respect the wisdom of my elders, Father. But—"

Their father spoke hurriedly. Clay thought he was afraid to let Laughing Dog finish whatever he'd been about to say. "And tell us all—tell your brother—that you will bless your spears from this day on."

Laughing Dog's laugh was half nervous, half defiant. It rang out through the silence of the night. "I am not going to say that, Father." Gasps of astonishment went around the fire. He turned toward the circle and lifted his voice. "It is through the strength of my arm that I have provided you all with kills for many weeks now. I did not bless a single spear. If the spirits object, then why are your bellies full of meat? Why do you lie on fresh hides? Why should I give them the credit? Why should any of us? Would it not be better for us to accept the credit for success? The blame for failure? Would it be so terrible for us to ask ourselves if these are, perhaps, only stories we have told ourselves for far too long?"

It was utter heresy. To deny the spirits entirely, to question the gods themselves? Laughing Dog had always had an independent streak, but this was beyond anything he'd ever said before, beyond that one brazen claim in Cloud's tent. *We* will be the gods, Laughing Dog had said. Clay had hoped that it was simply the impetuousness of the moment. He wanted to jump to his feet, to press his hand across Laughing Dog's mouth before he could say any more, but far too much had been said already. With dread certainty, he knew what would happen next: his brother would lose his inheritance. He would no longer be treated as a son of the king, no longer enjoy the best food and clothes and pottery that the people had to offer. He would be disgraced.

"Laughing Dog!" their father said, but it was not the voice of their father. It was the voice of the King, powerful, commanding. It rang out above the fire and called down the stars. "Your words are not the words of my son." He paused for a deep breath, resignation settling in his craggy brow. "They are not the words of our people."

Clay felt his hairs rise, his skin tighten. This was worse, much worse. His voice bubbled up from within him unbidden. "Father, no!"

The King ignored him. A slow, steady drumbeat came from across the fire. "You tell us that you will not follow your people." The drumbeat was joined by another, a heavy, thumping, joyless tempo. It was the beat of loss, of mourning. It tugged at Clay's soul and pulled it along. "You tell us that you will not follow your King." Now all the drums had joined in. Clay had last heard it when his Uncle Six died. He remembered every time he had heard the beat before: a fallen child, the elderly gone to final sleep, a miscarriage, a festering wound, his mother's death. Each drumbeat chanted their losses in his heart. "You tell us that you will not follow your gods."

Laughing Dog stood very still against the flames. He did not look around at the faces of his people. He did not turn to glance at Clay. His back was erect, his head held high, his face determined. Clay could see, though, that he was trembling. Risking a glance toward Ant With a Leaf, he saw her own face set, her gaze focused into the fire. She was not looking at Laughing Dog.

"I will not risk the fate of the People of the Savanna to your foolish youth and arrogance. I cannot let your pride threaten our village, or anger the gods against us. Laughing Dog, you are now banished from the tribe." Once, and only once, the King's voice broke, his father's raw grief cracking through it. "You are exiled from our hunting grounds. I cast you out into the wilderness, until such time as you learn the wisdom you have forgotten, until the gods speak to you so loudly that you cannot ignore them any longer."

The King turned his back to Laughing Dog. "Go now. Take water and food. Take the spears that you have cursed. And do not return until you are a different man."

The drums grew louder and louder, their beats like the knocks of an axe into a tree. Laughing Dog stood stiff as a stone for beat after beat, and then he turned. He picked up his spear from the side of the fire. Louder. He kept his gaze distant, looking right past Clay; nor did he meet the eyes of anyone else as far as Clay could tell.

Ignoring the pain in his leg, Clay rolled to his knees and began to push himself upright—if not to follow after Laughing Dog, at least to embrace him and wish him a safe journey. He called out his brother's name, but a sharp look from his father and a shake of the head halted him, and he sat down again.

Louder. Louder. Clay watched his brother turn away from the fire, without food and without water, and venture into the darkness. His shadow disappeared into the night. Their father never turned to look after him.

The drums fell silent.

‿‿‿

When Clay had seen the rains only ten times, and Laughing Dog eight, their mother had taken fever. Cloud, who back then had had no white in her hair, had tended to her as best as she was able, but the sun was fierce, and the fever was fiercer still. On the third day, she died. The people sounded the beat of mourning. They built a pyre of acacia, and placed Clay's mother upon it, and sent her back to Wem. Then their father had gone into his tent to mourn, and did not come out until a moon had passed.

Now, too, he disappeared, remaining inside his tent through both the cool night and the hottest part of the day. Days passed and Clay did not see him, nor did any of the other villagers. Great Ram stepped in to serve as King in his father's stead, and he took to the role with a readiness and seriousness that Clay might have teased him for, had circumstances been different. He strode importantly about the village, wearing the King's hat of leopard skin and feathers and holding his head high, responding to questions and comments with a solemn expression.

Clay felt numb after his brother had gone. Feelings of guilt and anger with Laughing Dog wrestled inside of him. If he hadn't been so foolish as to accept the wager… But no. Laughing Dog had set himself down this path long ago. Odd little memories that Clay had never paid much attention to before suddenly presented themselves: his brother holding his head high when others were bent in reverence; always dancing the victories, but never the prayers; turns of phrase which had seemed innocent at the time but now were full of heavy significance. Clay ought to have known something was wrong long ago. They all ought to. Maybe others had. His father had; he was certain of that much.

Still, it didn't seem possible that Laughing Dog could be truly gone. It was as if he were only on a long hunt, or a search for new water, or a journey to another people to trade for goats or fine cloth. Clay found his eyes turning to the edge of village and the rolling hills of the savanna beyond, hoping to see his brother returning with a sheepish grin on his face, embarrassed at his own foolish pride. Or perhaps in the wilderness, the gods would have found him, and taught him his error. Perhaps in isolation, he would have discovered the wisdom of his people, or finally felt the strength of the spirits in every living thing around him.

But day after day went by, and still Laughing Dog did not return. Clay knew, deep in his heart, that his brother would not accept that humiliation. He would not return in defeat. He wondered if he would never see Laughing Dog again. Entertaining the thought made him sick to his stomach.

Distraction, however, proved both more frequent and less welcome than he would have liked. Cloud kept him busy throughout the day, setting him to weaving palm fronds, mashing nuts, and carving spears for the other hunters. At first he thought she simply wished to take his mind away from his brother and from his injury, but she was surprisingly firm and demanding. When he weaved the hunting walls too loosely, she struck at his hands with a leather strop, made him unpick them, and begin again. She instructed him in new methods of aligning the leaves so they looked like a solid wall, taught him to slick his fingers with palm butter so that the sturdier, less pliable blades did not slice them open. Sometimes she would call him into her tent and set him to stirring one of her foul-smelling decoctions, and while he did so, she would arrange her ingredients, lecturing him on various extracts and roots and their purposes, quizzing him on them after the fact. He tried his best to pay attention to her, but he hadn't much of a head for it, and besides, his legs ached to run. His mind drifted always back to thoughts of bounding like an antelope between the trees, spear held at the ready, the wind rushing past his ears. The dream would carry him away for a while and then let him drop like a stone.

Cloud changed his poultice at least once a day, and eventually taught him to brew up a new one and change it himself. The first time he pulled away the leaves binding his foot and saw the twisted, scabrous shape, he felt dizzy, and nearly vomited. The thing at the end of his leg could not truly be part of him. As days passed, the pain steadily lessened, though if he put any of his weight on it, it hurt all the way up to his teeth. He took one of Laughing Dog's abandoned spears, blessed it, and carved two separate pieces from it, fashioning a crutch that he could at least use to get around without hopping, though it was neither easy nor comfortable to do so. Even as he grew more skilled with using it to move about, an increasing heaviness settled across him. He cared little what task he was assigned to, and spoke little to others while engaged in it.

One afternoon, Cloud sent him across the village to assist the women in stripping hides from the morning's kills. It was not work that he found appealing, but he could scarcely complain; he did not bring in kills. At the very least he could help tend to them. And it was work in the shade during the heat of the day.

Slowly, painfully, he made his way across the village. He had nearly reached the work area when the tip of his crutch caught an upward-jutting tree root and sent him spilling forward to the ground. He wasn't hurt much, but a great anger and misery rose inside him nonetheless, pushing up past the heaviness that had been bearing him down and breaking out of him in a wordless cry of anger. He pushed himself to his knees, took up his crutch in both hands and swung it hard against the tree that had tripped him up. The crutch shuddered with the blow, so he reared back and swung it again, striking the tree over and over until the crutch splintered and broke.

For a while he knelt panting in the dirt. Then, using the tree for support, he pushed himself up to a standing position. Out of the corner of his eye he could see people watching him, but he didn't care. He turned and took a limping step, letting a little of his weight come down on the stump where his foot used to be. Pain bit through him, up his leg. He could feel something solid shifting in the flesh, a sharp, cutting pain, but it felt good, appropriate somehow. He limped again, and was rewarded with another keen blade of agony up his leg. It reaffirmed and validated every bit of fury and self-pity he was feeling. Each step hurt a little less than the previous, the pain growing duller and duller, though he panted with the exertion. Steadily he made his way out of the village, until finally he could limp no farther, and he fell to all fours. On hands and knees he crawled through the grass, feeling glad, grateful to be rid of the wretched crutch. He made his way, pulling himself up Gamewatch Rise, the large, grassy hill outside town. It was high and steep, and a good spot for watchers to survey the savanna, but not easy to climb on all fours. Clay labored to drag himself to the top, and when he reached it, he sprawled out flat, breathing heavily, staring at the sky. No gods smiled or frowned to him from its blue depths, so he sat upright, letting his foot rest. It throbbed in protest and bled a little; most of the leaves binding it had been pulled away by his exertions.

He ignored it and gazed out over the grass. There was a wind today, warm and heavy, promising rain soon. Soon Wem would call giant, dark piles of clouds to sweep in off the savanna and soak them all, but only the wispy ones wandered the sky now. He let his eyes settle on those, followed them as they crept westward.

A hand settled on his shoulder, startling him. The fingers were thin and bony. He turned. "Cloud. I didn't hear you coming."

Cloud sat down next to him, her earrings rattling in the breeze. "Went for a little walk, did you? Let me see that foot."

He bent his knee and let her take it with her rough fingers. She gripped at the ankle and examined his stump, shaking her head. "Foolish to walk on it," she said. "It will take twice as long to heal now."

"Doesn't matter," Clay said, looking away. "It'll never be good anyway."

"Is that what it is?" Cloud peered at him. "Come out here to beat the mourning for your foot, have you?"

"My foot," Clay returned bitterly. "My life."

"Funny. Don't recall a man's heart being in his foot."

"Well, mine was," he said with sudden conviction. "I ran, Cloud, that was what the gods made me. A runner. I was myself when I was out running a hunt. Joyful. At peace. How am I going to find that now? Weaving walls? Stripping hides?"

Cloud said nothing.

He sighed. "I was going to be the greatest hunter of our people. I was going to be somebody. Do great things. And now what?"

Cloud shook her head. "Sometimes it is hard to believe you and Laughing Dog are brothers. He would not be this way. He would not let some old foot stop him from becoming what he wanted to be."

Clay gave a bitter laugh. "He wouldn't even let the gods stop him. And look where that got him."

"He has his own lessons to learn, true. Too much fire and pride in that one. He looked to the gods too little. But you, Clay. Too much. You can't just wait for them to show you your way or to solve all your problems. You got to meet them halfway. Tell them what you want. Show them that you'll fight for it."

"I want to run!" he half-shouted. "But I can't. I never will. Never again."

Cloud put her hand on his shoulder again. "You see there? That's passion in you. You could do great things with it. Don't turn it against yourself. Don't have so much faith in your own weakness." She stood. "You made your way out here on your own. I expect you can find your own way back. Try not to ruin that foot any more than you already have."

Despite himself, Clay almost laughed. She was going to make him crawl back. It was harder to pity himself when Cloud wouldn't.

"The gods have got something for us all to do," Cloud said. "But if you just lie there waiting for them to tell you what it is, you're going to be waiting your whole life. So don't feel sorry for yourself too long." Then she left, walking down Gamewatch Rise, back toward the village. "Once you're done beating the mourning, there's some hide that needs stripping. I told them to leave it special for you."

Clay lay in his tent, feeling exhausted and strangely at peace. It was as though he'd vomited up something sour in his stomach, and the sickness and cramping was finally gone. The birds and the crickets sang in the darkness, and he was comforted to hear them. He thought of Laughing Dog, somewhere out in the wilderness to the north, and prayed that the gods would find him and guide him. He thought of hunting, and vowed that one day, somehow, he would find a way to feel the thrill and elation it gave him again. He would find something else. His eyes closed, and he fell into heavy and dreamless sleep.

When he awoke, it was still dark. He could not discern what had awoken him, and lifted his head. A figure stood crouched in the door to his tent, silhouetted against the moonlight. He peered, trying to see who it was.

"Hello?"

"You will come with me. You will not make any sound to your herd, or you will die. And then they will die."

Clay was instantly wide awake. Invaders from another people. It had to be. They didn't know the language well. The accent was strange, the voice husky and growling.

"Come now or I will kill you."

His spear was outside. There was no way he could get to it from here, and he had no knife. Shaking, he rolled to his knees and pushed himself up to one leg. The figure vanished from the doorway with an eerie fluidity. There was little light, but Clay had not seen any weapon. Maybe he could grapple the intruder. He wished now that he had not destroyed his crutch; it would have made a serviceable weapon. Quickly, he cast about for something in his tent he could use, but he could think of nothing. He hopped to the entry to his tent and looked out. No telling how many other intruders there might be. Certainly more than one.

"This way." The voice came from the south, toward the forest and around his tent. Clay hopped around it. He'd left his spear propped up against the side. He could probably get to it if they hadn't seen it.

His fingers brushed in the place where he'd left his spear and encountered only the rough hide of his tent.

"Your tooth stick is gone. It is too late to bite me with it. This way!" The voice growled more insistently.

Clay squinted through the darkness toward the figure standing there. The torch near his tent still burned with low embers, and between that and the moonlight, he could almost see. "I only have one foot," he said. "I cannot walk."

Eyes glinted green in the darkness, reflecting back at him. Into the dim light stepped an impossible creature, half man, half leopard. It was tall, powerfully built, and naked, its fur covered with rosettes, its weight balanced lightly on feline paws. A tail switched behind it. "You are injured," it said. "And weak. You cannot keep up with your herd. You are my prey."

Ascension

The creature was surprisingly weak and pathetic. Its eyes stared blankly around, sweeping past Doto without even seeing him. Had Doto not observed it moving about during the day, he would have thought it blind. But it did not sniff the air. Its ears did not twitch toward him. It groped about helplessly in the dark like an infant. How could a creature like this stand with the bearing of a god? Clearly Doto had been mistaken. It walked upright, perhaps, but it was no god. Its injury was proof enough of that.

From the safety of the forest, sometimes with his own eyes, sometimes with the eyes of birds, Doto had watched the bearer and its herd over the preceding days. It had hobbled pitifully about its nest, or crawled, mewling and sulking. This was what his father had been afraid of? This was one of Ogya's minions, this limping whelp? Perhaps the fire bearers were no longer the formidable creatures they once had been. But diminished or no, they yet had their flames, and at night, they would make the dead cry out. Their nest was full of the nauseating stench of burned wood. Doto had thought it best to move the thing's stone tooth away before waking it, but he had not dared go near the flame, even when it was low. He could not be certain that even now, Ogya did not peer at him through it.

With some amusement, he watched the creature grope blindly for its tooth, and then announced that it would not find it.

"I have only one foot. I cannot walk," the creature whined in its peculiar language. It was a complicated tongue, unlike any Doto had heard before, and he had needed many days of silent study and listening to the bearers babbling from afar before he had begun to comprehend it. Disappointingly, they talked of idle things: food; the deeds of other bearers; sex. They spoke of the gods, but little of their relationship to Ogya, and even less of their plans for the forest, which they seemed to regard with suspicion and trepidation, but not, as far as Doto had been able to discern, any antagonism. Whatever hopes he had had of gaining information for Kwaee had soon dissipated.

He could detect no scent of fear on this bearer, though of course that might be hidden by the ubiquitous reek of fire. Still, the creature neither cowered nor bowed before him. Plainly, it did not understand that it was confronted with a god. Perhaps, like a bird, it needed more light to see. Perhaps it *was* a bird, some sort of featherless, beakless thing. That might explain why it stood as it did. But no, the resemblance to Doto and his father in both shape and stance was too uncannily familiar for it to be a bird. Why was it so reticent to obey? If it had not been a fire bearer, he would have sent his mind into it, and urged it forward as he did with other beasts, but this thing was surely corrupted by Ogya. He dared not join his mind to its own.

If it could see him, he decided, it would understand that it was dealing with a god. He stepped forward a few paces, not pleased about reentering the potentially treacherous firelight, and was gratified to see the bearer cringe backward at the sight of him. The acrid stench of its sudden terror stung at his nostrils. "You are injured and weak," he informed it. "You cannot keep up with your herd. You are my prey."

That was right. That was the way of things. He prided himself that even when dealing with these aberrations, he upheld the laws of the forest. Kwaee would have been pleased.

The bearer trembled. Good. "Are you a demon?" it asked.

"A demon? Fool. Do you not recognize a god when you see one? You will follow me now, or I will destroy your herd." That was a bit of a bluff. The fire bearer he had selected was weak and injured, easily captured. Doto did not relish the idea of facing down a healthy one, one that might be armed with tooth and fire, much less a whole herd of them. But he thought the creature too feeble and frightened to suspect the lie.

The bearer gaped. "A god?" it said. It stood taller, staring at him with widening eyes, which Doto did not much care for. "That's impossible!"

"Do not speak to me about what is impossible. Follow me. Now."

The bearer hopped a few times, favoring its injured foot, its weight thumping loudly. Doto could scent healing flesh on it. He flattened his ears at the sound, hoping none of the other bearers would be alerted by it. But they were no doubt accustomed to this one hopping around its nest and would ignore it. He backed out of the firelight, leading the bearer toward the odd barrier of dead trees its herd had erected around their nest. There was a gap in this barrier now, thanks to him.

At first he had been concerned about how to enter. In the heart of the forest, his power would have been great, but the bearer's nest extended beyond the edge of his father's realm. Somewhere not too far beyond where he now stood, his power ended, the rich sensory knowledge of the forest he had always known ran into dull blindness. Beyond was the savanna, the realm of the god Sarmu, where he could not pass. If his prey were to escape past that edge of his power, he could not pursue it. And he would be helpless if Ogya's flames trapped him between the forest and the savanna. Caution was required.

He had used the smallest application of his power, shifting the soil, encouraging the dead wood to tilt, until he had been able to pull away a few of the dead branches, creating a hole in the wall large enough to creep through. Now he slunk back through it, relieved to be out of the firelight once more.

He led his captive bearer through that gap and into the forest, but the thing moved at a tedious pace, and after only a short time, his tail began to switch with impatience. He slunk a few paces ahead and turned about. They had scarcely left the bearers' nest. The circle of strange little things—which he had thought to be plants, but proved instead to be domes made of tree and bone and dead flesh—was still not far away. Any distance from the fires was progress, though; he felt more at ease now that the embers were little sparks in the distance.

The bearer seemed less at ease, however. It stopped in one place, panting, although the night was too cool for it to be overheated. It turned its head back and forth, eyes staring blankly. Of course, it could not see. How could anyone ever fear such a helpless creature? "Over here," Doto growled low, and it started as if attacked. It hopped again in his direction, and then its leg gave out and it went sprawling into the grass and leaves, awkwardly catching itself on its forepaws.

"I cannot walk," it complained. Doto thought the pitch to its voice was frustration. "And I cannot see. How am I to follow you? Lord," it added, with a more respectful note. At least it was learning.

"Why do you insist on walking like a god?" he asked it. "An animal walks on four legs and can move more quickly when one of them is hurt. You have no right to stand as we do."

It looked toward his voice in the darkness, picked itself up, and crept on paws and knees toward him. "You wish me to crawl, Lord?" It still moved with unacceptable slowness.

"Not like that," he told it with disdain. "On your paws." He could see as soon as he said it that the creature was incapable of moving in such a manner: its legs were too long, its balance too low for it to move on four feet. When Doto wished, he could crouch to move as the leopards of the forest that were blessed with his shape and appearance, but certainly this creature had no such ability. And even if it could crawl, he had no way to grant it sight in the darkness, at least not without risking Ogya's attention.

He wished his father had not commanded the retrieval of a living fire bearer. Dragging back a carcass would be simpler than herding this wounded thing all the way to Kwaee's temple. He pondered returning to the nest and retrieving another specimen that could move about on its own, but dismissed the idea as too risky. He'd been watching this one for days, and knew its habits and temperament. It had been hobbling around using a bit of stick, but then had inexplicably smashed it. He could get it a new stick to help it walk, but that wouldn't assist it with its night blindness.

The creature had mistaken his last command and managed to stand upright again. He sighed in resignation. There was no way around it: he would have to carry the thing for now. When crouched down, it was shaped a little like a monkey. Perhaps he could carry it on his back as a female monkey did its offspring. The idea was repugnant, but necessary, he supposed.

"Are we going much farther, Lord?" It hopped toward him again.

"Yes, much farther," he told it. He flattened his ears in distaste. "I will carry you for now. You will climb on my back and hold on." He turned his back and waited. The thing stumbled up behind him, batting its paws against his back as it groped for him in the dark, and then its fingers sunk into his fur, gripping. The sensation was odd and unfamiliar. Nothing in the forest ever dared touch him, save for his father when he had been just a cub, and Mother Fam's occasional earthy embraces, back when she had been with him, now so long ago. A tingle moved up his neck and down the backs of his legs. The bearer's paws groped up toward his shoulders and neck; for a moment he tensed with worry. Had this been foolish? Could the creature do him some harm even without its fire or teeth? He readied to whirl on it with tooth and claw, but no harm came. It hopped a bit, tugging at him, pulling his fur and squeezing at his shoulders unpleasantly. It was going to need some help. He reached behind to grip at its thighs, leaned forward, and hefted the bearer up, and then slipped his tail between its legs. Its weight spread across his back, and he let out a low growl.

"Am I too heavy?" it asked.

"I am a god," he told it. "To me you are as light as a little bird. I could carry ten of you through the forest with no trouble."

In fact, he had growled because, rather than reminding him of an infant clinging to its parent, the position had made him think of something else entirely. He was no stranger to the mating habits of animals. In the forest, sex was continual and ubiquitous; to be distant from it would be impossible. Birds, animals, insects, trees and flowers: the cycle of reproduction was all around. Doto himself had never experienced the urge. It must be something that gods did, or else he would not exist, but what prompted the behavior was a mystery to him. A few times he had sent his mind into creatures as they mated: once a pair of elephants, once tree frogs, and once a couple of bonobos. Each time he had found the experience both compelling and unpleasant—single-minded need consumed them, their brains directed toward a solitary purpose that drowned out all other consideration. In the case of the tree frog, the female had not even desired the mating and had fought it in a fit of pain and terror, but had been held down by the male. He had resolved never to engage with a mating mind again. Now he was holding a fire bearer atop his back like it was a rutting baboon. He shoved the ugly thought from his mind.

"Hold on tightly," he instructed it. "If you fall, you may be injured further." The creature's fingers cinched tightly into his fur, its arms about his neck. He crouched to bear more of its weight on his back, and began moving as swiftly as he dared. The burden on his back made his footfalls heavier. He passed through brush and around trees, the vines and leaves bending out of his way to permit him. Farther from the bearers' nest, the forest grew thick once more, and he had to choose his path between the larger trees more carefully, as they were too stiff to quickly move themselves out of his way without breaking themselves. The bearer bounced against his spine with his steps, its legs tricky to keep hold of as he moved. Its weight was no problem, but after a few minutes of it shifting from side to side and continually slipping down on his back, squirming its limbs the whole while, he began to think that it wished to fall off. "Keep still," he hissed at it. "You are being troublesome."

"Forgive me, Lord." The creature's words came out in short grunts as it bounced against his back. "It's difficult for me to keep hold. Have we much farther to go?"

He did not attempt to disguise the irritation in his voice. "If you continue to squirm and mewl at me, we will never get there."

It was silent after that for a time, for which he thanked Wem, but it continued to wriggle and shift on his back. Its grip about his neck and chest gradually grew looser and looser, and when Doto made a bound over a larger root, the creature's arms slipped from about his chest. It dropped heavily to the ground, landing with a startled yelp. In a flare of exasperation, he whirled on it. "Why did you let go?"

The creature lay sprawling on its back. It peered blindly up toward his voice. "I couldn't help it. I grew too tired. I held on as long as I could."

"We have scarcely come any distance at all." His tail lashed behind him. "You could not hold on longer than that?"

The fire bearer slumped backward. "I would have prayed for the strength to hold on longer," it said. "But I did not know…" It trailed off there, its forehead wrinkling. "Forgive me, Lord. You say you are a god. I know of Father Wem, god of the sky and creator of all, and of Mother Fam, goddess of the earth and of all living things. I know of Sarmu, who governs the savanna, and Kwaee, lord of the forest. I have heard of Atekye, goddess of swamps, and Mpo, who rules the great water. Forgive my ignorance, but which god are you, please, and what is your realm?"

Doto's fur prickled with wariness. The creature's words had a strange cadence to them, like recitation, and it knew many of his family. Why should it know so much? "My name is Doto," he told it. "I am…also a god of the forest." It need not know how little of the forest he governed, nor how weak his influence.

"I see." The fire bearer's brow wrinkled again. It rolled onto its knees and bowed low, spreading its arms before itself, and took a deep breath. Its next words were in a similarly strange and paced cadence, but at the same time unusually crisp in the air, loud, as if he were just next to Doto's ear. "Great Doto, god of the forest, please grant me the strength to do your will. Give me the endurance to last the trials that lie before me, that I may meet the night with your blessing."

"I will do no such thing!" he growled at it. The words had prickled at his hide, sparking in his fur and between his whiskers with electric potency. Never had any creature spoken in such a way to him. He was almost tempted to acquiesce from the sheer audacity of it. "Grant you strength from the gods? How dare you request such a thing from me? Use your own strength to do what I say."

It flinched as though struck. "As you say, Lord." It righted itself in that insolently upright stance and again climbed up onto his back, causing another wave of revulsion in him as it did so. He set off through the woods again, but this time the limbs about his shoulders trembled and strained as he moved, and he barely got very far at all before the creature again dropped off his back, sprawling right into the middle of a large bush. He turned to stare at it as it struggled on its back like a turtle turned over, arms and legs flailing uselessly. After a moment he seized its ankles and tugged it out of the bush until it lay on solid ground.

It panted for a while. "Forgive me," it said. "I need rest and sleep if I am to go on. Will you not allow us to stop for a while?"

It looked like a hunted animal. Sometimes it was possible to bring down a creature with a quick kill, but most of the time, prey had to be worn down, exhausted until it finally accepted death. Perhaps Doto had been treating the fire bearer too much like prey. Supposing it died on the trip? What would his father say then? *A failure. Weak, like your mother. A disappointment. Never show your face to me again.* Then he would be banished from his father's temple, and there would be nothing else for him for all eternity but the silent forest and the idle chattering of small gods.

No. He would ensure the thing lived. A different approach to their journey would be necessary. He wondered if they could afford to stop and rest here. Surely they were far enough from the nest that its herd mates would not be able to find it. Besides, the creatures slept. They would not even know he was missing until dawn.

"Very well," he said. "You can rest the night here. Tomorrow we will continue. And then there will be light, and you can walk on your own."

The creature opened its mouth, and then paused. "Yes, my Lord," it said.

Doto slept only if he desired to sleep, and he did not feel like it now, so he leaned up against a tree and watched the pathetic creature as it rummaged around, clearing a nest for itself, It then rested its head on a little mound, and for a while it looked around blankly into the darkness, but soon closed its eyes. Finally it lay still, its breathing slowed. Doto watched it in bemusement. How could it sleep in the middle of the forest floor like that? Did it not fear predators? Perhaps it thought Ogya would protect it. It would soon be disabused of that notion. It kicked and made strange, incoherent noises in its sleep. He could kill it in a moment, just as simply as desiring it dead. He was actually having to take care not to let it die by accident.

He wasn't sure now what he had expected of the fire bearers. As a cub, hearing tales of them, he had always envisioned giant, towering beasts with great teeth, wreathed in fire. Certainly not these blind, hairless monkeys that walked upright. How could such a pitiful, fragile thing be a fire bearer? How could it be one of the demons he had heard tales of since he was a cub, one of the great ravagers of the world, that had destroyed his father's dominion and elevated Ogya to power? What possible power could it possess that would make his father fear *this?* He could find no answer.

⌒⌒⌒

The birds were noisy long before the fire bearer woke. Impatient, Doto paced back and forth in the brush, and when the pale light of the morning began to filter through the trees, he nudged the creature awake. It grunted and stirred, then stared up at him with a stupid expression. "You're real," it breathed. "I thought I dreamed you."

"Of course I am real. Get up."

It seemed not to hear him. "Last night was so strange. So dark and confusing. But here you are."

Doto's tail twitched in annoyance. It seemed insistent on stating obvious facts. "Yes, here I am. And I do not wish to be here anymore. We have very far to go."

The bearer sprung to its feet, and then flinched in pain, its weight coming down too heavily on the wounded stump. It panted for a moment, then looked back up at him, baring its square little teeth. "I knew the gods had a plan for me. I knew it. And here you are, Lord...Lord Doto."

"A plan for you. Do you mean Ogya? Ogya has some scheme in which he has involved you and your mewling herd?"

The creature hopped a few steps forward on its good foot. "The god of fire? He has a plan for my people?"

Doto growled. Surely it was being deliberately evasive. "Why else would you serve him?" He looked about. "Find a stick like the one you had. It is time for us to go."

The creature nodded. "Yes, Lord Doto."

But still they could not go. Doto waited in growing exasperation as the fire bearer hopped pitifully about in the brush, poking through leaves and roots for a new stick. It experimented with several: one seemed to be too thin, another broke when tested, and many were too short. Soon the morning sun was glaring through the trees, and still nothing proved acceptable.

"Choose one and be done with it," Doto finally snapped at it.

"My apologies, my Lord," the bearer said, dipping its head low to him. "I do not wish to slow you further. If I had my knife, I could cut a branch suitable." A hopeful tone crept into its voice. "I don't suppose you could give me a new foot."

"That is an unacceptable thing to ask of the gods," he told it sternly. "It is strictly forbidden for gods to use their power to heal."

"Forbidden? Who would forbid a god?"

Doto halted at the question. A memory of a snarling, feathered face. Whirling through the air. Lines of fire burning on his cheek. His muscles throbbed now with memory of the pain.

He shuddered, and then realized that the bearer was staring at him. "It is forbidden!" he snapped, a predatory growl deepening the words. His claws flexed out, and the bearer flinched backward. Reacting this way to its question would probably be seen as unusual, Doto realized. It wouldn't do to have his captive regard him as less than in control. He straightened. "Even the gods are governed by the laws of the world. So I will not heal you. But I can give you a better stick than you could find on your own." He strode over to a nearby khaya tree. Its wood would be sturdy and strong. "Come here. Touch your wound to this tree and rest it there."

Obediently, the fire bearer hopped over to the tree. It leaned against it with one arm and watched him intently. Its eyes were wide and earnest, like a kitten's. He could see no trace of fear in them. Why should it not quail before him? Had Ogya granted it magics or protection of some kind? If so, and the bearer relied upon these, it would be greatly disappointed. Ogya's power would not thrive here, would not even work without a trace of the fire god's dominion: a bit of ash or charred wood. It would be amusing to see the bearer try to draw on fire magic here, in the thick of the forest, Doto thought, and then he reminded himself to be cautious. This was no mouse he toyed with. It was the ancient enemy, and it was not to be trusted.

But it would need to walk. He placed one paw on the bark of the khaya tree, closed his eyes, and sent himself into the wood, along the piping of the waters, up into bark and branch, down into the earth. That domain, that of soil and rock, was one he and Kwaee shared with Mother Fam, and even now he could feel the echoes of her there, her rich and exuberant presence watching from far away, as she watched all life. If she noticed him in the tree, she did not stir toward him, nor had she in centuries. Bitterly he recalled his last encounter with his foster Mother, and then, troubled, propelled it from his mind, focusing instead on his task. *Out, out,* he urged the wood of the tree. *Grow outward, spread, shape yourself.* Deep in the earth, he could feel the roots of the khaya pulling urgently at the water, at the soil. He could feel the sunlight transforming into matter throughout the tree. As if forming a young, green branch, the bark and wood of the tree extended outward, growing around the injured foot resting against it. Doto was gratified to hear the bearer's sudden intake of breath. Now it would be amazed at the power of its god. The tree groaned inside at the effort, and shook its branches, but its will was Doto's will; it could desire nothing but to obey him. Around the foot, up the calf and leg, the wood grew, the bark breaking to reveal the rich, burnished red-brown of the khaya wood, encasing the bearer's leg halfway to the knee. Below the stump of a foot, the wood extended in a curved spade, shaped roughly like a cat's paw. The tree shuddered again when the spade separated from it, and then bark crawled over the bare wood, sealing it up once more.

Doto pulled himself back from the tree and examined his work, paws on his hips. It was most satisfyingly done. It would not work half so well as a real foot, but it should prove sufficient to enable the bearer to walk without slowing their pace unacceptably.

The bearer gaped up at him in open astonishment, and then prodded at the wooden leg encasing its own. "This is remarkable! Thank you, Lord Doto, for this divine gift." It put the wooden foot against the ground and leaned on it, testing its weight.

Doto twitched his whiskers, proud despite the bearer's clumsy gratitude. "It is not a divine gift. It is so that I do not have to carry your clumsy little body on my back. Now you will walk with me."

The bearer took a few careful steps with the foot, and then several longer strides, laughing out loud as if Doto had said nothing. "It's amazing! This works so much better than a crutch. I could walk all day on this."

"Good." Doto pointed toward the heart of the forest. "That is exactly what I expect you to do. All day and all night, if necessary."

The bearer laughed again. "Right away, my Lord." It strode boldly forward and then the spade of the wooden foot slipped sideways on a patch of wet leaves and sent it tumbling face first onto the ground. Instead of howling or complaining, though, it began laughing again, now rapid and high-pitched.

Doto curled his lip, annoyed. This behavior was inane and incomprehensible. He wished again that Kwaee had requested a dead trophy rather than a captive for interrogation. "Get up," he growled. "We have a very long way to go. You would do well not to displease the gods."

The bearer stopped laughing immediately, and scrambled upright, looking chastened. "Forgive me, Lord."

"Let us go, then." He strode off through the forest, at a pace just a bit faster than he suspected the bearer would be able to match, and allowed himself a small smile as it hurried after.

The bearer's contrition did not persist for long. It took some time to grow comfortable walking on the wooden foot, but once it had, it adapted with surprising quickness, and soon it was running back and forth, making little jumps and laughing to itself when it landed. It seemed inordinately pleased with its new foot, and kept pausing to crouch down and touch it, muttering to itself in delighted tones all the while. Almost Doto regretted having fashioned the thing for it, but their pace was slow enough as it was. It would take half a moon to reach the temple at this rate, and possibly even longer if Kwaee decided to move it again.

His ears twitched. The fire bearer was rustling in the leaves far behind him now. Without turning, he said, "You will make haste. Or must I put my claws to your flanks to encourage you?"

There was a sudden series of crashing noises behind him as the bearer bounded through the leaves and then launched past him. The thing laughed as it flew by, too fast for its own legs, and slid head-first into the forest floor. It turned over, face smeared with dirt and leaves, still mewling with laughter as it bared its teeth at him.

Doto's tail lashed. "You make the parrots seem subdued and stealthy. Get up. Have you no concern for yourself at all?"

The bearer picked itself up, brushing leaves and grass from its legs. "My apologies, Lord," it said. "But this new foot is amazing."

"Well, of course it is amazing. A god made it. What else would you expect?"

"It's so springy and sturdy. Do you know, I think I could run faster with it than I ever could with my real foot? I almost wish I had two of them."

He growled. "That desire I could grant."

"But I'm having trouble getting used to it, so I keep falling. Still, it's wonderful to be able to walk again. To run, even."

"You ought to be more careful. There are many things in this forest that would enjoy killing you."

The bearer's brown face creased with a smile. "Surely not while their god is around. That would be very inconvenient for you, wouldn't it?"

Doto blinked in surprise. "There is a whole nest of your people back there. I can go and get any one of them if you die."

"Village," said the bearer.

He turned toward it. "What?"

"It's—we call it a village. What we live in, I mean. Not the tents. The tents make up the village. I live in a tent. My tent is in a village. Not a nest." The bearer hesitated. "—Lord."

Doto snorted at that and strode off. "Why should it matter to me what word you use?" he said over his shoulder. Of course, he had heard the bearers use the word, but it had not made sense to him. It was a nest. They lived in a nest, like the gorillas. There was no other word for it in the language of the gods.

The bearer hurried to move apace with him, its gait swift, but limping. "I didn't mean to offend, Lord. It's just—we thought we knew of all the gods. But we had never been told of Doto, god of the forest. So I thought perhaps Doto, god of the forest does not know of us. And you didn't seem to know that we can't see in the dark, nor that we need to rest and sleep. And you say we live in a nest, like birds, but it is a village."

"Many things live in nests," Doto said, in a louder voice than he had intended. He did not look over at the bearer. Roots snapped when his toes touched them, and brambles sprouted in his footsteps. "I know all I need to about you. You are a fire bearer. You serve Ogya, god of flames and destruction. You hunt and kill with stone teeth because your own are too small and weak, and you are too slow. You cover yourselves with the dead, and make them to cry out with dead voices. You make the black clouds. What else should I know, bearer?"

"Clay," it said.

He puzzled. Why would it speak of earth now? "I know of clay. I have seen it many times. The forest is filled with clay, the riverbanks lined with it. I have felt clay from the inside. I have felt it crush beneath the toes of the hippos and slather the bellies of the crocodiles. I have felt it accumulate and settle and bake in the sunlight. What do you think you can teach me about it that I do not already know?"

"No, Lord Doto," it said. "My name. My name is Clay."

Its name? Doto had heard the bearers in the nest address each other with confusing appellations, referring to each other as ants or stars, but he had thought them merely stupid. "Animals do not have names. Only gods have names."

The fire bearer stopped in its place. "But I'm not an animal." Its voice was quiet and curious.

"And what do you think you are?" he growled at it.

"You *don't* know about people, do you? You've never seen us before, Lord Doto."

Snorting, Doto turned away. "I have seen you things many times. But you are not very nice to look at, so I don't watch very often. And you are not beasts of the forest, so I have little reason to."

"I see." The bearer sounded careful now. "Well, you call us fire bearers, but we call ourselves people. We're not gods, and not beasts. We're something between."

"Either you lie," he told it archly, "or you are deceived. I know all about your kind. And I have been alive far, far longer than you, and seen much more. Whatever you believe you know about yourself and about your herd is nothing more than the fleeting dream of a gnat: here, and then gone. So be silent, and do not presume to educate your gods."

Happily, that seemed to shut the creature up. Doto stalked on, the vines and brambles on the forest floor melting away before him. The bearer followed closely, its brow furrowed. It was thinking, and that made Doto uneasy. No doubt it was scheming its escape, or perhaps devising a way to work some of its fire magic on him. There was almost certainly nothing it could do, now that they were deeper into the forest, but he still did not like it.

"Lord Doto," the bearer said after a while, "will you tell me where we are going?"

There could be no harm in its knowing, Doto thought to himself. Perhaps it would even be more tractable if it were told. "We are on our way to see the forest god, Kwaee. It is he who desires a fire bearer to inspect."

The bearer nodded. "So how far is it to Lord Kwaee? Am I really going to get to meet the god of the forest?"

"I am a god of the forest too," Doto said, his voice stiff. "It is quite far. And the distance may change. Kwaee's temple moves about."

"So we could get there and he'd be gone? What does he do, just pick up the whole temple and move it? *That* must be a sight."

"Wherever Kwaee chooses, that is where his temple is."

"So why doesn't he come to us?"

"A god doesn't come to you!" Doto snapped. "That is not how it works."

"You did," the bearer pointed out. "Where's your temple? Are we in it now? Is this it? It doesn't look like a temple to me."

"Will you ever be silent?" He hadn't meant to snarl and turn on the insolent creature, but it was just so infuriating. "Just close your—your muzzle, and…"

He trailed off. Something was not right in the forest. There were sounds that shouldn't be there, and sounds that *should* be there were not. He peered through the shade. Everything was still, the only movement insects swarming in the shafts of pale light that broke through the canopy. The birds were unnerved. The trogons only hooted louder to threaten invaders, but the parrots were suddenly still and timid.

"And what?" the bearer said loudly.

"Be silent!" Doto hissed. He crouched low in the brush, and his rosettes began to catch the light and shadow in entrancing ways, turning him invisible, so that eyes would slide just past him. Where, he realized, they would latch onto his captive, who stood there, brown skin gleaming with sweat, hide and colorful bits of plant or something swathed around its shoulders and hindquarters. It would be easily noticed.

"I must conceal you," Doto informed it. "Be still."

He pressed his palms to the soil and closed his eyes, sending himself down into the earth and the trees. He climbed up through root and trunk, spread into a thousand branches. High above, the sun was already hot on his leaves. The canopy swayed with his breath. Far away, he could feel Kwaee's unseeing awareness, the resistance as Doto invaded his father's terrain, the body that was his power. The trees would not help here. They were too rigid, too mighty to easily bend. Lianas would do. He extended up into them, dozens of grasping fingers reaching for the treetops, suffocating the trees they clung to in order to push their leaves into the vital sunlight. With a god's power, they could move. He sent into them the will of the python, and the vines coiled down out of the trees. He gave the bearer a warning stare—*be silent*—just as the lianas curled around its ankles, waist, and neck, but the fool thing still cried out in alarm.

Doto's vines constricted, hefting the bearer's weight and then hoisting it into the air. It struggled at first, but then went still, letting the lianas elevate it up into the higher branches, wrapping about a larger limb and securing it there, all of its brightly-colored wrappings covered. From below, it looked just like a small and knobby bit of tree bark. Inside his vines, Doto could feel the thing panting in fear. It was a pity he couldn't keep it bound for the entire journey.

Something heavy trod down upon him, broke his back painlessly in half under its huge foot. A fire bearer. He withdrew his senses from the trees, from the lianas, from the sapling snapped by the bearer's foot, and darted behind the tree to which he had bound his captive. Silently he extended his claws and dug them deep into the bark, slinking up and crouching along the branch to which the bearer was bound, just above it. His eyes searched the forest.

A trio of fire bearers crept from between the trees. They were brightly adorned with the colorful scraps they favored, their tooth-sticks held at the ready. Two were looking to either side, and a third seemed fascinated by the ground, watching it intently, as though about to pounce on a mouse or beetle. They were followed shortly by four more. One stood tall and proud, walking closely next to one who appeared aged, with slumped shoulders and a stiff gait, white filling its hair and whiskers. It was covered in more of those bits of dead animal and brightly colored plant, with a collection of teeth from some large cat hanging about its neck, and it was shaking its head back and forth. Doto recognized these bearers from the nest.

"It's my father!" the bearer exclaimed loudly. "He's looking for me! Father!" His voice carried easily through the forest, and a flock of martins roosting in the tree took to the air in sudden alarm, their wings rustling.

Doto growled low and reached under the branch, clamping his paw tightly over the bearer's muzzle, his claws sliding out to prick the soft flesh of its throat in warning. Through the lianas gripping it, he could feel it squirming frantically, but the vines held tight.

Below, the bearers were looking about. They had plainly heard the cry.

"It's him," the aged one said. It peered with rheumy eyes deeper into the forest. "I'd know his voice anywhere."

"I heard it too, father," said the tall one. "But how can it be? He could never have made it this far on his own. And without his crutch."

They would not depart without an explanation for what they'd heard: that much was plain. Doto scanned the tree branches. There was what he needed: a grey parrot, huddled down on a branch, feeling threatened by the strange, encroaching creatures. Doto sent himself out to it, settled in its mind. He didn't like going into parrots; they made him feel chatty for a while afterward, but this was necessary. Its confused brain sensed him there and tried to peck at him, its stupid, frightened psyche hammering with ineffectual little stabs of resentment. He ignored it, spread its wings, and sent it flapping down toward the bearers, tapping into its instincts and memory to control its flight, the forest floor reeling and swaying below. He landed it on a branch above them, feeling its talons sink into the bark, and opened its beak. "Fatah!" he encouraged it to say. The voice was a reasonable approximation of his captive's. "Fatah fatah fatah!"

All the bearers looked up toward the bird. The tall one grunted. "Just the forest playing tricks on us," it said. "A parrot. It does sound very much like him, though."

"No," the aged bearer said, its voice firm. "It wasn't a parrot I heard. It was him. It was my son. Do any of you dare tell me I don't know my own son's voice?"

The other bearers murmured to each other, and the tall one put its paw on the other's shoulder. "We all saw the bird make the sound, Father. I know you want it to be him. But you need to consider the possibility that he is gone."

"He is *not* gone!" The aged one's voice was angry, but trembling.

"But you saw the tracks. A great cat, bigger than any we have seen. A struggle on the ground outside camp. And then only the cat. A wild beast has taken my brother. You must know that this is true. What else could it be?"

The aged one shook its head. "But what of the other tracks we found later on? The footprint and the strange mark. They could be from someone walking with a stick."

"Those could have been made by anyone and anything," the tall one said. "There is no reason to think it's Clay. He couldn't have traveled this far in one night. Not the way he walks. We need to turn back."

"No!" The aged bearer stood taller. It stepped forward, its stride weak but full of purpose. "I will not leave here until we find him. I will not lose two sons in one moon. I will not."

The foremost bearer, the one that had been staring at the ground, continued moving forward until it reached the trunk of the tree in which Doto and his captive were hiding. It crouched just below them, moving the grasses and saplings about with its fingers. Doto dug his claws into the flesh of his captive's throat, warningly. Not a sound. It swallowed, the bulge of its larynx sliding against his fingertips.

Methodically, the bearer paced around the tree, inspecting the soil, the leaves. It moved in a spiral, outward, carefully choosing its steps.

"What is it, Beetle?" the elderly one asked.

The other stood, scratching at its chest. "No more tracks," it said. "The cat stopped here. The man with it. I can find no more trace of them." It looked upward. "Unless they took to the trees, I cannot say what happened." Its eyes scanned the branches, passing over the spot where Doto and his bearer were hidden, and then back to it. "There!" It pointed upward. "What is that?"

The vines were not enough to conceal the bound bearer. They would be discovered. Panic flashed through Doto. The bearers would throw their tooth-sticks. Or they would use their magic to burn the tree with Doto inside it. He muttered low to his captive, "Not a sound, or I drop you on them," and released its muzzle, gripping the branch. Then he turned, his claws sinking into the wood as he rotated himself around to hang under the bearer, putting its body between himself and the mossy tree branch. He shielded it from the bearers below, his rosettes playing with the light, shifting—a cloud of deception that passed over his captive to conceal it from its herd's eyes.

His prey was trembling against him, its breaths shallow and frightened, puffing into his face, dampening his fur. Its lithe body pressed against his own, the heat of it, its smooth skin sliding against his fur. A strange urge rose in him, the urge to seize it, to satisfy some rising appetite that he could not identify. The sensations were troubling and distracting, so he pressed them away, turning his head to look down.

The bearers below were searching the branches of the trees, their paws above their eyes. "I see nothing," one finally said.

The tracking bearer frowned. "I—I could have sworn I saw something. A trick of the light, perhaps."

"No!" the aged one shouted, stepping forward, clenching its paw into a fist. "No, a trick of sound, and then a trick of the light? Do you not understand? He is here. He is right here! The forest itself is trying to conceal him from us."

"Father!" The tall one rushed after it, gripping its shoulder again, and then said in a lower voice, "Father, listen to what you are saying. The forest, concealing him from us? This is madness. You cannot talk this way. You are King."

Straightening, the older bearer answered, "And you are not, son. Not yet. You think I could ever forget my position? After I was forced to send my youngest away? I will not lose this one too. I will not." It stepped forward, pulling free of the paw that gripped it, and came almost to the tree where Doto remained hidden.

Doto tensed, ready to drop down, to fight or flee, but the bearer stopped and crouched down, pressing its paws to the ground, dipping its head low. It was silent, for a moment only breathing, but Doto could feel something odd, a rising tension in the air, like the prickle before a lightning strike. The creature spoke words then, breathing them out so low they should have been inaudible, and yet the forest hummed with them, the branches of the trees sang at their syllables, the air in the leaves rustled in their tempo. Each word was a splash of a stone into a still and quiet pool.

"Gods of the forest," the bearer spoke, "Gods of rock and earth, gods of tree and vine and grass, gods of all that crawls and burrows, climbs and flies, gods of cloud and sun and moon, Mother Fam, Father Wem, hear me. You are in all places, and see all. Use your sight to find my lost son. You carry the storms from the south on your breath. Use that breath to guide him home to me again. Just as you return the gazelle to us after the rains, so too return my son to me. Restore what is lost, keepers of the earth. Restore what is lost."

Doto stared down at the little fire bearer prostrated on the ground beneath his tree. What could grant it speech that had such power? He had never felt anything like it before. Perhaps this was why his father dreaded them so. His senses crept out toward the fire bearer's mind, hungry to know what it felt. He could hear pain in the words, terrible longing and desperation, and it tugged at old, forgotten memories. Mingled with the pain was a hope, an upward reach of its spirit. All he had to do was touch it to remove all its pain and longing. It was the keen of a hungry kitten calling for its mother, the rasp of a dry throat moments before the cool relief of water. All he need do was touch. He would feel it too. The joy and respite would be his to share. The gratitude would bloom up through him. Touch. His power welled up within him to answer the old man's request.

"Fatah!" cried the parrot, remembering the word that had been placed in its head before. "Fatah!"

Doto's trance was shattered by the raucous cry, and he wrested his mind away in shock. What had he been about to do? Touch his mind to that of the bearer? Make himself vulnerable to any of its unearthly powers, and worse, reveal himself to the unquenchable blaze of Ogya's regard? He shuddered, and the forest shuddered with him, trees dropping dry branches, birds taking to wing with annoyed calls.

The bearers below stared about the trees in wonder. The elderly one stood upright, his motions slow. "The gods have heard me," he breathed.

"You must hope they have, First Claw," the tracking bearer said, "for the trail goes no farther than this. I have no trace to guide you beyond this spot. If we travel any farther, we will be wandering blind."

"I cannot abandon my son!" The old bearer's voice shook.

The tall bearer came forward and put his arm around the old one's shoulders. "You are not abandoning him, Father. You have beseeched the gods to return him. You must trust that they will do so. Perhaps they will return both your lost sons."

The older one looked into his face for a moment, watching for some expression or sign that Doto could not discern. Then he sighed. "I am so tired, Ram." He took the other's arm. "So tired. Let us return."

The other bearer nodded. Together, the group turned back the way they had come, their steps slow. They spoke no more words, retreating in silence. Doto listened with the forest's senses to their departure. The expression of the old bearer's face tugged at something deep within him, still. The words he had spoken had held some kind of magic; that much was plain. But what sort of magic could awaken this feeling within him, this peculiar yearning? He longed for something he could not name.

Once he was certain they were gone, he dropped out of the tree, landing lightly on all fours on the soft earth. He sent himself up into the lianas again, feeling his captive still squirming and hot in their grip. Carefully, he uncoiled them, extending them back down to the ground again, releasing the panting bearer and sending it sprawling.

It was squinting, and tears ran from the corners of its eyes. Doto knew tears. They had matted his fur when he was younger and Kwaee had been cruel, or when Doto had once again failed to please him, or when he'd sat alone and not known how he should fill day after endless day. But he had never seen them on an animal before. Elephants could make tears, Mother had said, when they felt great sorrow, but Doto had never witnessed this. The bearer furrowed its brow and wiped the tears away with the back of its paw, leaving streaks of dirt. Blood stained its jaw where Doto's claws had pricked the flesh. He felt again that uncomfortable yearning, a desire to reach out, to answer the blood and tears in some way. He did not like it.

"Get up."

The bearer got to its feet. "My father," it said. "He looked so weak."

"Fatah," the parrot nearby commented.

The bearer turned, taking a few steps back the way they had come. "I have to go to him, Lord Doto. He needs me."

"And why should I care what a fire bearer needs?" Doto's muzzle twisted in a sneer. "Why should it matter to me even as much as the life of an insect or a blade of grass? Those I let live and die as they must. Why ought I to help one of your miserable herd?"

The bearer was staring at him like a lost kitten. "Because…because, Lord Doto, we serve you. We worship you. My people are devoted to you."

Fury at this outrageous lie boiled in Doto's chest; in sudden rage he snarled and lunged at the fire bearer, who, startled, toppled backward to the ground. Doto crouched atop him, his paw closing about its throat, claws digging into the bearer's skin once more. The scent of blood burned in his nostrils. He leaned forward until his whiskers brushed the bearer's cheek, their muzzles inches apart. "Your people are murderers and traitors. You are monsters, every one of you, and once Kwaee is done with you, I will personally tear you apart and swallow your heart. Then I will hunt down your nest and order my trees and brambles to destroy it. I will send leopards to capture and slaughter your people. They will die like squealing pigs, and their tooth-sticks will not save them. Then my vultures will pick their bones, and there will be nothing left of you for your god to find but stains for the rains to wash away."

Thunder growled above the canopy as he stood, the sunbeams fading with the approach of the afternoon storm.

Sparks

Laughing Dog had not had a full swallow of water in two days, and the flies were determined to get what was left inside him. He regretted leaving so suddenly, without taking food or a water skin, but the looks on his people's faces as he strode out into the wilderness with nothing but his spear had nearly been worth it. He had shown them that he was brave, bold, that he relied on nothing but the strength of his hand and mind. He had stalked out of his people's village with a stern and righteous anger. Now, though, he would gladly trade that moment of triumph for a little moisture on his tongue.

Upon leaving the village, he had briefly considered turning south and hiding himself in the forest. There would be water there, at least. But the forest was strange to his people, and they did not know how to live in it. Hungry things prowled beneath its branches. There were dangerous marshes, poisonous snakes, and dark magics. The food in the forest was unusual and risky. Laughing Dog could not survive in the forest. The savanna, though, was safe, familiar. And there his father would expect him to suffer. But Laughing Dog would not suffer. He would grow harder, stronger. He would prove to his father that he could not be beaten.

When he and Clay were young, the People of the Savanna had lived in a village far to the north. For as long as any of them could remember, they had settled there, on a little rise above the broad plains. There they could see so far in each direction that on some days Laughing Dog swore he could see the great waters where the sun cooled herself from dusk until dawn. There his people worked and played, feasted and danced. There he had gone on his first hunt. He had learned from Uncle Six how to skin a zebra, how to track game to watering holes, how to play the xalam, how to balance a spear so that it would fly true. And every year, when the rains came, the plains would turn lush and green, and spread with yellow flowers and broad white mushrooms. Birds would flock by the thousands to wade through the tall grasses. Game would thunder through in herds so large they could not be counted. His memories of those times were happy.

But one year, the rains did not come at their usual time. Far to the south, they could see the dark of clouds, but even there, no shadow of rain. The early sun turned into a late one, and still no rain had fallen. Everyone thirsted. A young runner, ignoring the cautions of the elders, ate the mud from a watering hole, and the water in it was bad. He vomited and shat all the bad water out, and then died. It was a troublesome time for his father, too. The people blamed him for not appeasing the gods. Laughing Dog knew this was foolish. His father was a devoted and worshipful man, but the people were angry and needed a reason. Many talked about moving the village farther south, following the rains, but his father had said no. They must wait for a sign from the gods.

A traveler came through the village, looking for food and water, and the people shared what they had. He told them that drought had spread in all directions, and that his own village had died. His own people told new stories, of gods that had forgotten them, of gods that were only dreams. The adults had ushered all the children away, sending them to chores or play, but Laughing Dog was fascinated, and crept back, hiding behind his father's tent and listening through the wall as the traveler spoke of the lost gods, the death of stories, and the rise of the strength of man. He wanted to ask the stranger more questions, but when he woke the next morning, the traveler had continued on his journey, searching for a land where rain still fell and game still ran. Laughing Dog always wondered if he found it. Perhaps his bones baked in the sun.

One night, lightning struck the savanna very near their village. Laughing Dog saw the blazing white spear of Father Wem flash against the sky, with a furious roar louder than anything he had ever heard. Lightning, but no rain. Where it landed, an orange light rose, a distant fire. Not distant enough. The people of the village began to shout and gather their skins and clothes and food, rushing all around him. The orange light grew and grew until it seemed that the whole of the north was burning. They fled, then, before Ogya's hunger could consume them all. Laughing Dog remembered, to his shame, sobbing in terror and despair as they left their village behind. They never returned.

The journey across the savanna in search of water seemed to last forever. The people headed south, in search of the clouds they had seen. Their march was slow; the elderly could not move quickly, and children had to be carried. They had to stop many times in search of game, or to refresh themselves when any source of water could be found. After countless days, they finally found a place where the rains still came, where streams painted streaks of green across the plains and game grazed, and the people praised Father Wem and Sarmu. They drank until their bellies were ready to burst, until the water came back up again, and they drank again, and feasted.

There they made camp, and stayed through the year, and two years, but in their third year, the rains were late once more, and once more they saw the clouds to the south. This time the elders convinced the King to move the people much sooner, and so again they packed up their belongings and followed the rains. The year after that they traveled again, and after that once more, and so on, every year, until they made camp on the edge of the great forest, where his father said that the rains must come always, because so many trees could not grow without much water. Living there, he said, they would never have to move again.

But now Laughing Dog had had to leave his home, this time on his own, traveling back north, away from water, following the traces of his people over the many years of his life. Somewhere far to the north was their old home that he had left as a child. The gods his father revered had driven them from it, so he would return to show them he stood on his own. He would prove his strength. He would find the burned scar where a village had once flourished, scoop up a handful of that ashen earth, and bring it back to his father, uttering no prayer, seeking neither help nor guidance from the gods. "You see?" he would say. "Even the gods must respect us if we are strong."

So he journeyed, traveling in the mornings and evenings, resting at night when darkness prevented him from finding his way, taking shelter during the heat of the midday. Along the way, he used the tricks to find water that he had learned on the people's migrations. He used a branch to dig up snake plant and squeeze the root for the precious drops of water it held. From a day's journey away, he saw a huge baobab and headed for it, cutting the bark away with his spear tip to reveal the wet, fleshy wood inside. He followed game tracks to watering holes and filled his skins with clear, running water that filtered through the lovegrass. The farther north he traveled, the rarer the sources of water. Twice now he had passed familiar sites, where his people had lived for a year or two, but had abandoned to drought. He didn't know how far north he could go. The ground beneath his feet was dryer than any he could remember, coarse and gritty, and plants were rarer.

Now he had no water left. He could not find snake plant. He dug up others, hoping for fleshy roots containing moisture, but all he could find was dry: hard, brittle fingers that had not tasted water in some time. He had not seen any animal tracks in a full day. His tongue felt as though it were made of bark, and his eyes burned, gummy when he blinked. It had been days since he had made water. The moon was now the same shape it had been the night he had left his village.

He trudged on, but his steps were shorter, stumbling, and his mind was dizzy. Thoughts came more slowly. He had more trouble finding his bearings. Which way was south? Which north? He kept losing track as the merciless sun beetled across the sky.

Now he was back in the village. There was a feast, a great one, but no one would let him have any food or water. His father sat on the stool and looked down at him, eyes sad.

"Father," he pleaded, his voice hoarse, the croak of a stork. "I'm so thirsty. Let me have a drink."

"The gods say you cannot drink anymore," his father said. His words were distant and empty of feeling. "Go and sit by the fire." His finger pointed at a woven mat lying next to the flames.

Laughing Dog might have wept, but he had no water for tears. He crawled on all fours across the earth to the mat and huddled there. The fire burned at the back of his neck and arms, soaked into his braided black hair to lick at his scalp. He looked around for faces of his friends and relatives, for Clay, who had always guarded him, but he could make out none of them.

A figure appeared at the edge of the circle, too tall to be a man. It had a huge, panting body and great horns. An eland. A blue-feathered spear bobbed from its withers. It fixed him with a serious expression. "I will give you a drink of water, if you want it." Its mouth moved like a man's as it spoke. It lifted a hoof and tapped the ground, and where it struck, clear water bubbled up, filling its print. The liquid shimmered in the firelight.

Laughing Dog's throat lanced with pain. "Please," he begged it.

"First," the eland said severely, "you must admit to all here before you that you have no strength of your own. You must agree to subjugate yourself entirely to the will of the gods. You must promise never again to question their wisdom."

He stared at the water. He desired it so intensely. He needed it. All it would cost was complete surrender. And then he would be worse than Ram, who followed their father unthinkingly, or Clay, who had to ask permission for everything. His mouth felt as though it were filled with sand. He was not here. He was in the savanna. None of this was real. "No," he rasped.

Fury blazed in the eland's eyes, the light of the fire behind him. The fire's heat seared into Laughing Dog's skin, burning him. The eland was gone; it was just the fire now, arrows of heat bending around him, frying his skin. He wanted to scream, but all he could do was pant from the pain.

He opened his gummy eyes and could feel tiny grains of sand beneath the lids. The sun burned into his hair and back. His cheek pressed into the hot earth.

Eyes, large and brown and wet, stared back into his. They belonged to an eland, a calf that must have become separated from its mother. Flies crawled over it, nipping at its hide. Its sides heaved slowly with its breaths. The stink of it panted into his face.

Laughing Dog sat up weakly, and the thing's legs kicked in feeble terror at its realization that he was alive. It tried to bleat for its mother, but it was dying, and had no voice left. A thin, viscous rope of drool hung from its chapped lips to the dirt, and Laughing Dog wanted desperately to drink it. But there was a better source of water inside this animal. He took his spear from where it had fallen, and crawled over to straddle the eland, which put up a weak struggle, lifting its head, its hindquarters trying to buck. There was no fight left in it, and Laughing Dog's weight was crushing out its breath. It laid its head down with a sigh through its nares, its glassy eyes staring forward.

Laughing Dog gripped its snout in one hand, lifted his spear in the other, and punctured the calf's throat. It gave a low, helpless moan, and dark blood welled up from the wound. With eagerness that gave him new energy, he leaned down and pressed his lips to the calf's throat, suckling at the gash. Delicious, soothing wetness filled his mouth. It was hot and thick, but it was liquid. It burned his throat as it went down and left coolness behind. The calf's heart pumped, jetting the blood up into his mouth, soaking his chin and nose, the odor crisp and tangy. He swallowed again and again. Blood was full of water, but it would not keep. There would be no point in filling his skin with it. He would have to drink what he could now. He took what he could stomach, and then the calf's heartbeat failed, and no more blood came from the wound.

Nausea wracked him, burned at his stomach, and he turned, huddled like a child, holding his belly and trying to keep the precious fluid down. He rested like that, the sun burning at his back, until dusk.

In the cool of the evening he built a fire using the branches of a dead acacia, cut wedges of meat from the calf, and cooked them, chewing them for their juices before swallowing. He could feel strength returning to his limbs, clarity to his thoughts. He had been very close to death. His quest north had been foolhardy. Often his father or brothers liked to call him arrogant, but this time he found himself agreeing with them. Once his belly was full he would head south once more. He would not return home, though. Not until he found some way to prove that the gods would not beat him.

Fires were necessary even in the northern reaches of the sahil, that dry stretch of land between the Firelands and the savanna, and they were critical if you had a kill. The hyenas, his namesakes, wandered the night, and if they happened across you while you slept, they would nip at you, but could be easily startled away. If there was fresh meat nearby, however, the scent would attract them from great distances. Vultures, too, large and vicious, would attack the living and dead alike if they were hungry. A good, roaring fire would keep all these at bay.

Laughing Dog sat and chewed fatty, juicy gristle and stared into the blackness of night, keeping alert for predators. In these barren lands, there might be few, but with the dead eland lying nearby and the aroma of cooking meat in the air, he thought it best to remain watchful. For a time, there was only deepening darkness, but then eyes glinted back at him from beyond the firelight, not the lambent flash of a predator's gaze, but glittering red spots, unlike any eyes he had seen before. With slow movements, not looking away, he reached for his spear.

The eyes came closer, glinting as their owner turned away and back again. Laughing Dog lifted his spear, crouched at the ready. Then, out of the darkness, a man, an ordinary man, walked up to the fire.

"How are you?" the man asked. "Please, do not be alarmed. Will you share your fire?"

Laughing Dog kept his grip on his spear. "Who are you? What is your people?" he asked. The chances of finding anyone else this far north were tiny. The chances of that person being friendly were even smaller.

"I am just a traveler, alone. I have no people." The man's voice was strange. It was very friendly in tone, with no accent, but there was a roar of wind in it. The consonants popped and cracked when he spoke them. He came closer to the fire, which lit up his eyes and teeth, and gleamed on his chest and arms and legs, which Laughing Dog could now see were covered with gold bands and rings and necklaces. What he had taken for eyes in the darkness were two large red rubies hanging at his chest. They captured the firelight and sent it blazing back in refraction.

"Are you a bandit?" Laughing Dog asked him, letting the distrust sound in his voice. "You are a very rich man to be wandering the savanna by yourself. Where did you come by these gold and jewels?"

"My friend, I am no bandit. Look at me. I carry no weapons, while you have a spear. I have more to fear from you than you from me, would you not say? At least share with me the warmth and safety of your fire."

Laughing Dog nodded to the man, and lowered his spear, though he did not release it.

"I come from far to the north," the man said.

"Beyond the Firelands?" No one had ever traveled through the Firelands as far as Laughing Dog had ever heard. None could survive even a few days in that desolate place. Those who ventured into them never returned. Once or twice, travelers had come from the lands to the north, traveling east and south around the great desert to reach Laughing Dog's village. Like the man at his campfire now, they had short hair, reddish skin, and large round earrings, though theirs had not sparkled with gems as his did.

"I found a city," the man said. "Once it must have been vast and glorious and powerful, but only ruins now. Its people are dead, or gone, and most of it is in the sand. In the city is a palace of alabaster and lapis lazuli, and in that palace, a throne of gold. All around were many jewels and ornaments. I took what I could carry, as would any man. If I find my way to another city, I will be rich."

"If the gold does not weigh you down and burn your skin in the sun," Laughing Dog answered him. "Sit by my fire, then. Do not fear that I will rob you. I have no use for your gold. I am called Laughing Dog."

The man squatted by the fire, his hands on his knees. "I am Sedjet." His eyes glinted again as he stared with obvious desire at the chunks of meat sizzling on sticks in the flames.

"Please. I have more than I can eat." Laughing Dog pointed with his chin at one and the man took it, reaching into the flames with one mahogany-colored hand. The fire licked around his fingers, but did not appear to burn him.

He looked up, his bright eyes flashing in the firelight as he caught Laughing Dog's astonishment, and his face stretched in a wide grin. He had very large teeth, and he smiled so broadly there seemed to be more than a man should have. "Ah! A little trick I picked up. I could teach you how to do it." He sunk his teeth deep into the meat, and the juice ran down his beardless chin. He tore a piece away and swallowed without chewing, then immediately bit at another.

Laughing Dog poked at the fire with a stick, making sparks float up into the dark night sky. "You said you came from the north. I have been journeying to find a place my people lived once. We were stricken by a drought and then a fire. Did you find a place where the earth had been scorched, perhaps twelve rains ago? It might be regrown by now."

Sedjet reached into the fire for another stick of meat. "The north?" He laughed low into the flames. "The north is nothing but ash and sand. Nothing grows there. Nothing lives, not until you near the great water. It is all Firelands."

What he was claiming was impossible. Laughing Dog shook his head. "Certainly you are mistaken, my friend. My village was yet farther north of here. There can be no doubt of that. And we did not live near the Firelands."

Sedjet grinned at him again around his mouthful of meat. "I do not know where you lived in the past, but all north of here is rock and sand, now. There is nothing else. Savanna has become sahil. The bunchgrasses that grow in this land are the first plants I have seen for some time."

The man was carrying no water skin that Laughing Dog could see, nor any other supplies for such a journey. All he had with him was gold and precious stones. "Forgive me, my friend, but how have you managed such a voyage through the Firelands with no water or food?"

Without asking, Sedjet reached into the fire for the last stick of meat. "Ah. That is a tale."

Laughing Dog took his spear to cut more from the dead calf. Anything not consumed would be spoiled by morning. "I would be curious to hear it."

For a moment, he thought Sedjet intended to ignore him. The man ripped at the meat with his teeth, swallowing it in huge bites, letting the fat run down his fingers. When every last bit of cooked meat was gone, he licked his fingers clean. Laughing Dog was putting fresh skewers of eland on the fire before the man finally answered, "I told you of the palace I found, with the room full of jewels."

"Yes."

"I did not tell you that when I found this palace, I was aching with hunger and thirst. I prepared to leave, hoping to find a caravan from which I could buy food and water, when I thought, hold just a moment, Sedjet. If a caravan comes upon you alone and unarmed in the desert, covered in gold, they will surely kill you and take your wealth for themselves. You had better arm yourself. I had seen among the treasure a magnificent sword, sharp and deadly, so I decided to take it. But when I tugged at it, imagine my surprise when it did not move, but instead a deep and black hole appeared in the sand beneath my feet. What could be down there, I wondered to myself, and so I climbed down. Below was a dark room, filled with many skeletons, lying as if felled in the middle of a great battle. In the fingers of one, I found this."

Laughing Dog did not see Sedjet take anything from within his clothes or elsewhere, but the man's fingers were now outstretched, closed around something. He opened them and revealed a diamond as large as a shea nut, catching the blaze of the fire even more brightly than the rubies on his chest, bending the flames so that they seemed to be caught within the stone. The glitter drew Laughing Dog in. He could not look away from it.

Sedjet rolled the diamond back and forth across his fingers, making it dance along his knuckles like a playful star. "As soon as I picked it up, all my hunger and thirst vanished. Strength filled my bones. I climbed out of the hole and felt I could walk in the midday sun and never feel the heat. I could travel through the heart of the Firelands and not require a drop of water. Such power it held." He looked up at Laughing Dog, his eyes glittering. "And all I had to do was reach out and take it." The diamond rolled into the center of his palm, and his fingers curled around it, snuffing out its light.

Something was lost when its spark vanished; some beauty disappeared from the world. Laughing Dog longed to gaze upon it again. He looked away into the night, the images of the fire and the glint of jewels burned into his vision, ghostly shades of green and red that slid across the invisible sahil. "Ridiculous," he snorted. "A magic jewel that takes away all hunger and thirst."

Sedjet shrugged. "Think what you like. But then how did I come here? Why would I invent such a tale?"

"It's a good story, anyhow," Laughing Dog said.

The man gazed covetously into the fire at the meat cooking there. "Perhaps you will tell me one of your own, from your people," he suggested.

"My people listen to stories too much." Taking the meat from the fire, he gave some to Sedjet and, wary of his guest's greed, kept the rest this time. For a while they ate in silence, but after being prodded several times, Laughing Dog finally relented and told some of his people's tales, though not the one he'd heard last. Soon, however, his full belly coupled with his exhaustion caused drowsiness to overtake him. He lay down a little ways from the fire, half-listening as Sedjet related impossible tales of wandering the Firelands and the surrounding areas, stories of great battles and flooded cities, lost relics and angry gods. His eyes closed.

He awoke to the sound of an animal snorting and smacking as it tore at the carcass. He kept very still and cracked his eyes open. The fire still blazed brightly a short distance away. Whatever was after the fresh meat was so hungry that it had not been deterred by the flames, and that meant it was probably quite dangerous. Startling it could prove a fatal mistake. Quietly, Laughing Dog let his fingers stray behind him, feeling for his spear, but they found only hard earth, not even a stone to hurl.

The snorts and hungry growls of the animal sounded like a jackal, perhaps, or a hyena. Nothing he couldn't chase off, at least if there were only one. With painstaking slowness, he turned his head toward the sounds.

He froze in horror. It was no jackal. Every hair on his body stood upright, sweat crawling across his skin. His mind twisted, his stomach lurched, refusing to accept what he was seeing.

Sedjet crouched on the ground, but his body was hideously contorted, wrenched backward, his hands and feet planted on the earth, his chest pointed upward, face grinning emptily toward the sky, gaze blank and unseeing. In the firelight his features were warped by shadow, his teeth seeming to stretch all the way back to his hairline. Like a preying scorpion, he scuttled from side to side on his hands and feet, dipping the back of his head down toward the carcass. Something protruded from his scalp, something that snarled and snorted, bit and tore at the corpse, pulling away bits of meat. Laughing Dog could see Sedjet's bared throat bulge as it swallowed.

A shudder rippled through Laughing Dog, and he was helpless to stop it; fear paralyzed him. The monster paused its gorging. Sedjet's body moved toward him, back-splayed fingers pointing in his direction, his head lifting up to turn his human face away. Out of the close-cropped hair on the back of his skull grew a muzzle like that of a hyena, covered with short fur, stained with blood, gristly ropes of eland meat dangling from its jaws. It sniffed the air toward him, and then emitted a low, gurgling growl.

Laughing Dog's paralysis was broken; in terror, he scrambled backward on his hands in an unconscious imitation of the monster's own pose, moving toward the fire. His eyes danced across the ground—his spear was nowhere to be seen.

The thing that had been Sedjet stood upright in one swift, unnatural movement, its body ignoring its weight, bending upward until its human back was facing him. The muzzle poking out of the hair on the back of its head drooled red. It took a jerking step toward him.

"Get back," Laughing Dog shouted at it, terror strangling his voice. "Get away, demon!" He groped at his thigh for his knife, and remembered he had left it back in the village. There was no weapon anywhere nearby, not a stone nor branch. The world outside the fire was dark, and if he ran out into it, he would be unable to see anything. He would fall and be set upon by the demon.

It snarled again, leaning toward him so deeply that he expected to hear its reversed spine snap. Its hands groped toward the stars in futile clutching motions. Then it lunged, taking bounding backward steps toward him.

Driven purely by instinct, Laughing Dog grabbed at the closest thing to him—a large and heavy acacia branch—and pulled it out of the fire. Its underside was soft white ash and glowing ember, and seared into his palms and fingers with immediate pain, but he scarcely noticed. He rolled onto his back as the demon leapt over him, and swung the branch as hard as he could. With a crack and a shower of sparks, it connected solidly with the thing's side and broke in half. The impact wrenched the blazing log out of Laughing Dog's hands, tearing the burned skin away from his palms and fingers. The demon snout yelped at the blow, the beast careening sideways into the campfire. It landed among the blazing branches, cracking them, sending sparks and embers skittering across the earth.

The fire was not a big one, no larger than an arm's length across, but it flared and roared when the demon fell into it as though it had been fed dry grass. Laughing Dog rolled to one side on his elbows, his hands already screaming with pain, as the sudden cloud of flame billowed over him. The blaze of the fire lit the savanna brighter, the orange glow dancing infernal shadows across the flat ground. Within the flames the twisted shape thrashed and flailed, kicking out sparks and ash that clouded the air, howling and screeching horribly.

Then it lay still. Laughing Dog crouched on the ground nearby, watching. It might yet move again.

The flames around it diminished, shrank down to hands and then fingers of fire gripping a dark, unmoving shape. The sudden dimness of light made it difficult for Laughing Dog to see anything but small flames outlining the shape of a man. These then shrank, flickered, and went out, leaving him to sit alone in the sahil by a snuffed-out fire, a half-devoured eland carcass, and the ashen corpse of a man that had become a thing and attacked him. The desert was as quiet as death, and the visible light came from the glimmering stars and the still glowing embers illuminating a faint circle around his destroyed campfire.

His hands throbbed with pain from his burns.

There could be more demons out there, waiting for him, and he had no idea where his spear had gone. All the same, he couldn't remain near the fire where that thing still smoldered. The reek of it, charred and sickly sweet, made his meal rise in his stomach, and he turned and voided it into the sand, though he could not afford to lose it. Tomorrow, he would certainly die. Tonight, however, he crawled away and sat a little distance from what remained of his fire, hugging his knees, his destroyed hands turned upward so that the charred flesh didn't accidentally touch anything else and sting. He waited in the dark and listened in terror for the sound of anything else that might approach in the night.

As the hours went by, the remaining embers winked out one by one, and then he could see nothing but the stars. The searing in his hands intensified; between the gnawing pain and unrelenting fear, he had no chance of sleeping. Finally, after a night that would not end, he saw the sky turn pale, and turned to greet the coming sunrise, more grateful for the light than he could ever remember being, though the land was still too dark to see.

The pale faded into white, the surrounding sky to rich blue, drowning out the stars. The horizon—a dark black border, flat and featureless—was broken only by the grasping claw of the dead acacia tree from which he had taken his firewood. After a while, gold bordered the dark horizon, and finally, as it brightened, the land grew light enough to see. He got to his feet and hunted around the surrounding area for his spear. He found it thrown a good distance from the fire, and took it gingerly between the burned parts of his fingers.

The eland carcass lay on its side. It stank already, and its insides were a mass of black flies. Laughing Dog could not tell how much of it had been eaten, nor did he care to know. The rest of it was useless to him anyhow. He took cautious steps as he moved toward the fire. A man-sized lump of white ash lay across the middle of it, smears radiating away from where it had flailed. He lifted his spear and poked lightly at it with the haft end, and the lump crumbled and fell apart, raising a white cloud. He darted back from it, not wanting to let any of it touch him, or worse, enter his nose or mouth.

Nothing of the demon had persisted. He could see no remnants of a body, no clothes, nor the gold and jewels it had carried. Everything had turned completely to ash. It was dead, then, destroyed. He crouched next to the fire pit as relief blew through him and out his mouth. It was followed by a sense of giddy elation. This would be a story he could bring back to his people. He had been approached in the night by a demon. It had attacked him and he had destroyed it. And better yet, he had done so without a single prayer for assistance or guidance from the gods. He, Laughing Dog, had killed a demon with his bare hands.

But no. They would think him a liar. None would believe his tale, even if he could make it back alive, which was doubtful. Already he felt weak again, thirst scraping at his throat. He had lost much of his meal and the precious water it contained. The last place he had found water was nearly two days' walk away, perhaps more in his weakened state, if he could even find it again. All the same, walking back was his only hope. Perhaps he would find plants to suck for moisture. Perhaps he would find another lost animal. At the very least, he did not want to spend another night in these haunted lands.

The sun cracked open the horizon, golden and glorious, chasing away the terrors of the previous night. It would be several hours at least until he found himself damning its thirsty beams. He would not lie here and wait for it to cook him. No. He would go back. And he would bring his people the tale of his journey.

Again he prodded the ashes with the haft of his spear. Perhaps not everything had been destroyed; some souvenir, some proof of his visitor might yet remain. The lump disintegrated further, raising another cloud, and as it cleared, something glinted in the golden sunlight. Laughing Dog ducked around the cloud and crouched near the fire pit, taking his knife and digging it into the ashes next to the glint, nudging something solid. Out from the white dust rolled something brilliant and sparkling: the diamond the thing had shown him last night, the magical artifact it claimed eradicated all hunger and thirst. An obvious lie, considering how greedily it had eaten.

Laughing Dog's throat felt like leather. He reached for the gem, took it between his fingers. It was heavy and cool, and where it touched his burns he felt no pain. He stood, hefting it in his palm. It weighed more than it should. Once, when he was a boy, his father had taken him to a strange place where the gods were said to have lived, a great hollow full of dead trees, mostly broken pillars lying in heaps across the ground. His father had taken up a piece of wood and placed it in his hands, and he had been astonished to feel that it was not wood at all, but converted by the gods into stone, heavy and solid. That was how this diamond felt. Not like a stone at all, but like something somehow heavier and more solid than stone itself. He closed his fingers around it.

Immediately the dryness of his throat receded. The gnawing empti-ness in his stomach dwindled and vanished. He inhaled deeply in astonish-ment, and the dry desert air did not tear at his throat and tongue. Moisture flooded his mouth, soothed his dried and gritty eyes, and he blinked them several times in astonishment, licked his lips and felt the slippery sensation of his water on them. His thin skin fleshed out with the fullness of the rains, and his thoughts, previously dizzy and desperate, became clear again. Strength flooded through his limbs. He felt his sunken belly flatten, his thin arms and legs fill with muscle they had lost.

In shock, he staggered backward a few steps. He squeezed his newly strong hands into fists. The burns on his palms and fingers remained, but they no longer caused him any pain, and he found something yet more odd: there was nothing in his hand. He opened his fingers. The diamond had vanished. In desperation, he dropped to his hands and knees, running his fingers over the sand to try to find the gem in the morning light. He could not lose this new strength, this alleviation of all his suffering. He could not.

"Do not be afraid," said a voice. It was a man's voice, deep and reso-nant, seeming to come from everywhere, but it sounded much like Sedjet's had—with a roar of wind, and cracking and popping around the edges of the words. "You have not lost my gift. I have put it inside you, so you will never lose it."

Laughing Dog looked up, turning. "Where are you?" he asked. "Who are you?"

"I am Ogya," said the voice from everywhere, "and I am with you."

Old Stories

6

For Clay, home had never felt so far away. He missed the village at the edge of the forest, and more than that, the wide savanna. Rain had been falling for nearly the entire day. Out in the open, the downpour would have been even and steady, but here, under the canopy, it collected in the great leaves and branches and poured in rivulets and miniature cataracts to the ground below. He found avoiding the heavier patches of rain all but impossible. The air was white with haze and water that matted his hair and ran down into his eyes, so that he kept having to wipe them to see. Streams coursed along the forest floor, nearly deep enough to reach his knees in spots, and even in the shallower puddles, the mud was thick and sucking, and the hard wooden paw affixed to his injured foot sank down and stuck.

As their pace slowed, so Lord Doto's impatience grew. He seemed utterly unaffected by the rain, his fur just as light and fluffy as if no water touched it, and he somehow never took a step into the deep water, nor did the mud cake on his feet. He did not speak much to Clay, except to growl at him if he stumbled or slowed.

Clay thought of his comfortable, dry tent, raised on a mound of earth so that the water would run to either side, the hides protecting him from the downpour. He thought of smoked antelope and sorghum and juicy pear. Sometimes on rainy days, he and his brothers would be invited to their father's tent to sit around the fire in the center and sip palm wine and hear stories. He longed to be there now.

How foolish he had been, yearning to meet the gods. He had met one now, and that god despised him, had told him that he and his people were monsters. This was beyond understanding. All his prayers, every dance, every humble request that the gods might share their world with his people, all of these had been meaningless? Laughing Dog's exile for nothing? The very notion of it confused his steps, his feet straying as he slogged after his captor. Lord Doto was a god; the forest's pliant bending to his will left no doubt of that. But why had Clay never heard of him? Why was the name of Doto not included in the prayers and dances of the people? Maybe he was angry with people and called them murderers and traitors because they had never prayed to him. But Kwaee, the great forest god, was venerated by the people. Perhaps he would recognize Clay as a true and humble servant and set him free.

Clay pinned his hopes on that, imagining the encounter, the mighty forest god Kwaee, standing as tall as three men, frowning down at Doto, informing him of his grave mistake, that the man he had brought was neither murderer nor traitor. This was one of the faithful people. Lord Doto would be shocked, chagrined at his error, but did not even the gods sometimes go astray, fight and squabble among themselves? Were they not, in their own ways, just as flawed as their followers? In return, Doto would offer Clay a gift, anything he should wish from the powers of earth or sky. Clay would demur, then, saying that it was his pleasure to serve the gods in anything, and both Kwaee and Doto would be so pleased with his devotion that they would return him to his village immediately, with his foot healed good as new and faster than ever before. His father would be overjoyed to see him, and amazed at his tales, and he would be named emissary to the gods for his entire village.

He pushed away the misery of the rain with these comforting fancies, and by the end of it, he imagined himself guided by the gods to find Laughing Dog in the wilderness, who would be so taken with wonder and astonishment at seeing them with his own eyes that he would fall to his knees in contrition and tearful joy.

As the daylight faded, however, so did his daydreams. The rain had eased, but their pace had only quickened, and hunger sucked at Clay's empty stomach. His limbs were weary, and the stump of his foot, which had fit so perfectly into the wooden paw before, now ached and chafed, the edges of the cuff digging into his lower leg with every step. When the rain stopped, mosquitos and biting flies filled the air, stinging at his arms, legs, and neck. Exhausted, he tried to call to Lord Doto for a break, but the god ignored him, not even responding save for a quickening switch of his long, spotted tail.

Clay had been deceiving himself all these hours. He was not headed toward glory. He was headed for death. Doto himself had sworn it. He had vowed the obliteration of Clay's people. Surely gods kept their word. What reason would they have to lie? Briefly, Clay entertained thoughts of waiting until the god's attention was elsewhere, turning and running back to the village, warning them all to pick up what they could carry and move as far from the forest as they safely manage before divine wrath rained down on them. This notion, though, was hopeless. Even were he not so weary and his foot uninjured, and even if it had been midday, the blackness of night not so near, he could not forget what Lord Doto could do with the forest, the way he could make it come alive. When Clay was a boy, he had heard old tales of trees moving, even walking around, and the images had featured prominently in several of his more memorable nightmares. Seeing it with his own eyes, however, was far worse than a dream or imagination. When the trees and vines had animated and reached after him, he had felt a primal and unthinking terror. He'd shaken with fear as the lianas kept him pinned to the tree branch, only Doto's whim preventing him from a deadly fall. He shuddered again, recalling it.

He thought then of seeing his father, always proud, always in command, reduced to an aged, stooped figure pleading for his son's life. Clay had longed to call out to him, to run to him, but instead he could do nothing but struggle against his bonds, trapped in the unyielding, rough grip of the lianas about his limbs and chest, barely able to see past the fur of the leopard god concealing him.

The whole event itched at him. Why had Doto bothered to hide him at all? If, as he said, Clay's people were traitors whom he intended to slaughter, why not kill them there? Surely he could have brought the forest to life, strung them up by vines, raked them with thorns, shattered them with rock, or even summoned wild beasts to hunt them down? And yet, Lord Doto had done none of these things, but instead chosen to disappear and leave no trace behind. Why? An answer echoed at the back of his mind, first in a quiet whisper, and then with the roar of near-certainty: Doto was afraid, not just of Clay's people, but of Clay himself. He had taken care to hide himself and Clay from the trackers, and gripped Clay's throat to keep him from calling out. And after they'd left the village, he had carried him a great distance in the dark before pausing to allow him sleep. Perhaps it had been a coincidence, but perhaps Doto had feared the people finding him. And what was it the god had said when he first appeared? That he had taken Clay's "tooth stick" so that he could not bite him with it.

This was the most puzzling of all. A being who could command the forest to his will and lift Clay as if he weighed no more than a leaf should have no reason to fear him. What could trouble a deity so? Surely only another god could cause a god grievance. One name had come up several times during their journey: Ogya. Doto seemed concerned about the god of fire, worried of some scheme or plan. Perhaps he thought Clay might use the power of the god against him. Could Clay use this to defend himself somehow, or perhaps bargain for his life? It was what Laughing Dog would do, he thought. It was also reckless. One didn't challenge the gods. They were to be obeyed, however difficult their commands might be. He had paid for challenging them once, for testing them in the hunt. He would not make that mistake again. His hope, if he was to find his way back to his people, was not to fight Lord Doto, but to communicate with him. The gods were not fools. They would not behave irrationally.

He looked ahead at the resolutely silent, stalking form of Doto, whose tail swayed with his impatient steps. "It will be dark soon," Clay ventured. "We will have to stop for the night."

Lord Doto did not turn, though his spotted ears flicked back. "We will not be stopping." His voice was hard and emotionless.

"Forgive me, Lord Doto, but you will recall that I am unable to see at night."

"I do not forget so quickly. There will be light by which you will see."

Clay wondered how this might be done, and despite his situation, found himself curious to see this magic. He looked up at the sky, still heavy with clouds, the greys deepening with twilight. Roosting ibises croaked in the treetops, calling to their fellows to join them. The birds would rest for the evening. Surely a forest god would understand that all creatures needed to do so.

"Lord Doto—"

"Be silent."

Clay's shoulders sagged with weariness and a growing despair. It seemed Lord Doto truly did despise him. He continued to walk, and each step was heavier than the last, the wooden cuff biting into his calf a little deeper, rubbing dirt into it. Pain and hunger and exhaustion welled up inside him. He was lagging behind Doto's rapid pace, and could not compel himself to move more quickly.

Doto sensed him faltering, turned, and ordered, "You will keep up with me. You will waste no more time."

It was unjust. He had done everything the god had asked, everything within his power, and even requested strength to follow, and been refused. He dared not argue with divinity, but the words came out anyhow. "But I cannot continue, Lord Doto. I need rest and food. Without them I cannot go on."

"And yet you must," Doto said in a breezy tone, continuing his pace. "You must forget about being hungry and tired and follow me. You think you have reached the limits of your strength, but I assure you, you have not. A frightened animal will run itself to collapse if it fears death, and then pull itself even farther to escape it. You have strength left in you. You will find it when you know your survival requires it. You will keep following me, now, or you will die."

The protest rose behind Clay's lips. He almost argued. He almost told the god, "No," and stopped in place. But that would have been arrogance, and the gods demanded obedience. "Yes, Lord Doto," he said wearily. He forced himself to take a quicker step, and then another, calling on whatever hidden reserves of energy the god claimed were there. His legs ached and his foot hurt, the wooden paw dragging along the ground.

He made it perhaps another hundred paces or so at the faster speed, and then collapsed, hitting the ground before he knew he was falling. It didn't even hurt. It felt good to lie there, his weight off of his feet, his legs shaking with exhaustion.

"Get up," Doto ordered, just above him.

"Yes, Lord Doto," Clay said again, opening his eyes to see the leopard standing above him, eyes narrowed in annoyance. Bracing his palms against the ground, he pushed himself to his feet. Doto turned, the tip of his tail brushing against Clay's legs, and started forward again, but Clay had barely taken five steps before his muscles shuddered with exhaustion and he fell forward once more. This time a rock dug painfully into his ribs, bruising them. He lay panting, so tired he wanted to cry.

A clawed foot nudged forcefully at his shoulder. "Do you play games with me? Stand and follow. You are not even trying."

Obediently, Clay tried to get up, but his legs were shaking, and his toes skidded along the muddy roots of the ground. His body refused to rise a third time. "Lord Doto, I cannot," he said. "I have no more strength."

The foot nudged under his shoulder, lifting him and rolling him onto his back. He stared up at the broad, shaggy branches of the canopy, the gloomy grey sky, and the angry face of Doto. The great cat dropped into a crouch over him, paws gripping his shoulders and pinning them to the ground. His fur smelled rich and earthy. He put clawed fingers around Clay's neck. His fangs glistened with saliva. "You will get up and follow me now," he said, "or I will tear out your throat. I will go and get another fire bearer who is more tractable and obedient than you."

Clay swallowed, feeling the bulge of his throat slide past the god's grip. "Please, Lord Doto," he said, "just let me go home. My people need me. My father needs me."

For what? a nasty voice in the back of his mind asked. *You are no use to your people. You can't run. You can't hunt. You can't even look after your brother. What good are you to any of them?*

The god scowled. "I will not let you go. You will come with me, or you will die."

"Then I will have to die. I can't walk any farther." It was the truth. He might be able to get to his feet, but he would not be able to take more than a few steps. His legs were heavy with weariness. He thought of his poor father never knowing what happened to him; his brothers, who would no doubt mount another search that would never find him. He wished he were back there to say goodbye to them. And here there would be no one to burn his body and send him to his ancestors. He would lie and rot in the jungle. Or perhaps, he thought morbidly, Lord Doto would consume his carcass.

The god's pink tongue licked over his fangs. He leaned down as if to bite at Clay's throat, and then stopped, his brow creasing. "You are a very bothersome creature," he said. He sat up and released Clay's neck. Clay rubbed at his punctured skin with one hand. Was he not to die, then? Would a god change his mind so easily?

Doto stood and turned away, his tail swaying slowly. "It would be very inconvenient for me to go back to your nest and find another fire bearer. You know this, and would risk your death to test me."

"No, Lord Doto," Clay protested, leaning up on his elbows. "I spoke the truth when I said I couldn't continue."

Doto's tail went still, and he looked back. "Perhaps you did. Any creature would have obeyed me to preserve its own life. We will stay here for the night. You will have rest. And tomorrow, we will continue."

Clay sighed in relief. "Thank you, Lord Doto. You are most generous."

"I am not generous! You have won no favors from me. I let you rest only because it is practical. You will have only the sleep necessary to keep our journey to Kwaee's temple swift. And after we reach it, I will most certainly kill you."

"I understand."

The god turned and crouched to stare at him, leaning closer and closer, as if to peer at some tiny detail on his face, or to look behind his skin. "You are very strange creatures, you fire bearers. In the grip of a predator, you neither struggle nor surrender as prey should. Instead, you speak to the predator and ask that it release you. No other animal does this. Why do you?"

"I don't know," Clay said. "I just know that we're different than the animals. The tales tell us that the gods made us different. But you are a god, surely you must know how all things were made."

"What do you mean, how all things were made? They are being made around us now. They are born and they die. They sprout from seed and wilt."

"I mean at first. When the first things were made."

"There are no first things," Doto said firmly. "The trees have always been, and the gods, and the forest, and the fire bearers."

Again Clay felt the urge to contradict rise behind his lips. The tales told that Wem, the Sky Father, had scooped the people up out of the muddy earth and formed them into shapes and baked them in the oven of the sun. And some he had baked for too long, and some not long enough, but the people, Clay's people, had been baked just the right amount of time, into living flesh, by the magic of Wem and the magic of the sun and set loose on the land to live and love. It was the tale he had grown up knowing by heart. But who would know the truth better? His people, flawed and frail, or the gods, invincible and all-powerful? He let the story die inside him, and grieved its passing. "Our people must have been wrong, Lord Doto. We have many tales of the gods from the years. Maybe not all of them are true."

"Likely none of them are. What could animals know of the gods?"

"Maybe nothing," Clay admitted. "But the tales are important to us. They are our past. Don't you have stories of your own that are important to you?"

A surprised look passed over Lord Doto's face, his round, golden-green eyes going wider. Despite being a god, with face and muzzle of a leopard his expressions were so open, so plain, that he might have been just another person. "Of course I have stories of my own," he said. "They are not the sort of stories that a mere beast would understand."

"I would listen anyway," Clay offered.

Doto leaned closer, his pointed ears perked toward Clay. "You would? Why would you do that?"

"If they are a god's stories, then they must be true. They must be important. And then I could take those true stories back to my people so that they could learn them."

Doto's expression hardened. "Except that you will not be going back to your people." He turned away again, standing. "Because you are going with me to Kwaee, and then you will die. If you are truly so tired, you should rest now. We have a very long way to go."

⁀⌃⁀

The next morning, Clay felt as though he had barely slept, and his legs still ached with fatigue. His sleep had been heavy, but too short, and the ground was damp and uncomfortable. Biting flies and mosquitos had crawled over him while he slept, and when Doto curtly roused him in the early dawn, he woke to find his skin mottled with welts. He could not remember a moment when he had ever felt more miserable. To worsen matters, there was a stabbing pain in his toes—but in the toes of his left foot, which no longer existed. It seemed patently unfair that a foot that he could no longer use should feel such pain. But there was nothing to be done about it. The gods commanded him, and would accept nothing less than obedience, so he stood, tried to shake himself awake, and followed after Doto's stalking form. His pace was slow this time, slower than yesterday, and no matter how forcefully Lord Doto commanded him to follow, he could not muster any additional speed. He had just found a tolerable rhythm to his stride when the rain started pouring down on him once more. The only mercy was that after a time, Lord Doto seemed to sense that he was moving as quickly as he could, and left off his continual orders to hasten.

Around mid-morning, the rain grew so heavy that Clay could no longer see nor follow Doto, and then his foot stuck in the mud and he fell forward. He tugged at his leg, but the angle was wrong, and the sodden earth sucked at the wood surrounding his foot. He was too exhausted to pull it out. Despairing, he sat back and waited for Doto to be angry with him. He didn't have to wait long before the god to appeared out of the rain, his fur as dry and fluffed as though the day were sunny and breezy. With strong paws, he gripped Clay's leg and tugged it up out of the mud. Then he put his arms around Clay and hefted him to his feet, his chest pressing into Clay's back as he did. "Come," he said.

He led Clay a short distance away, to the base of a tree with a wide, gnarled trunk, its upper branches high out of sight. The spot near the trunk was sheltered from the downpour and dry, and when Clay huddled against the rough bark, the whole thing bent slowly toward him, blocking more of the rain. He half-panicked, fearing that it was falling and would crush him, but it moved no farther.

"I allowed you to rest," Doto said once he was settled, "but you move no faster today."

"I'm sorry, Lord Doto. I have been going as quickly as I can. I'm afraid I need more rest than I had. I'm not used to sleeping on the ground like that. And I'm hungry, too. I think I will need food if I'm to go much farther. I want to obey," he added. For now, though, he was glad to stop, and not to feel the rain on his face and shoulders. He imagined how he would have responded if someone had told him five rains ago that he would be sick to death of water. He probably would have thought them mad. Here, the shelter of the tree was comforting—not so comforting as the coziness and safety of his tent, perhaps, but still welcome.

Doto stretched out his back and shoulders, and Clay tried not to stare. God he might be, and with the face and fur of a leopard, but he was still man-shaped, and quite nude. Clay thought of his nighttime fancies of Left Rabbit and forcibly reminded himself that such thoughts were perverse even when gods were not involved. Wildly blasphemous, when they were.

"Why do you want to obey?" the forest god asked him. "You are the enemy, fragile and easily fought though you seem to be. I have taken you from your home, and I have told you what I intend to do. Why did you not try to escape in the night? Why do you want to follow me now?"

Puzzled, Clay answered, "Because...we're supposed to follow the gods. We're supposed to obey them. I and my people, we've prayed to the gods and done what they asked all our lives. And our ancestors before them, and their ancestors before them."

"But these gods do not compel you to act?".

"No," Clay said. Why would Doto not know the answers to these questions? "But if we ignore them, we usually regret it. The gods control every part of our lives. It would be foolish not to listen to them. There could be a flood or a drought, or a crazed animal. We could starve. The ground could swallow us up, or the flies consume us."

Doto lifted his head. "So. You worship us because you fear us."

"No!" Clay protested, then admitted, "Well, yes, in part. But that's not all of it. Of course we're afraid of what the gods might do to us. But we're also grateful."

"What do you mean, grateful? What is this?"

Clay looked up into Doto's large eyes, rich green circles ringed with yellow, full of blinking curiosity. "I don't know how to explain."

"Try."

Sighing, Clay closed his eyes, and reached into his memories. "Back when our people lived on the savanna, I would sometimes wake up early, before the sun. I would leave our village quietly, not waking anyone else, and walk a long distance away. There I would stand out in the middle of the grasses and wait. The birds would sing around me. The air would be cool and still. All around would be the early morning light, the dark sky with a few bright stars still showing in the west, and maybe the face of the moon. Then the sun would rise up above the grasses in the east, a bright orange fire. And sometimes with the sun, Father Wem would send a wind racing to meet it. I would see it make the grasses nod and bow in great lines across the savanna. I would see it bend the trees. It would pick up nesting birds and toss them into the sky. And in these moments I would understand that just as we dance for the gods, so the whole world dances. The grass, the wind, the sun, the birds, the grasshoppers leaping from blade to blade, it's all dancing. It's all worship. And then the wind would pick me up too, and I would run with it, along the ground, along the heads of the grasses. I would run like I was flying, like if I ran fast enough, I could catch the sun. I was so happy for everything that the gods had given me that I had to dance too, along with the savanna. That's what I mean by grateful. It means that sometimes I see the goodness of my life and I can't quite believe it. I have to thank someone for it, and thanking only makes it better. I don't worship the gods out of fear. I worship them out of joy."

Doto drew himself up importantly, head back, eyes narrowed. "I am pleased that I am not afflicted by this joy. It makes you behave in foolish ways."

For a moment, Clay forgot that Doto was a god who had kidnapped him and threatened to kill him and his family. For a moment, he felt only great pity. He put his hand on Doto's arm. "That's terrible," he said. "A life without joy."

Doto hissed and pulled his arm away. "Do not touch me, foolish fire bearer," he snarled. "What need has a god of your petty vulnerabilities? Why should I want a silly wind to force me to dance?"

"Because," Clay said, looking down at the mud-covered piece of wood at the end of his leg, "it's the best thing that there is in life."

The march went onward. Clay was still tired, but not so much now as he had been in the morning. Lord Doto had allowed him to rest until the rain stopped and beyond. He had been silent after their conversation, ascending with athletic ease a nearby tree and sitting with his back to Clay, his tail switching. The discussion had seemed to discomfit him for reasons Clay could not understand. Clay had fallen asleep in the shelter of the leaning tree with the sounds of rain all around him, and when Lord Doto had finally awoken him with the nudge of one foot, he had felt far more rested, though far hungrier as well. They had continued with little conversation.

"Are you feeling grateful now?" Doto asked him after a while.

Clay looked up at the sky, or what he could see of it between breaks in the treetops. The color was a deepening blue. The afternoon was already beginning to fade into evening. It would be his third night away from his people, and two days since he had eaten anything. "Not at the moment," he admitted. "I've been taken from my home to be killed. I'm hungry and tired."

"You are always tired," Doto observed. "So maybe you are never grate-ful either. But you are far from the savanna and cannot run. All your people left the savanna and came to the forest. Why? Did Ogya tell you to?"

"The gods don't talk to us. Not like you are now. Not directly. We have to pray that they will show us what they want."

"And they showed you that they wanted you to go to the forest?"

"I suppose. Father Wem stopped sending the rain where we lived. And then great fires came. They burned our village, and we had to come south to find water."

Lord Doto slowed his pace, falling back to walk beside Clay, his ears perked. "Tell me more of these great fires."

So as they walked, Clay told him of how the savanna had once had great rains and rivers that ran through it, but how when he was young, the rivers had begun to grow dry. He told of how one day they could no longer grow sorghum, and the antelope had to migrate much farther, visiting their village's hunting grounds less often. He told of how, after Laughing Dog was born, the rains came later and later every year, until finally the plains were dry and bristly, and they could see the red of fires burning far away at night, like little sunsets. Then the fires came to their village, and they had to leave. He told of the great hardship they had suffered, the long journey, the terrible hungers and thirsts year after year, until finally they came to the edge of the forest, where the rains did not just come some of the time, but regularly, and how now the people could live comfortably, and could drink when they wished to, and always find food to eat.

"And even after these great fires came, you still serve Ogya?" Lord Doto inquired.

Clay hesitated. He did not want to admit that his people could be, at times, less than devoted. "Some do not. A few of those who lost wives, hus-bands, or children because of the great fires are very angry with Lord Ogya. They will not pray to him anymore. Others volunteer to say their blessings to the fire god for them, so that he will not curse them further in his wrath. But it is a hard thing to honor a god who causes someone terrible pain." He looked up at Doto as he said this.

The forest god seemed to be considering these words. His tail swayed slowly above the forest floor as he thought. "This is a very interesting story you tell me. I think my father may be pleased to hear it."

Clay knitted his brow in confusion. "Forgive me, Lord Doto. You say I should tell this story to…Father Wem? But surely he sees everything."

Lord Doto's eyes widened. "Yes," he said. "You should tell all your life's tales to Father Wem, for it pleases him to hear them. And since you will be telling tales anyhow, perhaps when we reach Kwaee, I will have you tell *him* that story as well."

"I don't understand. How will telling a god that my people can be faithless sometimes make him think well of us? Would that make him believe we are not the murderers and traitors you said we were?"

Doto looked back with a sneering expression. "I am all but certain you are," he said. "You are fire bearers. You light your sticks and make the black smoke and the Cry of the Dead. But you do not seem very threatening to me, nor do you seem to be so fond of Ogya as the tales say you once were."

"What tales?" Clay asked with interest.

Doto ignored him. "It might be that you have changed from the people you were. If I had time, I would go to see Sarmu to ask him about your people and what you have been doing in the savanna. But there is no time for that. We must hurry to Kwaee's temple. Especially as you are so feeble and cannot travel for long without complaining."

Clay felt sudden hope. "Then you will allow me food and rest, Lord Doto?" His stomach ached at the mere thought of a meal.

"It would seem I have no choice, unless I wish to drag you to Kwaee myself. But you will stay here while I find food for you. I have seen the things that your people eat, and I can find them faster if you are not stumbling around all over the place and screeching like a baboon."

"I don't screech like a baboon," Clay protested, but Doto had already faded into the background, invisible. Watching him vanish was like suddenly noticing that one could see the stripes and shape of an animal hidden, resting in sun-dappled grass, and then losing it again, its outlines and features melting into the detail of the world around it. One moment Clay could see him as plain as day, and the next his eyes slid past, unable to tell the god from the surroundings.

"Lord Doto?" he called out. "Are you there?"

No answer.

So. He was to have food and rest, and perhaps a chance not to die. It was a minor victory, but a victory nonetheless. He felt a surge of elation, and then a deep and overpowering weariness. He wanted nothing more than to lie back and drift off into sleep. But the forest was dark, the ground wet and unpleasant, and if Lord Doto brought meat, it would need to be cooked. Clay would need to build a fire and a bed. Fire would come first, and provide light as he searched for dry bedding. Heavy rains had soaked everything, and so finding wood to burn would not be easy.

He took his belt from about his waist—it was lined with bright blue stones and little white shells, and had once belonged to his grandfather, who had visited the great water. He tied it high in a bush so that he could see it and find his way back to the clearing, and also as a message to Lord Doto that he had not run away. He would not like to see the god's anger if he thought Clay had fled him. Methodically, he made his way in a spiral about the clearing. He found a huge, mottled tree of a type he did not recognize, and using a flat stone, prised up pieces of its bark. Beneath were many hair-like strips of wood that would work well for kindling. He snapped away twigs that had been sheltered from the rain in the shadows of larger trees, broke sticks that he could scrape the bark from with a sharp stone, and found a few larger pieces of deadwood that were older and damp, but that he reckoned would burn once they had dried in the fire.

Once he was satisfied with his collection, he returned the clearing and assembled his fire. He lamented having no knife with him, for the going was slow and laborious with the stones he could find, and his knuckles were bruised and torn by the time he had stripped damp bark and prepared the wood to his satisfaction. He notched a plank, placed a stick in the notch, and spun it by rubbing it between his palms until a thread of smoke rose up and the bark scrapings caught light. Soon he had a small, snapping flame that spread and began to dry out the damper wood, and the sight of it gladdened him. Back home, his people would be lighting their own fires about now, gathering around to cook food and make jokes and talk about their days.

But there would be no jokes around his father's fire tonight, he reflected. It had been only two days since he had been taken—too soon for mourning his death. But by now, they must all believe him gone forever, dragged off into the forest by a great cat. It might be true, he realized with a prickling of the hair on his arms.

Firewood there might be, but he had less luck locating any dry bedding material. The ground was soggy, with no apparent hollows containing shrubs or leaves that had been sheltered from the rain. Soon enough the light was too low for him to continue searching, so he made his way back to the fire and sat down. The scent of smoke made him think of cooking food, and his stomach twisted in hunger.

"Traitor!" hissed a voice from the darkness.

He looked up, peering out beyond the flames into the dark forest. The huge trunks of trees were lit by yellow firelight, angular shadows flickering behind them. Everything beyond was swallowed by an engulfing blackness. "Lord Doto?"

The voice seemed to come from everywhere, or at least, not from any specific direction Clay could identify. "You feign hunger and exhaustion to send me away so that you can try to fight me with fire? You will fail. The forest is wet with rain; you cannot burn it. And soon your little fire will go out, and then your god will not be able to help you."

So. The forest god feared fire that much. Clay knew Doto did not care for Ogya, but had not realized that he hated even a small flame. "Lord Doto, please, I did not mean to offend you. There is no reason for alarm. I have summoned no god here. It is only a small fire I built for warmth and light, and to cook my food."

"Fool," spat Doto from the darkness. "Can you really not know that Ogya lives in every flame, that he can see you from every spark? Wherever there is a fire, Ogya has power, and you have brought him here into my forest. You have given his fingers hold inside my domain."

Clay stood up beside the fire, feeling it burn the moisture from his damp and muddy knees. "Forgive me, Lord Doto. I swear to you, I did not know." He paused. He did not want to go the night without fire, but if he didn't win back some portion of the god's favor, the next day would be far worse than a night without light or a dry place to sleep. But Doto was prideful; there could be little doubt of that. After a moment, he added, in a supplicating voice, "If you are frightened of the flames, Lord, I will extinguish it immediately." He lifted his foot as if to kick the fire apart.

There was a long silence. Green eyes flashed in the darkness beyond the fire. "What is done is done." A figure resolved from the shadows, and then Doto slunk toward the fire. He carried an armload of bright orange fruits that Clay had never seen, and the slain carcass of a young pig. Regarding the flames with a wary expression, he paced toward them at angles and then moved away again, ears flattened, nose wrinkling. Eventually he seemed to find a place that suited him, and crouched down, resting a decent distance away. "If Ogya has seen me, then there is little I can change about that. Let him see me here, and burn in impotence. He will know I have you in captivity. Perhaps that will make him worry a bit." He spoke directly at the fire. "As well he should."

Clay felt a little surge of satisfaction. The god's pride could be pricked, after all. The thought of manipulating a god was blasphemous, but for the moment, at least, hunger and relief left no room for regrets. He sat down again next to the fire, but his eyes were on the food Doto had brought. His mouth watered.

The leopard god caught his gaze and put down the pile of fruits and the little pig. He did not come any closer to the fire. "These are for you to eat," he said in an indulgent tone.

Retrieving the food, Clay could see that the small pig had been slain with what looked like a bite to the throat, torn puncture wounds still slick with blood. He looked back at Doto but could see no blood on his muzzle, though darkness may have been concealing it. "You are gracious, Lord Doto. Thank you for this gift of food."

Doto snorted.

The fruits he had brought had a yielding, sweet, yellow flesh and were filled with many soft, slippery, black seeds. Clay found the taste almost overwhelming after a full day without food, and consumed one of them in a few hungry bites, licking his fingers. The meat. He would need to cook the meat. It would be difficult to skin and gut it without his knife. He thought for a moment, then turned to the god. "Lord Doto, as god, the best parts of this kill rightly belong to you. Please honor me by taking the heart and liver of this pig."

Doto's ears went forward. "I do not require food as a beast does," he said. His tone sounded stern, but there was a note of pleasure there as well. "But since you make this offering, I will accept."

Clay brought the carcass to him, turning away as the god took it and lowered his head toward it. He could hear slick, tearing sounds, and then Doto licking his jaws. He looked back. The pig had been eviscerated, the heart, kidneys, liver, and even other organs missing, ragged bite marks torn across the stomach. "Thank you for this honor, Lord Doto."

Doto grunted in response.

Cleaning and skinning as much as he could of the pig was still difficult, but he managed. All the while, his captor watched him with a suspicious expression. The expression turned to mystification as Clay spitted the piglet and suspended it over the flames.

"I have seen that your people do this to all their meat," Doto said. "You must offer Ogya a taste of every kill before you eat it. But you give me a taste before you give one to Ogya." He held his head high.

Clay turned the meat slowly on its spit, hearing it sizzle in the fire. "Cooking the meat brings out its flavor, Lord Doto. And besides, if we do not cook it, it will make us ill."

The god snorted. "As if you needed any more proof that you are minions of the fire god. He sickens you if you do not offer him your share of your hunt."

Clay paused with the denial on his tongue. Perhaps it was true. Perhaps the god did sicken them if they did not offer it to him first. No one had ever told that story before. "But it is only meat that we must cook," he said. "Why then does Ogya not demand a taste of our food that grows? Perhaps he does not care for that?"

Doto's expression darkened. "There is no food that Ogya does not enjoy."

The scent of the cooking pig made Clay's mouth water. "You could try some of this after it has been cooked. The taste might please you."

"And swallow any poisons Ogya might put in it for me? If you are trying to be clever, fire bearer, then you are an even greater fool than I had supposed. I will not let you deceive me. Already you have brought the black clouds into the forest."

"The black clouds?" Clay looked over at the fire. "You mean the smoke? But most smoke is white."

Doto wrinkled his nose. "It smells black."

Clay sniffed at the fire without thinking. He could smell the rich, salty flavor of the meat sizzling in the flames, and his mouth filled in anticipation. But below that was the burning of wood, the thin pervasive scent of char and ash.

"It is a bad smell," Doto said. "And it goes very far. Even animals that do not have a god's senses can smell it from a journey of days away. It is a smell that says here everything is dying. Go far, far away so that the fire does not catch you and kill you. Flee, or you will die. That is the smell of destruction and death. Everything that lives knows to stay away from it. Except you fire bearers. Not only do you not flee from it, you start it, on purpose. You sleep next to it, even when you know it could consume your nest and all who live in it. Even when it has," he added pointedly.

"But the fires we make are small and safe," Clay said. "They do not hurt us. The fire that burned our home was not started by us."

"Maybe some other fire bearers started that one," Doto suggested. "Because they were angry with you."

Clay had no real argument for that. The notion was preposterous, but how could he explain that to a god? "All right, so smoke is the black clouds. What about the Cry of the Dead you talk about? What is that?"

Doto looked back at him curiously. "It is the sound that comes out of the dead animals. I have seen your people make this sound. You touch your paw to the dead animal, and the dead animal shouts in pain."

Clay frowned. "We do not touch dead animals. Except to prepare them for food."

"You are carrying around pieces of dead animal now!" Doto exclaimed loudly. "They are wrapped around your body. You all have these pieces on you. You live inside little holes covered with dead animal. How can you tell me you do not touch them? I think you do not know your people so well as you think you do."

"Oh, skins," Clay said. The last comment from Doto made him uncomfortable. Skins weren't the same thing as dead animals. He didn't wear dead things, or live beneath them. They were just skins. But now, talking to Doto, it seemed strange, even unhealthy. The god had a way of altering Clay's perspective. Could a god's perspective even *be* wrong?

"Yes," he said finally. "We do use skins everywhere. I thought you were talking about the entire animal. Forgive me."

"Skins," said Doto. "That is what you use to make the Cry of the Dead. You touch the skins."

Touch the skins? "Oh! Our drums! It's—Lord Doto, it is not the animal shouting when we beat the drums. It's just a sound. Like—" He tapped with his knuckles against a piece of wood. "We take the skin and stretch it tight, and then when we tap it, we get a sound."

"You use the sound to say, here we come, we are fire bearers, and we will burn your forests and kill your living things, and these are the sounds of your dead to prove it."

"No!" Clay shouted, surprising himself. "No, Lord Doto. We beat drums to talk to the gods, and to remember the past. We use them for songs and prayers and dances. Lord Doto, I don't mean to argue you, but we have danced to drumbeats in honor of Kwaee himself."

Doto peered at him. "Why would striking dead things honor a god? These songs and dances, these are not things that a god does. We do not hear them, except from far away."

No songs. No dances. The gods had heard none of these. All that they had done over the years to honor and bless the gods around them had gone unnoticed. But no, that was inconceivable. "My Lord Doto, we have never danced nor sung in your name before, because we did not know it. This must be why you have never heard us. When I return to my people, I will tell them your name, and how you guided me and guarded me through the forest, and they will praise you, and you will see."

"Do not make assumptions about what will happen to you," Doto growled. Then, in a calmer tone, he inquired, "Why do you make the Cry of the Dead when you have these songs and prayers and dances? How will this sound honor me if I allow your people to make it?"

Clay shrugged. "The sound makes us want to dance. Have you never felt that before? When your blood moves faster, and you have to move with it?"

"This is like the wind thing. Drums make you grateful."

"No, Lord Doto." Clay hesitated. "Actually, it is a bit like joy, yes. It's like the earth's heart beats, and it picks you up and carries you with it, and you can try to keep still if you want, but it's so much better to let it seize you and spin you around." He looked down at his mangled foot and heard his voice break. "It's like flying."

"I have flown in the minds of birds many times," Doto informed him. "It is not hard to do."

Clay sighed. "I suppose not. If you're a god, nothing is hard to do. It must be very boring, being a god, and finding nothing difficult."

"Boring is not a thing that gods feel," Doto said after a considerable pause. "But sometimes being a god is…frustrating."

"Why?"

The god looked into the forest. "Because everything that is not a god is so very small and stupid," he said in a bitter tone. He reminded Clay, for a brief, blasphemous moment, of a petulant child. "Nothing can say anything or do anything that is worth a god paying attention to. But a god must listen anyway. The birds will make the same sounds every morning and night. The trees will fight each other for sun. The animals will screech and hiss and eat and mate, and all the time they do not understand anything that a god might want to say or do, but I just have to keep listening, and listening—" He broke off there, staring at the ground. "And they are all so very small and stupid. And it is frustrating, sometimes."

Clay sat still, taken aback. He silently turned the meat on the spit. "Do I frustrate you, Lord Doto?"

The god looked up, gazing at him through the firelight. "No," he said slowly. "You are troublesome, and you complain a great deal, and you hardly know anything at all. At first you frustrated me. But now I think you are something different. At least it is interesting."

Uncertain how to respond to that dubious compliment, Clay turned his focus to the fire. The pig was browning on the edges, so he took the spit out of the flames and tested the meat carefully. It was well-cooked, hot, the outside skin dry. With his fingers, he gingerly tore away a bit of the meat and placed it in his mouth. The rich, restorative flavor flooded his senses, so that for a moment he could think of nothing else. His stomach clamored for him to swallow, but he took his time with it, enjoying it.

He tore off another piece and held it out toward Doto. "Are you certain you will not try some, Lord?"

The great cat sniffed at the air; his pupils, round in the darkness, fixed on the strip of cooked meat. "No. I will not put something touched by Ogya inside me."

Clay shrugged and popped the morsel into his mouth, chewing hungrily. He needed to force himself to eat more slowly, or he might be sick. "I don't understand," he said around the bite. "You said that all animals know to run from fire. But if that is true, then why did they bring fire to us in the first place?"

Doto's ears twitched. "Bring fire? Animals do not bring fire."

"Once they did." Clay looked into the flames. They burned orange and yellow and blue, sparking and crackling around the wood. The larger logs were smoking more as they dried out. Through the fire, he could look back into his past, into a thousand story circles, his people around him, his brothers fighting him for the best spot. There was a tale told so often that every child knew it by heart.

"Long ago," he said, "man travelled in places far beyond the savanna. He walked in the high places that climb to Father Wem. Do you know the high places?" He paused here, for here the children would answer, but there were no children. He felt a reverence at uttering the sacred words to a god of the forest, the threads of the spirit world lifting him up, tugging deep within him.

"Some have seen them, but they are far, far from here. Here the warmth of the sun spills out and pours over the land like honey, but up there, in the high places, the warmth of the sun runs down, far down, into the valleys, and so the high places shiver, and the breath of Wem blows cold. Man was colder than he had ever been, so cold that he thought he might die. Happily, man came across an antelope, and said to himself, 'This antelope has thick fur and the cold does not bother it. I will kill it and take its skin, and then I can wear it and be warm.'

"What do you know of the high places? You know that up in the high places, all are close to Wem, and can speak to each other as brothers. There in the high places, the antelope heard man, and understood him, and said, 'Please do not kill me, man. I do not wish to die.'

"'But I must,' said man, 'or I will die from this cold.'

"The antelope thought quickly, and told man, 'If you promise to spare my life, then I will bring you something from the gods, a little piece of their power, so that you never need to be cold again, and you never need to fear the darkness again.'

"Man was not sure he could trust the antelope, but he felt pity for her, and so agreed. Then antelope used her long legs, yes, and her powerful hooves, yes, and danced up the rocks and cliffs to the highest parts of the high places, where no man could ever follow. Higher and higher she danced until she was standing up with the clouds and the sun. Then she made the greatest leap an antelope has ever leapt. She soared over the clouds and the lands far below, until she landed on the very sun. She leaned her head down and scooped up fire into her mouth, for back then fire was as safe to touch as water, and then she jumped back down to man.

"And man built his first fire, and kept himself and antelope warm. And he carried the fire back to his people. But Ogya, the god of fire, was very angry at this theft, and so he cursed man, and all beasts, so that if they ever came too close to fire, it would burn them, and cause them terrible pain. With antelope he was especially angry, yes, and he sent his flames to burn her back bright orange, and that is why to this day the antelope has an orange back, and why nothing will frighten her so much as a burning torch."

Clay finished, realizing he had unconsciously adopted the sing-song voice and rolling cadence of the Teller when he spoke. He had told the tale as if to children, and felt a flush of embarrassment. All the same, the story felt good to tell. He felt closer to home, closer to his people. Speaking the familiar words had felt like the gods speaking through him. He looked up at Doto with a smile.

Doto was staring at him. "That," he said, "is a very stupid story."

At first Clay didn't understand what he was saying. Stung, he stammered, "Well, there is some exaggeration for the telling of it, but the gist of it is true."

"It was so wrong and stupid that I cannot understand how anyone could say it without shame. Have you not ever seen the sun? Have you not seen how high up it is? Nothing could ever reach that. And if they did, they would burn into ashes."

"But the high places—"

"Are not even a tiny bit high enough," said Doto. "I have soared in the minds of eagles, who fly higher than any other birds, and the sun is a thousand times higher. And then you thought that an antelope could carry fire in its mouth? It is so very stupid. Baboons are less stupid than that." He twitched his tail.

Clay poked at the fire miserably. "But it is a tale of our people," he said.

"And they think this is a true story?"

Clay thought of Laughing Dog, protesting the absurdity of the tales before the fire, banished for his insolence. He had been right all along, and the people had punished him for it. How many others doubted the truth of the tales but dared not voice their disagreement?

"I—not all of them do, I guess."

But how could the stories not be true? It made no sense. How else could they have become stories? Truth was what made something a story, and a story is what made something true. No matter how he tried, he could not think around it.

"So some people in your nest have a different story about where fire came from?"

"No, I…" Clay remembered that when his people had lived to the north, sometimes they would be visited by travelers from other tribes. The wanderers would bring goods from beyond the Firelands, from the great waters, and even farther. And when these people visited, they would sit at the fires and hear the stories of Clay's people, and they would tell their own. Some of these stories were very strange, so different from the stories Clay had heard that they were difficult to comprehend. He remembered that Great Ram, then just barely old enough to go on hunts, had laughed at these tales, had tried on at least one occasion to correct them in their false beliefs. But their father had put a hand on Ram's shoulder. "All tales are true," he had said. "Our guest grants us the gift of his people's wisdom. Do not dishonor yourself by refusing this gift."

Clay could have kicked himself, were his foot still undamaged, for his arrogance. He had thought to tell a god of the nature of the world, but had never asked the god for his own stories. "Tell me, Lord Doto, of the truth, then? What do the gods say of how people got fire?"

Doto regarded him with glittering eyes. "How fire bearers got fire? There was no time when they did not have fire; they are called fire bearers. Before you had it, you were not fire bearers. You were something else. A strange bird perhaps, or a naked chimpanzee. But long ago, before there were fire bearers, or any other beasts, there were only gods. And chief among the gods were Father Wem, who rules the sky, Mother Fam, who governs the earth, and Ogya, brother of Father Wem, whose dominion is fire, and everything that has burned. And Father Wem and Mother Fam made the world together, the great water and the forest, and filled them with plants and animals. Where new places were made, new gods were born to govern the plants and animals there."

Clay considered how this story contradicted what Lord Doto had said before, about the forest always being there, and about nothing ever having been made. All tales were true, his father had said, but how could both of these be true?

Doto spoke slowly, with pauses between his words, as if speaking a story he had not heard in a very long time, and struggled to remember. "Ogya coveted Kwaee's power, for the forest is very large, and all flames in the world were small. Ogya lived in the spark, in the heat on the rocks when the sun shone brightest, in the lightning bolts, and the ash, and deep in the belly of the land. But Kwaee ruled the entire forest, and it covered nearly all the land from great water to great water. There was no place on the ground where he did not have dominion, and the trees of the forest grew so high, you could climb for a day and never see the sunlight. More than anything, Ogya wanted this land and its power for himself.

"One day a herd of miserable beasts wandered through a burned field. They were feeble, and weak, and slow, and died very easily. Ogya lived there in the char of the field and he called out to them. 'Serve me, and me alone,' he said, 'and I will give you power beyond that of any of the other animals. Help me, and I will teach you how to make fire.' The beasts agreed, and so Ogya granted them his power. The only thing they needed to do to make fire, he told them, was to destroy a little bit of the forest. Each branch from each tree could make a flame. And so Ogya taught his new servants, the fire bearers, to take power from Kwaee and give it to Ogya himself.

"The fire bearers obeyed his every order. But they did not just make small fires here and there. They did not take only branches. They lit their branches aflame and turned them on the forest itself. They burned entire trees just to see them turn into ash, and then they burned whole copses. And Ogya was pleased with how they spread his dominion and rewarded them. Mother Fam herself went to warn the fire bearers that they were destroying everything in their world that sustained them. She warned them that they burned their own food, that they filled their air with smoke. But the fire bearers were maddened with their power and would not be stopped. They laughed and beat the Cry of the Dead as they set the forest ablaze. The night sky was lit by their flames until it was as bright as day. Kwaee's body burned, and he could do nothing. With every tree that joined the black clouds, his power lessened, and Ogya's grew. The trees fell, the animals and birds were swallowed by the black clouds, and when the fire finally passed, not even ash remained. Only rock and sand were left behind, hills of it as far as one could travel. These sands became the Firelands, and it was there that Ogya dwelt, his domain many thousands of times larger than once it had been, his power mighty. And in those Firelands, nothing lived but his fire bearers, whom he preserved with his magic. But the fire bearers would not stop there. One quarter of all the forest they had burned with Ogya's magic, and he drove them on, urging them to burn more and more, until the Firelands covered the entire world, and Ogya ruled all but the great water.

"But Mother Fam did not wish to see all the plants in the world die, and so she went to the forest god. 'Kwaee,' she said to him, 'were the trees of your forest not so close together, the fire could not spread so easily. Now one fire bearer can light one tree, and a thousand or more will burn. If your trees were farther apart, then they could burn only one tree at a time, and you and I could grow them back faster than they could burn them.'

"'What can I do?' asked Kwaee. 'I am the forest, and in the forest, trees grow close together. Someday I will have no place left to hide my temple, and Ogya will burn it, and I will die. How then can I stop him?'

"'Sacrifice,' answered Mother Fam.

"And so Kwaee let his trees die, all around the edges of his forest, for a journey of a hundred days in every direction. It pained him greatly, but he gave up some of his power to save his domain. And where the trees fell and died, a new kind of land was made, a land where the trees were farther apart, and there were grasses and bush and sand. Here the fire could not spread so easily, and it was not burned, so Ogya had no power there. The fire bearers tried to burn it for him, but only one tree at a time burned, or grasses, and the fire god's great advance was stalled. A new god was born, Sarmu, the savanna god, and he vowed to protect his own lands, and so the forest, from Ogya's unending hunger."

Doto fixed Clay with a hard gaze. "But even though Ogya was slowed, he was not stopped. Every year a little more of the world burns, and Ogya grows in power. Every year the Firelands creep south. One day the savanna will be gone, and Ogya will be at the forest once again, and he will use your people to burn it into ash until there is nothing left of the world. And that is why I call you murderers and traitors. You have left a scar across the world with your torches, and you will not rest until it has covered all of it. Then Ogya will have no more use for you. He will take his power away from you, and let you die. And there will be no more Kwaee or Sarmu, no more Mother Fam. There will be no more animals, no more trees. There will be only dead sand and rock, a silent world, and Ogya, burning in endless hatred because there is nothing left for him to devour."

Clay stared into the fire, watching it suckle greedily at the branches, consuming them. He thought of Ogya peering out through the flames at them, of the little pit of char he would leave behind. "Then this is why plants grow faster out of ash. It is Kwaee recovering his lost power from Ogya?"

Doto nodded. "That is how it is."

"I see." Clay chewed a piece of meat, thinking. He had never heard anything like this story before. In none of his people's stories had Ogya ever been so monstrous. In some he was mischievous, a trickster, but never had he heard of any god waging war on the others. It was unthinkable, and even more senseless to imagine that people would try to burn down the whole forest and turn the world to Firelands.

"Lord Doto, I don't know who these fire bearers were from long ago, but they could not have been my people."

"You built a fire," Doto pointed out, gesturing toward as if to bat it out. "That is proof enough that it was you. None of the animals can make fire except the fire bearers."

"We use fire, true, but we love both the forest and the savanna. We depend upon them for everything: for our food, our clothing, for shade."

"We are both in agreement then that you are foolish for serving Ogya," Doto said.

"But you said Ogya's power sustained the fire bearers. That they were able to live in the Firelands where no other animals could. But none of us could live in the Firelands. We would die in only a few days."

The leopard god stared at Clay, and then sidled backward into the darkness a ways, farther from the fire. "Renounce him then," he said quietly.

"What?"

"Renounce Ogya. Vow never again to serve him. Do not pray to him, do not dance for him. Never make another fire."

Clay almost could not understand Doto's words. Could the god be serious? This was blasphemy. Surely it had to be a test, to see if he would be so arrogant as to renounce a god. "I cannot do that. I would die. I depend on fire for light to find my way in the dark and to keep away the animals at night. I need it to cook my meat."

"You see?" said Doto, with a triumphant tone to his voice. "The power of Ogya sustains you."

〰️

Clay had held out a faint hope that his brother or other hunters from the village might catch up to him again, though what he would do if they found him, he wasn't sure. The next day, however, eradicated that hope. Doto woke him at the crack of dawn with a brusque push and a "get up." The fire had burned down into an accusing spot of ash. He kicked dirt on top of it to ensure that no remaining cinders could spark a blaze, though most of the forest was still too damp for that. Doto watched him with a bemused expression. Then they left, heading south at a steady pace, and soon they were moving through terrain that would have been impassible without the escort of a god. The trees were of many sizes: some big around as baobabs, some thin and tall; but they all reached for the same sunlight, growing clustered so closely together that Clay would have had to climb all the way up into their branches to squeeze past them. Thick brambles with wicked-looking thorns clustered in huge patches. Between all of these hung curtains of heavy vines that swayed with the movements of the treetops. Clay could hear the screech of monkeys leaping about far above. In spots, the trees broke, allowing sunlight to beam down, and there, tall, broad-leafed plants crowded each other, sparring for the light. Their leaves were coarse and roughly edged. Clay could just as soon have pushed through a rock wall as through those thickets. If he had had the sharpest knife to cut the plants away, it would still have taken him days to travel what they did in a few hours.

Any remaining doubt that Doto was a god of the forest vanished: he stepped toward the great trees as though they were not even there, and with a terrific creak and the shaking of branches, they bent aside to permit his advance. The movement of these giants of the forest was both awing and innately frightening. They should not move, and yet they did, their massive limbs bowing, their roots crawling like pinned serpents. Doto did not even seem to notice their movement; he stepped between them and made noises of exasperation when Clay hesitated.

They moved on in this way, the forest prostrating itself before Doto. Vines drew aside, brambles slithered away, the great thickets parted like opening tents. Through all of these they moved, and behind them, the forest closed again, leaving no trace of their passage. Clay moved in silence and wonder, distracted by both the fantastic fluidity of the forest around him and thoughts of the story last night. Everything that he knew of the gods and the world around him had been questioned. His people stood accused of allying themselves with an ancient evil, and he could not even deny that they offered worship to this god. He had sat next to a fire he built with his own hands, a fire that had stolen power from Kwaee and given it to Ogya, who was not a benevolent trickster, but a malevolent, world-consuming monster. His thoughts were in disarray; like a handful of beads too small to hold, they kept slipping through his grasp and spilling everywhere, and when he tried to collect them, he only lost others. When he thought of where they were going and of what might happen to his people, his gut knotted, and the pig meat that had tasted so delicious last night felt sour in his stomach.

Distracting him from all of this was his foot. The wooden paw that had fit so comfortably at first now ached with each step. His leg was reddened and swollen around the top of the cuff, and it throbbed. Somewhere inside the paw, it itched badly, but the pain almost drowned it out. He tried to adjust his gait to ease the pressure on his leg, but this caused him to limp badly, and by midday, he was moving at half the pace. If Doto was annoyed at the slower travel, he said nothing about it. By the early afternoon, however, the pain had grown so bad that Clay finally collapsed on the ground, clutching at his leg. He lay against a tangle of weeds that had drawn aside for them, gasping, trying to keep little tears of pain from the corners of his eyes.

Doto came over, looking down, and Clay waited for rebuke. Instead, the leopard god crouched, his whiskers twitching as he sniffed. "You have a new wound."

"Yes." Clay showed him his leg, the swollen ring of flesh against the cuff leaking blood and clear fluid against the wood.

"I did not intend this to happen. We should have put some soft leaves or grass in there to stop the wood from biting it. Or maybe a little bit of soft pelt to pad it." He set his golden-furred fingers against the wooden paw and it separated in two, right down the middle, but the wooden pieces did not drop away. Doto pulled at them, tugging them away from the foot, and Clay felt his skin stick to them. The leg beneath was crusted with dried blood that had run down and congealed inside. Immediately it itched more strongly, and Clay reached down and scratched at it with both hands, flaking away dried blood. The air felt good against his exposed skin.

"Are you sure you cannot heal it?" Clay asked.

Doto narrowed his eyes. "I could do it. But I told you, the magic is forbidden."

"Yes, you said that before. And when I asked who forbade you, you grew angry. I didn't understand why." Clay prodded gingerly at the swollen flesh with one finger. It hurt, but not too much to touch.

"You ask many questions," Doto said. "I never know for what reason. You should not care why I will not heal you; only *that* I will not, and yet you want to know why anyway. No animal or bird asks questions like this."

"You speak to the animals and birds?" Clay asked in astonishment, and immediately regretted the question. Of course a god of the forest would speak to animals and birds. He was part of the forest himself, half animal in appearance. It was easy to forget sometimes; Lord Doto walked like a human and spoke like one. He gestured and changed his expression like a human. Despite the coat of fur, the feline head and tail, the blunt paws, it was sometimes difficult not to think of him as just a person like Clay's people. In his way, he was even handsome and striking, though Clay supposed that it made no sense for a god to lack beauty.

"Sometimes," Doto said, apparently not regarding the question as strange. "But they don't have much to say. Parrots are dull. Elephants never shut up. And baboons are simply foul."

"Can you teach me to speak to them?" Clay asked, surprising himself. Excitement tickled at his fingers at the thought of it, moving through the forest, conversing with the creatures as no person had ever been able to do before.

Doto stared at him. "Why should I do that? Why would you want to?"

"Why would I not want to? Maybe you know everything that they would say to you, but I don't. I guess you've lived in this place for hundreds of lifetimes, but to me it's amazing." He reached his fingers toward the tree-tops. "Look at this forest! Until we moved here, I spent my whole life out on the savanna. It's beautiful there, but very flat, and very plain. You can travel great distances and never see any changes. If you are as tall as I am, you are a giant on the savanna. But here in this forest, the trees reach higher than—I don't know, higher than maybe fifty of me. You can walk at the height of the sun and not see daylight. You can hear things moving through the brush all around you, catch glimpses of them dancing across the branches above. There are bright flowers and sweet smells and strange fruit. At first I thought this place was sinister and kind of scary, but now I don't understand why none of my people live in the forest."

"Kwaee will not allow it," Doto said. He stood and began to pace through the grass, searching the ground for something. "Because you are fire bearers. He makes the forest dangerous for your people. You are safe because you have traveled with me, but were you alone, then snakes would have bitten you, or a leopard hunted you down. You might have been pricked by poison thorns, drowned in mud, or torn apart by angry baboons. None of your people may live inside the forest for very long."

He crouched, plucking something from the earth, and came back to Clay's side with a pair of large, flat mushrooms, round and dark brown on top. He broke the stalks away. "Gods do not use their powers to heal," he said. His fingers gripped at the skin of Clay's leg, moving deftly as they pressed and wrapped the mushroom caps to the wound encircling the calf. Their texture was firm and stretchy, like aloe leaves, and though their pressure made his flesh throb, their coolness soothed it. Doto bound the caps in place with a few long, flat leaves and strips of grass stalk. "To take away a wound from another is not part of the laws of life, and gods exist to uphold the laws of life. They define us. Come. I must make a new foot for you. The old one is dead now and will not shape itself for me again."

He stood, and did not offer Clay a hand of assistance, so Clay hopped on his good leg, following him to a nearby tree. There, like before, the god set his fingers to the wood. He closed his eyes in apparent concentration, and the wood of the tree flowed up around Clay's foot, moving as mud after the rain, encasing it and layering itself around the mushroom pad Doto had made for him. Then the wood stilled, the bark of the tree sealing over once again.

"Try now," Doto suggested, and Clay set the wood foot against the ground and eased his weight onto it. The pressure made his wound ache, but there was no more hard bite of wood grinding into it; the pad was far more comfortable.

He turned a grateful smile up to the god. "It's good. It doesn't hurt so much anymore. Thank you."

"You can walk on it?" Doto asked, ignoring the appreciation. "You can move more quickly again?"

"I think so."

Doto nodded, and without another word, he set off again, making a brisker pace. Clay hurried after him. The pad eased the pain in his leg; the wooden foot no longer ground into his wound with each step, but deep in the muscle, he could feel his injury throbbing, burning. He wished Cloud were here. She would make a mash of herbs to rub into it and help it to heal. But Cloud was far away, in the village with all his people, and she would have heard the reports of those who had followed his tracks into the forest. No doubt she thought him dead. Perhaps they would mourn him around the fire. He wondered if Ogya would watch them and laugh.

〰

That night they stopped in a small grove of ebony trees whose roots starved the ground and kept it clear of other brush. Clay could see the round, flat tracks of forest elephants meandering through the open spaces between the trees. Before going out to hunt, Doto permitted him to make another small fire. There had been no rains that afternoon, and so the task of gathering wood was considerably easier than the previous day. Clay even found a cluster of thick, soft grass to harvest and lay down as a pallet.

By the time Doto returned, Clay had a sizable fire blazing. Doto kept a careful distance from the flames at first, skulking outside the grove, before finally he seemed to make up his mind, and approached, tossing a pair of fat, white-speckled guineafowl, their necks broken and lolling, over to Clay.

He had also brought a few handfuls of black berries, carried in a bit of hollowed out log, which he set on the ground several paces from the fire.

"Thank you," Clay said, and began stripping the feathers from one of the guineafowl.

Doto said nothing in return. He stood and gazed out into the forest, his tail swaying in rhythm with the movement of the branches above as the breeze tugged at them.

"Would you like some of the cooked meat tonight?"

"I did not want it last night," Doto said. "There is no reason why I should want it tonight."

"You don't ever change your mind?"

The god looked over one spotted shoulder at Clay. "No."

Clay hesitated to ask the question, knowing it bordered blasphemy. "What if you're wrong about something?"

"Gods are not wrong," Doto answered stiffly.

"Not even Ogya?"

The great cat narrowed his eyes. Clay had offended him, he supposed. "Ogya is mad," Doto said. "Madness is neither right nor wrong."

"Then surely it cannot be wrong to offer prayer to a mad god," Clay said.

"Neither right nor wrong. But maybe very stupid."

Clay sat in silence, not wishing to annoy the god further. He stripped the fowl of their feathers, and solicited Doto's help once again in gutting them. He spitted the birds and ate the berries while the meat turned golden over the fire. The berries were tart and sweet, and not entirely ripe, Clay thought, but he made no mention of this.

He was surprised when Doto broke the silence. "You say your people serve all the gods."

"Yes, Lord Doto," Clay answered. "The gods rule everything in our lives, from the passing of the sun to the creeping of the smallest insects. Any of these things may cause a change in our lives, so it is sensible for us to venerate the spirits in all things."

"But you did not serve me, because you did not know my name."

"No, indeed, Lord Doto, we had no inkling that there was more than one god of the forest at all."

"Well, there are!" the god snapped, with a peevish tone to his voice. He stood tall, rolling his shoulders back, chest out. "Two gods of the forest. Kwaee rules, yes, but he sequesters himself in his temple, and seldom ventures outside of it. Throughout all of the forest, I, Doto, guide the land and uphold the natural law. Your people should serve me as well."

Clay blinked up at him, puzzled. Why this sudden announcement? Was Doto about to let him return to his home? "Of course we will, Lord Doto, just as soon as I can tell my people of you."

"And you will beat the Cry of the Dead in my name? You will sing of me, and dance to me? You will serve food in my honor, and whisper for permission from me before you enter the forest?"

"Of course, Lord Doto. All these things."

Doto's pink tongue licked the sides of his jaws as if in hunger. "You will do it now."

"Now?" Clay asked hesitantly. He had not seen this expression on the god's face before. His ears were back, his gaze intent, a look of unguarded eagerness in his eyes.

"None outside the forest know my name," Doto said. "And yes, the animals of the forest serve me in their way, but I want to feel the worship of a fire bearer. I want to know this thing that your people do for all the gods but me."

Unsure, Clay got to his feet. "My Lord Doto, I have no drum, and I cannot dance much of a dance with only one foot."

Doto rubbed at his chin. "You need the drum for this…joy. For gratefulness?"

"Yes, in a way."

"Or you could have the wind. You could have other things that make the joy. Those would make you dance."

"Well, yes."

"I cannot make wind. I am not god of the sky and air. But I can make something like it. And then you will be grateful to me, and you will dance."

Clay opened his mouth to explain that it didn't work like that, but the god had already closed his eyes. He put his clawed fingers to the ground, ears twitching, tail swaying gently.

Nothing happened at first, but then the leaves at the tops of the ebony trees twitched—first one here, then another there, and then all of them, as though snared butterflies attempting to escape. The twigs of the trees bent backward, then the branches. The sound of their movement was a hiss in the canopy. The effect spread outward to the surrounding plants: lianas bent in an imaginary wind, branches swayed, trunks leaned as though pulled by a mighty gale, though all around the air was still and warm.

It was no wind. It was no sunrise and a healed foot and a dance across the grasslands. But Clay's heart was filled with wonder, his eyes wet. A god was reaching out to him, moving the forest to earn his worship. Not his people, not the priests and elders, but him. For the first time in his life, he felt as though a prayer had been answered.

"Now," said Doto, as the illusion of wind settled, "you feel grateful. Now you will dance for me."

How could he refuse? "There are no songs written to you, Lord Doto. But I will try."

The great cat nodded, stepping back. "Near the fire. Let Ogya see that you serve me."

Clay closed his eyes. A god had asked for his worship, and he had no songs. He took a deep breath, trying to find them inside himself. He smelled the rich scent of the ebony trees, the roasting of guineafowl, the thick smoke from the fire. The hairs lifted across his arms and thighs. He would be the first man ever to pray to this god. His song would be the first composed to Doto, and the god himself would stand before him to witness it. He thought of the prayers of his people, sung out to Kwaee and Sarmu. He stilled his mind, listened for the drumbeat of his heart to guide the rhythm of his words, and found it, driving his blood through his body. He sang.

The forest has come to greet the savanna
and spill into it the blessings of Doto the mighty.
You are the god who dares to stand before the flame.
You are the god who can bend the forest
with the movements of your fingers
and before you the oldest of trees must bow.

He shifted from foot to foot, taking little steps, feeling the rhythm of the dance he could not hear, letting it guide him for the first time since the eland had crushed his toes.

If you do not will it, we will never see you.
You stride through darkness and daylight without tiring.
In your land Father Wem smiles and never holds back the rain.

The dance had come to him now, and he obeyed it, ignoring the pain in his foot and leg. The air hummed around him like a storm. There was no circle of people to chant responses to his lines, but the forest echoed his words back to him all the same.

Mighty Doto, you speak to the people
as we speak to each other.
You bring us the wisdom of the gods.
You bless the people with your greatness.

He opened his eyes, the dance still pulsing in his fingers. Doto was staring, his jaws slack, the lightning that hung in the air standing his fur on end. His eyes flashed firelight back at Clay. Clay panted for breath, feeling the throb in his foot. He looked down, and then he saw: around Doto's toes a carpet of grass had grown, thick and lush, spreading out from him in tendrils. Vines sprouted from it, twisting upward, red and white flowers splashing into the green. As Clay watched, the patch of green spread further, reaching toward him.

"Again," Doto breathed. His voice was heavy with wonder. "Sing it again."

And so Clay sang again, finding with ease the words he had sung before, calling them out more confidently now. His voice rang through the darkened halls of the forest. And as he sang, Doto rose on his feet, stretching up until his toes barely touched the ground, his arms spread wide, palms up. His eyes were closed, his expression rapt. Clay danced, beyond pain now, moving around the fire, springing from foot to foot, raising his arms as he spun and sang. The green crawled out, away from Doto, filling with life. Saplings sprung up in the twining arms of the spreading patch, shooting up several feet in an instant. The magic spread to a nearby ebony tree, and thick lianas coiled around it, bright orange flowers bursting from their stems as they climbed. Clay spun around the fire and landed in a patch of soft green grass, his toes sinking into it. He did not take another step. Grasping vines and spiraling stems crawled about his foot and climbed his leg, the grip of growing plants pricking at his flesh. Yellow flowers bloomed about his shins, and one larger vine coiled around his waist. He gasped in surprise and sudden fear.

Doto opened his eyes and dropped into a crouch. He turned around, staring at the newly formed and verdant field of grasses and flowers. Then he strode toward Clay, ignoring the campfire still burning nearby, and gripped his shoulders, holding him in place. The god's paws were powerful, harder than stone. "This praise. This song." He paused, brow furrowing.

The air smelled like the savanna during the rainy season, bright and raw and fragile green and yellow. Clay felt the pain in his leg once more, and shifted his weight to the other, leaves tickling at his thighs when he moved. He stumbled with the weight of Doto's paws on his shoulders, and caught himself, his hands about the leopard god's waist, fingers sinking into thick fur, his chest pressing to Doto's.

"The fire bearers will sing this song to me every night?" Doto seemed unbothered by the contact, gazing down at Clay, his mouth inches away. That scent of rain was in his breath.

"My people will sing to you, yes, when they know your name." Clay tried not to think that he was being held by a god, tried not to feel the sudden surge of elation, tried not to bury his face against Doto's strong chest and breathe deep. His grip about the god's waist tightened. "But I will sing it to you, Lord Doto. Every night."

A grin lit up Doto's face, and the expression startled Clay, not because it was filled with fangs and whiskers; despite the god having the features of a great cat, his expressions were strangely, unmistakably human. What was startling was the expression itself: Doto had frowned, stared, snarled, and even pouted, but not once before had Clay seen him even hint at a smile. "For I am Doto the mighty," he cried to the treetops, "who dares to stand before the flame!"

Clay smiled back at him hopefully. "Doto the mighty," he agreed. "God of the forest."

"God of the fire bearers," Doto said in a determined tone. Then, more gently, "God of Clay."

It was the first time Doto had said his name, and it resounded through his body as though he were the skin of a drum, making his bones ache with his own name, vibrating his teeth, and tugging at something deeper, as though lifting him out of his own body. "God of Clay," he whispered back. He lifted his gaze to meet Doto's and then stared.

Sprouting from the god's brow, just above his eyes, was a small, bright blue feather.

The Fall of Laughing Dog

Madness had claimed Laughing Dog. Something in the blood of the eland he had drunk had swallowed his mind. Then he had dreamed a man walked out of the darkness and changed into a demon. Or perhaps there had been a man in truth, and madness had made him into a demon in Laughing Dog's eyes. Perhaps he had struck an innocent man and knocked him into the fire, burning him alive. Perhaps he was a murderer now. Certainly there had been no demon, no magic jewel. The voice that spoke to him from the air was not real; it was a delusion, a figment of his madness, as false as the shimmer of water on the horizon. It called his name, over and over, claiming to be the god of fire, and he struggled to ignore it.

He walked across the sahil, heading south, trying to find his way back to his people. The madness made his limbs seem filled with strength. He felt no hunger nor thirst, and for that, at least, he was grateful to it. He wondered if he were truly wandering through the desert at all. Maybe he was lying by the ashes of a spent fire, baking in the sun, and all these travels were but the feverish glimmer of a fading consciousness. But maybe he really was traveling across the dry sahil. It was possible that, even mad, he might find water and recover. He might make it back to the village, where Cloud could give him something to make him well again. He would repent it all. He would recant. He would accept the will of the gods, and bless the whole world and everything in it, if only the voice that came from everywhere would go away.

"You will not ignore me forever, little man," the voice said.

Laughing Dog gave no reply. He scanned the horizon for trees. He was seeing more of them now than he had a few days ago, which meant he was headed in the right direction. How he had survived the journey south with no food or water, he did not know. It should have been impossible. Perhaps he had found sustenance and quenched his thirst from the roots of plants—or more likely from Sedjet's water skins—and the madness had erased the memory from his mind.

"You are a stubborn one, I know," said the voice. Its tone was calm, unhurried, but always with the snaps and pops of a flame consuming its tinder. "I have watched you from a thousand fires. I saw you on the night you left your camp. Delightful. So strong, so bold. So full of passion and defiance. You will not be ruled by anyone, will you? You will not let anyone hold back your strength. Not even the gods. We created you to be slaves. Did you know that? Oh, yes. Serve us, praise us, dance for us. Ask our permission for everything. The gods are very, very vain, little man. Praise is our milk. Worship, the sweetest meal we consume. And what delightful cooks your people are. We grow fat on them."

A wind was coming off the desert, blowing to his back. It was hot and dry, and stung his flesh with the tiny bits of sand carried upon it. It rustled past his ears, but it did not drown out the sound of the madness. Of course not. The sound was in his head. He guarded his eyes with his hand, and kept on.

"But not you, Laughing Dog. You refused to feed us your delicious devotion. You spurned us. We could not accept it. So we whispered, all of us, in the ears of your people while they slept. Kwaee, on a breath out of the jungle. Sarmu, stealing in from the savanna. Fam, in the rustle of leaves, and Wem, singing down in the moonlight. You had to be punished for not serving us, for not giving us your slave's wages. We turned your father against you. We made him despise you. We put the words of banishment in his mouth."

"You did no such thing!" Laughing Dog snapped. He could not help himself. He knew it was insane to argue with a voice from his own mind, but the claim was so pernicious, it demanded a response. Perhaps if he could point to the lies of the madness, he could quell it. "My father and my people needed no encouragement from the gods to turn on me. The foolishness of their own faith was enough. I will not be deceived into blaming the gods for their error, not even by madness."

"No?"

"The responsibility for my father's actions rests on his shoulders, just as credit for his accomplishments belongs to him. If the gods truly exist, they are distant and unseeing. I will not curse them for my own misfortune and the misdeeds of others."

"My, my, my." The voice chuckled. "Such a strong will you have, Laughing Dog. You think yourself bold. Independent. But I will break you."

Laughing Dog set his teeth. "You will not."

"Of course you intend to resist me. It is who you are, little whelp. But stronger men than you have struggled against me, and I consumed them. I kept them alive while their bones burned. Their screams filled with smoke, and I savored them. Now they are part of me, their strength mine. What are you, little man, compared to the might of a god?"

"If you were truly a god, and not a voice in my head, why would you say these things to me? Why would you not simply burn me alive? No, you have no power. You are just the chattering in my dying mind."

"Do you think so?" The voice sounded amused. "Let us see what you think when I take my strength away from you."

In an instant, the fullness in Laughing Dog's limbs was sucked away. His arms and legs wilted into narrow bones wrapped in grass-thin skin. He collapsed, his face hitting the hard, hot ground of the savanna. Hunger gnawed at his gut like a lion consuming him, red and white bolts of pain flashing before his eyes. His tongue and mouth dried into things of bone and wood, his eyelids growing gummy and crusted. He struggled to breathe, to form coherent thought.

"Without me," said the voice, "you will die here. Scorpions will chew on your flesh while you can still feel. Vultures will pick out your eyes."

Laughing Dog rasped his reply, and every breath burned of fire. "If I die here, your gem will be lost. No one will ever find it here in the sahil. A sandstorm will bury it. It will be your last torment."

There was silence for a heartbeat and four, and then suddenly his pain vanished, his hunger and thirst so distant as to have been imagined, his mouth moist, his limbs full of strength once more. "Clever boy," said the voice. "It would be inconvenient for me to have my little fetish lost in the sands. A fragment of my power, buried forever. No god cares to lose power. But surely now you see that I am real, that I am not just a voice in your head."

The sudden, crippling pain and the swift approach of death had shaken Laughing Dog, but he was determined not to let the madness know it. He kept his voice steady, getting to his feet and continuing his forward stride. "That proves nothing. This strength, this absence of hunger or thirst, is only another side effect of my madness. That the madness should recede for a moment to show me the true world? This isn't proof that a god dwells inside me. It's proof that I'm mad."

"If you are mad," the voice said, "then why do you walk with such purpose? Where is there to go, if you lie dying in the desert? Why fight with me at all?"

Just in case, Laughing Dog thought fervently. Just in case there is a chance I might survive. I must not give in.

"Such pleasures I could give you, little man, if you would allow me. How could those pleasures harm a man who is dying?"

"They're lies," Laughing Dog answered with conviction. "I would rather die with my eyes open than live with them closed."

"Ahhhh." The voice crackled like sizzling fat. "Those are the words of the humans I remember. Once, your species was strong, hungry, ambitious. You would not remember. A thousand thousand men lived between that time and now. But once, humans were strong enough to challenge the gods. They strode this world like giants. They ruled all the beasts, and named them. They hunted the lion and the elephant without fear, and if the rains did not come, they would tear open the earth to bring the great water to them. Such creatures they were, little man. They laughed in the faces of the gods, and so we stole their power. We cut them down to tiny size, made them slaves, made them serve us."

Laughing Dog was silent. He had never heard this story before. But of course, it was not a real story. Just another invention of his insanity.

"The things we did to them. The boils we put on their skin, the flies we sent to bite them, the insects to eat their crops, the disease to make them sleep themselves into death. It was so very funny." The voice's laugh was the roar of flames torn by the wind. "And now look at you, crawling across the surface of the world like ants, begging and pleading the gods for every little mercy, every blessing we might grant you. You cannot eat a meal without craving its permission, cannot scar a tree without begging forgiveness. Even the beasts are not so subservient. They take what they need because they need it. But not humans, no, you are less than all of these. You are pathetic, groveling, miserable creatures."

"Not I!" Laughing Dog shouted to the empty savanna.

"No," the voice returned. "Not you, Laughing Dog. You dared to think yourself powerful. You dared to think you were yet capable of challenging the gods. And now you are exiled, lost and dying."

The voice laughed again, a giggle of cruel glee. Laughing Dog turned his thoughts away from it. He set his eyes to the horizon and pressed toward it, the little group of trees so far away. He might reach them by nightfall. He set his mind on it, shutting out the voice. Think only of the trees. Think of the water you will find there, sweet water that can soothe your fevered thoughts, restore your sanity.

"You're thinking of water, are you?" said the voice calmly, a low and casual crackle. "Oh yes, Laughing Dog, I know your mind. I can see into it when I choose to. You have no surprises from me. I know all that you are. I can tell you now that I do not love water. You will displease me if you drink it. Perhaps I will take my gift away from you again, leave you wasting, gnawed at by hunger and thirst."

"Of course you don't want me to drink," Laughing Dog scoffed aloud. "Because you are madness borne of drought, and you seek to preserve yourself. When I finally take water, you will become just a flickering memory, a fever dream lost in the morning."

"I do not wish you to drink," the voice observed sternly, "because I am the god of fire, and I do not care to be quenched."

"A god who can be repelled with a mouthful of water isn't much of a god at all, is he?" Laughing Dog asked.

The voice remained silent, though whether because it was sulking at this question, or for some other reason, Laughing Dog had no idea. Then he scowled. Already he was deceiving himself into thinking the voice an actual person, with motivations and emotions, rather than the delusion he knew it to be. He continued on, and the voice did not speak again.

As he neared the vegetation-filled area, he could see more and more trees, and, he noted with a rising heart, what appeared to be water, not the deceptive, sky-kissing mirror of a mirage, but the darker glass that betrayed a true oasis. Could this be the Deraji-Wem waterhole? That had been a four-day journey southeast of their village when he was a boy, but then the land had been furred with grasses and occasional trees, not bone-dry and parched as it was now. Drawing closer, he could see that it was, in fact, Deraji. He recognized it by the shapes and heights of the trees, the way the oasis was nestled in a little dale in the sands, a bowl intruded upon by the looming, round edges of the dry sahil. Deraji-Wem was, to his people, a mystery of the gods, for it was an oasis visited neither by streams nor by frequent rains, and yet its waters had never been known to run low. Its name meant "Kiss of Wem," but Laughing Dog suspected the waters had a more mundane source. Perhaps they bubbled up from beneath the ground. He had heard a traveler tell of a place where this had happened, trickles of clear and fresh water gushing from a hole in a rock. The traveler had believed that all the world was a great water, and their land merely a mote that floated atop its waves. That notion might be ridiculous—after all, did not any rock tossed into the water sink immediately to the bottom?—but that there might be secret channels beneath the earth, Laughing Dog thought possible. The rains fell, and they disappeared. They must go somewhere.

The heat-warped images of trees and plants resolved themselves into clarity as he approached. In the middle of the sand and the arid-white sahil, the brilliant, spiking green of vegetation glowed with life and abundance. White and yellow birds perched high in the palms, calling in brash tones to each other, but Laughing Dog could see no other wildlife. Normally, around a waterhole, especially in a dry area, one would find uncountable animals surrounding it: antelope, giraffe, oryx, and buffalo. Lions might scout out a corner to prey on the gathering thirsty and keep the wild dogs at bay. Mongooses would climb trees in attempts to surprise unsuspecting birds. Elephants would wallow in the hole, turning the water brown, fouling it with their filth as they rolled in it. Hares would steal about in the farther grasses, trying to find safe routes to the water while avoiding the predators. Underfoot, sometimes dangerously close to being trodden upon, gerbils and rats would scurry about in an ecstasy of feasting.

Deraji had once been such a waterhole, and though people had sometimes tried to keep the wildlife at bay so that the water might remain safe and usable, it had been a futile effort. Now, though, if there were any wildlife at all, Laughing Dog could not see it. No longer surrounded by true savanna, Deraji could not be called waterhole. No, it was an oasis, an emerald drop of life glittering in the middle of the sahil, somewhere between Firelands and savanna, where most animals did not gladly venture. "What has happened to the savanna?" Laughing Dog wondered out loud.

"I ate it," announced the voice from everywhere with a tone of remembered satisfaction. "I gobbled it up."

It had been silent for so long now, Laughing Dog had almost forgotten about it. "You seem to have missed a spot," he pointed out irritably.

"Yes. A little too damp for my liking." It made a resentful popping sound.

Laughing Dog began the descent into the little valley that cradled the oasis. He had to squint his eyes against the reflection of the sun blazing up at him from the waters below. Water. He could scarcely believe it. He almost wished, now, that he could feel the terrible thirst from before. The sight of water after a trip across the savanna ought to inspire immense joy and relief. He should long to dash down the hill and splash into it, to feel its cool touch flood his throat and relax his belly. Now he felt only a sense of anticipation, a hope that it might dispel his madness and drown the impossible voice in a tide of returned sanity.

He strode toward the water. As he approached, he could now see that he had been mistaken when he thought Deraji empty of all life but plants and birds. On the opposite shore of the oasis sat a small camp spread out in the bushes. There were two people, and they had an animal with them, like a zebra, but shorter and stouter. He could not make out whether they were man or woman, and they did not see him when he lifted his arm to them. He would go to them, once he had drunk. They might have food to offer. He had not thought himself hungry, but his belly panged at the notion. Perhaps even the sight of water was beginning to drive his madness from him.

"I told you," the voice said as he drew closer to the water, "that I do not wish you to drink."

Was that a note of anxiety in the voice? Laughing Dog did not reply to it. It was nothing. It was not a fire god. It was not a voice. It was just a madness, a stain across his perceptions, one he intended to wash away. He could smell the water from here, clean and delicious, unsullied by the droppings of animals. It glittered with sunlight. He was so near he could feel its coolness in the air, the slight damp picked up by the wind against his skin, on his tongue.

The voice became a roar. It was a conflagration whipped up by wind and fed by a million grasses. It was the bellow of the blaze that had come roiling across the savanna to eat Laughing Dog's childhood home so long ago. In it, he could hear the gurgling screams of Sedjet being consumed by fire. There were others, too, other voices, howling in insensate torment. "This is your final warning, Laughing Dog. I have lent you my strength so far. You know I can take it away."

The last, desperate pleas of insanity attempting to preserve itself, he told himself. The witless rage of a fractured mind. He would cool it soon. The oasis was but one hundred paces away. He fixed his gaze on it, pushing toward it, past coarse-edged, fanning leaves that scratched at his thighs, past fragrant stalks of thyme, past acacia and date palms.

"Very well, then," the voice roared.

As before, hunger and terrible thirst raked at his belly and throat. His limbs shook with weakness and he collapsed to the hot ground. The sun burned into the back of his head. He lay gasping in shock and astonishment. The madness wanted to preserve itself badly. It wanted to kill him rather than let itself be flushed away. He set his teeth. He would not let that happen. He tried to pull himself along the ground toward the water. He barely moved an inch.

"Surrender to me," the voice crackled in his mind with a gleeful edge. "Swear to take no drink. Swear to serve me, and I will grant you my strength to use however you like, so long as you do not oppose my will."

"I will not swear," Laughing Dog rasped. His voice might have been the wind rattling grains of sand against a tent. He set his fingers against the hard earth, grasping for a handhold. He found an acacia root and tugged himself forward.

"As it pleases you." The voice had an uninterested tone, but behind it, Laughing Dog could hear barely restrained fury. And, he thought, a touch of panic. Heat and aridity burned at his eyes. His lips cracked and blistered. "I have no fear letting you die here. Out there in the desert, my fetish would be lost in the wide paths, buried beneath the sand, never to be found again. Here I think I may be picked up later tonight, perhaps by those people across the water. One of them will serve me, and I will grant them the might of a god as reward. By the time they reach you, you will be shriveled old bones, dragged off by the wild dogs."

"Not if I reach the water." He pushed himself forward again. The hot, cracked ground burned his arms and belly. The roots of thyme and blades of lovegrass scratched at his dragging flesh.

"You will not reach it. It is too far. You have no strength left. But I am not a merciless god. Yield to me, and I may yet take pity on you. I may even allow you a small drink, though I do not love it."

Laughing Dog set his teeth. They felt loose in his jaw. "Never." The word was barely a croak. He pushed himself inexorably toward the water. The sun beat down cruelly against his skin. He felt as though his brain were boiling in his skull. He had no saliva left, his mouth dry and rough as wood. His eyes stung, their sight nothing but a bright, blurred haze whose intensity sent a stab of pain up into his forehead. He could smell the water from here. He did not need to see it, so he closed his eyes, but this was scarcely better. It felt as though tiny, sharp granules of sand clung to the insides of his eyelids.

"Die then," said the voice acidly, the hiss of water flung across embers. "Fry in the sun like a caterpillar."

Laughing Dog had no need to listen to it. It was only fleeting a thought in his mind, a flailing and desperate insanity. He would have his drink. He pulled himself forward. His limbs felt made of stone. They seemed almost impossible to move. But to cease the attempt would be death.

"You are not even headed toward water. Do you know that?" the voice returned to him with a pleasant, amused tone. "You think you're at an oasis, but it's all a trick of your mind. A trick of me. I'm not Ogya at all. Just a nattering voice you've conjured out of loneliness and thirst. You're still lying by your bonfire, out in the sahil. That's what you're crawling toward. The embers of your own fire. When you reach it, it'll catch that dry skin and hair of yours. You'll smell like a pig when you cook, though there's not much fat on you. That's what I've been trying to save you from. Crawling into your own fire."

Laughing Dog hesitated. The voice had admitted it was madness. He considered the possibility that this might actually be the truth, and then decided that he didn't care. Either he would drink of water or fire. Either way, the madness would be purged. Either way, he would cease to live in delusion. He pushed himself forward along the ground. He could feel the coolness radiating away from the water now. The ground was softer with it. He opened his eyes again and saw the blaze of the sun reflected back at him from the surface of the oasis. It was still so far away. It would be easier to die here. Easy just to set his head down and let the sun cook away the last of his senses. Or better yet, to submit to delusion, to surrender his will to the voice of madness in his head, to take its strength back into his limbs and run the remaining few steps to the water, or imagine he did, imagine he was sinking beneath the cool, soothing surface of the pool. Anything would be easier than to lift his arm again, to claw at the ground with breaking finger-nails, to move another inch. He reached forward, and his fingers dug into softer earth, damp and warm. The sun performed a warping, twisting dance before his eyes. He was almost there. A few arm lengths away.

Abruptly, his strength returned to him once more, the crippling thirst and hunger gone. His hazy sight clarified. The sun bobbed across gentle ripples in the water before him. The earth was stained dark brown with water that had soaked into it. The voice from everywhere was bold and jubilant. "Well done, Laughing Dog. You have bested me."

He heaved himself up onto his knees distrustfully. His arms felt strong and capable once more, no traces of the scratches and burns on his dark brown skin. "Have I?"

"Yes," said the voice, resonant with congratulation. "You resisted every temptation and every threat. You drove yourself past your own pain and weakness, and for that, you shall be rewarded with my power."

Laughing Dog did not quite believe the voice. "And I do not have to surrender to you, as you threatened before? I am not required to serve you?"

"Only if it pleases you," the voice said in a magnanimous tone. "You shall have the power of the fire god at your command."

For a moment, elation had flooded his thoughts, pride at having bested this god, but these latter words expelled it. This was no fire god, he reminded himself. This was madness, and that he was forgetting it was a frightening sign. He turned toward the water.

"No!" the voice shouted. It seemed to shake the trees, send heat waves rippling through the air. "I will grant you all my power, but you *must not drink.*"

And thus, Laughing Dog thought, surrender to the insanity and die. No. He stepped toward the water and fell to his knees, his hands splashing into the shallows. The liquid felt foreign, impossibly cool, wet beyond wetness, the edges of the surface like blades cutting into his weathered skin.

"Drink," said the voice, "and you quench my fire. Would you willingly destroy power that might make you as a god among men?"

Laughing Dog dipped his lips toward the rippling mirror.

"No!" the voice roared, and again he heard the voices beneath it, the screams of a thousand men and women and children dying in a blaze, the bellow of the flames across the savanna grasses...and something deeper and older. He heard forests burning, the crash of centuries-old trees crumbling to the forest floor in flames, smashing smaller trees below them. He heard the sizzle of a thousand thousand meals, the crack of lightning in the rain, the impossible explosion of a mountain boiling with dazzling fire. Then he drank deep. The water was sweeter than honey in his mouth, in his throat. The fire mountain went dark. He swallowed, and the thunder faded into memory. He swallowed, and the hiss of rain across the burning forest quenched its embers. His stomach panged as it remembered the touch of water, and streams wended across the burning prairies and drowned their tongues of flame in cold mercy. One by one, the voices of the dying went silent in his mind.

His stomach soured and ached; he turned away from the water, crawled a few steps, and then vomited clear liquid onto the hard earth, his belly not yet ready for such generous portions of what it needed. He hunched, heaved, and spat up again, and then he turned and sipped more slowly, allowing his parched stomach time to adjust to its cool relief. Then he crawled into the meager shade of a date palm and closed his eyes, waiting for his mind to be soothed by the restorative water.

He could not know whether he had drunk anything at all, whether the trip to Deraji and the liquid in his gurgling belly were anything but another delusion. But it seemed to him that it had been a very long time since he had drunk the blood of the eland calf. He did not think he lay dying by the cold remains of a fire or a stinking carcass. He should have been dead already, were that the case. He waited, with his eyes still closed, feeling the shadows of the palm move across his legs. He felt neither better nor worse.

A woman's voice, gentle and concerned, spoke above him. "Are you all right, traveler?"

He opened his eyes. The oasis had not gone away. The sun flashed on the water before him, blinding him. A figure stood above him, against the sun, and he lifted his hand to shade his eyes. The woman was dressed in robes of white and green. Her head was wrapped in green and gold cloth, her skin reddish brown, like that of the people from the north. Like Sedjet, Laughing Dog thought warily.

"Yes," he answered. "I'm much better now." He got to his feet, and found that he stood much taller than the woman. Without the sun in his eyes he could see that her slight smile was concerned, but friendly and open. Her features were soft, unburned by the sun. He could not tell for certain, but he thought she must have seen at least thirty rains, though her skin bore little evidence of age. She lifted her hands, and he saw that she held a broad leaf bearing yellow dates, plump and freshly picked.

"You must have traveled some distance," she said. "I thought you might be hungry. My husband and I saw you arrive from across the water. We feared you were ill, from how you staggered and crawled. He did not want me to come to you, in case you carried plague." Her eyes scanned down Laughing Dog's chest and arms. At first he thought she admired him, but then realized she was checking his skin for boils.

Annoyed, he told her, "I don't have plague. I'm a little weak, is all, because I've traveled a great distance with very little water or food." He looked down at the dates she offered, and felt a fierce pang of hunger. He took one and bit. The crisp sweetness of the fruit flooded his mouth, sugar and spice mingling with his welling saliva. His shoulders and back slumped at the unexpected pleasure, and the woman gave him a concerned look. "It's good," he told her. He finished the date, spitting the stone to the ground, and took another. "Thank you."

"You are welcome." She lowered her eyes. "I am called Sara."

"I am Laughing Dog."

She frowned, no doubt at the strangeness of his name. "Since you are well, my husband Yakeb and I would be pleased if you would join us at our camp."

He swallowed the flesh of another date, its sweetness so rich and overwhelming as to be cloying. "It has been quite some time since I've enjoyed the company of others," he said. He thought of Sedjet's distorted face grinning up at the night sky. But that had been just a nightmare. "I'd welcome the opportunity for conversation, and a story or two."

"Please, then, follow me." She offered him the rest of the dates and he cupped them all in his hands. The flesh of his palms and fingers was pink: seared, but healing. This puzzled him. If he had truly burned his palms in his encounter with Sedjet, how could the flesh be healing so soon? Perhaps some disorientation from his madness still lingered. He would need to be sure to eat and drink all that he could. He followed Sara, feeding the dates one after another into his mouth, crushing them between his teeth to release their nectar.

The woman's hips nudged her traveling robes from side to side as she moved, and he decided that he desired her. She was much different than Ant With a Leaf, his promised. Ant was a tall runner, with a stern and unforgiving beauty, and he had felt his blood blow through him like the wind when he looked at her, or when they had stolen quiet moments together alone, entangled in each other's arms. This was different. Sara was gentle, quiet, utterly unlike Ant With a Leaf. He felt as though he had selected her for desire, chosen her as, during their hunts, he selected a running animal. There, he thought. That is where I will throw my spear.

Would Ant think it a betrayal, he wondered? But what would that matter if he were never able to return home? In the sahil, one enjoyed sweetness where one found it.

He followed her, his eyes tracing the hints of her shape through the robes. Abruptly he chastised himself for thinking so; this was another man's wife. What he was considering was unthinkable. If Cloud had been here to catch him staring at the woman, she'd have walloped him across the shoulders with that great stick of hers. She'd done it before, more than once, when she'd caught any of the village's boys giggling lewdly, and she'd taken special measures to ensure that both he and Great Ram took their share of stripes, sons of the King or no—or perhaps because they *were* sons of the King. She had had no tolerance for lasciviousness, reminding them that if they did not prove themselves to be honorable men, their own promised wives had the right to refuse them. The only one who usually escaped her wrath had been Clay, but he had never had any interest in women at all, as far as Laughing Dog could tell. There probably wasn't room for any lust in his head, what with all that sanctimony that filled him. A blow from Cloud's stick was preferable to one of Clay's lectures any day.

And yet he found himself wishing that Clay were here to lecture him now. He missed his brother, with his well-meaning guidance and hesitant smile. Whatever his faults, Clay had always looked out for him. Laughing Dog had seen him start to his feet when he was exiled. He had been ready to follow him out into the wilderness. An ache of homesickness passed over him. He missed fried caterpillars and palm wine and the rich scent of leather in his tent. He missed Clay, and Great Ram, for all his haughtiness. He missed his father, and even Cloud.

The sun was settling toward the horizon as Sara led Laughing Dog around the edge of the water, and when he drew closer, he could see a little white tent there, and a carpet of crimson and gold spread across the earth. A northern man with a thick black beard and white robes was crouched down, constructing a fire. Occasionally, he looked over his shoulder at the two of them, and when they were a short walk away, he waved and shouted a greeting. Laughing Dog did not reply back to him; faced with the man whose wife he had just been considering, he felt a little uncomfortable.

The camp was nestled among date palms, not far from the water, on a flat clearing with little brush. The animal Laughing Dog had seen before stood nearby: a thing like a zebra, but smaller, more heavily muscled, squat and grey. It lipped boredly at nearby grasses and disregarded the people. The tent was small, and of a white material that Laughing Dog had never seen before. It was not made of skin, nor of the cloth that the weavers of the northern peoples were renowned for, and he could not discern how the couple had managed to bring it along, for though it barely looked large enough for two people to lie down in, it still appeared much too heavy and unwieldy to bring on a journey across the desert. Perhaps they had found it here.

When they entered the camp, the hunched-over man suddenly exclaimed in wordless triumph, a thin wisp of smoke rising up his little pile of sticks. "There we are! So, we shall have light and coffee tonight after all! I was not certain I could get anything here to burn!" His robes swelled around his great bulk, and Laughing Dog could not help but be impressed at the sight of him. This was a well-fed man, obviously of great wealth. His beard was thick and bushy, and it parted for his smile, his dark eyes sparkling jovially above it.

"So, my dear wife has brought me another stray, I see." He bustled toward the two of them, heavy arms spread wide, draping his robes like the wings of a fat stork. "Welcome, traveler, welcome. Please. Sit and enjoy our fire. Share our food. I am Yakeb, this is my wife Sara, who I will hope has introduced herself, although I cannot be certain. She is very quiet much of the time."

The woman allowed herself a quirked smile, and in this easy expression, Laughing Dog could now see the lines of age in her face, crinkling her eyes and curling around her mouth. "You think so only because you drown me out, Yakeb," she said, and her husband roared with laughter as if this were the greatest of jokes.

Laughing Dog held his head high. "I am Laughing Dog. I gratefully accept your invitation, as I've been traveling for many days with no respite."

"He says he has had neither food nor water," Sara said, giving her husband a direct stare. She looked back to Laughing Dog. "You must have been very hungry. The dates seemed barely to touch your fingers."

"Well, say no more," Yakeb announced. "Tonight you will have meat and fruit and bread."

"I will be glad of it," Laughing Dog said truthfully. He peered with curiosity at the carpet. He had heard of them, but his people did not make them. His aunt had traded for one, back when they had lived in the north, but it had been left behind in their village when they fled the fires.

Sara caught his gaze. "Please," she said. "Sit. Be comfortable. I will bring you food."

"Thank you." Laughing Dog settled himself down gingerly on the carpet. The texture was strange and prickly. He decided he did not like it, and when Sara went to retrieve things from the large bundles next to their animal, and Yakeb had turned back to tend to his fire, he surreptitiously relocated himself to the ground. "You come from the north, I see. Where are you traveling?"

Yakeb did not look around. "Ah yes. My wife's family is with another people, beyond where the sun sets on the Firelands. We are journeying to see them. We would have taken a boat, but traveling across water does not agree with my stomach, and so we are on foot."

"It's a very long journey to the other side of the Firelands. I don't know of any who have traveled so far."

The man's cheerful tone abandoned his voice temporarily. "Yes, the journey used to be much shorter, they say. The Firelands are spreading. I have heard tales of whole cities swallowed up by the sands."

"I have heard those tales too," Laughing Dog said cautiously. He remembered Sedjet's report of a lost city in the sands. "Have you ever seen such a thing?"

"Not I," Yakeb said. "But our village has moved three times since I was a boy. Three times! The sands grew closer, the rains grew scarcer, and we had to leave. The Wandering Folk used to visit our village once a year, trading some of their livestock for cloth, jewelry, and other goods. But after the last move, it took them two rains before they found us again. And there were not nearly so many of them. I think they suffer too."

Sara came up behind Laughing Dog and put her hand on his sun-weathered shoulder. Her touch was gentle, delicate. She offered him thin sticks that had skewered meat of a type Laughing Dog did not know. He sniffed at it, smelling odd spices. The meat was shriveled and dry. He wondered if it had spoiled, but suddenly he was too hungry to care. He tore at it with his teeth, finding it unusually salty, so heavily seasoned that it did not taste of meat at all. It was tough and chewy in his mouth, and he had to let his saliva wet it before he could swallow.

Sara seated herself nearby on the carpet, expertly folding her robes about her legs as she did so. It was an odd habit of the northern folk, to cover themselves so much. Laughing Dog did not understand it. To bind and swaddle one's limbs so would make it difficult to move about easily. Why anyone would limit herself in such a way was beyond his guess. "And what has brought you traveling across the sahil," she asked him. "Did you lose your food and water?"

Laughing Dog wondered how much to tell them, and then decided most of his story was not worth explaining. "I was on a personal journey. It's usual among my people to find food and water as they travel, but it's far scarcer these days than it used to be."

"It is fortunate you found the oasis!" Yakeb exclaimed. "We saw you approach, and you appeared half dead. We feared you might be ill."

Laughing Dog thought of the voice that had followed him, the madness that had claimed to be Ogya. He had not heard it since drinking the water. That proved it, then. Only crazed imaginings born of too much heat and not enough to drink. He felt a tickle in the back of his mind. Water extinguishes fire. He pushed it out of his thoughts with another bite of salted meat. "I was fortunate indeed. And even more fortunate to have happened upon such hospitable travelers."

Sara lifted a date to her soft, pink lips, parting them, and Laughing Dog found himself watching intently. His stomach growled again with hunger, and his loins pulsed with lust. He was not certain which he coveted more: the date, or those lips. Suddenly certain that Yakeb would catch him staring and grow angry, he looked away.

"Where are your people now, Laughing Dog?" Sara asked.

Around mouthfuls of dried meat, Laughing Dog replied, "They are far to the south and east of here, on the edge of the forest. Perhaps seven days' journey if one is fleet. My father is King First Claw."

"A king!" Yakeb's ruddy cheeks glowed with enthusiasm, black beard spreading around his broad grin. "Then it is royalty we have welcomed into our camp this evening! Perhaps we are the fortunate ones."

"Royalty?" Laughing Dog repeated quietly. "Not really. That would be my brother, Great Ram. He'll be King when our father passes. Even were I first-born, I've always believed that it's what a man does, rather than who bedded his mother, that is the mark of greatness in a man."

Yakeb shrugged at this statement, as if the political sentiment were a spider's web that might cling to his robes. "Well spoken, I suppose. But there are many ways to be great, and sometimes greatness is just being in the right place at the right time. Certainly a king is wealthy, though, and there is nothing wrong with that."

Thinking of how he had admired Yakeb's rich weight and fine clothes as he had entered the camp, Laughing Dog found he could not argue. "That is true. And Great Ram will make a fine king. He's very much like our father."

Sara spoke then, her voice calm and curious. "Great Ram, First Claw, Laughing Dog! Your people have such strange names. Please do not take offense," she hastened to add, "but among my people, the hyena is considered an ill omen."

"Among mine too," replied Laughing Dog, "in some tales." He thought of the hyena snout snarling at him from the back of Sedjet's head and shuddered. A nightmare, a bad dream. That was all it had been. "And in others, a good omen. There's room for good and ill in all creatures, they say."

"True enough," Yakeb agreed heartily, slapping his knees with his broad palms.

Laughing Dog looked down and found to his dismay that he had eaten all the dried meat. His stomach complained to him as intensely as if he had had nothing at all. "Is there more meat?" He knew that it was rude to ask, but the necessity of his hunger was blinding him to finer courtesies. Sara and Yakeb exchanged glances, and then Sara stood. "I will fetch you bread and fruit," she said. "We forget how long you must have traveled with nothing at all. How hungry you must be!"

This was not what he had requested, but he smiled politely anyhow. Anything to fill his belly would be welcome. "Thank you."

"And later we will all have coffee," Yakeb announced. "A marvelous drink! It quickens the mind and renews the spirit. Have you had it before?"

"Only once," Laughing Dog said uncomfortably, remembering a foul and bitter sip from a cup shared with him by a trader, the same who had once talked to him of the strength of men over the gods. He had always wondered why anyone would drink the stuff.

He must have made a sour expression, because Yakeb laughed uproariously. "A man grows to love the taste after a time! But its flavor requires familiarity, true enough. You know, they say its name comes from the old words for 'no hunger.' A good drink for when one has little food."

Sara returned with a flat, white circle of bread with a handful of fruits, primarily dates, but also tiny, black, wrinkled things, and a round, red, papery fruit he did not recognize. He set these in his lap and sank his teeth into the bread as Sara seated herself next to her husband. He had not had bread since he was a boy, and his people had grown grain in the floodplains near their village. That had been soft, rich, and flavorful. This was hard and bland; he found it difficult to tear away pieces with his fingers. Nonetheless, it swelled delightfully in his mouth, and when he swallowed, rested heavy in his stomach. He took greedy bites of the sweet, juicy dates to wash down the dry bread and filled his mouth with more, his stomach aching with pleasure. He looked up to see both Sara and Yakeb staring at him. Guiltily, he wiped juice from his chin with the back of his arm and forced himself to eat more slowly. It was difficult, though. Thoughts of the food demanded his attention. He occupied himself with the small, wrinkled fruits, chewing them deliberately. They were sweet and, like the meat and bread, dry.

"You said our names sound strange to you," he began, trying to rid the air of the awkward silence that had fallen as he ate, "but yours would sound strange to us as well. It's hard for me to hear meaning in them beyond their sounds."

"Our names do have meanings," Yakeb said, seeming cheered that conversation had resumed, "though we think of them little. My name comes from the old words meaning 'struggles with gods.'" He chuckled. "Though I assure you, I do not intend to do anything of the kind! They leave me alone and I leave them alone, and that suits me well enough. Sara, here, her name means…" He trailed off. "What does your name mean, my jewel? I do not know that I have ever asked you before."

She gave him a fond smile. "It means little queen," she said. "And I have found plenty of other ways to let you know that is who I am."

"That you have!" Yakeb bellowed a laugh. "Not so little a queen either, if you have anything to say about it."

Laughing Dog turned his eyes toward Sara. She sat proudly, her back straight, meeting her husband's eyes. You could be my little queen, he thought, were I to be King instead of my brother.

She nodded to Yakeb and patted his hand. To Laughing Dog, she said, "But our names do not mean much. They are the names of our ancestors, and so we honor them by keeping their names."

"We don't always know the significance of our names either," confessed Laughing Dog. "Our mothers name us the first thing they see after we are born. It's said that the gods send them what they need to see to name us properly, so that we may serve them best. It's the custom for our women to give birth under an open sky, so that they may be receptive to a sign from the gods." He grinned. "Although I suspect it's more so we do not have many, many children named Tent Roof."

Yakeb guffawed with laughter at this, but Sara leaned forward, her brow creasing in interest. "But that is fascinating! And do the names often prove to have significance later on? Do the gods truly show a woman what they wish her to see?"

Shrugging, Laughing Dog answered, "Who can say? Certainly sometimes the names seem to be meaningful. My mother opened her eyes upon a huge mountain ram, standing tall and proud, far from the high places where it lived. My father said he knew from that moment that my brother was destined to be a mighty king after him. But more likely, we find significance in our lives because of the names, rather than the reverse. Had my brother been named Mongoose instead, we would all talk about what a skilled hunter he was, quick and nimble. You see."

Yakeb poked at the fire with a stick, sending a puff of smoke upward. "Well, how about you, Laughing Dog? Your mother saw a hyena when you were born?"

"So she says. Standing up on a ridge, black against the night sky." He had the image in his head, had always had it, since before he could remember. A boy's name image was *his* image. It was what he saw in his mind when he thought of himself.

"And has it proven significant for you, in your life?"

He thought of the snarling muzzle in the back of Sedjet's head, growling at him, and shuddered. Again and again that memory kept returning to him, false though it must certainly be. He could not purge it from his mind's eye. "Perhaps, but no more so than a flame might be, or a spear, or a purple grenadier, or an eland, or a smiling woman."

"Why do you tell them lies, Laughing Dog?" a voice hissed from out of the fire. He knew the sound of it as he knew the taste of his teeth. It was the voice of his madness, the voice that had hounded him through his thirst. His hair stood up on the back of his neck, a crushing terror pushing down on his lungs and belly.

"You're not real," he muttered, low.

"Forgive me," Sara said, leaning closer to him. "I didn't quite hear."

The voice laughed the sound of snapping sticks. "I'm real, Laughing Dog. I'm a god. You cannot defeat me."

"I can," he growled. "I'll drink again." He looked up at Sara's puzzled brown eyes. "I mean, I think I need more water. Please excuse me." He stood and went down to the edge of the oasis, ignoring the worried glances she and her husband exchanged. He crouched by the water.

"Do not drink, Laughing Dog," the voice beseeched him. It was not coming from the fire, as he had thought before. It was as if someone was standing right behind him, whispering the words into his ears. "With my power, you could have anything you desire. I could make you King, instead of your brother. Is that what you want? I could give you armies at your command." Slyly, it added, "I could even give you *her*. I know you desire her."

"What can madness grant me," Laughing Dog demanded of it, "but the pity and scorn of others? You saw how they looked at me just now." He realized that he still spoke to the voice as though it were another person.

"You must know by now that I am not madness," the voice said, crackling with heat. "You have drunk. You have rested in the shade. You have eaten. No, I am a god. I was silent for a while, Laughing Dog, because you drank after I bade you not to, and quenched my voice. But I am not a little campfire you can put out with your piss. I am Ogya. I am the heart of the conflagration, the soul of lightning, and deep beneath the sand you stand on, I burn eternal, snug in the belly of the earth."

He did not hear the passion in its voice so much as felt it, deep within his own mind: the blazing fury of a caged beast, so monstrous and enormous that he was but a speck of dust in its vision. He felt its seething, endless desire to grow and consume everything, a maddening, compelling drive that would never be satisfied. He knew it was not insanity, not the fever of thirst or heat, that spoke to him. It was something else. It was the voice of a demented god.

He was shaken by this realization. The gods spoke to men after all. In some misguided way, his brother and father had been correct. But he was not, however, daunted by this fact. He did not fear the voice. Even a speck could fell a charging beast if it blinded its eyes or choked its throat. God the voice might be, but he would never surrender to it. He crouched down to the water, dipped his face to it, and drank deeply. Again he heard the voice roar in wordless fury, hissing steam. It faded to a whisper, and then to nothing. He drank again, drowning it a deluge of water.

There was silence, and yet still he drank, until his belly stretched and ached with fullness.

"Well, Ogya?" he said aloud.

There was no answer.

"Do you listen still, or have I drowned you for good?"

Nothing.

"God or madness, it's all the same to me. I will never yield to you. I will never grovel for your power and blessings. All that you promised me, all that I desire, if I am to have them, I will have them through the might of my own arm. I will owe nothing to you. Seethe in fury all you wish, if there is anything left of you to seethe."

With that, he turned and strode back to the camp, where Yakeb and Sara were leaning toward each other and speaking in low tones. When he returned, they sat upright, and Yakeb inquired, "Is everything all right, friend?"

Laughing Dog looked back and forth at the two of them suspiciously. What had they been talking about? His strange behavior, no doubt. He wondered if he had frightened them with his odd mutterings and sudden trip to the water. Had they heard him speaking to Ogya down there? He did not think they could have—he had taken care to keep his voice low enough not to carry back to the camp. He set himself down in his spot and answered in an airy tone, "Everything's fine. I just needed more water. There was…a ringing in my ears, as happens sometimes when one has not had enough to drink."

Yakeb nodded sagely. "This has been my experience as well. A little disorientation is to be expected, I'm sure. The sun of the sahil can cook a man's brains if he is not careful. A little rest, and you'll be fine."

Laughing Dog felt his stomach growl. A moment ago, it had seemed full to bursting, but now it sucked with hunger. He looked about for his meal and realized belatedly that he had eaten everything that he had been given. "Rest, yes," he said. "And food."

Yakeb and Sara exchanged another glance, and then the husband cleared his throat. "Perhaps it would be best," he said in a reasoning voice, "to let your stomach settle first. You have eaten a great deal after a long period of privation, and I have seen many a man grow ill from overeating after such an ordeal."

Crossly, Laughing Dog responded, "I have not overeaten. I have great experience with traveling long distances on little food and water, and I know my capabilities as well as my needs. I regret any rudeness, but my hunger demands that I request more of you."

Yakeb poked at the fire, his expression visibly uncomfortable, though Laughing Dog could discern no reason why he should be distressed. Gently, Sara said, "The trees here are plentiful with dates. With a little climbing, we could retrieve more, but for now, let us rest and enjoy the evening."

Laughing Dog did not think he could enjoy the evening very well with his stomach complaining to him as it was; nor did he think dates would quell its pangs half so well as meat and bread, but to protest further would have been ungrateful, so he kept a diplomatic if somewhat surly silence.

For a time, there was no conversation, and the three of them awkwardly avoided each other's gazes, but eventually Yakeb, whose jovial nature would apparently brook no inhospitality, broke the silence with an enthusiastic and probably embellished tale of his homeland, and when he did so,

Sara seemed to relax and be at ease once again. Laughing Dog's hunger only intensified, but he forced himself to smile and laugh and comment along with the story as Yakeb told it, and after the man was done, he reciprocated with one of his own people's stories about the rabbit and the spider. Laughing Dog was no Teller, but he thought he delivered a fair rendition, especially as neither Yakeb nor Sara seemed to know how to properly enjoy a story; instead of making interjections at the right moments, they simply sat in silence, listening. He supposed it was the way of their people.

At the end of his tale, the sun was beginning to set, and then Yakeb and Sara fetched their own meals from their baggage. Laughing Dog politely requested more meat and bread, as by that time, his stomach ached with hunger so compelling that he could hardly think of anything else. The couple seemed reluctant, but after some quiet discussion with her husband, Sara doled out another portion of meat and bread that Laughing Dog deemed unfairly small. Had the two of them visited his village, they would have been welcomed with a great feast; they would have been sent to bed with bellies stretched and aching. He glowered at the portions and tried to eat them slowly so as to make them last and trick his hunger into thinking it was being provided more than it was, but in very little time, all his food was gone, and he was scarcely more satiated than before he had eaten. Sara and Yakeb themselves ate very little—most likely, Laughing Dog thought, to shame him out of requesting more. He could hardly ask for larger portions than his hosts allowed themselves. No doubt they planned to secretly indulge in second helpings after he was asleep. Well, they were not the only ones who could skulk around after dark.

As evening turned into night, he and Yakeb kept the fire fed and traded tales, and from time to time Sara would contribute her own. Her stories were from the west and bore similarity to the tales of Laughing Dog's own people, but Yakeb told of legends and histories of the northeast, and these were strange and exotic to Laughing Dog.

After a time, the flames of the fire grew low, and Yakeb and Sara said their good nights and retired to their tent. The little shelter was so low to the ground that Laughing Dog could not imagine what it would be like to sleep under it. Uncomfortable, he thought, with the white fabric so close to one's face, bouncing one's own breath back. It must be very stuffy. He found a soft patch of earth and settled down into it, staring up at the stars. After all this time out in the hard-packed dirt of the savanna and sahil, even that was comfort. He lay quietly with his thoughts, waiting for his two hosts to go to sleep, and considered his battle with Ogya over the last few days.

So. The gods spoke to men after all. It had not been madness that had rattled through his mind in his journey across the sahil, but the voice of a god. And it must also have been the power of a god that had restored his body from hunger and thirst and preserved him through his travels. Ogya had wrested the strength away from him to coerce him into submission, but Laughing Dog had not faltered. He had defied the god and drunk deep, extinguishing the flame of Ogya's wrath, leaving him with all the strength that the god had granted him. He, Laughing Dog, had bested a god. He felt almost giddy at the thought. What would his people say if they knew? As soon as he considered the question, he discarded it in disgust. They would call him a liar. They would call him arrogant. No, this little victory would have to remain his own. And what if the voice of Ogya returned? Why, then he could drink again, as simple as that, flooding it into silence once more.

He crossed his arms behind his head, feeling the restored strength in his limbs. With so easy a method of dismissing the god, perhaps he could even bargain for more. Grant me strength, he could say, or I drink again. The power of a god at his beck and call. Who among his people would challenge the strength of men then? It was a thought worth considering.

He was still hungry, though. Perhaps the restoration of his body from starvation had created this great need within him. He lay silently and listened. Insects chirruped rhythmically around the water, but even the birds were quiet now. He waited, watching the stars glimmer before his eyes. He was sleepy, but he wanted food more than slumber. The faint sound of snoring came from the tent. So Yakeb was asleep, then.

Cautiously, he rose. The fire burned low with dim red flames, but the moon was a cupped calabash overhead, so there was enough light to see. He looked around. The tent was still, the animal that his hosts had brought with them standing with its head lowered. It was not moving, and though it was standing, Laughing Dog thought it slept. He took quiet hunting steps through the low brush—years of hunting eland had taught him to move without waking a slumbering beast. He found the packs that Sara had retrieved the food from. They were made of a rough cloth, tied with cords. Laughing Dog was not used to knots, but his fingers were clever, and he managed to undo the strings and pull the sack open. He reached inside and prodded around until his fingertips found the familiar texture of meat and bread, bound within a thin cloth. Seizing the package, he withdrew it and unwrapped it. There was less food there than he had expected—perhaps twenty of the dried skewers were wrapped up in the cloth. There must be more in the other bags. He withdrew one and sank his teeth into it. The meat was dry, but salty and delicious, and his hunger rose to meet it.

"Here," said Yakeb's voice, "what are you doing?"

Laughing Dog turned to see the portly man crawling out of the tent. The light snoring stopped, and he realized it must have been Sara the whole time. Yakeb had suspected him, been waiting for him to help himself to the meal he was due as a guest. "I'm hungry," he informed the man. "You greedily hoarded the food you ought to have offered me as a guest, and so I'm sparing you the shame you would have bought for yourself had I died of starvation."

Yakeb's expression broke in astonishment. "But you have eaten enough for three men!" he exclaimed. "My wife and I have shared more than we could afford with you already. We have meager supplies remaining, and it will be difficult for us to manage the journey across the sahil with what we have left. Already I fear we will suffer greatly from hunger before our journey's end. I am sorry for your misfortune, my friend, but I must ask you to return the meat you have taken from us to the bags and leave us be."

The blood was hot in Laughing Dog's face. Either this was an outright lie, or his host had begun this journey woefully unprepared. Admittedly, when he reflected on it, the amount of food he had consumed seemed more than sufficient, but it had proven woefully low in nutrition, filling him so little that he felt he had barely eaten at all. This food was not his—he knew that—but he would not allow himself to die of starvation in the desert simply because his host was a liar or a fool. "No," he said firmly. "I need this to survive. It is as simple as that."

Yakeb's hand moved inside his robe, and he withdrew partway the haft of a knife. A bright blade glinted in the moonlight; it was not stone, but the hard and shining metal favored by the northerners. "My friend, I must insist that you return our food and leave us be. It grieves me to express such inhospitality, but I am prepared to defend our supplies if you give me no choice."

Laughing Dog looked up and down Yakeb's frame, taking stock of the man. He was fat, yes, but fat men could be strong. Beneath the drapery of the billowing robes, it was difficult to discern his athleticism. Nonetheless, Laughing Dog was hardened by years of hunting and travel. Such a difficult life allowed for none of the softness that padded the other man's form. He decided that knife or no, he was not afraid of Yakeb. "I am a great warrior of my people," he told the man, "and you are a fat man alone in the savanna. If you wish to live, you will go back inside your tiny little tent and hide until I am gone."

Dismay sagged the man's face, but then his mouth tightened with resolve behind his black beard. "I am sad to hear you say that." He drew the knife all the way from his cloak. It was longer than the knives Laughing Dog had seen before, its blade half again as long as his hand. Its keen edge gleamed in the moonlight.

Laughing Dog regarded it warily, dropping a little to lower his center of gravity, ready to spring to either side should Yakeb come at him.

The broad man held the blade with one hand, just below his ribcage, and lunged forward. Laughing Dog slid to one side, keeping the bags of supplies between himself and Yakeb. He had abandoned his own spear somewhere back in the arid reaches of the sahil. It would be good to have it now, but this man did not look like he knew how to fight. "Please, my friend," Yakeb entreated him. "Just go. Leave me and my wife in peace."

"If I do," Laughing Dog answered, "I will die. I need your food to live."

"We need it more," Yakeb insisted, circling the packs. The animal had awoken, and regarded them both with an uneasy stare. "I sense you are a good man, but in a difficult place. Please do not do this thing. Once you have lost this, once you surrender this part of yourself, you can never get it back. It is not worth it."

Laughing Dog watched the man move in the dim light. He was not aware of his own feet below his bulk. He might trip on a stone. "The only good men alive are those who have never been in difficult places," Laughing Dog said. He made as if to dart to the right, and Yakeb swung clumsily in that direction with the blade. Laughing Dog reversed direction and moved to the other side, behind Yakeb. He had been right; this was a man who had little experience with a knife. He would be easy to defeat.

No sooner had he thought this than Yakeb recovered, spun, and lunged with the knife in the other direction. Laughing Dog crouched low below the wide swing and sprung backward, letting the heavy man's momentum carry him forward and cause him to stumble. He kicked out with his foot at one knee. Though the voluminous robes made it difficult to tell exactly where the man's legs stood, he felt his heel connect, buckling Yakeb's leg. With a shrill cry, oddly high-pitched for a man of his stature, Yakeb tumbled sideways to the ground, the knife glinting in the moonlight as it was flung. The animal made an alarmed sound and trotted a little distance away.

"Yakeb?" a voice said, soft, but cracked with concern. Sara rose up from the tent, looking toward both of them. "What's happening? Is everything all right?"

The man pushed himself up on his hands, crawled toward her on his side, terror showing the whites around his eyes. "Sara!" he called out. "Get out of here! Run!"

Fool, Laughing Dog thought, wrapping his fingers around a heavy stone. Never turn your eyes from an opponent. He lifted the stone up to the height of his chest and then thrust it forward as hard as he could. It struck Yakeb's forehead with a dull thud.

Sara screamed wordlessly. Yakeb slumped to the ground, eyes staring upward. His legs began kicking, as if attempting to carry him away from his aggressor while lying down. His hands shook against his belly. Then he was still, his gaze unfocused.

Laughing Dog backed away, suddenly uncertain. He had never killed anyone before. Not a man, anyhow. Sedjet had been a demon sent by Ogya. This was different. His heart ached with pounding.

With shaking steps, Sara came toward him. Wordless, she crouched down by her husband's body. She clasped his cheeks in her hands as though she could tug his soul back into his body through them. She looked into his unseeing eyes. She brushed the back of her hand across his forehead, and her knuckles came up with dark stains that Laughing Dog could see even in the dim moonlight. She took his limp hand in her own.

When she looked up at Laughing Dog, her cheeks were wet. "You killed him," she said. Her voice was shaking now, but not with grief.

"He left me no choice. He attacked me. He would have killed me had I not defended myself."

"He was on his back!" She spat the words at him like they were knives. "Unarmed. And you murdered him!"

Her accusations sent a deep, hot fear running through him. It had been self-defense. It *had*. Had he not thrown the rock, Yakeb would have scrambled after the knife, and then Laughing Dog would have faced an armed opponent once more. He had done the only sensible thing in the situation. What else should he have done? Fled, with neither food nor water nor provisions? Surrendered? No, had he surrendered, Yakeb would have surely killed him anyway, just to ensure that he didn't try again to take their food later on, even tracking them from the oasis. His rising sense of guilt eased. It had been the only way. His actions may not have been kind, but they were necessary.

"What was it you wanted from us, bandit?" Sara demanded. "Our riches? We have none, save for a few bolts of fine cloth that were to be gifts for my sisters."

"I'm no thief!" Laughing Dog protested. "I care nothing for your riches."

"Then what?" She stared at him in broken bewilderment for a moment, and then a look of horror dawned on her face. She scrambled backward along the ground, on the heels of her hands, away from her dead husband. "You won't take me without paying a dear price," she told him. She was shaking. "I'll rip your eyes out of their sockets. I'll pull off your ears."

"You think I mean to—to force myself on you?" Laughing Dog asked incredulously.

"Why else would you kill him?" Sara hesitated before speaking the last two words, no doubt to make herself believe that the act had been murder, rather than self-defense, so that she could hate him. Well, let her. Laughing Dog didn't want her.

Except, he thought, he had. His desire for her had been intense and hungry. And, he thought, looking at her through the emotion that twisted her face, even angry and distraught, she was beautiful. If she were to accept him, even now, he would take her in an instant. It was her accusations that made her now so unappealing. And her shaking. It made her seem feeble, weak.

"I told you," he said. "He attacked me. He came at me with a knife."

"Yakeb is a gentle man. I have hardly known him to raise his voice to another man."

This was not surprising to Laughing Dog. Plainly, Yakeb had been in few, if any, fights in his life. "Believe what you will. I have told you what happened. And I have no intention of taking you. Nor doing anything at all with you."

She looked at him in silence for a moment, and then crawled back to her husband's body and buried her face in his chest. Her narrow back shook with unvoiced sobs. This was, somehow, worse than the accusations.

"Look," said Laughing Dog. "I very much regret what happened. It was never my intention. I swear this to you."

She did not respond. Her fingers gripped at her husband's robes as she wept.

"If there's anything at all that I can do to help you, you must tell me. I will do anything within my power. I would not hold your husband's foolish acts against you."

Still nothing. Laughing Dog found her silence strangely frustrating. Could she not hear that he was trying to make amends, trying to help her? He tried again. "What happened is a terrible, unfortunate thing. Come with me, and I'll help you to make it across the sahil to a safe place. You won't survive on your own. You need my help."

She gave no response, but continued to soak her husband's robes with her tears.

"Please," he said. "Listen to me."

Nothing.

Flushing with anger, Laughing Dog turned away. "Very well, then. Suffer and die under the sun on your own, if you wish." He reached into the open packs and plucked out a generous helping of meat, then rummaged around for more. He found only wrapped bread, like he had been served earlier. There was no other food. Guiltily, he returned some of the meat, and took only a paltry few pieces of the bread.

"I am taking some food," he told her, "but I have left a great deal more than half for you."

Still she did not respond. He looked down at her, frail and shaking against a fat corpse, and any remaining attraction melted away. She was feeble, powerless. Disgust roiled in his stomach. How could he ever have found her appealing? "You ought to be grateful. Now you just might have enough food to make it across the sahil."

Sara gave no reply, nor did she even move. Laughing Dog realized she would probably just lie there, grieving senselessly, until the sun cooked her to death.

He took two of the water skins and strode away from her, giddy and a little nauseated after the confrontation. He made his way down to the oasis. He would fill the skins, take the food, and be on his way. Moonlight would be bright enough for travel tonight. It rippled on the water as he approached. He heard the sound of birds taking flight behind him.

Then there was a keen bite into his back, just below his right shoulder blade, a deep and searing line that made him duck and turn instinctively. Sara stood there, holding Yakeb's knife, which now dripped with Laughing Dog's blood. Her eyes were narrowed and hard, her teeth bared like a wild dog's.

"You stabbed me," Laughing Dog said in astonishment. He could feel his hot blood running down his back. It tickled at his side. The line of pain from the wound blossomed into a dozen lines that lashed at him if he moved his back at all. "You stabbed me."

He had no time to say anything else. The crazed woman lunged at him again, striking downward with the knife. He caught her wrist in his left hand, pulled her forward, and punched at her with his right, his back flaring with intense pain at the motion. Her head whipped backward, and she immediately collapsed in his grip, lifeless weight.

He let go of her wrist, and she slumped to the ground, the eyes that had fascinated him earlier in the day staring up past him. She was dead. It was impossible. He had not struck her hard enough to kill her. It had been a freak accident.

Leaving the woman lying by the water, Laughing Dog stumbled up to the little camp and huddled by the fire. He stared at the luggage. The animal. The little tent. The carpet spread out by the fire. The shadowy lump on the ground behind the luggage.

It hadn't been his fault. None of it had been. They had both attacked him. He had only been fending for his own life. A man was allowed to survive. There was no injustice in that. A man was permitted to do what was necessary to survive. All the same, it would not be good for him if someone happened across the oasis and discovered the bodies. Someone who found this scene might think it had been murder, or bandits. So far as Laughing Dog knew, his own people were closer to Deraji than any other. A traveler moving east from Deraji might come across his village next, with tales of a slain couple at the oasis. And then people would remember how Laughing Dog returned with a knife wound. It would be inconvenient. There might be questions. In a way, it was fortunate for him that Sara had attacked him. He wasn't pleased about being injured, and the memory of her falling dead at his feet made him feel sick. But had she been alive, and made it back to her people, she would certainly have told them of the man who had killed her husband. Murder, she had called it, and murder was what she would have told her kinsmen. No, it might be unpleasant, but it was better this way.

He cut strips of Yakeb's white robes away and wrapped them around his middle, staunching the flow of blood from his wound. Then, struggling, he dragged the fat man into the tent, cursing his weight. His injury screamed its pain so intensely during the ordeal, he had to take regular pauses so as not to pass out. After, he went back down to the water and retrieved Sara's body, pushing it into the tent alongside her husband.

Then he took a branch from the fire and touched it to the carpet, wondering why anyone would bring so heavy an item on such an arduous journey anyway. It was foolish; the two of them had both been foolish to make such a journey ill-prepared, and then to attack an unarmed man. It was small wonder they were both dead. When the carpet was burning steadily, letting off thick clouds of black smoke, he set the tent alight as well. There. Now anyone who came along would think that the couple had been careless, left their carpet too close to the fire, and been burned alive in their tent.

He tossed the branch back into the fire and watched the tent go up in flames, the blaze licking and consuming everything it touched. Deep in the recesses of his awareness, he could hear some part of him laughing at the spectacle.

He felt that every part of his body was too cold, a sensation that was rare and strange to him. He rummaged through the luggage, looking for anything of value. There were clothes, rolled up bits of odd cloth, and clear stones with liquid inside. Nothing besides the food held any interest for him, and anyway, if he brought unusual things back to camp, there could be questions. He bundled up all the food, tucked Yakeb's knife into his belt, filled his water skins, and set off.

After he had gone a short distance, he looked back. The fire on the tent and carpet was still burning merrily away, billowing thick clouds of black smoke. Again he heard laughing somewhere in the back of his mind. Abruptly he realized it must be Ogya, observing his handiwork. So the god was not completely silenced then. That was all right. Laughing Dog had proven he could control him. The god held no power over him. To prove it, he took a little sip of water from his skins and tore his gaze away from the fire.

He was tired of starvation and thirst and demons in the night. He was tired of arguments with gods and bloodthirsty travelers and his own mind. He thought of his camp, warm and friendly and inviting, and his people, his brothers, his father. He didn't hate them for exiling him. They'd only been trying to do what they thought was right. They thought they understood the truth of the gods, but they didn't. They were teaching false ways, all of them—the same false ways they had been taught by their own ancestors, by Tellers distracted by fanciful tales. All the people were being led astray. Sooner or later the other gods would turn on them as well, and they would be helpless. They wouldn't fight back. They would just sacrifice, plead for mercy. He had to go home. He had to show them all how to fight back. And he could bring the strength of a god to wield against their enemies. They would love him then. They would all love him.

Forsaken

Kwaee's forest was wide, and it was empty. There were countless plants and animals and insects, all madly crawling around in an orgy of life, but they were always the same. None of them spoke to Doto and surprised him. None challenged him. And his father just sat in his temple and did nothing. The emptiness of the forest had taken him, made him dull and angry and listless. Doto thought it had begun to take him as it had taken his father: the passions he had once felt failed to move him any longer. He cared little how he spent his days; no activity or ordeal moved him more than any other.

But for three nights now, the fire bearer had danced for Doto. The experience was like nothing he had ever felt before. The rhythm of the dance sent waves through the earth and air of the forest, and they came together around Doto and crashed into him, filling him up, making him feel both giddy and powerful. Far away, he could feel his little copse of trees, his own tiny temple, spreading into the forest, sending down roots, sprouting shoots of new trees. He felt larger; he felt he could send the roots of his forest down into the land and snap it into two pieces. He felt as though he could snuff the menace of Ogya out with one foot. If the praise of one fire bearer felt like this, what would the praise of all of them be like? How great and glorious could he become? Could this be what Kwaee felt every night?

He crouched on a branch, his tail swaying, and gazed down at the slumbering form of his captive. With a fingertip he traced the edges of the bright blue feather that had sprouted from his forehead, feeling its grip deep in his brow. It was a sign of divinity that he had never borne before; of all the gods and goddesses he had met, only Kwaee grew the divine plumage. And now he too bore it, all because of the dance from his little prize.

There had been no fire this night. The moon had provided enough light for the bearer's weak eyes—at least when the treetops, in obeisance to Doto's wishes, bent aside to admit it and illuminate their path. Forgoing meat for the evening, the fire bearer had agreed to a meal of various fruits and seeds, explaining that it did not need to scorch these with flame before consuming them.

Still it required sleep, however, and these nights spent waiting for it to recover from the apparently fatiguing act of simply being awake were both annoying and tedious to Doto. He did not like sitting around doing nothing, and so he let his mind go out into the forest, into the grass, trees, insects, birds, and wandering animals. He felt with mild disinterest their frail pains and desires. He felt the wind tickle his branches. He felt the cool kiss of the moonlight on his leaves. He felt his talons sink into the flesh of his prey, and he felt himself seized, his terrified life bleeding away into helplessness, and then nothing. The only thing he would not feel was his fire bearer. Worship or no, he did not dare enter the mind of a creature corrupted by Ogya. It might be like mud in a stream. The thoughts of two gods might mingle; or Ogya, being a far more powerful god, might simply flood him away.

What a curious creature the fire bearer was. It was not at all like the stories of demons Kwaee had related to Doto, when he was just a cub. There seemed to be no malice or deceit in it, and aside from building fires, it had made efforts neither to attack Doto nor to escape. Not that it could move very fast on that wounded leg. Their pace over the days had been slower and slower, the bearer's limp growing more pronounced. Twice Doto had broken the wooden paw apart to pad the wound with new mushrooms and soft plants. He had urged the bearer to lick the wound clean, but either it would not or it could not, and Doto was not about to lick it himself. Still, it would not have done much good. There was a stink in the wound, an odor Doto recognized quite well. He had not often scented an animal with that stench that had not died soon after. It was the smell of infection. The fire bearer was likely not going to live much longer. It would make it to Kwaee's temple, Doto thought, but not for much beyond that. Half a moon, perhaps.

Doto yearned to use his power to heal the wound. There was a compulsion in him that he did not understand, urging him to send his magic into the fire bearer, knit the flesh back together, purify the rot, make the skin smooth once more. His desire to do this was strong, but healing was one thing he could never do.

Once, when he had been a cub, still small, his copse just a tiny clearing of saplings, he had found a young genet that had been trampled by some larger animal, though by what exactly, he did not know. It was only an infant, squealing in pain and fear, calling for its mother. No mother was anywhere to be found; she had abandoned it, perhaps knowing it would not survive. Its legs and tail were crushed, bleeding and twitching uselessly. It had released its musk in its terror and reeked of fear. Doto had felt pity for it, had crouched to take it up in his paws. Its eyes were pale blue and frightened. He had sent his mind into it, had felt where the breaks in the bones were, found the tears in muscle and ligament. He could fix this, he thought. He could send his power into the little cub and put it back together. It would take a lot of his energy, but he could do it.

He had gathered his focus, and was preparing to use his magic to heal the little cub, when a heavy paw slashed across his face and muzzle, tearing open his hide, sending him sprawling to the ground. He hissed in fear and terror, the wounded infant in his paws sent flying to one side when he fell.

Kwaee stood over him then, a huge and menacing shadow. Doto's blood dripped from his claws. He could feel the injuries on his cheek and muzzle mending themselves, but he was too astonished to know how to react. Kwaee had struck him before only rarely, and only for the most grievous of offenses.

"And what do you think you are doing?" his father demanded.

"Please, Father," he begged. "I was only trying to help the cub. It's hurt." Doto still cringed to think of the way he had groveled and pleaded back then. It was no way for a god to behave. Not even a young one. Small wonder that his father had felt scorn for him.

"And what of it?" Kwaee had snarled at him. "Why should this matter to you?"

He was terrified. Seldom had he ever seen his father so angry. "Because, I…" He didn't know the answer, could not explain why it mattered. "Because," he finally replied, "I can help. And then it will stop hurting."

"Sympathy." His father snorted at him. "You got that from your mother. And where is she now?"

He had felt tears in his eyes back then, strange things, hot and wet, soaking into the fur around his muzzle. It was hard now for him to recall them, the feelings that had prompted them. "Dead, Father."

"Dead," Kwaee had agreed. "Because of her own weakness. Is that what you want, Doto? To be dead, like your mother?"

Doto sniffled. "You said that a monster killed her. Can monsters come into the forest?"

"Not monsters, no," Kwaee said. His voice grew calmer, and he looked out into the forest, past Doto. "But healing will make you weak, Doto, so weak that I cannot protect you. Do you understand that? You think you can take away that little cub's pain. But you cannot. All you can do is move it.

Where is its mother? Do you intend to care for it for the rest of its life? Or will you leave it, healed, to starve?"

"I—" Doto began, but his father cut him off.

"And suppose it is healed, and survives. It will only die later on, of an injury, or starvation, or something else. You do not take the pain away. You only move it. And what of all the prey the cub will catch over its lifetime? What of all the times it will seize a bird in its teeth, or rake a rat with its claws? What of all that pain that now happens because you saved this cub's life? Is that what you want?"

His father's questioning made him feel frustrated and confused. "Father, no, I was not thinking of all those things. I only thought that there was a cub in pain, and I could help."

Kwaee's voice was gentle then, almost fond, and he had crouched to look Doto in the eyes, his golden-green gaze serious, his ears forward. "Listen to me, son. The gods enforce the laws of nature, and nature is merciless. If you are to be a god, then you must think of all these things—not only a single wounded cub, but the whole forest that it lives in. Those who are wounded and do not recover on their own must die. That is the way of things. It is how they must always be. You must promise me that you will never stand in the way of that. You must promise to me now that you will never, ever use your powers to heal another creature. Use them to serve your will. Use them to grow the forest. Turn the wind, fly on the wings of birds, ride the backs of elephants if you like. Eat anything and everything that appeals to you. But never, ever heal anything. To heal something is to give it your magic, and that magic belongs to gods, not beasts. Do you understand?"

Doto had not understood, but no would not be an acceptable answer. He had nodded, lowering his eyes. "Yes, Father."

Kwaee had taken Doto's chin in his paw, gripped it firmly, and turned his face upward, so that he looked into his father's eyes. "Promise me now. Promise me that you will never heal another living being's injuries."

"I promise, Father."

"Good."

His father had been strangely gentle with him that day, even fond. He had led Doto away. The little genet cub had lain where it had fallen, and its tiny cries for help had pierced through the forest, finding Doto's ears from far away, and his memory from farther still.

On reflection, Doto found his father's explanation unsatisfactory. Why should he not use his power to heal this fire bearer? How did it make him weak, if the bearer's dance only made him stronger, and healing made him able to dance? And what was so terrible about moving a little pain around, as long as it helped Doto to reach his goal sooner? He scowled down at the sleeping creature. This whole journey could have gone much swifter if he had just healed its wounded foot at the start. But then, he reminded himself, he was the one who had chosen an injured bearer. That was the way of things.

All the same, if the bearer seemed about to perish before they reached Kwaee's temple, he decided that he would disobey his father. He would mend the bearer's foot. Having to go all the way back to retrieve another fire bearer, simply because this one died, would smack of carelessness to Kwaee. Afterward, if the creature lived or died, that was none of Doto's concern.

Originally he had hoped to kill it, once Kwaee was done with it, but its story about its home being destroyed by fire was an unsettling one. If the bearers worked with Ogya, why would he destroy their home? Why would they seem to have no knowledge of their alliance with him? Doto had watched their nest for days, but he had never heard any special prayer or obeisance paid to the fire god, nor had he seen them starting fires beyond the little ones about the nest. Certainly they were not what he had imagined: great horned beasts that belched out black clouds and set everything they touched ablaze. And if that were not true, what else had Kwaee told him that might be false?

This last thought troubled him, so he discarded it as unhelpful. No. He would convey the fire bearer safely to Kwaee, as directed, and then let it live or die as it would. He would have no further use for it. He traced the feather sprouting from his brow. The touch of its soft edges was almost a tickle. He was pleased with his feather, and the dances. But if the fire bearer died, there would be no more dances. The new plants he could feel growing in his copse might die. The thought did not appeal to him.

He let his mind drift away again, into the life that made the forest a forest instead of bare earth. Somewhere, a porcupine lay dying. He resided in its mind, felt its heart struggle to beat, to push blood through its body; felt its breaths grow shallower, emptier, until the light of its awareness faded away. Bats dropped dead out of the air, their hearts failing. Birds tipped from trees and fell with splayed wings into matted leaves, *piff piff piff*. Monkeys clawed at their hides in debilitating fever and went still. An alligator, its tail caught in a tangle of roots beneath the great river, drowned. Mice were snatched up by owls, gobbled by golden cats. A thousand in a few minutes died from predation or starvation or exhaustion. Saplings asphyxiated from lack of sunlight. Grass was torn up by roving, hungry dik-diks. And all around him, a million million insects, each a bright, beady pinprick of desperate and flailing awareness, fell from the air or were crushed under-foot or were torn apart in the waging of their tiny insect wars. They were exploded by parasitic fungi, eaten by bats, by porcupines, by birds, by other insects, by everything. The forest flowed with death; it hummed with it. The sound of the dead raining down upon the forest floor was ever-present and unceasing.

But he did not want this fire bearer to die. Why not? What difference could it possibly make? He struggled to find the answer. If the fire bearer were to die, it would just lie on the ground. It would not dance for Doto, true, but also, it would not ask all its irritating questions. It would not ar-gue, nor limp, nor build fires, nor tell stories. It would be still, and be eaten by birds and insects and other beasts. Doto found himself discomfited by this thought. The forest might be empty, but it was less empty with the fire bearer in it.

Aloud, he made a small hiss at the irritating fire bearer for placing these sorts of unpleasant considerations in his mind. He decided he was tired of waiting any longer. They would continue. If the bearer did not limp too badly, perhaps they could be at Kwaee's temple before sunset. And then? Perhaps Kwaee would want to kill him. And then, Doto knew, there would be no trip to the mountains. Kwaee would stay in his temple, surly and reclusive. Nothing would change. The world would go on as it always had, and the fire bearer and everything he represented would be gone. Probably Doto's feather would fall out too. Back to the way things were. That was what he had to look forward to.

Rolling off the tree branch and dropping to the ground, he crawled forward on all fours and prodded at the bearer's shoulder with one paw. "Wake up," he instructed it.

The bearer groaned and rolled in its sleep.

Doto growled. "Wake up, fire bearer. It is time to go. The god of Clay commands you to wake up."

"Yes, Lord," it mumbled. It rubbed at its eyes and got to its feet, mov-ing stiffly.

"If we make haste, and Kwaee does not move his temple, then we may be there before sunset this day." Doto turned and set off, keeping his senses aware for how swiftly the bearer moved. The creature was often slower in the morning, after sleeping, but it hastened soon enough. It was limping worse today than yesterday, but if all went well, this would be the final day it was required to hurry on its injured leg.

Doto kept it moving, giving it a terse word of command whenever it fell too far behind, but he could tell that his captive was struggling to obey.

Still, with Doto's urgings, they made decent time. It was only around midday when Doto's ears pricked, picking up the distant roar of the Asubonten. His shoulders slumped, his tail going limp behind him. He had forgotten it entirely. With some difficulty, he could get himself across, but he could not manage the fire bearer as well. He had never had to consider the difficulties of traveling with a mortal creature before. He felt almost ashamed at all the things he had never understood. They needed rest. They needed food. And of course they could not cross huge stretches of water. He cursed himself for not thinking of it.

"Is something the matter, Lord Doto?"

At the question, he became aware that his pace had faltered. He straightened his back. He would not let the bearer know this had not been in his plans. "No. I am simply considering our best route forward. Normally I would continue straight, but with your foot, you may not be able to follow. We will see."

With that, he continued. The air grew muggier and thick with flies and mosquitos. These did not dare bother Doto, but his worshiper swore and slapped at them constantly. This was amusing for a time, but after a while, the biting insects were slowing the fire bearer's pace even further, and its constant exclamations, slapping, and scratching were becoming tiresome, and so Doto silently compelled the insects to leave Clay alone, and after that, they continued in relative peace.

As they approached the Asubonten, its roar steadily increased in volume, until finally they moved out of the trees onto the flood banks of the great river. Of all the rivers in the world, the Asubonten was the greatest. In places it was angry and swift, but here, it was fat and peaceful. Doto could step into water without bother, but the farther he moved into the river, the farther out of the jungle he walked. Were one able to step on the surface as on earth, the Asubonten could take a day's journey to cross at its widest, and at the pace he and the fire bearer had been traveling, it would be even longer. In the middle of these wide stretches, his power would grow weak, and he would be vulnerable. This was the greatest protection of Kwaee's temple, the barrier that Ogya's bearers could not cross. No fire could travel over the surface of the great river, nor even burn easily in the air near it. Neither could any land animal travel to the other side to bring Ogya's flame with it. And Doto, when he traveled across it, stepped out of the forest and into the domain of the river goddess.

The river here would not take a day to cross, but its far side was distant still, and while Doto's keen gaze could pick out details on the opposite shore, he doubted very much whether the fire bearer's weak eyes could see much of anything that far away. Even the trees on the other side would be a dark green hedge. In between was the river, brown with mud and blue with the sky and green with the trees. Despite its peaceful surface, it ran swiftly and with power. Skimmer birds banked their black and white wings over the water as they hunted for fish, and along the shores, martins and swallows clustered in enormous, whirling flocks, diving and swooping around each other as they feasted on insects.

Clay stared at the river in astonishment and, Doto noted to his surprise, fear. "Is this the great water?" he asked, his voice low and meek.

Doto snorted. "Do not be foolish," he said. "It is *a* great water, but it is not *the* great water that Sister Mpo rules. This is the river Asubonten, and all rain that falls anywhere in the world comes here."

Staring at the water with an apprehensive expression, Clay ventured, "Why have we come here, Lord Doto? Is this where Kwaee lives?"

Doto's tail twitched in amusement at the mere thought of such a thing—his father, rising, drenched, fur dripping, out of the muddy river. "Of course not. Kwaee's temple is on the other side. We must cross."

Still looking trepidatious, the fire bearer limped a little closer to the river, his eyes darting back and forth. "I have never seen so much water in all my life," he breathed in wonder. "I did not know so much water existed. But how are we to cross it? Can we wade through it?"

Doto actually laughed. "Wade? Certainly not. Bearer, that water covers a valley so deep that the water would be over the tops of trees if they grew there."

The bearer shuddered and shrank back toward Doto, putting a paw against his arm. Doto nearly shrugged it away—how dare it put its filthy fingers on him?—but then he decided that the creature was already injured, tired, and frightened enough. It would not be helpful to rebuff him just now.

"I can walk across the surface," Doto said airily, "being a god. You will have to…" He frowned. He tried to think of the word for "swim" in the bearer's tongue and could not summon it. There must not be a word for it. And why should there be? The fire bearers, minions of Ogya or not, lived out in the savanna. They would never have need of such a word; and if they could not say it, then certainly they could not do it. Even if they could, his fire bearer was injured. He gestured toward the wooden paw. "You will have to let me take care of your own passage across."

So that was it, then. Another challenge, another difficulty in complying with Kwaee's demands. Surely his father must have known this problem would present itself. Doto could not go back to him now and say, "Apologies, Father, I got him most of the way here, but then the river stopped us." No. Kwaee would accept no excuses. He would be angry, and cast Doto out into the empty forest, alone forever.

He frowned, pondering. Were the river narrow enough, he could simply carry the bearer across using the trees, but here, even if the giant trees of Dua Bera grew along the river banks, they would not be tall enough to help the bearer reach the opposite shore. Any journey up or downstream would be a time-consuming detour, with debatable outcome. Upstream, the river narrowed into a fast and winding course through a high-walled canyon. There it was narrower, but even more impassable than their current spot, and the path alongside it climbed up into mountains and more difficult terrain. Downstream it widened until, much farther away, it met a crashing series of cataracts and rapids that continued to the west for a journey of a dozen days at least. It would have to be here, or they would go so far out of their way that the bearer's injury would kill him before they ever reached Kwaee's temple.

He growled in annoyance at the river. Anything they might encounter in the forest, he could handle, but this was not his terrain. Well, perhaps he could make it his terrain. It would be dangerous, and might have consequences for him later, but it was the only way he could imagine continuing on their journey.

Stepping up to the edge, he crouched and set his paws on the ground. He sent his mind out into the earth, down deep into the muck and mud, and below. He burrowed his consciousness through clay and rock, finding the ground beneath the river. This, too, was not entirely his territory. The earth belonged to Mother Fam, as the sky to Father Wem, but earth and sky were in all places, and neither god guarded as jealously their territory. Earth and sky were shared with all. Doto found stone deep under the river. *Rise up*, he told it. *Rise, heap yourself higher, stretch your neck up to bathe in the water and dry in the sun.* He would raise up pillars of rock to make stepping stones for the fire bearer. He felt the cool of the water as stone obeyed, erupting through the silt of the riverbed into a rising pillar, and just as suddenly, he felt awareness and resentment from the river surging against him. This was what he had feared. Still, he encouraged the pillars of rock to elevate. His fur bushed out. The air hummed with electricity.

Then his power was cut off, his awareness of the stone going blind. The water of the river rose up before him in a great, silvery hump, and broke. Eyes breached the surface of the river, huge yellow circles each as wide across as Doto's reach from fingertips to toes, black slits for pupils. The water rushed away from dark green scales covering a massive head. Fanged jaws so large that they could nip up elephants for treats emerged, rivulets streaming from their sides. It was Asubonten herself, goddess of the river, the crocodile who drank the night, and she was angry.

She reared herself up to a great height, towering over the riverbanks, her shadow falling across Doto. He heard Clay cry out in terror, and looked over one shoulder to see the fire bearer scrambling backward, nearly tripping over his feet in an attempt to get away, but never daring to tear his gaze from the monstrous goddess.

Water poured around Doto as she tipped her head down to regard him. He deflected the streams with a casual nudge of his power. The goddess stank of river muck and fish.

"Why do you meddle with the bottom of my river, little godling?" she demanded. She spoke in the language of the gods, her voice hard and bold, with only a hint of the croak of the crocodile beneath it. It was so loud that Doto folded his ears back involuntarily, and like a waterfall, it drowned out the cries of birds and the sound of wind.

He did not appreciate being called godling. "Because I must cross your waters, Sister Asubonten." He put emphasis on the word sister, to remind her that in the eyes of Father Wem, they were equals.

"Must you, now?" she asked. Her voice was calm, but deafening in volume, and coming from jaws that could snap up his entire copse in a few bites, it did not sound calm at all. "And this requires you to pierce my bed with your stones, does it? Do you think I will be pleased with your little mountains burrowing through my blood and altering my flow, hmm? Why do you not simply skip across my skin like a strider bug, as you have done so many times before?"

"Sister Asubonten, if my tiny stones have disrupted the flow of your great river, I beg humble apologies." The goddess was in a poor temper, and she would not appreciate his needling, but he had found her remarks unduly patronizing.

He oughtn't have antagonized her. The goddess lifted her great scaled tail up from the river, sending birds arcing away from it alarm, water pouring to either side. So massive was her body, so long her tail, that the far end of it was shrouded in mist and haze from the river. Then she slapped it down against the surface of the water, the thunderclap that followed so deafening that Doto stumbled backward, clutching at his ears. Waves of water followed, massive walls many times taller than Doto himself, stunning birds out of the air, sending fish flying, flooding the banks of the river up and downstream.

"Nothing disrupts the flow of my river for long," Asubonten roared. "My might is greater than that of any other god. Let Kwaee put his temple in my path, and I will scour it from the earth. Let Ogya blaze the forest before me, and I will send him hissing into extinction. If Fam herself puts her earth and rocks in my way, I will wear them down. Water will always have its way, little godling. Remember that when you think to put yourself before my might. I can clean your muddy little spot of sticks off of Fam's face in the time it takes me to exhale."

"Then," Doto said calmly, "I will have to be sure to keep my little spot of sticks uphill of you."

The goddess glowered at him from one slitted eye. "Well then, why do you raise stones from my bed?"

"Certainly I could travel across your surface, but I have a captive I bring to Kwaee." Doto pointed back toward the fire bearer, who was sprawling, terrified, in the mud. He thought of the genet cub then, fallen where he had dropped it after the blow from his father, and ached with remembered pity.

Asubonten peered with interest. "So you have. And what is it you have brought to Sister Asubonten? A fire bearer, is it? So. Kwaee has decided to scratch at that old itch, has he?" She settled down into the river, lowering through no means that Doto could discern, waves surging up onto the banks as she sank. "And he has his little cub to do all his hunting for him. Well, well. It has been a long time since anyone saw any of their sort around. How did he even know they were about any more? I thought he did not turn his eyes outward anymore. Always he stays woven up in his little basket of trees."

Doto's fur bristled across his chest and back. Little cub? How dare she? "It was I who alerted Kwaee to the return of the fire bearers," he informed her, "as it is I who governs much of the forest in his stead."

Asubonten gave a great, heaving chucking, her deep voice booming through him. "And yet your own divine terrain is still so tiny. Just a little grove I could squash beneath my belly."

Flushing, Doto forced himself not to rise to her insults. The goddess was not always in such an ill temper; on some days, she could be quite pleasant. But that was the way of the river, tempestuous or peaceful, depending on the day. He attempted to engage her again. "I am sure you too will see the importance of the news I bring about the return of the fire bearers."

The goddess waved a scaled paw, her webbed fingers flicking river water and muck into the trees, sending them swaying and cracking. "The fire bearers do not concern me. That is your father's war, godling, not mine. Let them come. Let them burn the forest. It does not worry me. They will not burn my waters."

"True," Doto said, "but what of when the rains wash the ash of my father's corpse into your waters and make it thick with sludge? What of when your fish die, and your insects boil, and your birds starve? My father has told me of the rivers that once flowed through the north. Where are they now?"

Asubonten hissed in a deep breath. "Gone," she admitted. "Nothing but sand and bone now. Ogya grew so strong that his blaze kept even Wem out, and no more rains came to feed the rivers. True. But the fire bearers will not come this far south. Things were different, then."

"Perhaps," Doto allowed. He had not existed in the time the goddess spoke of. If things had indeed been different, he had no idea how. "But in case things are not so different as you think, it is best if I bring this fire bearer to Kwaee. He will know what to do."

The goddess chuckled again at that. "Oh, I suppose he will. Kwaee always knows what to do with fire bearers, doesn't he?"

Uncertain as to her meaning, Doto did not respond to this. "So you see that I must bring the fire bearer across you, as he wishes."

With a slight rise up out of the water, Asubonten leaned forward to peer at Clay, who emitted a low groan of fear and crawled backward even farther from the river banks. Her great nares widened as she sniffed at the air. "The one you have brought is sick. He will not live for a very long time."

Her cavernous jaws gaped. "You should give him to me, and go and fetch another one. I will make sure this one does not go to waste."

Deciding he did not care to argue with her any longer, Doto shook his head. "No. It will take far too much time. I have come a long way already. I will not go back and fetch another, only for you to stop me at the river again. I must cross. If you do not wish me to raise stones so that my captive and I can reach your far shore, then perhaps you will stretch out from one bank to the other so that we may journey across you."

The goddess seemed to smile at that, but her jaws were always grinning, no matter her temperament. Nonetheless, there was a trace of amusement in her voice when she answered, "You have grown much bolder than when I first met you, godling. The trait suits you well. But no. I will not let anything interrupt my path, and certainly I will not lie across my own body. That is a forest sort of thing to do. Always the forest fights itself. Beast devours beast, tree fights tree for sunlight, son and father spar. It is in your blood and bark, little copse, and it is both what makes you fierce, and keeps you small. You wage war on yourself. But I am the river, and the river never fights itself. The river goes where it goes, with all its might rushing to meet the sea. No force can oppose it. Not even me."

"Then how am I to reach my father?" Doto asked in exasperation. "Your waters are a tooth cutting into the heart of our forest, splitting us into two. Tell me some place I can take my captive to the other side."

Asubonten leaned down very close to him, her webbed fingers squeezing into the mud of the riverbank, her jaws a great cave filled with jagged stone. Her fetid breath blasted his fur back as she spoke, but he stood straight and unflinching before her. "It is a poor sort of god indeed who cannot find a way across a river with his pet ape. How you cross is of no concern to me, as long as you do so without interrupting my path. Do not think I do not know how your father steals from me. His trees and bushes suck up the water that is rightfully mine. His forests grow fat on the rains that would make me grow stronger. So go, little copse. Find your own path."

She turned to sink back into the river. Doto started forward, the flush burning in his cheeks, but before he could think of what to say, Clay stepped past him. The fire bearer's scent was sharp with fear, but he strode as though he did not feel it.

"Great Asubonten," he said in his own language. "I am not worthy to stand before you."

She paused, regarding him with one curious, yellow eye, one foot in the river, her jaws parted. When she spoke again, it was in the fire bearer's tongue as well. "You have heard of me, fire bearer?" Surprise registered in her voice.

Dropping to his knees on the muddy river banks, the fire bearer bowed low, as he had to Doto on the night he had been taken. "All my people have heard of you, great Asubonten. Your tales are from long ago, but none could forget them. Are you not Asubonten, who carries the rains to the great waters so they do not drown us all?"

Doto felt a strange emotion prickling through him. He did not want his fire bearer prostrating before this goddess who had just refused and insulted him. He put one paw on the bearer's shoulder, tugging him up. "Here. That is no concern of yours. You are my captive, not hers."

"Leave him be," the goddess roared in fury at him. The force of her breath and voice was so great that it nearly toppled Doto backward, and behind her, the river swelled in sympathetic anger. His ears went back, his tail switching behind him, but he let his bearer go. Perhaps she could learn for herself how troublesome his captive could be.

In a grand tone, Asubonten said, "It pleases me to know that I am still remembered by your people. I feel their praise still, sometimes."

"And gladly it is given," the bearer said earnestly. When he spoke his next words, they gained that electric clarity that he could sometimes invest in them. "Mighty Asubonten, the wonder of beholding you staggers me. In an instant, you could flood me away, or quench a lifetime of thirst. Please grant us a way to journey onward without being swept away by your power. Show us the path forward, so that I may meet this night with blessing."

Doto turned his head to the side in annoyance at this foolishness, but the goddess gave a little shiver. The water in the river calmed, lying flat and still, so motionless it looked as though it did not even flow.

"It has been long since I heard such a prayer, fire bearer," Asubonten said. Her eyes were unfocused and distant with recollection. "To me it is like fresh rain. Alas, even by my will I cannot still my waters enough that you might cross. But there is one place where crossing would be easier, and it is not very far from here. You might try continuing your journey there."

Search his memory though he might, Doto could not think of any place she might be referring to. "Where is that?" he demanded, stepping in front of the bowing fire bearer. "What is this place? Why did you not mention it before?"

"Abansin," the great crocodile said, eyeing him. "Take him to Abansin." She eased back into the water, ripples moving away from her giant body beneath its surface. "Farewell, fire bearer." Gulls lit on her head, and then flew off again as she sank. "May you fare better with Kwaee than the others did."

Then she was gone.

‸‸‸

"But what did she mean, the others?" Clay asked for the third time. He was wincing with his steps. Their journey was difficult going for him now, and had been for much of the afternoon. They were following the river upstream, but the way was steep, and he seemed to tire quite easily. Doto had to be judicious in selecting their route, choosing paths that were not too filled with boulders, nor ones that ended in cliff faces that needed climbing. The fire bearer's ability to jump was woefully inadequate, and even small rises that a leopard or deer could make easily gave him enormous trouble. Twice now Doto had instructed lianas to coil about him and hoist him up some of the more difficult climbs, but in many places, suitable plants did not grow nearby. Always next to them, Asubonten roared, gushing down massive cataracts. To Doto, the voice of the river sounded faintly mocking. His tail lashed when he considered how she had spoken to him.

"I told you already," he answered Clay. "She was deceiving you, trying to make you fight me, because that sort of thing amuses her. There have been no others." At least, he considered, not as long as he had been alive. The encounter with the goddess had troubled him, and not only because of her rudeness. She had hinted at knowledge of events he did not share, and that made him uncomfortable. What he did not know, he could not guard against. Nor could he be certain of not appearing foolish in front of his captive. He turned and took the bearer's paw in his own, hoisting him up a small cliff face. The wooden foot was not much good for climbing.

"Our tales are full of the gods playing tricks on each other. But she sounded like she was talking of something specific. Does she mean when the fire bearers burned the forest, like in your stories?"

"That is possible. A forest will not let itself be burned without fighting back. Kwaee would not have been friendly to the fire bearers."

"Oh," Clay replied in a small voice. For a while, he was blessedly silent, his thoughts, whatever they might be, his own.

He was probably worrying about what Kwaee would do to him when they got there. But that was only because Doto had frightened him with his threats, telling him how he was a great enemy, how Kwaee hated him. This might have been the case before. Almost certainly. He thought of how much he had hated the bearer at first, yearned simply to kill it and be rid of it.

But now the bearer could tell Kwaee of how his village had burned, of how his people served all the gods. His father would have to understand. Doto had worried that Clay might not have the nerve to explain himself to Kwaee, but after seeing how boldly he had confronted Asubonten, he had fewer concerns about that. The fire bearer had proven to be surprising. Surely his father would see that. He must.

"What is this place, Abansin?" Clay asked, stirring him from his contemplations. "You looked unhappy about it."

Doto sighed. "I am unhappy," he answered, "because it means a detour from our journey. I had hoped to have you in Kwaee's temple tonight." This was not entirely true. If they could cross the river in Abansin, it would be a detour, but only one of perhaps a day or two. But he did not wish to go to Abansin. It was an abandoned section of the forest, chaotic. Kwaee kept his eyes away from nearly all of the forest now, but even on those rare times when he did turn his gaze out and see the scope of his domains, he never looked into Abansin. He had told Doto never to go there, never to look into it, and never to speak of it. Once, Doto had dared peek inside, but without Kwaee's care, it had grown strange, godless and forsaken. The laws of nature had forgotten it, and after one look, Doto had avoided it as well.

"So it is just a narrow part of the river?"

"No," Doto said. "It is an old place, and unusual. I have seen it only once, and I do not like it."

"Oh." The slope they were ascending now was easier, but Clay still had to grip at roots and bushes to make his way up. He was panting with exertion. "How is it unusual?"

Uncomfortably, Doto answered, "It is a place forgotten by the gods."

"How can it be forgotten if everyone knows about it?"

"Because we choose to forget it," Doto said.

Clay paused for breath, then asked, "Why would gods choose to forget anything?"

"That is a question for gods, and not for fire bearers."

He had hoped that this would silence Clay, but his captive insisted on peppering him with questions about the place as they traveled, until finally, he told him that he would see it soon enough, and he would have to be silent until then.

They ascended along the side of the riverbank until they were quite high up. Clay, who said he had never seen any hill that was close to this high, kept giving fearful glances down the slopes, and when they drew close to the bluffs, he clutched anxiously at Doto's sides. Doto stood tall and strong then, assisting Clay with a steady paw. In general, he did not care for being touched, but it pleased him that the fire bearer trusted so completely in his strength.

After a time, the slopes leveled out, and they traveled over more or less even terrain. Great Asubonten had cut her river deep into the earth up here, winding it between high cliff walls. The sun was beginning to dip in the sky when the silhouette of Abansin finally came into view. It sat at the top of a hill, overlooking the river, the rising moon behind it. Doto shuddered when he saw it. Stone had defied nature here, spreading out huge and rising in broad, flat segments, tapering to a point at the top. The place was all angles and shapes. It was like a giant stone leopard ear, thrust up out of the ground, pricked toward the sky. Below, in the forest that clustered around its base, were many other odd stone formations, the curves and points of their unnatural surfaces only hinted at from between the grip of the trees.

Clay gaped when he saw the silhouette. "What is it?" he breathed.

"Abansin," Doto answered. "And we must go there."

His fur stood on end as they traveled closer. Soon they could make out the shapes of the smaller stones hidden in the trees, arranged in rows. They were squared and hollow, and vines and roots twisted in and out of them like clutching fingers. Each would be big enough to walk inside of without difficulty, though the thought of doing so made Doto's flesh crawl.

Clay's face lit up when he saw the place. "It can't be. Lord Doto, it can't be!"

"And yet it is." Doto tried to tear his eyes away from the place, and could not. There was more wrong with it than just the strange stones. The forest was confused, there. Hostile. Mad.

"But these are buildings! Some people made these to live in."

Doto stared at him in astonishment and confusion. "That is not a true thing. I have seen what your people live in. The mushroom things."

"Tents, yes, we live in tents. But we did not always. We made homes out of wood and straw and clay. And in other places, my father said, they make homes out of stone. He drew pictures for us."

"No fire bearers have lived in the forest," Doto said. "Perhaps they have copied their own buildings from what is here."

"But how could that be true, if they never saw them?"

Doto said nothing. The fire bearer's questions were troubling, and any answer he might give could seem ignorance.

They continued on, moving further into Abansin. The terrain prohibited them traveling close to the river here, so Doto was forced to guide them in the unnaturally straight paths between the buildings instead. As they progressed, so the wrongness of the place intensified. The air felt thick in places, and moving through it was more like wading than walking. Stones shifted beneath Doto's paws as though slippery. Grass bent too easily in places, like fur, and in other places it jutted up stubbornly as though made of wood. The sounds of bird calls were too deep, guttural, and what few insects buzzed through the air careened erratically.

"You're right about this place," Clay said, with unease in his voice. "I don't know what it is. The trees, maybe. They grow at strange angles. It's like my eyes don't want to see them, somehow. It hurts to look at them."

"It is everything," Doto told him. "Everything is wrong here. This is what happens to a place when a god stops tending it."

"Yes," Clay agreed, "but more than that. I think...I think something terrible happened here. Look at the buildings, all full of holes. And see how the trees and vines are woven in and out of them? They've actually cracked the stone."

"Trees can break stone with time. It takes many years, but I have seen it."

"But do they grow sideways to do it?" Clay pointed out buildings where trees had seemingly bent at right angles to puncture the walls, then grown upright again. Others he indicated were encaged and crumpled inward beneath the bases of trees. "Or lift up their roots to crush them? And vines, can they grow cleanly through stone like that?"

"It is possible," Doto said. "Everything is wrong here, as I said." But he shuddered again, and did not stare at the buildings. Beneath their feet as they walked were broad stones, flat and square, joined together. He did not care to feel their surface against the pads of his feet. Clay's wooden foot made clicking sounds against them as they walked.

"It is a road," Clay said, catching his stare at the strange intersections of lines in the flat rock. "People build them to walk on, I have heard. I am certain that people—that fire bearers lived here." He pointed to odd, squat objects of stone. "Stools for sitting on. And fire circles. And I have seen spears and knives lying about."

"Fire circles in the forest?" Doto said scornfully. "Kwaee would never have allowed that. It must be something else." The air had begun to carry his own voice differently. Now, instead of his deep, confident pitch, it sounded twisted, high and thin.

Clay looked back at him with worry, and the curled black hairs on the back of his neck lifted as though he had hackles to raise.

The buildings were placed ever closer together the farther they traveled into Abansin. They crowded the sides of the path, their shapes even more distorted in the slanted sunlight of the early evening. Doto turned to peer into their dark openings, but then imagined the hollow, glittering eyes of forgotten fire bearers staring back at him, and quickly looked away. His eyes scanned the trees: twisted into unnatural shapes, their bark was gnarled and malformed. Their branches were stunted, worn and rounded in peculiar ways. The grass, too, was frayed around the edges. Moss hung unevenly off the stone structures. The plants weren't decayed. Like stone, they were worn, eroded. His brow furrowed.

"Nothing grows here," he realized aloud. "And nothing dies. The trees are the same as those that grew here many ages ago. The grass under your feet is many lifetimes old."

"How can that be?" Clay stepped closer to his side and looked about fearfully.

Doto shook his head. "The forest grows and withers because the forest god makes it grow and wither. When there is no god to tend it, everything stops."

"But you are here now," Clay pointed out. He turned to look back, and then brushed his fingers against Doto's side. "Look." On the road behind them, thick patches of green had sprouted up, bunched grass and bright flowers and twisting vines. "Your footsteps," he said, and in the middle of the last word, his voice dropped into a deep, barely intelligible growl. He clapped his paw to his mouth with a horrified expression. "What is it?" he rumbled.

"The wrongness of the place," Doto told him, his own voice high and almost birdlike in comparison. He folded his ears, hating the sound of it.

"Can you fix it?"

"It will go away when we are through," Doto answered, although he was not entirely certain that was true.

"No." Clay's voice sounded so deep that it might have been the bellow of Asubonten, were it not so quiet. The timbre of it obviously distressed him. "I mean, can you fix this place? If it needs a god's attention, maybe you can heal it."

Doto considered. "With time," he decided. "Not now. Now we must get through, before this place disturbs you too greatly."

They followed the road. It met intersections, branching off into side roads, which were lined with even more buildings. The place was large, far larger than Kwaee's temple. Had this been some sort of temple for another god? For the fire bearers themselves? Or only a giant nest?

Occasionally the fire bearer would exclaim over some object he recognized, such as earth or stone that had been shaped into hard, curved surfaces—pottery, he called it. There were animal hides here and there, like those that the fire bearers wrapped themselves with, worn and somewhat bare, but showing little signs of rot. Carved bits of wood were everywhere, fashioned into configurations that must have had some functional purpose. Doto did not ask Clay about them. He wanted never to return here, to have nothing to do with this place ever again. Besides, neither of them cared to speak and hear the alien voices that came from their throats.

The shadow of the large, pointed structure rose before them, and the road widened into a broad square, filled with stone structures, including perfectly round, stone tree trunks that rose high above their heads. The path ahead was filled with bones. Clay gave a sudden, booming cry of dismay and rushed forward in his limping gait, falling to his paws and knees before a heap of them.

The bones were all of the same species, and from their shapes and Clay's reaction, Doto guessed that they were the bones of fire bearers. They were still stained dark brown with blood and stray meat that had never rotted away, but they had been picked clean by scavengers. Skulls gazed bewilderedly from wherever they had fallen, limbs splayed wide where they had been dragged by predatory teeth. There were thousands of them. They clustered in piles, mounded around the pillars, spread to the surrounding buildings. Doto's keen eyes could make out more figures inside the buildings, some of their round heads still undecayed, their limbs raised to the walls as if clutching at them in terror.

There could be no doubt as to what had killed the creatures: the forest itself had slaughtered them. Vines twisted in and out of the skeletons, thrust through ribcages, coiling snakelike through jaws and eye sockets. Saplings had burst through the stone paving of the square and speared bodies where they stood. Skulls were crushed by roots thrust up between the stones. One skeleton lay fallen halfway beneath one of the broad stones, as though something had seized its legs and begun pulling it underneath. Doto looked up toward the tree branches, and saw long bones still entwined in their wooden limbs—legs or arms, perhaps.

Clay made as if to touch a nearby bone, and then jerked his fingers away. "What could have done this?" he asked, his voice mercifully normal in pitch for the moment, though shaking.

There was nothing to say. Doto had seen Abansin before, but never looked inside, never traveled so far within as to find this spot. And there was only one thing that could have caused such devastation. Hearing it, though, would do his fire bearer no good, so he did not answer. Instead, he admitted, "I did not know this was here. I have never been inside Abansin before." He did not know how Clay would respond to this confession. A god should know everything. He should not admit ignorance. Ignorance was weakness.

The fire bearer did not acknowledge his admission, however. He simply stared out through the forest for a few moments, then stood, took a few deep breaths, and then asked, "Which way from here, Lord Doto?" He kept his gaze away from the bones scattered across the flat rock around them.

Doto pointed across the square. "The path will go down to the river. There we will find the stone tongue, and we can cross over that."

They picked their way across the square, Clay taking special care to avoid nearing and especially touching the bones. He smelled of fear again, and kept casting nervous glances toward the vines and trees lest they come alive again. Doto could have told him there was no need to worry; that if not infused with the will of their forest god, they would not move; neither growing nor shedding a single leaf that the wind did not tear from them. He could see no way in which explaining this would help. Besides, he reminded himself, he did not need Clay to be comfortable in order to transport him to Kwaee. He required only obedience.

They passed beneath the shadow of the huge, pointed building, and the road widened, heading into a slope downhill. As Doto had expected, this path would lead to the river. He was grateful to leave the bones behind him. There was nothing particularly upsetting about carcasses, fire bearers or otherwise, but Clay was right: something terrible had happened there, and the echoes of it were everywhere. Doto did not care to imagine what mad things the twisting of nature here might do with a lot of old fire bearer bones.

Clay was silent but for the clicking of his wooden foot against the stone, all the way down the road to the river. The farther they traveled from the center of Abansin, the more the ambient strangeness abated. Sounds returned to their natural pitch; the air no longer felt like thick honey in Doto's lungs. At the bottom of the hill, the river rushed swiftly and furiously through its narrow canyon, its roar a welcome, ordinary sound, for all it reminded Doto of Asubonten's haughtiness. Across the canyon, the stone tongue jutted, a spit of rock that arched over the river like a fallen tree, the gap to the far side wide enough that few would be able to leap across. An antelope might manage it, but not a leopard, and certainly not a fire bearer. Doto could get across easily of course, but still he did not care for it. It looked as though it ought to collapse in the middle and plunge into the swift waters below, and what power prevented it from doing so, he could not discern.

If the fire bearer was impressed or astonished by the stone tongue, he made no sign of it. He had been apparently incapable of remaining silent for any length of time during most of their journey, even when chastised, but now Doto found himself wishing he would just say something.

"We cross here," he told Clay. He walked up to the edge of the stone tongue and peered down. The river churned below, hungry and deep. Falling in would not kill him; as long as his temple survived, he could not die, but he could be carried a long way away, into territory where his powers were weak. He did not like to stare down into another god's domain. The far side of the river had another, shorter tongue protruding from its banks, its edges broken and jagged. He could grow the two pieces together again. The connection would be thinner, but he could make it hold.

Crouching, he braced his paws against the stone and sent himself into to it. *Out, out,* he sent to the stone, but as the feelers of his divine senses moved out and toward the stone, they were repelled. He could feel the air about, the moss and algae growing on the rock, the tiny sprouts of grass jutting up from the cracks, but not the stone itself. His mind slid past it as though it were not there. He frowned at the stone's implicit insolence. For whatever reason, his power could not affect it. Perhaps it was stone brought from the sea—Mpo's stone. Its very presence unnerved him. He stood at the gap and stared to the far side.

"This stone is no good for my magic," he told Clay. "I will toss you across. It is not so far that you might hurt yourself." He measured out the width of the tongue. Yes. The opposite side was broad enough that there was little risk of Clay falling off either edge.

Click, click, click. He turned to see the fire bearer shuffling backward, casting wide-eyed glances toward the river below. "Don't throw me across," Clay begged, his paws raised. "I'll fall. I'll fall into the water and die."

The acrid odor of his fear stung Doto's nostrils. "I will not let you fall," he said, trying to sound reassuring. "I can easily throw you to the other side. You will be fine." He strode back down the tongue and took Clay's wrist in his paw, tugging him firmly toward the gap. The fire bearer snatched his paw away.

"I changed my mind." His voice was rapid, panicked. "I don't want to go across the river. I don't want you to throw me across. I don't want to go see Kwaee. Please don't make me. He's going to kill me, Doto. I know he's going to kill me."

Doto tried to make his voice reasonable. "Kwaee is not going to kill you, fire bearer. He specifically told…he specifically requested that I bring you to him alive."

"No," Clay said, shaking his head, still backing away. "You saw up there. You saw the bones. He killed them. He killed all of them. There must have been hundreds of people. That's what Asubonten meant when she talked about the others. She meant all those people that Kwaee killed in Abansin."

"That might be true." Doto said the words slowly, reluctant to voice them and give them reality.

In a despairing voice, Clay continued, "It's like you said before. The gods hate us."

"The gods do not hate you," Doto said, thinking quickly. "It is the fire bearers of old that they hated, those who burned the forest, who aided Ogya. These must have been who Kwaee killed."

"How can you think that is true?" Clay shook his paws toward the canopy. "Those people were *living* there. They had homes made of stone, not tents they could pick up and leave with. Stone buildings that must have taken many, many rains to make. Why would they burn the forest around their own home?"

"Because they served Ogya. And they would have done anything that he commanded them. Minions of Ogya do not need the forest to survive. They need only ash and sand and heat." Privately, he doubted his own words. The fire bearer was right; these creatures had been living there for some time. How could any beings live so deep in the heart of the forest, be surrounded by the pulse of its life, eat and drink of it, breathe its air for so long, and yet still serve the god of the desert?

"But you think I serve Ogya too," Clay said. "Only Ogya. You call me fire bearer. You said you would kill me and all my people. You think I want to burn the forest down."

"But I don't think that anymore!" Doto realized he had raised his voice. He felt, he realized, like when his father had accused him of some imagined crime or fault. He was better than this. He needed to show Clay that he was. And yet he was sounding like a fool. "I have heard your stories, and you have told me how Ogya destroyed your village. I have seen how you behave. You light fires, but you burn only dead wood. Whatever your people are, you, at least, are not one of Ogya's minions from the tales of the past." He realized the truth of his next words as soon as he spoke them. "You danced for me, Clay. I believe you. And I will tell Kwaee that I believe you too."

Not quite understanding why he did so, he reached out and took Clay's paw in his own, enfolding the slender, brown fingers in his thick, furred grip. "I promise you that Kwaee will not kill you. And I promise that I will not let you fall."

Clay's brown eyes gazed searchingly into his own. "All right."

Doto nodded, resolute. "All right." He led Clay back up the stone tongue. Their pace was slow, for the bearer was still full of fear, taking short, timid steps, his wooden paw clicking on the stones. By the time they reached the gap, the bearer was clinging close to his side, fingers clutching at the fur on Doto's chest and back.

Below them, the river surged, spittle-white around dark rocks that jutted up from the bed, worn smooth by time and water. Its roar was merciless and unceasing.

"I'm going to take you by the waist and leg," Doto said, shouting above the sound of the water, "and swing you once, and then toss you across. I'll land you right on the stone on the far side. It is not so far a distance that it should hurt you. Just land on all fours. Do not run or roll when you come down. You will be fine."

"Please, no," Clay murmured. His voice was low, but Doto's keen ears had no trouble picking up his words. "I'm afraid."

"That is good," Doto shouted. "It will make your reflexes faster." He disengaged Clay's clutching paws from about him. The bearer struggled and tried to cling again, but he was no match for a god's strength. "Do not hold onto me when I toss you, or you could alter my aim." Clay stiffened and then went still.

Doto had no concern that he might miss with his toss, unless Clay thrashed or squirmed at the last second. He hefted the fire bearer, hooking his right arm about Clay's waist, left around his leg. He broadened his stance for leverage, setting his toes against the stone. Clay shook in his grip like a frightened hare. He swung back, then took a swift step forward and pitched Clay through the air, stepping back again quickly to catch his balance, his tail jerking to the left. Like a monkey leaping across tree branches, Clay arced through the air, turning as he did so. He came down on two feet, not four, and there was a cracking sound. The wooden foot snapped, and his leg slid beneath him, bending sharply. Both arms flailing, he pitched to one side and dropped toward the waters below like a diving bird.

When Doto wished to, he could move very quickly. He wished to.

A loud, creaking, rustling sound came from somewhere in front of him—almost a roar—but he had no time to pay attention to it. He streaked to the edge of the gap, braced his toes against the lip, and bounded across, catching the far side with one paw. With the other he caught Clay's wrist, the fire bearer's weight bouncing hard in his grip. They swung out over the river, only Doto's firm grip on the stone precipice keeping them from dropping into the roiling water below. His tail whipped about for balance. Clay cried out in panic as they teetered over the brink, reaching up to grab at Doto's paw with his own free one, clinging tightly to it. His brown eyes were wide. "Don't let me fall," he begged. "Please don't let me fall."

"I am keeping you from falling," Doto pointed out crossly, and then the edge of the stone tongue cracked under his fingers, the rock partly dislodging under his weight. He wasn't sure what to do. With only one arm, he couldn't climb back onto the rock, and it wouldn't respond to his power. Clay's fingers dug into his paw.

"Hold tight," he said. "I am going to swing you up. When you reach the edge, grab on and hang there. Then I can climb up and pull you to safety."

Clay's fingers slipped in his grip, and the bearer hoisted himself up again, catching hold of his wrist. "I don't think I can grab it," he said.

"You have to. Ready." Doto ignored Clay's protests and pulled him back into a swing, but with the shifting motion, the rock he was clinging to broke again beneath his fingertips, and gave way. He scrabbled for a grip, dropping a little, the weight of the bearer yanking at his arm as he caught himself on another piece of stone. The falling rock bounced against his side and dropped into the river with a small splash. Swinging was not going to work, then.

"Please don't let me fall please don't let me fall please don't let me fall." Clay reached higher, trying to climb up his arm.

"Don't do that," Doto growled. "You're going to make me slip." Even as he was saying the words, he changed his mind. "Wait. No. Can you climb up my arm and put your arms around my neck?" he asked.

"I don't know," Clay said, even as he reached up higher to try again. His paw squeezed at Doto's arm and slid down to the wrist again. "Your fur is too slippery. Can you bend your arm up?"

Doto was not thickly built and heavily muscled like the lions of the savanna. He was lithe and compact, but he was a god, and his strength knew no limits. With Clay dangling from his wrist, he curled his arm upward. Paw over paw, the fire bearer climbed toward his elbow like a monkey swinging from a tree branch, and then Doto lifted his arm higher so that Clay could reach his shoulder and neck. With some difficulty, Clay managed to climb up and reach around Doto's neck, his brown-skinned thighs encircling his waist, just like that first night when he'd ridden on Doto's back, unable to find his way through the dark woods. Doto reached up with his free paw and grabbed onto the edge of the stone tongue just as the rock he'd been holding began to give. With both paws for leverage, he was able to pull both himself and Clay up onto the solid surface.

Clay slid off of his back onto the stone, then rose to his paws and knees, panting heavily.

Doto got to his feet and frowned at the stone tongue. "I think we should get off of this unnatural thing before more pieces of it break out from under us."

Clay didn't answer. He was gazing out at the forest with an odd expression. "You said you wouldn't let me fall," he said in a dreamy tone.

"And I didn't," Doto agreed. "I—" He broke off as he followed Clay's gaze. The road traveled off into the forest only a short distance before breaking up into individual stones, swallowed up by tree roots and bushes and mounding earth. But the forest itself had moved since the last time he had looked at it. Every blade of grass, every vine, every stalk and stem and sapling and trunk was canted toward the river, trees leaning so far they looked as though they must be broken, leaves and branches all extended, reaching out toward the exact place that Clay had toppled over the edge of the stone.

That had been the strange creaking and rustling sound that Doto had heard just as he made his leap across the gap. It had been the forest itself seized with the power of his will, reaching out with all its fingers to catch Clay, just as Doto had promised.

They made camp once they had put enough of a distance between themselves and Abansin. They would not reach Kwaee's temple that day, and darkness was setting in. Still, Doto could feel Kwaee's closeness, a prickle in his fur. They were on the edge of the awareness of the forest god now.

So close to the end of their journey, Doto felt an optimism that surprised him. Temperamental his father might be, but Doto had done exactly as he asked, and better, would be bringing only good news. He had a live fire bearer, not only able to answer questions, but willing. And the answers to those questions were the best answers they could have hoped for. The fire bearers no longer served Ogya—at least not in the slavish devotion they once had. They were well-disposed to the forest god and eager to serve him. They would not burn the forest—would not even consider it, for to do so would be to destroy their shelter and food. The old enemy was gone after all. What better news could he deliver?

He thought of his father's promise. Worthy, he had said Doto would be. Worthy to sit at his side. They would rule together. He played the old dream over in his mind, his own moabi tree next to his father's. They would talk. They would hunt together again, as they had sometimes when Doto was a cub. And then...

And then what? The dream tasted stale in his mouth. He stroked the feather on his forehead, looking over toward Clay.

His fire bearer had been quiet that night. Doto thought it inadvisable to allow him to build a fire so close to the temple, and especially on the other side of the Asubonten, so he fetched more edible fruits and roots for him, but Clay had barely eaten anything. Sitting in the moonlight, he stared at the sky or off in the distance, to the north, back the way they had come.

The wooden foot had cracked severely from his bad landing on the stone tongue, and so Doto fashioned another from khaya wood. The wound stank so badly that he flattened his ears and turned his nose away from it. The flesh was purpled and swollen, and the blood in the veins around it was dark, spidering up his leg in ugly patterns. Doto knew this would be the last time he would make a wooden foot for the fire bearer. Even if Clay lived for days more, he would not walk on this leg again. It was almost useless. There would be no more dancing, either.

Doto would sit on his throne next to his father, and the fire bearer would die. And then what good would his throne be? His father might let him claim the fire bearer as a prize, perhaps. He might even forgive the transgressions of the fire bearers and allow them safety in his forest. But he would never, ever allow Doto to heal Clay's foot. It was forbidden magic. Gods did not carry scars, but his muzzle burned with remembered pain. No. The fire bearer would never dance again, and he would die. Doto said nothing to him of this, but a strange heaviness settled across his shoulders and in his chest.

And when after a time of sitting by himself, Clay came over and sat next to him, and leaned against his side, he neither scolded the bearer nor pushed him away, but instead put his arm across the smooth brown back next to him. To his surprise, a little of that heaviness across his shoulders lightened.

The next morning, however, his thoughts were still troubled. He had sat on a tree branch while Clay slept and watched him, knowing he might not have another chance. Clay must have sensed his mood, because he was quiet most of the morning. They traveled in silence together.

Doto made certain to walk more leisurely, slower than their pace had been the entire journey so far. In part, this was because of Clay's injury, which was now so severe that he could only hobble at a faltering pace. Doto kept beside him, sometimes allowing the bearer to lean on him, enjoying the feeling of the bearer's arm on his shoulder. But that arm was unusually warm to the touch, and Clay's breathing shallower. He had eaten nothing this morning, saying that he wasn't hungry.

Doto found he was in no particular hurry to arrive at his father's temple, either, and so was content not to rush. Around mid-morning, Clay stumbled and fell, and was too weak to get up again, and so Doto crouched and lifted him with both arms, carrying him against his chest.

Clay's fingers brushed against his cheek softly. "You could have carried me like this the first night, when I couldn't walk, and I couldn't hold onto your back."

"It is not how one carries one's prey," Doto said. "I would never have done so."

The fire bearer smiled and rested his head against Doto's shoulder. "I am grateful, Lord Doto."

"Grateful?" Doto asked. "Like when the sun comes up and the wind rises and you run?"

Clay closed his eyes. "Yes."

They reached the edge of Kwaee's temple before the sun was at its height. The intoxicating flow of power that surrounded it was thick as sap in the air. Doto knew his father would not respond well toward seeing him cradling the ancient enemy in his arms like a mother cat with her kittens, and so he set Clay down. "We are nearly there," he told him. "You will walk now."

"This is it?" Clay gave a grunt as he stood up on both feet and re-garded the deep, emerald hollow that held the temple. "What is he like? Is he like you? And what should I say? How should I talk to him so that I don't offend him like I did you?"

Doto had no easy answer to these questions. Kwaee was like Kwaee. He was a god of the forest: moody, unpredictable, and usually angry. For most of Doto's younger years, he had been the only god Doto had known besides Mother Fam. Only when Doto was much older had he encountered other gods in his travels through the forest.

"It will be difficult not to anger him," he admitted. "But remember that you are bringing good news for him. If he asks you, tell him how your people worship him. Tell him about the burning of your villages, and that you do not serve Ogya except in small ways. Tell him how you need the forest and would not burn it. But do not speak to him unless he asks you a question. Never argue anything he says or contradict him. That is a bad habit of yours. Your ears are very small and you do not move them as much as you should, but try to keep them perked and focused on him so that he will know you are paying attention."

Clay stood up on the toes of his good foot to peer down into the hol-low, then hunched down. He smelled of fear. "What if he doesn't like me?"

"I didn't like you. But you turned out to be interesting. Kwaee is an old god, and has known many fire bearers. He will see that you are differ-ent quicker than I did." He wondered if his reassurances were true. He had been optimistic the day before, but now, standing on the border of Kwaee's sanctum, he toyed with the urge to turn, to take his fire bearer away from this place and not look back. He gave Clay a little nudge on the shoulder with one paw. "Come. It is time."

Together, they stepped into Kwaee's temple and moved down the mossy, verdant slopes of the hollow, Clay picking his way cautiously, fa-voring his leg. Doto dizzied with the rush of primal forest energy flowing around them. The ground here was softer, thick with ferns and loamy soil puffed up by continually trickling springs, and the sun floated across it in dreamy shapes formed by the swaying weave of tree limbs above.

Above the dark green pond Kwaee sat in his towering throne. Though normally he would be sprawled out among the gnarled roots, today he sat upright, watching them intently as they approached.

Clay's eyes widened when he saw the forest god. "He's huge," he whispered to Doto.

"And he hears everything you say," Doto muttered back. "Be silent."

His warning was too late. Kwaee rose from his throne, his divine plumage spread proudly, and strode forward to meet them at the edge of the pond. At first he barely glanced at Doto, but then his eyes fixed on Doto's brow and narrowed.

Doto fought an urge to lift a paw and cover the feather growing there. "I have brought you the fire bearer, alive, just as you requested," he said to his father in the language of the gods.

Clay dropped to his knees and bowed low, spreading himself prostrate before the god. He was trembling with fear, or perhaps the illness.

"Yes, little enemy," Kwaee said. He spoke in the fire bearer's language, but with an accent different than Clay's, the words lilted, and sounding nearly foreign to Doto's ears. "I am huge, for I am not only this body, but this temple, and the whole forest you have taken so very long to travel through. You are honored beyond most of your wretched kind, as I allow you to enter here, in the deepest of my heart. Stand up. Let me see you."

Clay obediently got to his feet, staggering a little as he did. His eyes barely met the god's chest.

Kwaee's nose wrinkled. "You are injured."

"Yes, Lord Kwaee."

"And dying."

Clay said nothing, but looked toward Doto. Doto turned away so as not to see the desperation in his eyes.

Kwaee crouched and sniffed at Clay's black, woven hair, at his shoulders and chest. He stalked around him in a narrow circle, looking him up and down, his tail twitching. Then he gripped him in both paws, lifting him up, staring intently into his face, his golden eyes wide and searching, turning him from side to side. His ears flattened further and further as he inspected the bearer.

Clay squirmed in the grip, clutching at the god's paws and forearms, and then cried aloud as Kwaee abruptly dropped him and he fell to his hands and knees on the mercifully soft soil.

"Well, son," Kwaee said in the gods' language, "it looks like you managed to surprise me after all. It had been so long, I thought perhaps the fire bearers had killed you."

Doto shifted his weight from paw to paw, worrying. It was plain that Kwaee was in a poor mood. Still, he might be cheered by the good news they brought. "I took time to observe the fire bearers. I studied them to see what our ancient enemy was like, what their plans for the forest were, and how Ogya might still work through them. And then our journey was much more difficult than I had expected."

"Difficult? Why? You are a god. How did this little enemy inconvenience you so greatly?" He regarded his unsheathed claws with a bored expression.

"Through his own fragility," Doto admitted. "It was right to choose one who was wounded, but then he could not walk very fast."

Kwaee tapped the wooden paw with the claws on one foot, ignoring the way the bearer shrank away from him. "Yes, I see you've done some favors for it." His gaze traveled back to Doto's forehead. "And it, you. Had a little fun with your catch, did you?"

Doto laid his ears back and felt the feather flatten against his forehead when they moved. He was still not accustomed to the way it raised or lowered with his expressions. "The assistance was necessary to bring the fire bearer here. He was wounded, and could not travel on his foot. Had I not rendered this assistance, we would have taken even longer than we had."

"I see," Kwaee said in an understanding tone. He stalked toward his throne, his back to Doto. "So that's why it took you the better part of a moon to return to me. You had to let your wounded little animal drag itself through the forest day after interminable day."

"I…" Doto faltered. "Yes, there was no other way to bring him here."

"*Him?*" Kwaee growled. "Not him! It! It's a thing. A beast. A treacherous minion of Ogya. Or did you forget?" He sat himself in his throne and leaned back, his bared claws digging into the gnarled bark of the moabi. "Why did you not simply grab it by the throat and carry it to me? Why did you not drag it screaming across the forest floor?"

"And supposing I had killed it by accident?" Doto's blood heated, his own claws unsheathing. "I couldn't easily go and get another. Its nest was alerted. They even followed after! Father, you told me time and time again how dangerous they are! I was only being cautious!"

"Cautious? And was it caution that led you to coddle it, shelter it? Guard it? You probably even hunted food for it. As if it were an equal. As if you were not a god at all, but a beast like it."

"But that's what I came to tell you!" Doto protested. "The bearers, they are—they are different now. They're not the vicious minions of Ogya they once were. They don't want to burn the forest. Ask it for yourself. They're not beasts at all!"

"Aren't they?" Kwaee raised one brow. "I smell death on that one. Its life will be short and miserable, like all its kind. It will die soon. How is it not a beast?"

Doto faltered. "It...it can do things. It can dance, and talk in ways that—"

"Prayer?" Kwaee leaned forward in his throne. "Did it pray to you? Did the words feel important when it spoke them? What did it say?"

"Nothing! It didn't say anything, it just...it just asked for strength."

Kwaee's face stretched in a fang-filled grin. "And then you helped it. Didn't you?"

"But—yes, but only to get it here. That's all. It wasn't because of the prayer. It was my choice."

"Oh, son." His father's voice sounded almost pitying. "You don't understand. You think you know the fire bearers better than I. You arrogant little cub. Don't you see that that's their power? That's how they betray us. It's not the fire they wield. It's the way they get inside you. Then they destroy you. The fire bearer has done to you what they always do. It's made you trust it. It's gotten you to do what it wants."

Could that be? Doubts winged through Doto's mind. Had all their journey been just some magical trick of the fire bearer? But no, Clay had suffered greatly on the journey, and for what reason? To die in the forest? It made no sense. "He wanted me to take him home, but I didn't. I brought him here, like you said. Why didn't he use this prayer to trick me into returning him? Anyway, if they are so dangerous and insidious, why didn't you warn me of that? Why didn't you tell me how they could trick us?"

Kwaee kneaded his claws into his throne. "I had to see for myself if they would still do it. If they would use their power against us."

"But that's what I'm trying to tell you about, Father. I've spoken with the fire bearer about this during the whole journey. I know he wouldn't destroy us, and I don't think his people would, either. Once, perhaps, they served Ogya alone, but not now. They revere all gods, even you." He frowned then, doubts creeping into his mind. "You must feel their worship of you. Perhaps they are too far away?"

Kwaee stared at him for a moment, at the place just above his eyes. "You bear that feather on your head and you tell me they have not tried to affect you."

"A feather like yours?" Doto asked.

Kwaee's eyes narrowed into slits. He stood before Clay and spoke again, this time in the language of the fire bearers, his voice gentle and reassuring. Doto knew that tone as a perilous one, often preceding an attack. "And what is your name, little animal?"

"I am called Clay, Lord Kwaee," Clay answered in a small voice, looking up to meet the god's eyes, but still trembling.

"Clay," Kwaee repeated, as if trying the name on his tongue. "In your language, it means 'dirt,' does it not?"

"Yes, Lord Kwaee. A special soil found where water has flowed. Finding it is good fortune; it means water may be found nearby. And we can make things of it as well."

"Can you?" Kwaee purred indulgently. "Why, so can we gods! The older stories say that Father Wem shaped your species out of clay, as he did all the animals. So which are you, fire bearer? Dirt? Or an animal?"

Clay looked over toward Doto for some kind of confirmation or reassurance, but Kwaee was behaving strangely. Doto was no longer sure what the right response would be. "Please, Lord Kwaee," Clay said, "I do not believe myself to be either."

"Then you are poorly named. You ought to have been named 'Neither,' or perhaps 'Traitor' or 'Deceiver.' Do any of those names sound truer to you?"

Clay lowered his eyes. "Great Kwaee, I have heard that you believe my people serve only the fire god Ogya and long to continue some old war between the forest and the Firelands." He spread his paws. "Once, perhaps, it must have been so. None of us have memories that exceed those of the gods. But please believe me that this is not now the case. My people pray to all the gods, for we depend on all of them." He looked up again, his gaze steadier now. "We would not survive without the forest. We depend upon it for food. And before that, we depended on the savanna. We never would have burned it on purpose. In fact—" He looked over at Doto again before continuing. Doto gave him an encouraging nod. "In fact, many of my people are angry with Ogya because he sent a firestorm across the savanna, driving us from our homes. Some of us were killed. It is true that we serve him and pray to him still, but so we also give honor and prayers to you, Lord Kwaee."

The tall leopard god's brow knitted with sudden interest, the plumage folding as if into a single feather. "You say that you lived on the savanna until Ogya sent a fire."

"Yes, Lord Kwaee."

"And because of the fire, you moved closer to the forest?"

"Because of that and the droughts, yes. We moved nearer to the forest for the water and food we could not find elsewhere."

Kwaee snorted. "And still you claim not to be minions of Ogya?" he demanded. "When at his behest, you have brought your miserable, stinking species and their flames and black clouds to the borders of my forest, where you burned them long ago?"

Clay's mouth hung open in dismay.

"Fool! Ogya has used you to bring his flames to my dominion. Witting or no, you are still his minions, and you will attack. You will burn my forest if I let any of you live. You will try to destroy me just as you did so long ago. And I do not believe you are so innocent of all this as you pretend. I know your tricks, your sentimental little deceptions." He leaned down and hissed through clenched teeth, saliva dripping at Clay's toes. "It is too late for you and your people. I will set my forest against you. I will flood it with my hatred for you. If any of your people set foot within the reach of my trees, their bones will be broken. I will tear them apart with my vines. The beasts that dwell within me will rove my borders and destroy any interlopers or trespassers. Your people will move back to the savanna, or they will die."

"No!" Clay cried aloud, horror in his eyes. "Please, Lord Kwaee, we serve you faithfully."

Knowing it was foolish to speak up, Doto found he still could keep silent no longer. "He speaks the truth. He and his people do worship us. I have seen it myself."

With narrowed eyes, Kwaee turned on him. "Yes, I see that you have."

"We do," Clay insisted desperately. "We dance in your honor, Lord Kwaee. And I confess that our people did not know of a second god of the forest, but if you allow me to return, I swear to you that we will dance in Lord Doto's name as well."

Kwaee paused, an unreadable expression writing itself across his face. "God of the forest?" he asked in a disbelieving voice. "Doto, a god of the forest?" He gave a short, barking laugh. Doto hunched backward, his ears flattening.

"So the little captive fire bearer danced for his forest god, is that it?"

Clay looked back and forth between Doto and Kwaee in plain confusion. "Yes...yes, Lord Kwaee."

"And did you do this of your own initiative? Or did he request it?"

"He—he asked me to."

A terrible, cruel smile stretched Kwaee's muzzle. "Of course he did. Just as you wished him to. And you, obedient little fire bearer, did as he requested. "

"How could I refuse the request of a forest god?"

"Ahhhh," Kwaee said. "But he is not a forest god."

Doto's tail curled tightly around his left ankle.

Clay blinked several times. "I don't understand. Not a forest god?"

"No." Kwaee's voice was filled with mock pity. "No, not a forest god at all. Well. Unless you consider a little stand of trees a forest. And who does? No, Doto is really more of a…I suppose you would say a copse god. Perhaps a grove god. It is a tiny little space. Even you, fire bearer, with that injured foot, could travel through it in the space of twenty breaths. And you say he convinced you that he was a forest god. How disappointing." He turned that cruel grin toward Doto. "He probably didn't even tell you that he is my son."

"Son?" Clay shifted his weight onto his injured leg and stumbled backward.

"Tell him, Doto," Kwaee purred.

Doto breathed in deep, lifting his eyes. "It is true. Kwaee is my father. He is the god of the forest, and it was at his command that I came to retrieve you. I have never seen fire bearers before, never seen the world outside the forest." He met the fire bearer's injured gaze. "There were many things I thought I knew that I did not. And I thought you would not listen to me as much if you knew that I was Kwaee's son."

"And not a very good son," Kwaee added. "Even for a copse god, he is very weak and frail."

"Father!" Doto could not keep the cry from his throat, his cheeks burning with shame.

Kwaee pretended not to have heard him. "Always weak, always inadequate. I had such hopes for him, fire bearer. He should have been strong and merciless. Together we would have ruled this forest and grown it ever beyond its borders. We would have pushed the savanna north, shrinking the Firelands until Ogya was forced away entirely, back into the belly of the earth where he belongs." With a look of disgust toward Doto, he said, "Instead he proved to be feeble, crippled with sympathies like his mother. But I am a forgiving god. I care for my son. I gave him a chance to prove his strength by bringing back one of your people. I wished him to show that he could resist your deceptive ways.

"I expected his return in less than the passing of three suns, but nearly a moon later, he finally comes crawling back with you, a pathetic, dying, witless excuse for a fire bearer. And not only does he bring back the poorest specimen he can find while taking far too long to return, he betrays me."

"I never betrayed you!" Doto cried in astonishment. "Everything I did was for you."

"Everything? Is that why you spoke to the servant of my oldest enemy as though he was your equal? Why you let him trick you into befriending him?"

"Yes!" Doto's face was hot. "I thought he had information that you did not know, that you would be pleased to learn that the fire bearers were different than they used to be."

"And," Kwaee continued as if Doto had never spoken, "was it me you were thinking of when you had this creature worship you, night after night? Did he beg you to dance for you, or did you beg him?"

"I…" He could think of no reply.

"Did your little grove grow a little larger? Did you feel new trees sprouting, spreading and taking over *my* forest?" All pretense of politeness was gone now, fury cracking Kwaee's voice.

"I—yes, I did," Doto stammered, "but that is not how it was."

"Not how it was? My son was not colluding with an agent of my sworn enemy to usurp my own forest from me?" Kwaee roared. "Then what in the name of Wem is *this*?"

With that, he lunged toward Doto. Doto told himself to stand tall, to face the attack, but even as he was telling himself that, he was flinching backward, hissing, his fur bushing out. With two fingers, Kwaee seized the bright blue feather growing from Doto's brow and tore it out in one deft movement. Doto's vision blurred. A god could feel pain, but it was rare. Few things other than another god could cause it, and it had been many hundreds of years since Doto had felt it—not since he was a young god and Kwaee had punished him. Now the stabbing shock of pain deep into his forehead overwhelmed him. His vision blurred, and he heard himself yowl in shock and agony. Far away, his temple shuddered and groaned, the new saplings that had sprouted there withering where they stood. Clay, too, cried out in wordless distress.

Doto staggered backward, clutching at his forehead, feeling the hot ooze of his blood soaking through his fur. A red drop of it fell from the end of the blue feather as Kwaee slowly twirled it between thumb and forefinger. He could not understand what had just happened, nor why.

Kwaee let the feather drift to the ground as though it meant nothing. "You're a disappointment," he said. "A miserable, weak-willed disappointment. But I'm going to help you. I'm going to free you from the influence of this creature. Understand that what I do now is mercy."

Kwaee strode down and pounced onto Clay on all fours, gripping his slender, brown neck with one paw. He stood upright, lifting the fire bearer in the air by the throat, his fangs bared. Clay's legs kicked desperately, his paws tugging uselessly at Kwaee's fingers.

"No!" Doto shouted in panic. He bounded toward Kwaee, not thinking about what he would do, half-expecting he could somehow pull Clay away from his father.

"Get back," Kwaee snarled at him, and a heavy branch of the tree swung down, striking Doto in his chest and knocking him backward several feet.

He landed on his side in the leaves and went rolling into the pool with a splash. He floundered in confusion, losing his bearings in the water and mud, out of direct contact with the power of the forest, though it flowed all around him. He found his footing in the muck and dragged himself out of the pool, his fur dripping, heavy with water.

Kwaee still held Clay by the throat, choking him, his muzzle twisted in hatred. The little bearer was tiny by comparison, his kicks growing slow and weak. Doto wanted to help, but could do nothing. Here in the heart of Kwaee's temple, he was helpless.

The god of the forest stared up into the fire bearer's eyes, and then his expression changed. His plumage lowered, his snarl softened. He bared his teeth, clenched in one last effort, and then dropped Clay to the ground again with a growl.

Clay lay on his side, wheezing faintly.

"It is sick and dying," Kwaee said in the fire bearer's tongue. "There is no pleasure in killing it. I cannot stand to look at the pathetic wretch, and I do not want its corruption polluting my temple. Get the thing out of my sight."

Doto stood, letting the water vanish from his fur. Puzzled, he asked, "You're not going to kill it?"

"No," Kwaee said. "It is your prize. Take it away from here and do whatever you wish with it. Your choice. It would be a mercy to kill it. It is wounded. Diseased. Keep it like a suffering pet for the rest of its miserable life if you want. But there is one more thing about the fire bearers that you should know."

"What is that?" Doto asked through the shock. He rubbed at his forehead where pain still throbbed. He could scarcely force himself to listen.

Kwaee grinned nastily. "They killed your mother."

Doto dropped his paw to his side. The temple was silent as the air before a thunderstorm. "That cannot be true," he breathed.

"Oh, it is quite true." Kwaee stalked back to the moabi tree, one foot crushing the blue feather beneath it. "It happened at a place not far from here." He settled back into his throne and said in a sly tone, "I think you might have had to go there before you came here. A place called Abansin. Your mother was there when she died. Died at the fire bearers' hands."

"Father?" Doto asked. He felt lost, helpless.

"It is a fact, son. The fire bearers killed your mother. And so I killed them, all of them, in vengeance. I struck them down with my forest, each and every one, and cursed their city with my absence. So if you would honor me, and honor your mother, then you know what you have to do."

He drummed his claws on the bark. When he spoke again, in god-tongue, his voice was gentler. "Son, listen to me. I know often you do not understand my anger. But it always has a reason. I understand how this fire bearer has deceived you with its magic. What do you think happened to me so long ago, when they killed your mother? I am not without forgiveness. So I will make one final agreement: should you choose to prove your strength and kill your little fire bearer, then I will welcome you back. You will sit with me in my temple and rule beside me."

He looked up toward the broad leaves of the canopy above that sheltered his temple from the light of the sun, the wind, the outside world entirely. "Of course, if you choose anything else, you will have chosen not to be my son. You will never enter my temple again. You will never speak to me. You will be alone in your miserable little life forever. I will disown you utterly."

Doto's Heart

Lying in Cloud's tent after injuring his foot, Clay had suffered a fever that had produced warped dreams and strange imaginings. These had not been real, but he had not been able to tell at the time. Once again, an illness pounded through his body. Over the past few days, he had felt his fever intensifying, making him dizzy and light-headed, turning his stomach against thoughts of food.

Doto had not permitted a fire the last few nights of their journey, but Clay had not minded. The thought of meat did not appeal to him. The fruits he had been able to keep down, but his illness had worsened, and weakened his steps. He had tried to conceal this from Doto, and for all but the last morning, it had not been too difficult. But now the sickness was putting dark images in his head again. Everything that happened was another fever dream. That was what it had to be. He could not have met the god of the entire forest, nor seen him fight with Doto, nor heard him promise to murder Clay's whole people.

And Doto could not now be shoving him forward with uncharacteristic brutality, snarling at him to keep up his pace if he wanted to die quickly rather than slow. That was not the Doto he had come to know over the past several days.

He stumbled and fell, climbing the mossy bank that led up from Kwaee's temple. "Get up," Doto growled. Clay felt a hand grip at his braids and hoist him upward again, making his scalp blaze with pain. He cried out.

No, this was not his Doto, the one who had proven to be oddly gentle and curious behind his thicket of pride. This was not the Doto who had shivered with rapture as Clay had danced, who had put his arm around him and held him close the previous evening, who had carried him in those strong arms that last exhausting step of the journey. It had to be the fever.

Except, Clay knew, hobbling out of the temple and down into the thickness of the forest, his leg throbbing with pain, no feeling remaining in the lower part where his ankle had once been, it was not the fever. He was not so far out of his mind as that. This was happening to him. It was not a dream. He was not still on the journey to meet Kwaee. Nor was he, as he sometimes fancied, still lying in Cloud's tent, recovering from the injury of the hunt, with all that happened after just a dark and confusion vision. He was here—sick, wounded, and probably dying, but here. He had failed to please the gods. His people would suffer for it. He felt his tears hot on his cheeks as he staggered toward whatever place Doto would deem suitable for his death.

He thought about just dropping here, falling to the ground and refusing to get up, but he knew he could not do that. Even now, he could not bring himself to disobey the gods. They might hate him and slay him, but he could not refuse their commands. It was wrong. Almost he laughed out loud to himself, thinking of how angry Laughing Dog would be to see him now. His brother would not submit to the gods like this. He would turn and fight, even if it were futile, even if he knew it meant his death. That was who Laughing Dog was. But Clay was always devoted. Even now.

For some time Doto propelled him through the forest, snarling and shoving at him when he moved too slow. He summoned all of his energy to keep moving, but he could tell he was nearing the end of it. Soon he would fall and he would not have the strength to rise again, however much he might wish to. Then, in a place where the trees grew thin, Doto gave him a hard shove against his back and sent him sprawling into a soft bank. Bewildered, he rolled over to blink up at the god.

"Why are you lying there?" Doto snapped. "Get to your feet this instant. We are not far enough from Kwaee's temple yet." His tone and words were harsh, but his golden-green eyes were wide and earnest, and even as he spoke, he gave a meaningful shake of his head. He silently mouthed the word "No."

Clay lay still, more confused than hurt.

"You will not rise?" Doto's voice was loud, carrying far beyond him. "Very well. You may have a short rest. But then you must continue to the place where you will be killed."

Clay leaned up on his elbows. Doto motioned him to lie still with one paw, then began casting about the clearing, staring into the grasses and shrubs, selecting items seemingly at random. He found a long, hard strip of bramble, a gnarled bit of bark, some dark purple berries, the bones of a bird, red earth from the ground, and other bits of plant and stone. Assembling these in a hasty pile, he then curled his tail, took its spotted length in one paw, and plucked a few strands of fur from its tip. He then added those to the assortment of objects, scooped them together in his paws and squeezed hard. His eyes closed, his breathing growing more measured as he appeared to concentrate. When he opened his paws, he held nothing like the pile of leaves and rocks and bone that he had scooped together. Instead, nestled in his velvet pads was a small carving of a leopard. Its eyes glittered green and yellow, and its rosettes shifted in the light. It was so lifelike, Clay almost expected it to move. Sprouting from its back was the long strand of bramble, still sharp with many thorns, attached in a loop.

"Get up now," Doto shouted, more at the forest than at him. His paw pressed down against Clay's chest, which was slick with sweat from the fever and the heat of the day. "I said get up!" He paused. "No? Then so be it. I will kill you here." Then he dropped the figurine and loop around Clay's neck.

As soon as the object touched Clay's skin, the forest altered. He could not discern what was different about it. The trees still towered above him in the same way, their branches drifting as before. The grasses still bent in the same direction, and the birds called the same songs. But everything was altered. The ground cradled him more comfortably. The little bush in the small of his back no longer pressed into or irritated his skin, and even the thorns on the bramble around his neck did not scratch. The air was clearer, purer in his lungs, and it carried the sounds and scents of the forest to him more plainly. He rubbed the sweat from his face with one hand. He reached up toward Doto's chest, and all about him, the stems of grasses bent to follow his movement, reaching along with his arm. "What—?" he gasped. He curled his fingers around the little figurine hanging from his neck. "What is this?"

Doto leaned toward him and kept his voice low. "It is a fetish. A little piece of my power. You heard Kwaee. The forest has been set against you and your kind. But when you wear this, the forest thinks you are me. If Kwaee ever opens his eyes and looks beyond the borders of his temple, he can find you. But as long as he keeps his gaze turned inward, the forest will not recognize you. It will behave toward you as it does with me. You must be cautious with this gift. The forest wishes to please me. Sometimes, when I feel strong emotion, it may act beyond my bidding. The fetish carries only a small part of my power, so it will not have the same effect, but it will be enough to protect you, and enough to warrant care. And more importantly, Kwaee will think you are dead. He will not feel you within his boundaries."

Clay's fingers brushed against the god's arm, sliding through the soft fur there. "But you were supposed to kill me. Your father ordered you to. He said—" He almost couldn't finish the words. "He said my people killed your mother."

"Yes." Doto's voice was still low and quiet, but it went hard. "And he was lying to me."

Against his judgment, Clay asked, "How do you know?"

Doto looked away, over one shoulder. "I just know. There is so much he never talked about, never told me until just now." He frowned. "It does not matter."

"And because of that, you're not going to kill me?"

The golden-green eyes shifted back to him. "Yes. That, and…you gave me a feather. He took it from me. I trust you more." Doto gripped at Clay's injured leg with strong, padded fingers. "There is one more thing I must do. It will not be safe for you here. We have a long journey to make, and you cannot make it on that foot. I do not think you could travel very far at all. I am going to have to heal you."

"Heal me?" Clay could scarcely believe what he was hearing. "But you said that it was forbidden!"

"Forbidden by Kwaee? He has disowned me."

"What do you mean?"

Scowling at the ground, Doto answered, "He said if I did not kill you, I would no longer be his son. Very well. I am not."

Clay slumped back dizzily. He thought of Laughing Dog marching out of the village by the order of their father. "You lost your father because of me?" He lifted his hand to brush his fingers through the fur on Doto's cheek, and the god did not pull away.

"Do not think yourself so important as all that. He had been cruel and shut away for a very long time. Not much changes except that I am no longer beholden to his orders." His eyes saddened, and he reached up to rub at the wound where his feather had been. The fur was dark and clumped with dried blood there. "And I suppose I will only ever be a god of a little copse, not a proper forest god as I told you."

Clay brushed at his cheek and neck fondly. "But you're my god. I will praise you above all others."

"Not if you die," Doto said. "Kwaee could never give me a satisfactory reason not to heal another. And you are dying. I…do not wish this to be so."

He stepped backward, still crouched, and took the wooden paw in his fingers. Clay could not even feel it at the end of his leg anymore. The thing fell apart, revealing the sticky, pulpy mass of bandage and injury beneath it. Clay looked away in revulsion, but not before he saw the dark veins running up his thigh, the swollen flesh. Doto delicately picked the dressings away with his claws. "Besides, there is another thing to consider here. Kwaee cautioned me against healing those whom I found injured in the forest. It is wrong for a god to interfere with the world around him. But this sickness in your leg is my doing. I made you walk on the wooden foot. It gashed and cut your leg and rubbed dirt in it. If not for me, you might never walk, but you would not be dying. At least I must undo the damage I caused."

He lifted the leg, but Clay could not feel the places where Doto's fingers touched; he had lost all sensation there. Around the edges, though, pain seared into muscle and skin, and he breathed faster through his mouth, trying to keep from crying out. "All right," Doto said. "I am going to try now. I have never done this before. I do not know what will happen." The god breathed deeply, and closed his eyes in concentration. The tip of his tail twitched slowly.

The air around them changed. Clay could feel something in it, like water flowing, like blood pulsing. It felt as though a great storm were approaching after a long drought. The trees creaked above him, and when he looked up, he saw their branches rocking mightily in a strong wind. The gust picked up below, swirling fallen leaves and twigs around them, blowing at his hair, at Doto's fur, eerily cool. "Doto," he said, frightened, but the rising wind blew the name from his lips. Goosebumps prickled across his arms and thighs, and the hairs on the back of his neck lifted.

Doto's eyes opened and went wide. He pulled his clawed fingers from the ruins of Clay's leg, and when they parted, bright stems of light jumped from between them. He gasped and gripped again, all his fur lifting across his body, making him seem larger and rounded. Clay could feel the hair on his head rising as well, stiff against the cyclone surrounding them.

Like the crack of faraway thunder, Doto's words cut through the wind and scatter of leaves. "Take what is mine." He spoke the words slowly and dreamily, as though he did not hear his own voice. "Out, out, into bone and flesh, into blood and scar, take what is mine." His fingertips traced over pulped skin and twisted, unrecognizable flesh, past a brown and purple stub where once Clay had had a foot, and beneath them the white light arced, like lightning, but slower—lightning made of honey.

The words had not been spoken in any language Clay had ever heard before, but he understood them all the same. He felt the change before he saw it. The fever that had been building in his blood the last few days broke all at once; his skin felt cool, as though he had been standing in fresh rain. The uncomfortable twisting of perceptions that had been churning in his mind was gone as though it had never been, just a bad dream fleeing with the passing of night. He had been sick, he realized. Very sick. And now he

was not. Energy flooded his limbs, as though he could run for twenty days without rest—he wanted to jump up and seize Doto in his arms.

Then his leg began to itch. At first it was just a tickle, a crawling of ants across the surface, and then the itch ate deeper, the ants gnawing their way down through muscle and bone. He wanted desperately to scratch at it, but he feared that if he touched his leg, his skin might tear away, or worse, whatever magic Doto was working might be countered. He clenched his fingers hard around the stalks of the bushes beneath him. The ants grew to beetles scurrying along his bone and burrowing beneath his skin. The ruined flesh on his leg twisted and shifted, the swelling receding, the scars flattening out. The color of his skin lightened from purple back to a healthy brown. Then the tips of bones, white and smooth, protruded from his stump of a foot, stretching outward, pink tendrils of muscle weaving around them. Clay shuddered and looked away, staring at the sky. It felt as though his skeleton were being extracted through his foot, a deep, awful ache, tugging and pulling and extending. He groaned and clenched his toes—he had toes! He looked back at his foot and saw that it did not look like a human foot yet; indeed, at the moment, it more resembled a paw, but it was a foot nonetheless. He splayed his toes, wiggled them again, and gaped in elation as he saw them respond.

It was when his toenails began to grow back that he realized something was going wrong. They were not shaped like toenails, but like little curved thorns. Claws. He was growing claws on the end of his foot, a foot that had only four toes. In panic, he called out Doto's name, but the god did not respond, lost in his magical reverie, his eyes staring through Clay and through the ground into some place in his own mind. Even as Clay watched, the skin on his foot and leg lightened in color and became mottled. With another wave of terrible itching, fur sprouted from it, covering his foot, winding up to a thin, narrow ankle that did not resemble his own in any way, sending creeping bands of fur like climbing vines that wound halfway up his thigh. The fur was golden and covered with dark brown rosettes. His foot and lower leg were those of a large leopard, exactly like Doto's.

The itching stopped. The energy faded from the air. The wind died down. Doto lifted his fingers from Clay's leg and looked up at him. There was a deep weariness in his eyes. "Did it…" he began, and then seemed to lose track of his words for a moment. "Did it work?" he asked finally. Then, before Clay could answer, Doto's eyes rolled up into his head and he collapsed heavily to the forest floor.

Everything was very quiet. There were no sounds of birds or insects, only the pounding of Clay's pulse in his ears and his rapid breaths. Doto had used forbidden magic and now he lay face down in front of him. On hands and knees, Clay scrambled over to him, feeling the unfamiliar sensation of the ground brushing against his new toes. Doto sprawled on his back, arms spread out, unmoving. His eyes were closed.

"Doto!" Clay gripped the ruffs of fur at the god's cheeks and lightly shook his head, but the golden eyelids remained closed, the neck limp. He called the god's name again, shaking his chest, trying to heft him up into his arms, but still, Doto was heavy and unmoving. His chest rose and fell, so at least he was breathing. Clay shook him again, but still, there was no response.

Stay calm, he told himself uselessly. Stay calm. So you've got a leopard foot now, there's a passed-out god in front of you, and there's another, more powerful god out there who wants you dead. You have to remain calm, not make any more noise than necessary. Doto will wake up soon. He has to. And then we can escape.

He rested against Doto's unconscious body, letting his heart slow down, his breaths come more easily. At least you can walk now, he told himself. He hesitated. Could he? He pushed himself upright and carefully got to his feet, feeling for the first time in more than a moon the texture of earth and plants beneath his toes, even if, strictly speaking, they were not his toes. The bottom of his foot was padded. Carefully, he put his weight down on it, feeling his new toes spread out. His heel did not reach the ground. He felt as though he were standing on tiptoe. Experimentally, he took a few steps, and found that walking felt both natural and unusual at the same time. He was *walking*. He took a few more steps past the prone leopard god. His gait was strange and uneven, but not uncomfortably so. Despite limping for so long, this new foot knew how to move for him. He did not have to learn how to use it; he just wished to step forward, and he stepped forward.

Elation danced through his body. All at once it did not matter that he had a beast's foot on the end of his leg, that his leg was wrapped with leopard fur. He could walk again. He could probably even run. He looked back at Doto, and then took a few running steps, and found himself moving with a powerful grace, his balance adapting to the irregular gait, body shifting forward in a stance he had never run in before. He ran again, stretching his legs out, his feet carrying him in bounding leaps. He bounced off a tree, changing directions in midstride, the claws on his toes catching at the bark and tugging at the bones in his foot. He was fast now, he realized, faster than he had ever been before his injury. He tried to suppress a giddy laugh, but it bubbled out of him all the same. He made circles around the clearing, half running on the ground, half caroming from tree trunk to tree trunk. His people had never seen anything like this before. The next time he hunted, he wouldn't have to run against a herd of eland, facing their charge. The others might have to, but Clay felt certain now that he could run with the herd, chase them down. He might be faster now than any fire bearer that had ever lived.

In excitement, he raced up a nearby tree trunk a few steps and flipped backward. In midair, he realized his mistake: the fetish looped around his neck whipped back and fell free. As soon as the loop left his neck, the forest went dim. It was as though he had suddenly plunged underwater: just as the forest had come alive and clear when Doto had given him the fetish, now his vision seemed blurred, his hearing muffled. Scents vanished from the air. He landed on his feet easily enough, but then stumbled backward, falling onto his elbows in the soft turf.

The forest loomed over him as though watching him with a surprised and suspicious regard. The trees creaked, and his breath caught in his throat. All around him, the plants were moving. Even with his dulled senses, he could see the shifting of branches and hear the rustle of leaves as roots burrowed beneath them. He cast about for the fetish. Where was it? He couldn't see it among the earth and fallen leaves. Why did it have to be brown? Why not bright red?

The tree he had flipped from actually leaned toward him, bending its whole body, emitting a deep, tortured, splintery groan that filled Clay with a gripping terror. Trees should not be able to make noise, and especially not *that* noise. Its limbs angled toward him, the great wooden giant looking as though it were about to fall on him. He wanted to run, but running would be a mistake. There were trees everywhere. He could run nowhere that they would not catch him. Unwelcome images of the carnage at Abansin flashed in his mind. Trying to lie as still as he could, he scanned the forest floor with his eyes. The branches lowered toward him, leaves and twigs pawing at the ground near him.

There. He spotted the small wooden carving of the leopard lying nestled in the leaves a few feet away. Carefully, he tried to scoot himself toward it. The tree groaned again, its thick branch brushing against the ground, sweeping toward him. Panicked, he made a sudden lunge and grab for the figurine, sliding across the forest floor. His fingers brushed its smooth surface, and then the ground boiled beneath him, twisting and writhing. Roots thrust up from beneath the earth, squirming like a mad cluster of wooden snakes. Before he could make another attempt at the fetish, earthy, wooden coils slipped around his ankles. The wood drew back at the touch of his feline ankle, but the other held fast, chafing his skin. With the heels of his hands, Clay pushed backward, trying to tug his trapped foot free, but the grip of the roots was unyielding. They began to pull his foot down into the cool earth. Roots squirmed beneath his hands too, and he pushed himself upright, standing and bracing himself with his leopard foot, trying to pull the other out of the ground.

Thin, flexible branches lashed around his shoulders and elbows, cinching tightly at the skin and yanking his arms upright. He half-screamed, half-shouted in terror, and then he was pulled upward, his shoulders aching with pain. His left foot pawed uselessly at the ground, even as the wooden fingers tugged the right deeper beneath the soil. His shoulders felt as though they were about to be dislocated. Vines that had before hung listlessly from theirs branches probed outward and crawled around his chest, tightening and pulling upward, making his midsection stretch until he felt it would come apart. He would be torn in half by the forest. He cried aloud again in pain and terror, but a thick liana insinuated itself around his neck, which still ached from Kwaee's powerful grip. It cinched tighter and tighter. His tongue felt too thick for his throat. He couldn't get a breath. No, he would not die from being torn in half. He would first be strangled by the forest and then torn in half. His arms flailed uselessly, tugging against the wooden grip that had seized them. His leopard foot, the only part of him free to move, pounded against the ground. His vision tinged with red.

Firm arms slid around him, holding him from behind. Immediately, the coils of the roots and branches and lianas eased. He sucked in a desperate, choked breath. The air was so sweet that for a moment he forgot all else. His body slumped in the arms holding him, and he panted as the branches lifted away, the roots slithering back and burrowing back into the soil. Doto's whiskers tickled against his ear. "Where is the fetish?"

After being twisted about by the tree, Clay wasn't certain. He shook his head, panting.

"Do not be afraid. The forest will not harm you as long as my arms are around you. Where is the fetish?"

Clay looked about, then pointed in the direction he had seen it last. Keeping his powerful arms around Clay's chest, Doto backed toward the spot and scanned the ground. His spotted tail slid along the earth and then hooked under a brown bramble loop and lifted it up. He took it with one paw and dropped it over Clay's neck once more.

The world leapt back into clarity, Clay's eyes, ears, and nose showing the forest to him as a massive entity filled with endless life and death—but one no longer interested in him. The trees no longer bent toward him with intention, but merely leaned in the purposeless wind.

When Doto let go of him, there was a scowl on his muzzle. "Why did you cast aside the fetish?" he demanded. "Now that your foot is healed, you are ready to be rid of me?"

"No," Clay cried, astonished. "I didn't cast it aside. It fell off."

Doto gave him a suspicious stare. "You fire bearers, you have so many stories. But you are not very good at making them up at a moment's request. How could the bramble have fallen from about your neck?"

Feeling a sudden flush of shame, Clay confessed, "I was running. I was just so excited. I ran up a tree and flipped, and then the next thing I knew…the forest was trying to eat me."

"You were running?" Doto's interest became keenly fixed. "You are well. You can walk and run again?"

"Yes." Clay gave him a small smile. "It's amazing. I have a foot again." He looked down at it. Furry, unfamiliar toes twitched beneath his gaze. "I have a leopard foot." He sank down to the ground again, running his fingers through the fur. He could feel the fur on—*in*—his skin, feel the touch of his fingertips running through it. He could even feel the minor shifts in the breeze as it ruffled the fur. *His* fur. "Doto, why do I have a leopard's foot?"

The god sighed heavily. "I do not know for certain. I told you the healing magic was forbidden to gods. Surely this must be why. I think part of me has gone into you. It felt…strange to me. I did not care for it. And I did not like falling asleep like that."

"Do you feel all right now?" Clay asked with some concern.

"Something is different now, but I do not know what. But yes, I am fine. There is very little that can harm a god."

"It looked like Kwaee could."

His expression darkening, Doto answered, "Yes, and he means to harm you as well. You saw how the forest behaved when you no longer wore my fetish. Though Kwaee does not look beyond his temple walls, he will have other ways of learning that you are not dead, and he may try worse things to kill you."

What could be worse than a forest attacking you? "Like what?"

Doto's voice was hard. "Worse things. Things that can look past the fetish you wear. We should go."

Clay nodded and stood. "Are you going to take me home, then?" The thought gave him pause. He would have news for everyone about the gods, but it would not be good news. And he did not know how they would react to seeing him walking about on an animal leg.

"That may not be wise," Doto said, frowning. "Things have begun here. Kwaee has turned the forest against the fire bearers, and if he learns you are not dead, you will not be safe. Besides, it is a long way back to your village. I will take you to my own temple. It is a shorter distance, and you will be safe there. We can rest and talk and try to decide what is next." His ears twitched. "And then you can dance for me with that new foot of yours."

"Do we have to travel all the way there? I thought gods could move their temples anywhere in their territory," Clay ventured with some hesitation, not wishing to annoy Doto.

The leopard stiffened. "Yes, they can. But all this forest is Kwaee's forest. I can command it and direct it, but it is still his. There is a…small part that is mine." He struggled with this last sentence, his tail lowering. "That is across the Asubonten. If you can run swiftly enough on that foot I have given you, we might be there before dark."

"I am ready," Clay said. He was more than ready. He had not run in so long. For days every step had been a painful limp, but now he could move naturally once again. He longed to fly over the ground and feel the wind against his skin.

"Then let us hurry. Kwaee will not take long to discern that you are alive."

〰

They ran. Doto kept a reasonably short pace at first, but Clay was easily able to keep up, and so they steadily increased in speed. Clay knew that he was now faster than he had ever been before, but it had been a long time since he had run, and he had feared his endurance might have suffered; however, he soon found his pace to be unflagging, his limbs nearly tireless. He was not certain whether his arduous trek through the forest had toughened him, or whether the magic that had healed his foot had given him new stores of energy, but whatever the case, he was able to keep running at high speed for long stretches at a time. The feeling of running was still odd, though, and sometimes distracting. The toes on his left foot were shorter and thicker than he was used to—not to mention there being only four of them—and he could feel them flexing and gripping against the ground as he ran, the curved claws catching occasionally at a large root and giving a tug that pulled all the way up into his lower leg. In addition, his gait was bouncing and uneven, and while it was not uncomfortable to run in such a way, he supposed it must look ungainly, even laughable.

This thought did not much trouble him. He could run again. The destiny that a foolish wager and an unblessed spear had taken from him had been restored to him by a god. It was proof. The gods did listen, at least sometimes. They responded. They answered.

But also, they could be defied. Doto had stood up to the god of all the forest. He had cast aside his heritage and healed Clay's foot. And he had not done so out of selfishness or blasphemy, but for Clay, for his worshiper. He had stood up to Kwaee because it was right. Was it arrogance to do so? Blasphemy? Perhaps. But Clay was grateful nonetheless.

The forest flew by. The going was easier this time not only because Clay was healed, but also because the world responded differently to him. The bushes tugged themselves out of Clay's way, branches bending aside. Roots that might have tripped him up flattened themselves into the ground as he passed. Each time his toes came down, they landed in clear, soft ground. He had seen the plants move this way for Doto before, but now, they reacted to him the same way. Two days ago, a trip through a meadow filled with thick, tall plants with fat leaves might have been a struggle, but today the stalks drew apart like an opening tent before his stride.

The sensory information of the forest was overwhelming, and the more he paid attention to smells, sights, and sounds, the more he could glean from them. It was not that his eyes were keener, nor his ears sharper. It was only that he understood better what he was seeing and hearing. A musky scent something like cooked liver told him that okapi had passed nearby, and the mingle of a fresh, sweet odor and an earthy, sour smell hinted at ripening figs, as well as the vervets they had attracted. He could hear their urgent cries, calling to each other about the food and about possible roaming predators. His eyes, too, picked out details in the forest he might never have noticed before. Lizards that ought to have been too well camouflaged against the trees and stones for him to see were plainly visible. Insects swarmed around, hovering in clouds, marching along the forest floor, climbing plants, harvesting food, waging war against each other. On the journey to Kwaee's temple, the forest had seemed largely quiet and empty, but now he could observe the ongoing trials of life all around him. Shrews preyed on beetles in the underbrush. Insects perched on stems or leaves and quietly died. Birds raucously announced their presences to each other, calling for sex or warning each other to keep their distances. He listened to their cries with fascination, almost thinking that he could hear words in their trills and caws.

After what seemed a short time, Doto slowed ahead of him and then stopped. Clay came to a rest beside him, bouncing from foot to foot. He was astonished that he was not yet tired from their run. "Is everything all right?"

Doto nodded. "There is a cliff ahead of us. You have been running quite well, but I do not think even with my gift you can climb down it. I must find another way." He crouched to the ground, tail swaying, and closed his eyes.

Clay watched him for a moment, and then found himself distracted by sounds in the forest. He turned, listening to the bird calls. The more he listened, the more he was sure he could hear words in them. With one hand, he brushed at the figurine about his neck. That barbet, for example. It sounded like it was saying, "Stay away! Stay away!" And, perched high in the canopy where he would never have seen it without Doto's gift, a small green bee-eater seemed to be crying, "Here they come, here they come." He strained his ears, listening with interest. No, he was certain. He could understand them. They were calling to each other about the approaching god and fire bearer, warning each other of the threat.

Something chuffed and moved in the underbrush, catching his attention. A heavy shape pushed through the bushes. He sniffed at the air—a monkey of some sort. A big one. The leaves of a nearby fern bent and shook, and then a large creature, more than half his height moving on all fours, swaggered out of the underbrush. A baboon. Clay had seen baboons before—they had visited the village a few times, not long after the people had first moved to the edge of the forest. They had been destructive and curious, with little fear of the people, but after the hunters had put arrows in a few of them, they had fled and not returned. This one was larger than any Clay had seen before, its shoulders and barrel broad, its light brown eyes intelligent.

He dropped into a squat as it approached. "Hello there," he called to it, reaching out a hand. He wondered if he would be able to understand this creature as well.

The baboon came closer. It was not behaving as though it were afraid, but there was an uncertain expression in its eyes. It looked down at his leopard foot, and then up at his face again.

"Hello. Bet you've never seen anything like me before, have you?"

It approached with small steps. It reached out its paw and took his hand in its leathery, black fingers, giving them an experimental tug. Then it sniffed.

"Claaaaaay..." Doto's voice rose in alarm behind him.

The baboon opened its mouth wide, baring four huge, curved fangs, each the size of Doto's fingers. "*Trespasser!*" it screeched. "*Trespasser!*" Its grip tightened on Clay's hand, and it pulled forward, lunging with bared teeth for his face.

White knives flashed before his eyes, the monkey's foul, fermented-fruit breath puffing into his face as it toppled Clay backward. He braced his hands against its chest, trying to keep it back, push it away. The thing was nearly as heavy as he was, but it was agile, squirming past his hands to snap its jaws at his nose. Flailing and grabbing, Clay seized fur and skin in one hand, gripping its scruff and putting his arm perilously near its mouth. He managed to twist his grip to pull at its nape, but the baboon only clung to his arm and the back of his head with its paws and struggled to get closer, slavering jaws raking just before his face, spittle flecking his skin. With several side-to-side twists of its head, it yanked its neck free of his fingers and dove for his face once more. Its jaws snapped closed again, but just shy of his nose, as its weight was hoisted off of him.

Dangling from Doto's grip, the baboon squalled fury. Without a moment's hesitation, Doto turned, swung the baboon at arm's length, and flung it into a tree. Its eyes widened, its fingers hugging at the bark, and then it dropped to the ground with a thump and lay limp, jaws slack. Doto snarled at it in wordless triumph.

His heart pounding with fear, Clay sprang to his feet. "You said the forest wouldn't recognize me with the fetish!"

Doto nudged the baboon with his toes. "The forest won't. But the animals might, especially the smarter ones. Baboons are very smart. Kwaee must have sent them after you."

Them? Clay peered into the forest. Rustling noises made his ears twitch. "Doto," he began uneasily.

"We should run," Doto said.

From out of the bushes, three more baboons strutted, each as big as the one Doto had knocked against a tree. Their malevolent copper eyes fixed on Clay. He could smell the stink of them now. "Trespasser!" one called.

"Trespasser!" echoed a voice from the trees. Clay looked up. The leaves were shaking as dark shapes leapt across the branches. The cry was taken up by many more shrill, hate-filled voices, calling down from the tree-tops, repeated by many more on the ground below. "Trespasser! Trespasser!" The word flew through the air from all sides now, the screeching so loud it made Clay's ears ring.

"I said *run!*" Doto shouted at him, pointing into the trees.

He did not need to be told a third time. He turned on his toes and bolted. A scream of fury rose behind him. He heard the crash of heavy bodies bounding through the leaves at his heels and on either side. He did not know how fast baboons could run, but even with his improved speed, they were keeping pace with him.

A monkey howled in pain or surprise behind him, and then Doto bounded past him in a terrific leap. "Do not slow down. They will not harm me, but I could not fight them all off before they killed you."

Clay was already panting with exertion. From his left side, a dark blur of fur and bared fangs lunged at him. He ducked, and heard the baboon hit the ground behind him and go tumbling. "I'm not...going to...slow down," he managed between breaths. "Can't you do that...forest thing to... kill them?"

"Not in time! It requires stillness and concentration. We will simply have to run."

A hail of hard nuts and seed pods rained down on them from the branches above. One stung Clay's arm, and another whacked hard against his skull. As far as he could tell, none of them hit Doto. "I don't think I can...run forever," he panted.

"Neither can they. But you will not have to. If we can make it to the stone tongue, we can escape them."

The memory of swaying over the water in Doto's grip nearly made him sick. He'd been so helpless, so terrified. He didn't want to try that again, new foot or no. He looked back over his shoulder. Baboons were tearing through the forest after him, too many to count, charging masses of hair and teeth, screeching and screaming, "Trespasser! Kill the trespasser!" They leapt forward, bounding off of tree trunks, crashing into each other, snapping at each other's necks and heels in their madness. If they caught him, they would shred him into ribbons. The river was far preferable.

He struggled to run faster, but at top speed, his endurance was finally beginning to flag. He heard a deep, wet growl, and then sharp teeth grazed at the back of his leg. His heel cracked the baboon in the chin, knocking it upward and making him stumble, but he managed to catch his balance. Doto led him through wide paths of the forest, avoiding the larger tree trunks. Clay was grateful for this, as he did not think that, running at such a high speed, he could have dodged them all; in addition, there were fewer branches overhead for the baboons traveling above to navigate, and more and more of them were forced to leap to the ground. One lost its grip and, wailing, dropped to the earth just in front of him. He leapt over it before he could see if it was still moving.

They sped on, barely staying ahead of the troop of baboons. Clay's limbs had begun to ache with exhaustion, and he was panting heavily, the muscles in his sides knotting. They followed the open area between the trees, which led them along a flat ridge, then curved to the left and descended sharply downhill, the grade so severe that Clay feared traveling it at such a high speed. One misstep was all it would take to send him tumbling head over heels toward the bottom. Doto did not slacken, however; in scurrying steps that were half-running, half-falling, he sped down the open slope, and Clay could do nothing but follow after, trusting his newfound nimbleness to keep him steady. Their descent was terrifying, rapid and jarring, more like a series of quick jumps or a controlled fall than a run, but he somehow kept his footing.

The baboons were not all so lucky. He dared not look back, but he could hear their feet skidding in the earth and leaves as some of them tumbled. They howled in fury. Two of them rolled past his right side, flailing and grappling at each other, unable to stop their precipitous descent. They rolled into a pearwood sapling that had found root on the side of the hill and buckled around it with a cracking sound. One clung to it with both arms, feet scrabbling in the loose earth, and the other stopped flailing, its arms swinging limply as it continued to slide and roll down the decline. After that, the screeching behind grew more distant. He hoped that they'd left off the chase, but didn't dare look over his shoulder to be sure.

At the bottom, the steep descent leveled out into a more gentle slope, and Clay thought he recognized the area from their journey the previous day. Doto pointed off to the northwest. "Not too much farther! The Asubonten and the stone tongue are just down the next hill. Just a little farth—" His words were cut off as his toe caught an errant root and he tripped forward, falling flat on his belly and skidding along the forest floor, his tail stiff. Clay was moving so swiftly that he bounded right past, and it took several more steps before he could slow himself enough to turn around.

The god was still lying there with a dazed expression, shaking his head. Behind him, the baboons had reached the bottom of the hill and were barreling toward him, a dark grey swarm of hair and tails and flashing white sickle teeth.

Clay didn't think about it. He ran toward Doto, leaves kicking up beneath his feet. He reached the leopard's side and tugged at his arm, trying to heft him up. Doto didn't move. The baboons charged at them, and for a moment, he was out on the savanna again, a wounded eland bearing down on him. Only this was worse, much worse. He pulled at Doto's arm. "Come on!"

"What happened?" Doto said, frowning. "Did I sleep again?"

"You tripped!" Clay tugged the god upright. Doto was thick with muscle, and unexpectedly heavy. "Now come on! The baboons!"

The god's eyes went wide. He did not look behind him to see the charging troop, but instead gave Clay a shove backward. "You fool! They will not attack me! Run!"

Even as he said it, a smaller monkey leapt past him and grappled at Clay's chest and neck, sending him stumbling, already off-balance from the shove. He felt the heat of spittle and breath as the baboon sunk its fangs into his shoulder and bit deep. Staggering backward, he tugged at the creature fastened to his neck. It growled, its breath bubbling in his blood, and its grip tightened. Searing pain burned in his shoulder. "Doto!" he cried out.

The god crouched, one paw on the ground. Behind him, the rest of the baboons approached, hooting. "Kill the trespasser. Kill him. Suck out his eyes. Crack his bones. Scatter his flesh for the birds."

The baboon clinging to Clay's chest released its bite, leaning back and screeching in triumph, its jaws red, coarse fur flecked with his blood. It did not see the liana curl down from the tree branch above it. The tendril struck like a serpent, cinching around its chest in an instant. In surprise, the creature let go of Clay and was hoisted rapidly up into the air. There was a crunch as it met the tree branch above, and Clay was left standing free, panting, hot blood oozing down his chest and back.

The remaining baboons shrieked in rage and charged forward, but beneath them, thick, purple plants armed with long thorns rapidly sprouted up from the forest floor, winding about them, jabbing at their limbs and bodies with their knifelike points.

"Quickly," Doto said. "To the river." He sprang into a run.

Already the baboons were extricating themselves from the trap, and those not caught by it were picking their way around it. Clay needed no further urging. He ignored the pain in his shoulder, his aching sides, his pounding heart, and raced after Doto. They sped down the slope to the final decline. Beyond that was the gash of the canyon. The stone tongue jutted out over it, little more than a grey thread at this distance, and above it wound the road to the crown of Abansin, sitting against the ridge, the great pyramid nestled in among the trees. Clay did not like to think of going near it again, but between the baboons and the ruined city, the choice was easy. He followed closely after Doto, his feet finding their way between the remaining isolated stones that had once been the old road on this side of the river.

They reached the bottom of the hill and made a dash for the stone tongue. The threats of the charging monkeys were nearing behind them. Doto led Clay to the tongue, raced up its length, and leapt, flying through the air to land on the other side. Clay slowed to a stop, frightened and puzzled. How was he to get across? Had the god deliberately left him behind?

Doto turned on the other side of the gap. "Why are you waiting? They are coming! Jump across!"

Jump? It was impossible. No human could make such a leap. Clay looked down at his feet, curling his toes, feeling the strange scrape of the stones beneath the pads of his left foot. Maybe he could make it now. He looked over the edge of the gap. Far below, the water rushed, an impossible amount of water, more water than should exist in the whole world. It was unnatural, terrifying. He remembered his previous fall, swaying out over the current. He looked back toward the hillside. The baboons were racing toward him, all fury and teeth—it seemed that more of them had joined the troop from elsewhere in the forest. They would be upon him in a moment. He had no choice. He backed up a few steps, then a few steps more.

Don't think about the river. Don't think about the fall. Doto is waiting for you on the other side. Think of him. He curled his toes and then raced forward, sprinting toward the gap. The wind from the canyon rushed upward, cool with moisture from the river. His toes hit the edge of the stone tongue. He leapt, pushing off with all his strength.

He sailed through the air like he was flying, his heart rising in his chest. Below him, the green and white surface of the Asubonten floated by. The grey stone of the tongue rose to meet him, and he landed on his feet, staggering forward a few steps. Then he was standing upright, safe on the other side. The baboons crowded each other, racing up to the gap and scrabbling to a stop when they saw it, but they could not halt the momentum of their brethren, who jostled up behind them, pushing a good half-dozen of them over the edge. They screeched and flailed in panic as they fell toward the river, plunged into it, and were swiftly carried away, dark shapes floating on the surface toward the waterfalls downstream.

〰

They settled down a little distance from the river, but not so close that the strangeness of Abansin affected them. Neither of them cared to visit that place again, and now that Clay no longer limped, they could pick their way through the steep terrain around it. Clay was tired and hungry. Several days had passed since he'd eaten anything very satisfying. He found a tree with ripening fruit on it—odd, pear-shaped, fuzzy things—and shaking down a few, found them sour but tasty.

Doto was frowning, his ears swiveled back. He was brooding over something. Clay supposed it might have been the altercation with Kwaee, but his companion's mood had grown even darker since then. "Is it the baboons?" he asked. "Is that what is bothering you? That Kwaee probably sent them after me?"

The feline's brow wrinkled. "No. Though that is cause for concern. The baboons would have to travel a great distance to find a way across the river, if they can indeed cross it at all. But they do not live only on that side of the Asubonten. There will be more on this side, and they will find us. I must get you to safety. But that is not what troubles me. It is what happened when we were running for the stone tongue. When I…fell."

Could the god's pride really be that delicate? "It was only a little trip. It happens to everyone now and then."

"It does not happen to a god! All my life, I have never tripped on anything. I have never fallen. I did not even know what had happened."

"It couldn't just be a mistake?"

"You have seen how the forest moves for me. The grass bends before my step. Stems part, roots lower. It is how it has always been. But this time, a root lingered in my path."

Clay considered. "Maybe Kwaee is wresting control of the forest from you. Maybe he wanted the forest to trip you. Maybe he even suspects you gave me the fetish and wishes to turn the forest against you so that it will catch me."

"I had not thought of that," Doto admitted. "It could be. But I do not think so. What I spoke of, the way the forest bends before me? Now it does this for you. I have seen the tree roots flatten in your path. I have given you two parts of my power: the fetish and the healing. And I think that foot of yours has made you a little bit more of a god, and me a little less."

He laughed bitterly. "When you first met me, you asked me to give you my strength, and I refused. Now it seems I have done so without intending to."

Clay thought of the god's paws on his foot, the flow of power, the words murmured in an unfamiliar language. "Take what is mine," he repeated thoughtfully.

"What?" Doto gave him a sharp look.

"That's what you said. When you were healing me. 'Take what is mine.' And then I changed."

Doto shook his head. "I do not recall saying the words, but I think that I felt them. And now you move through the forest as though you belong in it. You stalk like a cat. And I am tripped up by my own trees." He scowled at the ground. "You should not have come after me. It was senseless to do so. You were in danger, not me."

"I'm sorry. I didn't think about it. I just saw that you fell, and I was worried about you."

"That was stupid," Doto said. Then, softer, he added, "But I was glad to see you come back. How is your shoulder?"

Clay prodded at it gingerly with one finger. It was still oozing blood, but not as badly. He ought to poultice it. "It hurts."

"You are always getting hurt. It is a bad habit of yours." Doto got up and leaned close to the wound, his whiskers tickling Clay's cheek. He sniffed a few times, then said, "I think it will heal on its own. I could do it for you, but I do not wish to risk losing any more of my power."

Clay smiled at the blunt declaration. "And I don't want to end up with a leopard shoulder. I really don't know what my people will think of this foot when they see it."

"If they are still alive," Doto said casually. "Do not forget that Kwaee has turned the forest against them. Perhaps they have all been killed already."

The blood drained from Clay's face. He had not even thought of that. His friends, his brothers, his father, his aunts and uncles and cousins could all be dead? Surely not. They didn't live *in* the forest; only nearby. If it came to life and started moving and attacking them, they would know to retreat. They had to. But now the thought was in his head, an unexpected specter. "I hope you are wrong," he whispered. "I really hope so."

"Oh. That would make you feel sad, yes?"

"Of course it would! My family, my friends, dead? Don't you know what it's like to lose someone?"

"The forest is filled with death. It is nothing to be concerned about. Death makes way for new life." Doto was quiet for a moment, then added,

"But I see what you mean. I do not have others that I care about. And if my fath—if Kwaee were to die, I am not sure I would be very sad about that, either. I have never lost something that I could not get back." Even as he said it, Doto's eyes wandered reluctantly toward Clay's leopard foot.

"What about your mother?" Clay asked. "Don't you miss her?"

The leopard stiffened. "I did not know her. She died when I was an infant."

"But how? I didn't think anything could kill a god."

"Very little can. To kill a god, you would have to destroy his temple, and a god can move his temple anywhere in his domain. So you would have to destroy his whole domain, and then destroy his temple." His upper lip curled. "As Kwaee was pleased to inform you, my domain is very small, so small that my temple fills it entirely. So with my mother. He told me that she was weak, feeble, and that is why she died. He told me that if I wished to survive, to grow my domains as broad and expansive as his, I must admit no weakness. I must be strong." He sighed. "Well, I have been as strong as I know how to be, and my lands have not spread beyond my temple, not one step beyond." His eyes met Clay's. "Not until you danced for me. When you did that, I grew. I don't know why Kwaee didn't tell me of that. Perhaps he did not want me taking over his realm. Or maybe he simply did not care to admit that his own power must come at least in part from your people. If he had told me of this dance, how wonderful it could be…" He trailed off, still staring into Clay's eyes.

Clay looked away shyly. "And your father told you that the fire bearers killed your mother?"

"Today was the first time he ever said that to me. He told me before that a monster had killed her."

"What kind of a monster?"

Doto sighed. "He never said. He would not talk about her much. He said I was like her. I always thought he meant that the monster would kill me too." He glanced at Clay. "But if you were the monster the whole time, then I think it is not very likely."

Looking up the road toward Abansin, Clay felt a prickle crawl across his skin, and the fur on his leg bushed out like Doto's did when the god was annoyed. "If she was killed up there, then no wonder Kwaee never looks at it."

Doto shook his head. "A god's body is her temple. Wherever that was destroyed is where she would have died. But surely it would not be that place of fire bearers. That could never be a god's temple."

"Then why kill them all?" Clay asked. "If your father was telling the truth, and fire—and my people—did kill your mother, then where did it happen? And what do all the bodies up there have to do with it?"

"I told you already that I believe he was lying to me about that."

"But why?" Clay persisted. "Why tell you that my people killed your mother if it was not true?"

"To turn me against you, of course. Kwaee carries a deep hatred of your people for burning so much of his domain long ago. I had hoped he would forgive it if he saw that you are no longer the same people, but plainly he will not. So he lied about how she died, thinking such a story would affect me, as though I had some sentimental emotions toward her."

"Don't you?"

Doto shrugged. "Why should I? I never knew her."

"I barely remember my own mother," Clay said. "Most of what I remember now is only glimpses. Her smile. Her walk when she was tired. Parts of the stories she used to tell. The way she cried the day I was playing and smashed the earrings Father gave her. But she still means everything to me. She's part of where I come from."

"Well, you are a fire bearer, and you are emotional about things. That is normal for you. Gods are different. More sensible. We do not become attached to things that do not matter to us."

Clay looked down at his foot and gave Doto a wry smile.

"That is different," Doto declared. "Of course I care about you. You are my sole worshiper. Now do whatever you have to do with your shoulder and let us make haste toward my temple before the baboons find you and eat you."

⌁

The journey to Doto's temple was swift. Doto kept up a steady pace, and paused for Clay to rest whenever he needed it. If more baboons were about, they failed to catch wind of Clay, for their progress continued unmolested. Only now did Clay begin to appreciate just how much Doto had gone out of his way to accommodate Clay's injury. The journey to Kwaee's temple had been long and arduous, but it had also been over fairly flat and solid terrain. Certainly there had been some slopes and areas with heavy rain, but on the whole, their path had taken them over an even and open forest floor. Now, with Clay unhindered, their route was more direct, and the going more challenging. The forest was far less uniform than the previous days had indicated. The two pushed their way through dense thickets of plants covered with barbed thorns and purple flowers that bent before them in submission. They passed through a swampy area where Doto said

Atekye shared dominion. There, out of the treacherous bogs, grew massive trees with corded wood, their roots jutting up from the water like knobby knees, forcing Clay and Doto to leap over the waters by jumping from root to root. Clay's nimble toes found easy purchase each time. Their path took them mostly uphill, and the air both cooled and lost humidity as they ascended, traveling through huge boulder fields and along the bases of jutting precipices.

In the late afternoon, they circled around a huge, flat lake. It was so wide that Clay could scarcely make out the other side and still enough that it held a perfect image of the sky within it. Rising above it was a real mountain, the first that Clay had ever seen. The white peak of it seemed to hold up the sky, and errant clouds crashed into its shaggy green slopes and slid down into the secret folds of its valleys. Doto pointed toward it. "We go up."

They climbed, their path winding back and forth like the leaves of a palm weave, taking them steadily upward. When Clay looked back over his shoulder, his head reeled at the sight of the ground so far away, and stems of nearby plants stirred at his discomfort, winding around his ankles and wrists to steady him. Never before had he imagined such heights, not even when telling the story of the antelope who brought fire to the people. Finally, he looked ahead to Doto and asked, "Are we going to the highest place in all the world? Is that where your temple is?"

Doto was standing atop a little rise. He beckoned to Clay. "Come here."

Clay picked his way upward and stood next to Doto. There he gaped. The mountain still towered above them, but beyond it rose a hundred other mountains, spreading from the farthest north to the farthest south, each reaching higher than the ones before, some completely white. Clay knew then that the world was so large that he could not understand it. It did not end at the Firelands or the great water. It went on forever. He could spend his whole life traveling and never see the end of it. He looked back over his shoulder and saw the forest spreading out behind them, dense and hilly and rich with life. Below them was the lake they had circled, the vast plain of water whose opposite side Clay had not been able to discern, now a shining disc the size of his fist. In the distance, he thought he could barely make out the Asubonten, but beyond that, nothing but more forest. He could see no savanna. His village would be but a speck out there, tiny, almost meaningless against the great vastness of the forest, the people who inhabited it even smaller. He wondered that a god could care whether they existed.

Doto nodded toward the vista. "All of that is Kwaee." He stared out over the endless treetops, and then turned and pointed up the slope. "And up there is me."

The vegetation had thinned as they had ascended the mountain, with more bushes and fewer trees, but along the slope a stream ran, cutting into the side, and cradled in the edge of the mountain was a narrow valley thick with forestation, a cup of dark green trees against the lighter slopes. The stream spilled into it from above in a waterfall, a thread that caught the light of the setting sun and dissolved it into a misty fan of orange. This was Doto's temple; it could be nothing else. The sight stirred happy feelings in Clay, like those of coming back to his own tent after days of travel, or seeing a familiar face after a long absence. The weariness of the journey ebbed from his legs, and even the pain from the bite in his shoulder dimmed.

Doto led him along the slope of the mountain. As they neared the grove, Clay could feel something in the air: the same vibration he had felt when Doto had healed him. It was like a heartbeat in the breeze or the approach of a storm, but it pulled at him, drew him closer. He longed to enter the little valley cradled against the mountainside. As they neared, he saw signs of young trees sprouting down the slopes, but these had withered and died, their leaves shriveled, bark split. Doto walked past them, between the trunks of larger trees, and those were tall and sturdy, their trunks unmarred by whatever had withered the saplings. Here he paused and turned.

"I have never let anyone in here before," he said. "Not my father, nor any other god, nor any beast." He glanced back over his shoulder. "Up to now, it has only been me."

Clay nodded and did not step forward, though he could not help peering between the trees into the glen. It was darker in there, thick with vegetation. "Doto," he began. When had he stopped calling the god Lord Doto? He could not remember doing so. "Doto, I understand if you do not want—"

The god's hand reached out to him, padded palm turned up. Clay took it in his own, and Doto pulled him gently toward the entrance between the trees. He stepped in, and as he did so, Doto's grip on his hand tightened, his breath drawing in sharply.

"Is it all right?"

"Yes. It is just that—I felt it. I can feel you now. It is something new."

Doto led him further into the glen, through leaves and grasses that curled around his body as he walked, neither hindering him nor bending before him. Each was perfectly formed, the leaves unmarred by blight or insect, each a paragon of plants. The trees stretched upward in majestic arches, their branches permitting few shafts of light to strike the ground. Against the bank of one tree, mushrooms grew in brilliant pipes of red and gold, and between two more strung a curtain of flowering vines splashed with violet, blue, and pink. Doto led him across a bed of bright green moss so thick and soft that it felt as though he were strolling across hare's fur. They reached the stream that Clay had seen before, its clear waters twisting and winding over white and grey stone, and here Clay knelt and dipped his face to it. He gasped in astonishment.

"What is wrong?" Doto asked. "Is the water not good?" He actually sounded anxious.

"Yes, of course," Clay said. "It is delicious. Water from a stream or pond usually tastes of the ground, but this tastes clean, like the rain. And it is...cold." He frowned. He had had to search for the word. "I have never felt a cold like this before." Again he drank deeply, and the coldness of the water spread through his throat and stomach. "It is wonderful," he decided.

Doto's feline muzzle stretched in a strange grin—one that bared pointed fangs, true, but unmistakably a grin. "Come. Let me take you to a place where you may rest."

They walked alongside the stream, following it to a deep, clear pool at the base of a high cliff. It was filled by trickles of water down the rock face, and by a cool white mist that hazed the air, beading on the broad leaves of the trees and dripping downward. The cliff was sheer stone, dark with moisture, and jutting crags led upward in what might have been a series of hand and footholds, their surfaces sprouting thick tufts of moss. Doto climbed up these, ascending the cliff face beneath a waterfall that had dissolved into mist halfway up. "Up here!" he urged.

Clay followed hesitantly, uneasy about climbing what was surely a treacherous path, but he found that when he put his fingers and toes onto the holds, the moss there gripped at his fingers and toes, making ascent easy. A short climb revealed a shallow cave behind the falls, and there Doto crouched waiting for him, sheltered from the water in the crevice. Vines with light purple and yellow flowers clustered the walls, and squat, white mushrooms and bright green algae grew between the stones of the floor.

Taking some care not to lose his footing, Clay climbed into the cave, finding it drier than he had expected. He was about to ask what it was Doto wanted to show him, but he then turned around, and the words died on his breath. Behind the curtain of water and the mist, the forest lay spread out below him, an endless plain of green treetops covering the hills. The sun was setting into the western horizon, and its dying light burned the water red and orange and made the whole cave glow. He sat down near Doto, transfixed. "It's beautiful. I have never seen anything like it."

"My father has the whole of the forest," Doto said, "and I only this place, but I have done well with it, I think."

"Did you make it look like this?"

The great cat stood and gazed down into his garden. "Yes," he said softly. "I made the water come this way. I grew the plants and directed the stream and made the cave. I could not even say why I did it. No one has seen it but me. Certainly not Kwaee. He would only snort and call it sentimental nonsense and probably compare me to my mother again."

"She must have been wonderful if she made places like this," Clay said. Doto turned and stared at him, and for a moment he was afraid he had offended the forest god.

"Wait here," Doto said, and then he dashed forward and leapt off of the edge.

Clay stood and nearly shouted in alarm before reminding himself, sheepishly, that the god would not be in any danger. He peered over the edge, but Doto was nowhere to be seen.

The sunset was a darker red by the time he returned, and he had in his arms—Clay had no idea how he'd climbed up the waterfall with them—a few large yellow and red fruits, so ripe that their skins looked ready to burst at the touch. "I thought you might be hungry," he said, setting the fruits at Clay's feet. "So I grew these for you." His gaze and ears were intently focused on Clay.

Reaching down, Clay took one. "You grew these? Are these you too?"

"Yes."

He slid his fingers over the taut rind of the fruit. "And you can feel it when I do this?"

"I can feel everything that you do here: every footstep, every shift of your weight, the air moving in and out of your lungs, everything."

Clay's skin prickled at the god's words, or perhaps it was the coldness of the water in the air. He found himself shivering.

"I felt that, too."

He lifted the fruit to his lips. "Will it hurt you if I eat this?"

"You cannot hurt me." A little of Doto's haughty pride returned to the straightness of his back, the tilt of his head.

Clay bit into the fruit, and its juice flooded his mouth, sweet and exotic and wild, its heady flavor briefly overwhelming his tongue and nose. He had never tasted anything like it in his life. Eagerly he took another bite. Only now did he realize how hungry he had been, not just over the past day or two, but since he had left his village so long ago. He greedily devoured the fruit and licked his fingers clean of its sticky juices. "It is amazing," he said, reaching for another. "How could you have made this?"

"I watched you as we traveled," Doto said. His grin was even broader than before, the expression odd on the face of the usually stoic and bossy leopard. "When you ate, I saw what you liked, and what you did not. It was not hard to guess what you would like most."

"I didn't think you were paying attention," Clay admitted. He bit into the second fruit and found it as delicious as the first, so juicy that its syrup ran down his chin.

Doto watched him eat with evident pleasure, and then tilted his ears to the sides. "When you are rested and full, would you dance for me again?"

Clay thought about it. He wiggled his toes, feeling their new thickness, the brush of fur against fur, the way the claws stretched out when they splayed. He could dance again, properly, for the first time since he had been injured. It would be a dance like Doto had never had before. "There will be no fire," he pointed out. "I could never light one here."

Doto leaned closer to him. "You can dance around me. I will be your fire."

Prodigal

"Laughing Dog?" Left Rabbit's grin wavered between joy and disbelief. "I saw you from afar, and I didn't even know it was you!" He paused, peering. "*Is* it you? Have you come back to us?"

Laughing Dog spread his arms in frustration. Not back for an instant, and the first thing out of Left Rabbit's mouth was stupid. "Of course it's me. Who else? Did you think me gone forever?" Instead of rushing close for a clasp of friendship, Rabbit stood still, staring up and down at him with a bewildered expression.

"But you're—you've been out in the wilderness, Laughing Dog. All alone! And you look like you've feasted for weeks. Did you find some trove of food you've been keeping a secret? But the King will be so happy to see you, you know." Finally he approached and gripped Laughing Dog's arm and shoulder. "Everyone thinks you're dead." He whispered the words as though they were a curse. "The way you went off without any food or water. Everyone was really upset about it. Ant With a Leaf was so angry. She said stubbornness had killed off another pretty man for no reason, and she would have to find another one. She didn't," he added hastily. "But she talked about it very loudly. And Great Ram won't say you're dead, either. But I know he thinks it."

"Plainly I am not dead. Though it doesn't surprise me much to hear everyone would assume I couldn't survive on my own. What about Clay? Does he mourn me too?"

Left Rabbit closed his mouth, licking his lips nervously. The whites were showing around his eyes.

Frowning, Laughing Dog stepped back. "What's happened? Did Father punish him as well? Is he all right?"

"Laughing Dog. Clay…your brother, he…"

"He what?" Laughing Dog realized with a twinge of guilt that he had thought little of his brother's plight while out on the sahil. Had his wounds worsened? Had he blamed himself for his brother's exile and come in pursuit?

"He's gone." Left Rabbit stared at the ground. "No one has seen him in a moon. Everyone thinks he's dead too. So, you see, your father will be so happy to know you are back—"

"Gone? What do you mean he's gone? Did he wander off? Where did he go?"

"We don't know. Some kind of animal dragged him off, is what everyone's saying. A big cat, a leopard maybe. They said it looked like leopard tracks, only bigger. No one's really sure."

"When did this happen? And why did our hunters not track this leopard?" Laughing Dog could scarcely believe what he was hearing. Clay, gone? It was unthinkable. Dark thoughts of his brother being torn apart in the forest, screaming, came unbidden to his mind, and he forced them away.

"Oh, of course they tracked it. The King went himself! And Great Ram, far into the forest, I heard, but it was a strange trail, full of mysteries, and after some distance, they lost it." Left Rabbit's voice broke with misery. "He's gone, Laughing Dog. People are saying the forest just swallowed him up. Your father—the King has been in his tent for days and days, and he doesn't speak to anyone. He doesn't even come out except to, you know, do his business. He took it real bad, what with you, and then Clay... He'll be glad to see you, for sure. I know I am. Maybe now that you're back, things will start to go right again."

Laughing Dog barely heard him. He had had plans, ever since he left Deraji and the nasty business there, and in his journey back across the savanna, he had time to formulate them. He had expected to be challenged by his father, by the village elders, by Cloud, and perhaps even Ram, for his right to return. None of them would believe he had spoken to the gods, much less bested one, though that secret, at least, he intended to keep to himself. But he could have boasted that he had spoken to Ogya, out there in the dark, on the edge of the Firelands, and that he now knew the old stories must have truth to them.

Clay would have been on his side. He would have stood up for him. The rest would be skeptical, but Laughing Dog would have told them what they wanted to hear: that they were right, and they would have accepted it. With the new strength and endurance that he had wrested from Ogya, he could become a champion among his people, and if Great Ram were destined to become King, then Laughing Dog could show him up by making himself the greatest hunter any of them had ever known. Then, one day, when they all knew of his prowess, and respected it, he would tell them the secret of how he had wrestled with Ogya in the sahil and won. He would show them that even the gods could be beaten to their knees if one were smart enough and determined enough. Then the people could learn to be strong. They could master the world rather than quail before it. And the next time there was a drought or a sickness, there would be no whining prayers to spirits that did not listen. There would be no sacrifices they could not afford, no inaction while they waited for signs from the gods. No one would sit in their village and just wait for it to burn before they left.

He had soothed his mind with these dreams during his journey, drowning out the mad mutterings of Ogya as long as he could, and then quenching the voice with sips of water when it grew too loud for him to ignore. His plans had seemed fine things, and he had looked forward to taking this first step when he returned. But his brother was gone, and probably dead, and no matter how frustratingly devout and self-righteous Clay could be, Laughing Dog found that the loss shocked him beyond grief.

"Laughing Dog?" Rabbit's voice reminded him he was not alone, not anymore. "Are you all right?"

"Clay cannot be gone," Laughing Dog decided. "Not dead. No. You would have found something. No animal could drag him off without leaving some sign. Blood. Bone. Perhaps he left on his own. Did you think of that?"

"Well," Rabbit began, but Laughing Dog didn't let him finish the thought.

"He was very upset about his foot and what happened. If he blamed me, then no doubt he blamed the gods too. Maybe when he saw me go off on my own journey to find the gods, he decided to do the same. You said the trail was strange. Well, of course it was. It was Clay attempting to deceive you. He wished to be left alone to think, or grieve, or pray. Perhaps he even intended to follow me and bring me back."

Rabbit scratched at his chest. "We didn't think of that."

"No, that doesn't surprise me. It's not the sort of thing he would normally do. But much has happened to Clay. Injury can make people behave strangely. Remember when your nephew fell in the field and hit his head, and then always complained of bad smells afterward? Maybe it's something like that." Even as he said the words, they rang false to him, but he rejected the whispering doubts in his mind as nothing more than Ogya's dark mutterings. "You'll see. One day soon he'll come out of the forest again, limping, and maybe a little sulky, but glad to see everyone all the same."

Frowning, Left Rabbit said, "Out of the forest? But if he went in there, he's dead for sure."

"Dead? Why dead? He lost a foot, not his eyes."

"But the forest would have…" Left Rabbit's frown deepened. "I forgot! You left before it happened."

"Happened? Rabbit, what else happened?"

"The forest. It turned against us. The Teller says the gods are angry with us again."

Laughing Dog stared at him in incomprehension. "What is this nonsense? The forest has turned against you? What can that mean?"

"I have never seen anything like it. It moves if you go near it. It attacks us. It tore apart half the village, Laughing Dog. Just pulled apart the wall like it was made of straw and started smashing tents."

"It moves?" Laughing Dog repeated in disbelief. What new madness was this? "That cannot possibly be true."

"I know it can't," Rabbit said miserably, "but you will never be able to tell that to Flint or Bramble or Mighty Ant or Six Star. They're gone. All gone. They were on a hunting party in the forest when it changed. And they never came back. Laughing Dog, the forest ate them! It's true!" he added hastily, seeing Laughing Dog's eyes narrow. "Bramble's wife Red Moth went to look for him. She says that a tree's branches grabbed at her. It broke both her arms. Everyone is frightened and afraid. We can't hunt in the forest any more, and there's not much game outside it. We're all so hungry. And even some of the trees near the village will move toward us if we get close, like they're angry. The gods want vengeance against us for something, but no one knows what we have done. We pray, we dance, and some of the elders have even given blood to the earth, but nothing helps."

Laughing Dog listened to this tale with increasing suspicion. Rabbit had never been bright and was prone to believe the worst sorts of superstition. The ordeal in the sahil might have changed Laughing Dog's mind about some things, but even so, this story defied credulity. "This cannot be true. The hunting party must have encountered some hungry beast in the forest. None of us know what creatures might live in there. And Red Moth, stricken with grief, could have met an accident with a falling tree and mistaken it for intent. The destruction of the town—perhaps elephants blundered into it, and people *thought* it was the forest attacking. But trees don't move on their own, Left Rabbit. You must know that."

"I know—I know I'm not always smart about how things work." Left Rabbit lifted his chin to look Laughing Dog in the eye. "But you're not always smart about stuff either. You were exiled, remember? For saying that things weren't true when they were."

Laughing Dog clenched his teeth, fighting down a sudden urge to strike the stupid hunter in his chin. He breathed slowly, letting his kindling rage subside before he answered. "That's true. I was banished to the wilderness for a time. A very good point, Rabbit. But because I went there and encountered the gods, I learned about them. I heard their voices. So why don't you and I go to the edge of the forest, just out of reach, where you say the trees move. If I'm right, we know that something else took our hunters. If you're right, then we can learn something new."

The man stared at him. "But Laughing Dog, you have been out in the wilderness for so long. Surely you want a meal and some water. Surely you wish to see your father and brother."

Hunger and thirst had not inconvenienced Laughing Dog for most of his journey, but now, at the mention of a meal, his gut twisted with sudden craving. And, he realized, he did yearn to see his father and Great Ram again, even though they had cast him out. The loneliness of the savanna had taken home in his soul, and Ogya's needling voice was far from companionship. He longed to see their faces again, to clasp them in his arms, and to rest and feel the safety and comfort of his tent once more.

"I do wish to, very much. But they did exile me for challenging the old tales. And now the Teller is saying that the forest has come to life against us, and that divine vengeance motivates it. It's so hard to believe, Rabbit." He turned toward the deepening shade of the forest to the south. "I have to see it for myself, or I'm just going to end up arguing, and next thing I know, I'll be banished again for stubbornness."

"I don't understand why you have to argue," Rabbit said unhappily. "But if you really want to see it, I'll take you there."

⁓

Near the forest's edge, the trees did seem to move and sway in a menacing manner, but that was likely just his imagination working Left Rabbit's fears into his mind. The man had stayed back some distance, in the more open part of the savanna, and despite Laughing Dog's ribbing and coaxing, he would not venture any further.

Laughing Dog looked over his shoulder and saw Rabbit wave. East of them sat their village, looking the same as he had left it, the wooden wall encircling it, or at least what he could see of it, concealing and sheltering the tents. Smoke was rising. They would be cooking. A deep hunger clutched at his stomach. For now he ignored it.

He took a few steps toward the forest, telling himself he was not afraid. But the trees looked dark and malevolent. He thought of all he had seen in the last moon, and the notion of a moving, angry forest did not seem so laughable. Still. He could hardly show himself as champion to his people if he feared standing trees. He would just walk up to one, pat it on the trunk, and smile back to Left Rabbit. That would be enough.

Near the edge of the forest, where the bushes began to grow higher and the savanna trees clustered more closely together, there was a rustle along the ground that made his heart leap, a slither that moved through the grasses, brushing them aside. Then a thorn vine—long, wickedly barbed, and twisting like a serpent—whipped through the air and lashed around his calf. To his shame, he cried out in terror, but the shout was knocked out of him when the vine tugged at him, pulling him off his feet and dragging him toward the dark, gaping forest. He flailed in terror, clutching at roots and stems, stripping their leaves away and pulling his fingernails backward. Rocks scratched at his back and leg as he was pulled.

He heard Left Rabbit call his name, but from a distance, too far to save him. He would have to save himself. The trees bent stiffly toward him, their branches stretching out in skeletal claws to clutch at him. He knew that if he were pulled beneath them, he would be killed. He groped for Yakeb's knife at his belt, tugged it free, and then lost his grip on it. It slipped from his fingers and the vine pulled him past it. No knife, then. He would have to claw his way free of the vine with his fingers. He curled toward his leg, getting a face full of leaves and grass. A rock struck at his forehead, but he ignored it. With his fingers he gripped at the vine, trying to pull it away. It cinched more tightly, the thorns gashing into his flesh, his blood welling up around it.

For no reason that he could discern, the vine stopped pulling him. He scrambled backward, trying to pull himself free, but the thorns were still hooked in his leg. Thin wisps of smoke were rising from the edges of their wooden grip. The green vines hissed and darkened to brown, withering wherever his blood touched them. They blackened, grew brittle, and then broke. He stood and backed away, gazing in astonishment. Smoke rose wherever drops of his blood hit the ground, circles of ash forming in the leaves and grasses, with edges that glowed red for a moment. Gingerly he prodded at the blood on his leg with one finger. It did not feel hot. He wiped his leg clean of blood. There were no wounds where the thorns had dug into his skin. He was unharmed.

And the forest was alive, which meant that Rabbit was probably right. The hunting party, gone. Clay, dead. The gods had turned against them, attacked his people, taken his brother. Grief burned at him. Could it be his fault? Could it be that the gods resented his conflict with Ogya, and were now taking out their vengeance on his people? A smug chuckle came from the back of his mind. In panic, he stood and hurried away from the edge of the forest, snatching up Yakeb's knife. Once he was a safe distance away, he ignored the astonished remarks of Left Rabbit and drained every last drop of his remaining water from his water skin.

⌒⌒⌒

The village was quiet. Normally at this time of day, the children would be out playing. People should be weaving, shaping clay, playing the xalam, cooking, or caring for the goats, but few engaged in these activities now. He could hear quiet talk coming from tents. Those who he did see expressed surprise and pleasure at seeing him, coming up to clasp at his arms or kiss his cheeks, but their eyes were haunted, their faces hollow. They looked afraid and hungry. He did see his promised, Ant With a Leaf, among them, stringing a new bow with eland gut. She gave him a high and proud stare, but did not approach him. Was there relief in her eyes? Hope? He could not decide. But it would not be her place to approach him until his position among the people was restored. Ant was independent, but she respected the gods. No doubt his exile had shamed her.

He passed the village's inner circle, the fire pit, the site of his banishment. No fire burned there now, nor did it seem one was being prepared for tonight. A returning prince ought to have a feast, he thought, and his hunger clutched at his stomach. Beyond the fire pit he passed the racks for drying hides. No one wanted a tent near that, for it frequently stank. So of course, this was where Cloud set her tent. The thick smoke from burning herbs and feathers and who knew what else effectively blocked out any outside odors. His own tent was some distance away, near those of his father and brothers, and he headed toward it, Left Rabbit scurrying anxiously at his heels like a lost puppy.

At the top of the hill, he saw the clear impact of the forest's violence: the village's shape had changed completely. Where once his family's tents would have sat, sheltered beneath the branches of the forest, a freshly built wall cut through, like a scar where a finger or limb had been lost. Some tents were missing entirely—Laughing Dog supposed that those had not been rescued when the forest came to life—while others, like his and his family's, had been moved, dragged safely out of the way.

Once there would have been a cluster of friends and relatives grouped around their tents, but now the area looked barren and empty. As he approached, Great Ram pushed aside the hide covering the entrance to his tent and stepped out. He was as tall and stiff as always, but his cheeks sagged with a weariness that had not been there before. On seeing Laughing Dog, he very nearly smiled, the corners of his mouth stretching, before he no doubt recalled that the brother he was so happy to see had been exiled for blasphemy. His features set into a severe slab. "Brother. You have returned to us at last."

"I have," Laughing Dog answered, walking up to clasp his brother's arm.

Great Ram gripped it with open affection. "And you have some new meat on your bones, I see. Well. If you are back, then you must have seen your error. The gods must have spoken to you."

"Indeed they have, my brother. They have spoken to me more clearly than I believed possible."

Surprise broke Great Ram's serious expression. "They have? And you have heard their guidance? You acknowledge their truth and are ready to bend before their wisdom?"

Laughing Dog had thought for many days about what he would say when he was asked this. "Ram, without the strength of the gods, I would have died in the sahil. It is only through their power that I have returned to you. Their wisdom fills my thoughts so that it nearly drowns them out. Where before I could not hear them, now sometimes I can hear little else. I am a new man."

His brother's normally austere face now broke into a broad smile. He crushed Laughing Dog to his chest with unguarded relief, his grip powerful. He had not heard the meaning behind Laughing Dog's words, and he never would have. That was Great Ram: dutiful, strong, and about as clever as a mushroom. "I am so happy to hear it, Dog. Father will be so overjoyed to see you home safely." He paused, and his face fell. "But you have not heard about Clay, have you?"

Looking back at Left Rabbit, Laughing Dog answered, "I heard he was missing, but the tale makes no sense to me. A forest animal dragged him away, but left no trace? How can that be?"

Great Ram shook his head sadly. "I don't understand it either, but that's what happened. It looks like Clay left his tent and encountered a huge leopard. Then he seems to have followed it for some time. The tracks were so strange. I could make no sense of them. The leopard seemed to have walked on two feet for part of the way, and Clay followed along. But he left his stick behind. And his spear—it was tossed off a good distance from his tent."

Laughing Dog considered this information. "And there was no blood from a fight or an animal bite?"

"None. Not that we could find anywhere. None of it makes sense."

"Perhaps it was not a leopard at all."

"Now, what are you saying, Dog? I know leopard tracks when I see them. If you are trying to suggest that I don't know my hunting, I—"

"No, of course I'm not saying that," Laughing Dog said soothingly. "I don't doubt you saw leopard tracks. But perhaps that's only what someone else wanted you to see. It could be our brother was not carried off by a wild animal, but kidnapped. Tracks can be faked, you know."

Ram stared at him in open astonishment. "But of course, how could I not have seen it? Fake tracks! That would be why it walked on two feet."

"Yes. And the kidnapper threw Clay's spear away before kidnapping him so that he could not fight back. Rabbit says you lost the trail in the forest. No doubt his kidnapper heard you coming and, slowed by our brother's crippled leg, could not outpace you, so took extra care to conceal himself and his tracks from then on."

"But none of us thought of this!" Great Ram exclaimed. "We needed you there, Laughing Dog. You were always the clever one. Too clever sometimes, I suppose. But why would anyone kidnap our brother and take him into the forest?"

"I couldn't say. Maybe to ransom him to our father? But we will have to ask Clay when we find him," Laughing Dog said casually.

"Then you think we might find him yet? You think he is not dead?"

"That is what I think," he replied, and was surprised to find that he half-believed it.

He was more surprised to see the glimmer of relieved tears in his brother's eyes. "But this is wonderful news. You must tell Father your theory at once! He's been so distraught since you left. And then when Clay vanished, he just kind of went away. I thought it might kill him. He hasn't been out of his tent in days."

Laughing Dog nodded. "Rabbit told me. I would like very much to see him now. And I can ask him permission to return home."

When they approached the King's tent, however, they were stopped by Cloud exiting, the wild tangle of hair atop her head looking whiter than Laughing Dog remembered it. Her eyes flashed when she saw him, but she lifted a hand before her mouth to caution them to keep their voices low. "The King is sleeping. He needs whatever rest he can get."

Laughing Dog didn't care for her interfering—who was she to stand between a prince and his father, after all?—but now was not the time to stir up trouble. Besides, perhaps his father truly needed the sleep. He was content to wait. He went back to his own tent, and found the air inside stuffy and stale from disuse, so he opened it up to freshen and went to sit near the fire pit. The entire while, Left Rabbit followed him, peppering him with questions about his time in the savanna, until he finally had enough of his lingering, and sent him to fetch some food. Then the village was quiet, eerily so. There was no sound of children playing, no chatter about hunts or when the next rains would come or how the youth were so much less responsible than the prior generation. There was only the savanna wind rustling over the village wall and around the tents, and hushed murmurs that did not carry. Laughing Dog stared into the ashes of the fire pit and wondered how many times the people had joined the circle since he had been exiled. The ashes looked old and flat. Surely there would be a feast to welcome him home.

"You're different," Cloud said.

He looked up. She was short, but she stood as though taller, her back arched as taut as the curve of a bow. She was wearing that old wrap of green cloth she always wore. He wondered that she hadn't ridded herself of it by now: it was dirty and full of holes, and it stunk besides, but she didn't seem to notice that any more than she minded the sticks and leaves that were always tangled in her hair.

"I have been alone in the savanna for two moons," he answered. "I heard the voice of a god."

"Yes, so Left Rabbit said." She studied him with an expressionless gaze. "You have been out in the wilds for so long, but you are fatter. Stronger. And something else."

Laughing Dog's skin burned under her stare. He did not like her looking at him like this. "More humble, perhaps," he suggested. "I thought the gods distant, uninvolved. Now I know they watch us closely. I've felt their power."

"And what do you think of that?"

This was a test. She was weighing his answers, and would make a recommendation to his father on whether he should be allowed back into the village. He had little doubt it was on her advice he had been exiled to begin with; his sentimental father over-valued her judgment. Well. First Claw would not always be King, and Great Ram had felt Cloud's switch enough times not to be fond of her.

"I do not like it," he answered her. "The gods are dangerous. We must take care with them. I know that now."

"Yes," Cloud said slowly. "Yes, they are. Well. Maybe you have learned a few things out in the savanna." Her expression softened. "We have missed you, Laughing Dog. We have needed you. Your brother's disappearance, and then the forest… It is too much. People are afraid. Some talk of leaving. But where can we go? The droughts and Firelands to the north, the angry forest to the south. We are trapped here. We must find a way to appease the gods. They must forgive us." She reached down and put a hand on his shoulder. "I hope now, after all this, you will finally pray. Ask the spirits of the forest to forgive us for whatever offense we have committed. Ask Kwaee to turn his wrath away. And that the gods who have taken our people, your brother, will return them home again."

Laughing Dog despised falsehood. It was almost always better to speak your truth clearly and be hated for it than to say what someone wanted to hear and win their favor. He wanted to tell her, no, we do not have to beg mercy. The gods can be beaten. They can be defeated. We can fight against them using their own power. But Cloud would never accept this. She was too old, too set in her ways to understand what he had learned. And if he spoke his truth to her now, she would only speak to his father, and if he were banished again, he could not help his people. So he lied. "Of course. I will seek the blessing of the gods once more. Perhaps they will forgive us."

She eyed him with obvious suspicion, but did not push the topic. "I am pleased to hear it. When the King has had some rest, I will let him know of your return."

Laughing Dog wondered if he had truly been deterred because his father was resting, or if Cloud had merely wished to interrogate him first. But she strode away and disappeared into her tent once more, and about that time, Left Rabbit appeared with a shank of cold goat meat, a bowl of boiled roots, and spiced hare with honey, along with a calabash filled with stale-smelling water. The food did not appear very fresh, but Laughing Dog was reminded of the gnawing emptiness in his stomach, and snatched the meal out of Left Rabbit's hands.

"I know it's not the feast you'd want," the hunter said in apology, "but it's all we've got right now. If this were an ordinary night, there wouldn't be much at all, but everyone knows you've been out in the savanna."

Laughing Dog saw the man's eyes flicker down toward his flesh-padded belly and back up again. *Others are hungry,* he had been too polite to say. *Children, mothers, hunters who need their energy.* Laughing Dog knew it. He had seen their faces when he entered the village. Right now he did not care; he ached with hunger. He slurped up the boiled roots, and slid the hare across his tongue, barely giving himself time to savor the precious sweetness of the honey. He stripped the meat off of the goat leg and cracked the bone to get at the marrow, licking the splintery hollow clean.

He looked up from his meal to see Left Rabbit staring at him, aghast. "I need to get my strength up," he said, "if I am to find my brother and our lost people."

"You think there's a chance?" Left Rabbit did not sound very hopeful. "Well, if the gods speak to you, then there must be. They could guide you through the forest if you pray."

"It's possible." Laughing Dog was hungry still, but he dared not ask for more food now. He could not afford to have his people think him greedy. Once they were asleep, he could find something else to eat.

"You expect me to guide you, Laughing Dog?" said the voice of fire in his mind.

"Maybe," he said aloud, unthinking.

Left Rabbit gave him a puzzled look. "Maybe what?"

He cursed himself. It was far too soon for people to begin noticing his new strangeness. "Maybe you could leave me alone for a bit, Rabbit. I have much to think about. And I wish to—to pray." He was delighted with this explanation. It was actually somewhat true.

"Oh, of course." Seeming encouraged, Left Rabbit crouched to collect the bowl and departed.

The voice of Ogya popped and crackled its amusement. "You think I would help you find your fallen people. They are dead, you know. Kwaee has slain them."

"And how do you know that?" Laughing Dog muttered, looking about to make sure no one else saw him speaking.

"I am a god, foolish boy. Did you think me blind, miniscule, limited to what you see through your own soggy eyes? It is only a tiny part of my power you have swallowed. I am far greater than that. I burn in the belly of the earth. I rule the Firelands and even Wem himself cannot quench me there. Everywhere there is a flame, I see. And I have seen that Kwaee has stirred up his old enmity with your miserable species. He means to destroy you. Every tree in the forest will try to crush you; the very blades of grass will slash at your skin. The insects will swarm out of the forest to sap your blood. The animals will creep out of its shelter at night to prey upon you, to tear your flesh from your bones while you sleep. If you do not flee its boundaries, your people will die, every one."

"Well, we can't leave," Laughing Dog said. "This is the only place rain falls consistently. This is going to be home. It's here that we have a chance of survival."

The voice hissed with satisfaction. "Then you will die. Kwaee will kill you. It's only a pity you have refused my help, fought me. I will enjoy watching you all suffer."

"Your help? What could you possibly do to stop this?"

"What could the god of fire do to fight against a realm composed of wood? Can you possibly be so dense? I would immolate it, boy. I would lick it into ash. I would spit in the eye of Kwaee until he surrendered before me and swore to serve your race eternally. I still might do this thing for you, despite your insolence, your drowning my voice with that filthy water. If..."

Laughing Dog did not like to be toyed with, and he was beginning to feel like a plaything. It wanted to *make* him ask. He would not give it the satisfaction. "If I swore that I and my people would serve you in turn, I suppose. If I begged. If I called myself nothing before you and humbly beseeched your aid."

"That would be an excellent beginning," Ogya crackled.

"I understand. I reject your generous offer." He reached down for the calabash and lifted it to his lips.

Ogya roared in fury. "Do not be a bigger fool than you have already been. Kwaee will kill your people. He will destroy you all without my help."

Laughing Dog did not let him rage further. He swallowed the stale water in deep, greedy gulps. The voice diminished into a hiss and then nothing.

The sky was darkening, the evening air filled with the chirruping of waking insects and roosting birds. Already he could see a few flames being lit across the village. He wondered if they burned in futile hatred of him. Let Ogya rage against him. He would never bend before the will of the fire god nor any other. He would keep his independence, whatever the cost.

⌁

He woke with a start when a hand touched his shoulder. He had not known he was so tired as to drift off, but he had, leaning forward with his elbows on his knees, his head hanging.

"The King is awake," Cloud said. "He will see you now."

Laughing Dog stood, shaking the weariness from his mind. "At last." He turned toward the tent, but Cloud gripped at his arm.

"Be gentle with him, please. He's not well. He is very fragile." Her usual severity was gone for the moment, her eyes pleading with him.

"Of course. He's my father. I care for him too, you know." He pulled his arm from her grip and strode away.

The King's tent had seemed larger the last time Laughing Dog was inside it. The flaps had been open to the air and light, and made the tent seem safe and comfortable. Now they were shut, and the inside of the tent was dark, stuffy, and foul-smelling, filled with a thick smoke that rose from a brazier burning some remedy of Cloud's.

It was difficult to see, and Laughing Dog squinted into the smoke and darkness, trying to force his eyes to adjust to the scant red light the brazier provided.

"Who is it?" a voice rasped from the corner of the tent where his father slept. "Who's there?" A shape sat up, and the light of the burning embers fell across his father's face.

It was only Laughing Dog's self-discipline that prevented him from recoiling in horror. The man that sat in his father's bed was dirty and gaunt. He looked as though he had not eaten nor groomed in weeks. His cheeks were hollowed, his lips drawn back, teeth protruding from an unkempt, crusted, black beard. "Son? Son, how can this be?" Awkwardly, shaking, he got from his bed, reaching for Laughing Dog with bony arms, his rheumy eyes lighting with joy as he pulled his son into an embrace. He was as thin and dried up as an old carcass, and he stank of his own filth. He wept openly against Laughing Dog's shoulder. "You have returned to me at last. The gods have given one of my sons back to me."

"Yes," said Laughing Dog. "I have come back. But father, you must lie down. You are ill."

His father nodded, still smiling, his skeletal grin scraping at the air. He allowed Laughing Dog to lay him back down on the bed. "Gods be praised. You have come back, my son, my little hyena. And the gods, they spoke to you? You heard their wisdom?"

Pity and dismay welled in Laughing Dog as he stared down at the creature that wore a mockery of his father's face. How could this be their king, First Claw, who had led them across the savanna after their village had burned? How could this be the paragon of strength and wisdom, the man he had both admired and feared as a boy, this doddering creature? Tears welled in his own eyes at the sight of him.

"Yes, Father. I wandered out far, past the savanna and into the sahil, with no food or water. I was very angry. I wanted to prove to my people that I was stronger than their exile, and I nearly died. It was then that Ogya, god of fire, came to me. At first I thought myself mad from hunger and thirst, but I ate and drank, and still I heard his voice. He spoke to me. He speaks to me still. When I stood before you last, I believed the gods distant, uninterested, if they existed at all. And now I know they are real."

"Praise Wem," his father breathed. He relaxed back into his hides. "The gods have been so angry with us, son. They have taken our people. Your brother…" His voice cracked. "My son. Clay. He is gone. Kwaee has taken him from us. We saw the tracks. The forest god stole him away." The streak of a tear glinted in the red light from the embers. "But now that you have seen the wisdom of the gods, we can appease them. You, your brother, I, and all the people, we will have a great fast. We will dance and sing for the gods, and sacrifice our food for them. We will prostrate ourselves before them. Then they will see us and forgive us. They will take back their curse. They will return Clay to us, and the others lost. All will be well." His eyes gazed up past Laughing Dog's shoulder to some imagined place beyond the roof of the tent. "All will be well."

So. All Laughing Dog had to do was bend beneath the gods, was it? The same bargain Ogya had promised. He looked down at his father, whose yellowed teeth showed between lips bent in a smile that beamed all the false reassurances the sick man had dreamt up for himself.

"No," Laughing Dog said. He had resolved not to mention anything of his conflict with the fire god in the sahil, but now, seeing this old and decrepit man desperately grasping for the faintest of hopes, his determination faltered. His father no longer believed in the gods with sincere faith; his beliefs were cobwebs to which he clung, as Cloud did that tattered old dress of hers. He would find neither strength nor solace in them, but only filmy illusion. Saying things would get better would not make them so. Better to confront the truth, whatever it might be, and truth was something only Laughing Dog could grant him. It was not hatred, not arrogance, but pity that drove him to speak.

"Father, I told you the gods spoke to me. But they are not what we imagined. Not what our tales say. They are monsters. Bullies. They care nothing for our worship and prayer. They only want subjugation. They want to control us. And I will tell you something else that I have learned. They fear us, Father. They fear us because they know that we can fight back. We do not have to accept their control."

The old man's eyes bulged. "This is madness, my son. Fight the gods? Why should you wish to fight them? It is impossible."

"It is not impossible. In the sahil, I wrestled with Ogya. He sought to control me. He tempted me with power, and threatened me with death, but I would not yield to him. And I beat him, Father. I won. I took his power for my own."

Shock contorted his father's shriveled face. With bony arms, he pushed himself upright again. "Blasphemy!" he whispered. He shook his head. "I saw it in you, even as a boy. You never revered the gods, the spirits of this world. You took without consideration, you acted without care for the consequences. At first, I thought it was only that your mother's death had stricken you harder than the rest of us, that you were acting out of anger and sadness. I took care with you, used a gentler hand, made more allowances. I thought that harshness would push you further away from us. I believed I needed to allow you to come to the gods in your own time. But all the ways you chose to spite them kept mounting. The stories you told the children. Clay's accident." He sighed. "I did not want to send you away, son. But I saw no other way. A man who cannot find his god among his people may find him in the wilderness. And now you return to me claiming you have changed. You have not changed at all. You are even now defiant. You would damn your own brother with your insolence? Would you damn us all?"

"Damn us?" Laughing Dog asked. "Father, I wish to save us. And we will not do it with prayers and prostrations. We will do it by fighting back. Do you think prayer stopped Ogya when he burned our village and killed our people? Did our dances and blessings and sacrifice move Sarmu to intercede for us? Did Wem send rain?"

He spat on the ground, moved to defiance by the force of his own words, ignoring the horrified expression on his father's face. "No. They ignored us. They left us to suffer and die. And if I had not fought my own fight, I would be lying in the sand with the birds picking my bones. But I fought Ogya. I fought the sahil. And now I am alive and before you. I will tell you how to save Clay, if he is indeed alive and taken by Kwaee, as you say." He knew he was risking banishment once more by continuing, but this was the way it had to be. His father had to see reason.

"We will show the forest god that he, too, must respect us and our strength. We will send our words to him, yes, but in a war dance. And if he does not calm his forest, then I have seen how we may convince him..." There was a low, growling noise coming from behind him, the sound of a predator, so close as to be just behind him, and he broke off, turning to catch it, his hand going to his knife. The ember light flickered in the empty tent. There was nothing there. He turned back to a faint cry from his father.

The old man was shaking. "You are not my son!" he cried. "You are a demon, a monster!"

Laughing Dog reeled back as though he had been struck across the face. He knew his father was stricken with illness and grief; he knew that he had said words the old man did not want to hear, and he had expected an argument, even a rebuke. He had not expected to hear this disownment. Still there was the growling sound behind him, but he knew there was nothing there. Just another trick of Ogya, no doubt, toying with his mind.

"I will destroy you, demon!" his father groaned, his shriveled lips pulled back from his teeth. From the side of his bed, he lifted a bared knife. Laughing Dog had seen it many times before. His father had had it since

Laughing Dog was a boy. With it, he had taught him how to quickly kill a wounded beast, how to gut it, how to strip the pelt away. It was the knife of a hundred early lessons in his father's strong hands. Now it was brandished against him.

"Father, no!" Laughing Dog raised his hands, forgetting his own knife, unable to comprehend that his father was about to attack him for nothing, for saying words that he didn't want to hear. The once proud and brawny King First Claw came at him like a skeletal spider, unrecognizing hatred in his eyes, his teeth and knife point bared. Were he not withered by days upon days of sickness and grief in his tent, he might have killed Laughing Dog then, but now he was feeble and frail, and the slash of his knife fell pitifully short. With one quick block, Laughing Dog knocked the weapon free, but his father clutched at him with both hands, dirty nails clawing at his eyes. He gripped his father's wrist; with his free hand he reached for the King's throat and squeezed. His father gagged and struggled. He raked at Laughing Dog's face, and Laughing Dog turned his head to the side to spare his eyes from the scratches.

He could pin his father now, hold him down, call for Great Ram to help. The man was plainly mad. They could restrain him, get Cloud to boil up something to clear the mind, soothe and calm him. The thought entered his head and fled.

No. Why should he do such a thing? He was not First Claw's son anymore; the old man had said so. His people were in thrall to their King. They would listen to his ravings. Laughing Dog would be exiled once more, this time for good. He could hear Ogya's smug laughter somewhere deep in his mind, somewhere beyond the low growl of the animal pretending to be behind him. He would not be exiled again. He would not accept his father's cruel and pitiless rejection.

The old man's throat bulged in his hand as he gagged, struggling. Laughing Dog kept his head turned away. He squeezed. He ignored the struggling, the pulls, the frail beating of weakened arms against his chest and the side of his face. He pushed the neck in his grip against the bed, forcing it down. Skinny legs kicked erratically. The wet, choking sounds grew fainter.

Then the growl behind him ascended into a loud, bestial roar. The world bent around him as he fell, his torso twisting painfully. Something must have struck him from behind. There was an animal after all. It had not been one of Ogya's deceptions. He was staring up at the ceiling, and was helpless to right himself. He heard his father draw in a great, sucking breath. His hands and feet scrabbled helplessly against the dirt floor, but he could not find his footing; vertigo made him dizzy. His vision swam.

There was another roar. His father screamed, a horrible, high-pitched shriek of pain and terror. Laughing Dog tried desperately to right himself, but still he could not; his body was bent strangely, jerking and twisting. His father screamed again, and this time the scream was cut off by a wet gurgle.

Hot liquid sprayed against Laughing Dog's neck and back, and the tent filled with the smell of blood. Whatever was attacking his father had *him* now, he was being shaken back and forth by something that moved with manic energy.

"Father?" The voice was Great Ram's, from outside the tent, raised in alarm.

Whatever had Laughing Dog dropped him. He collapsed to the ground and lay panting, confused, trying to shake the dizziness and terror from his mind.

The tent flap before him opened, and Ram entered, carrying a flame. He halted upon entry, staring in nude horror. "Father!" he cried. "Father!" Smoke began to cloud the tent.

Woozily, Laughing Dog got to his knees. Pulling the roof open to let the smoke out was something that he could do, so he did it. He didn't want to look around.

"Laughing Dog," his brother said low, shaking, "what did this? Did you see it?"

He turned to follow Ram's gaze. Blood spattered the inside of the tent. Sprawled halfway across the bed lay the corpse of their father, King First Claw. His eyes and mouth gaped toward the roof. His chest was torn open. Much of it was missing. Laughing Dog looked away, unable to bear the sight of it. "I didn't see it."

He remembered the look of terror in his father's eyes, the words "monster" and "demon" shouted—not *at* him after all, but *behind* him, at some creature that he had not been able to see. The old man had been sick and confused, and had been trying to save himself. And now Laughing Dog knew from what. "Father saw it, though," he said. "It was a beast from the forest. Kwaee sent it to kill us. It knocked me down and went after him. It would have killed me too if you had not come. It must have run off."

"Father!" Great Ram bolted from the tent. Laughing Dog could hear him retching into the grass outside.

The back of his head was warm and wet. He raised his fingers to his scalp, pushing them into the coarse, curled hair there, feeling for injury. He could find none, but his fingers came away with blood on them. The creature had been about to kill him, too. Great Ram had saved him.

Keeping his eyes turned away from the horror where his father lay, he stumbled out of the tent. There he found Ram hunched over, hands on his knees. He put his hand on his brother's back. "The forest god has killed our people, our brother, and our father. He very nearly killed me. This has gone too far. There can be no appeasement, no prayer, no sacrifice anymore. The gods have sent fire, drought, and now the very forest itself against us. We have no place left to go. We can no longer submit to their tyranny."

"They killed Father," Great Ram said despairingly. "Father is dead."

"Yes," Laughing Dog answered. He searched inside himself for the grief that he knew he ought to feel, but it was all too soon, too sudden. He could feel only anger, only hatred for the gods that had taken his life from him without his permission, without asking his blessing. The hatred blazed so hotly in him that he could feel nothing else. "And we will make the forest god pay for it. We will fight him. We will hurt him and hurt him until he begs us for mercy."

Great Ram looked over at him, shock and misery in his eyes. "How can we possibly fight the forest itself?"

"With fire, King Great Ram," Laughing Dog said. "We burn it down."

Communion

Doto lay along a branch at the top of a tall tree, gazing down into the clearing in his temple, watching Clay sleep. The little fire bearer was curled up on a bed of moss. Doto could feel the heat of his skin against the fronds of the moss, the rise and fall of his belly as he breathed, the weight of him on the ground, the rhythms of his heartbeat and pulse.

He reached up with one paw to finger the new feather that had sprouted from his forehead, sturdy, blue, a sign that he was worshiped, that he was loved. It was more than Kwaee had ever given him. For year after year he had maintained his father's forest, guarded and guided it, obeyed every order. He had memories of his father being gentle with him, of occasional kindness, but most of their past together had been filled with insults, cuffs, punishments, and casual cruelty.

Now Doto had a fire bearer. He had treated Clay as his father had treated him, but Clay had offered him gentleness, respect, and even devotion. Clay had given him a feather. And something else.

When Doto had healed Clay's foot, the fire bearer had changed, taking on a little bit of godhood. But something in Doto had changed as well. There was now within him, he thought, a little bit of Clay. A vulnerability. He could trip now. He could fall.

When first he went tumbling into the ground, he had not understood what had happened; he thought it might be a new trick of his father's, an attack. But the forest had simply failed to bend before him just a little bit. Just once it had not moved out of his way. It had challenged him, taken him by surprise. He had felt fury at its insolence for a time. But after that, while traveling with Clay, there had been something new. With every step, he was aware of that vulnerability, that his gait was not assured, that at any moment he might go careening toward the ground. The thought was exhilarating.

The forest had warped around him. It was no longer empty. He had become newly and unexpectedly aware of its breadth and power, a mighty living thing all around him that would not always obey him. Mastery of it was not assured. He felt small and massive at the same time: still a god, still brimming with the power to which he had become accustomed, but now no longer apart from the world in which he wielded it. He could not say why everything had changed, but it had. He was excited. There were other new feelings too, little thrills and lulls for which he had no names, because he had never experienced them before. He wondered if this was what it was like to go through the world as a fire bearer, navigating these odd rises of emotion at unexpected times.

He felt one of them now, lying here and gazing down at his sleeping fire bearer. He enjoyed it, as he had enjoyed the dance earlier, when he had sat in the clearing and watched Clay spin and leap around him, singing the song he had invented, twirling on the new foot the way he never could on the old. He had felt through the forest floor each touch of Clay's smooth and furred toes. The new emotion had bubbled in him, given him strange rushes of pleasure like he had never before experienced. He had enjoyed, too, the touch of Clay's teeth on the fruit that he had given him, his senses even part of that for a while. Picked fruit did not live for long, but while it lived, he felt it, felt the warm lick of Clay's tongue and the smooth slide down his throat.

Now, lying atop his branch, he felt Clay stir below. The fire bearer sat upright, looking about. "Doto?"

Doto rolled from the branch and dropped, wondering giddily as he fell if he might miss the landing, slip and tumble onto his face. He focused on landing gracefully, and felt a triumphant swell of pride when he managed it. His sudden appearance seemed to startle Clay, however. "I am here."

The fire bearer smiled. "Oh. I had a dream and then I thought you might be gone."

"I cannot be gone," Doto pointed out. "This is my temple. When you are here, you are within me, even if I travel far away. You will always be with me here." He settled down next to Clay, curling his tail across his toes. "Why did you wake when it is still too dark for you?"

"Actually, I can see a little," Clay said. "I don't know if it is just not as dark a night, or if something is different."

Doto leaned over to peer into his eyes. They did not have the wide, reflective roundness of feline pupils. "I do not think your eyes have changed. But my fetish might help you to see a little better. Is that why you woke? Because you can see?"

"Actually, I think I just woke up because I was cold. And then I wondered where you were."

Doto noticed, now, that the fire bearer's skin was bumpy, and the fur on his leg was standing up. "Your skin is trying to puff your fur out," he observed, "but you haven't got enough."

"I've never needed it. I've never been cold before." Clay leaned toward Doto. "You are warm, though."

"Yes," Doto agreed. "Gods do not get cold." Privately he wondered whether that were true for him anymore. The question was an exciting one. "You may share my heat, if you like."

Clay gave him a questioning look and then scooted closer, leaning into Doto's side. He breathed a long sigh and rested his head in the fur on Doto's chest, putting his arms around him. Doto recalled the night he had tried to carry Clay on his back, and all the uncomfortable feelings that had provoked. This was rather pleasant now, though. Was that another thing that had changed?

Clay's fingers stroked slowly through the fur on his side, producing oddly pleasant sensations. "You're so soft," he murmured.

"Not underneath," Doto felt obliged to point out. "I have sharp bits."

The fire bearer gave a soft laugh. "I wish I could do this all the time."

"You can. You have fur on your own foot now. Any time you want it, it is there."

"It's different," Clay said. His voice was slurred, sleepy. He nestled closer into Doto's side.

There was something about this situation that made Doto uneasy and excited at once. A strange instinct rushed through him, predatory and frightening. His body was preparing to mate; he could feel his arousal rising. This had never happened to him before. He had observed it a few times through other creatures, but never in this body. It was different: intense and compelling. He felt the urge not as a mere animal compulsion, but as desire. He was not sure what to do about it. "Clay," he said.

Clay twitched against him. He must have fallen asleep. "What?" He sat up a little, then sniffed. The scent of Doto's arousal was strong in the air.

"I am not certain, but I think I want to mate."

Clay sat up all the way, the sleepiness leaving his eyes. He looked down at the pink shaft rising up against Doto's belly. "Oh," he said. He didn't look away. "Oh. Um. Do gods...do that?"

"I have never wished to do so before. I think this is new."

Clay looked up at him. "Are you going to go someplace, or do you want me to leave?" He cast a fearful glance toward the borders of the temple, no doubt worrying about the dangers of Kwaee's forest.

"No. I think I want to mate *you*."

The fire bearer stared at him, brown eyes wide. "But—but I'm not a god."

"A small part of you is god," Doto reminded him.

"But I'm not *female*."

Doto shrugged. "I do not see why that matters unless you were hoping for cubs. Many beasts do not seem to mind about male or female much."

"My people mind," Clay said. He edged away a little distance, but he was aroused as well; Doto could easily scent it in the air.

"But it does not seem to matter to you. And who are your people to argue with what you want? Who are they to argue with what a god wants?" He prowled forward toward Clay. The movement seemed right, his instincts growing stronger, more insistent. Why was his fire bearer resisting in this way? Surely his own instincts must be as strong, if not stronger. Doto knew that there were many reasons why he ought to take care at this moment, but they seemed irrelevant, secondary to the pressing, driving need of his loins. He pushed Clay backward into the moss and crouched over him, breathing into his face and chest. His stiffness now ached with irresistible desire. Nothing but the desire mattered now. He would mate with his fire bearer. That was what nature commanded, and as a god of the forest he must yield to its laws. His paws tugged at the bits of hide that covered his fire bearer's middle, breaking them free.

"Wait," Clay said suddenly. He pushed at Doto's chest, a scent of fear mingling with his arousal. "I don't…" Then Doto felt the firm jab of the fire bearer's erection nudge into the soft fur of his belly. "God," Clay groaned, and then his smooth brown arms wrapped tightly around Doto's back, his hips lifting. Doto clasped him as well, holding him firmly in place until all his resisting ceased.

Then they moved, sliding against each other, every shift sending exhilarating physical pleasure through Doto. It was like nothing he had ever experienced before, at once satisfying and intensifying the instincts that compelled him. His fire bearer rocked and thrust beneath him, smoothing fingers through his pelt, over the hard muscle of his chest and arms, gripping at his rump, even nipping at his neck as though he were a successful predator, a thought ludicrous to entertain.

But this was all courtship, and not proper mating. Doto rolled Clay over, more roughly than he had intended to, making the fire bearer groan again. He crouched behind Clay, nestled behind him, and pushed in. Clay cried out at the sensation, but did not resist. Doto sank deep into him, pleasure like none he had ever experienced before rolling through him in waves, compelling his hips to thrust, his paws to grip, to stroke across Clay's sides and down his thighs. He reached for the fire bearer's arousal and found that touching there could produce interesting jumps and twitches in Clay, and around that part of him that was buried inside Clay.

They rutted. The instinct and ecstasy drove Doto to thrust more forcefully, more quickly, and as he did so, he could feel something happening in his temple and the surrounding forest, all the plants responding. Life was reacting to the arousal of a god, growing and developing. Every tree, every bush, every bunch of grass around was forming flowers. Great bell-like orange blossoms unfolded from vines, tiny white flowers began to pepper the trees. Bushes covered themselves in blooms of crimson and gold and violet. Massive green petals uncoiled from the earthen banks nearby.

Doto could sense Clay's surprise, could feel the unusual way his temple was responding, but could not stop it—did not *care* to stop it. He was lost in the giddy rush of his first rut. Clay gave a few startled cries and then bucked beneath him, his erection jumping as it spattered the ground, his insides gripping tightly at Doto. After a few moments more, the wave of intensity carried Doto higher, and then it released him. His body, his whole temple, contracted and then burst, the pleasure surging from him. As a deep satisfaction settled through him, he looked up and saw that the air in his forest had become thick and hazy. No, not haze. It was pollen. The blossoms everywhere had burst with pollen, drifting down to settle over everything in his temple.

His fire bearer nestled into his arms, shaking and panting, smooth skin dampened with sweat, and Doto held him close, allowing him to sleep.

His father would revile him for what he had done—the Doto of two moons ago would have reviled him. He had mated with a beast, with an unfurred, slinking ape, a minion of Ogya, the ancient enemy. He ought to feel shame and disgust, but he did not. Instead, peace settled through him, a calming of the blood. What he had done was right. Clay was his, and no god could tell him otherwise. For the first time in his memory, he wanted something he had.

〜〜

In the early light of dawn, when Clay stirred in his arms, they coupled again, this time more slowly. Doto eased the rough sensation with the application of slick oil brushed from the petals of the large red orchids that had grown in the night. His temple mated with Clay, vine and stem curling around legs and arms, petal and leaf stroking skin, soft moss enveloping the bearer's twitching shaft. He fed Clay fruits as he moved within him, feeling him from every side at once, swallowing him as he was swallowed, surrounding and filling him, embracing him utterly.

They sprawled afterward on the mossy bank of the stream, and Clay dipped his toes into the water, exclaiming at the cold. There, Doto stared at the thick clay layering the banks, and a thought occurred to him. "My father said that clay is dirt. Why are you named after dirt? Did your father and mother worship Mother Fam most of all?"

Clay shook his head, and drew a little spiral in the dirt with his fingers. "My people name their children after the first thing a mother sees after she has given birth. They believe that the gods direct her eyes toward what she needs to see."

"I have never shown any mother anything after she gave birth," Doto declared. "But maybe Father Wem does. So your mother saw dirt when she was born, and you were named after dirt?" He paused. "Is that a name of great honor with your people?" It didn't seem like it could be. But who knew what fire bearers liked? At least Clay had not been named after a flame or the black clouds.

Smiling, Clay said, "It was in the time before our village burned. The rains were coming less and less often. It had been a very dry season, and we were all looking for water. My mother insisted on helping even though she was with child. She feared that without water I might die. She and my brother Great Ram traveled most of the day looking for water, but had found nothing, and just as they were about to turn around, she felt me coming. She gave birth to me out there, on the savanna, on the hot earth, and when she looked up, the first thing she saw was rich red clay in the soil. Where there is clay, there is water nearby. This was clay from a stream bed. If she had not birthed me there, she would not have seen it, but because she did, my brother was able to follow the bed to a muddy patch, and there he dug and found water for my people."

Clay leaned against Doto's shoulder. "When I asked her, she always told me that I was not named after dirt, but the promise that we would survive. She said that my name was a reason for joy."

Doto looked at him seriously. "Then it is a good name for you."

When the sun was high, he grew fruits, nuts, and tubers for Clay to eat, never tiring of the sensation of being consumed by his fire bearer, of giving him obvious pleasure and satisfaction. They climbed one of Doto's trees and nestled in the crook of its branches, gazing out over the forest and lake below, and there, Doto stiffened again, their tree growing taller in its sympathetic response, and with one paw, he guided Clay's mouth down below the white fur of his belly, letting his bearer consume him that way as well. The ground of the entire temple was by now coated in a fine layer of yellow pollen. There, in the tree, Doto considered the events of the past days, his father's fury, the changes that had happened to him, and found a decision that was simple to come to.

"You will stay here in my temple from now on," he said the next morning. He felt Clay tense against the soft earth of his riverbank and knew that the bearer was about to argue this, but for what reason, he had no idea. So much of Clay was still a mystery to him.

"I love being here with you. But my people..." Clay's fingers brushed at the fur on Doto's chest, and then tightened, gripping it. He gazed out over the forest. "I miss them. I miss my brothers. I miss my father. I need to tell them what I have learned, about Kwaee, about you, so they can worship you as well."

"I want only you to dance for me," Doto declared. He did not know why he suddenly desired it so strongly.

Clay just smiled. "And if Kwaee has turned the forest against them, as you say, then I need to help them. They need the forest. I must find a way to change Kwaee's mind."

"Kwaee will not move on this," Doto told him. "He does not change his mind about things. It is useless to try."

"Maybe so. But I still have to. And just because he hasn't changed his mind before, that doesn't mean he can't. Maybe if we pray to him..."

Doto shook his head. "It will not affect him. We do not hear these prayers of yours."

"Are you sure? Because you've done everything I prayed for."

"What?" Doto frowned. His skin prickled.

Clay stretched out his foot, wiggling the furred toes. "You gave me your strength and endurance, just like I prayed for."

"That is coincidence. It was my choice that caused me to do this thing, not your prayer."

The bearer shrugged and nestled down against his chest again. "But I must find a way to help my people."

"You are safe in my temple," Doto pointed out. "Even Kwaee cannot enter here without my permission. Out there, he will find you. His baboons will kill you. Or perhaps he will send something else—biting flies, or wasps, or leopards, or elephants. I will not allow this to happen to you."

"You can protect me. And now I can run again, so the journey will not take so long. But I cannot stay inside here my whole life, Doto. Wonderful as it is, if I can't leave, it's a cage."

Doto felt a flash of anger. "I am not a cage!" he snarled. Throughout his temple, he felt thorny vines sprout from the soil.

Clay pushed at his chest, leaning away. His eyes were troubled. "Doto," he said.

Doto growled, his thorns growing longer and sharper, filling in the spaces between the trees. "Do not push me. You will lie down. You will mate with me and dance with me, and stay here in my temple. You are my worshiper. I am your god, and I command you, and you will obey me."

Instead of nodding and obeying, as he had always done, the bearer stood up. "No," he said. His voice was firm. His toes clenched resolutely on Doto's soil.

"No?" Doto repeated, staring. No? He sprang to his feet. "You do not say no! You cannot say no to a god! You worship. You obey. You bow down. You do what I tell you."

"I want to. I want to be with you. But my people. My father, my brothers. They're important to me. I must do something to save them. And Doto, what if things get worse somehow? I can't stay, even if a god commands me to. I have to do this."

Fury burned hot in Doto's face and ears. His claws unsheathed, his tail lashed. Never had any creature in all the forest ever dared to defy him. "I do not care about any of that," he said. "None of your stupid people or their far-away village. Only you. You are mine."

Clay just looked at him, his eyes sadder.

"You will worship me. Now."

"No," Clay said. "I won't."

"Yes! Dance for me. You will dance and then I will mate you. Dance now!"

Clay shook his head. "No."

Doto roared.

The fire bearer cringed before him, lifting his paws in front of his face. All around, the temple evinced his fury. Branches split, their broken ends jabbing down toward Clay. The brambles grew thicker, snaking out from between the trees, ready to twine around him and slice him to shreds. Beneath his feet, huge, jagged boulders erupted, sending him staggering backward, all of them ready to press together and crush him between them. The little brown fire bearer hunched, naked, in the middle of a prison of pain, shrinking away as the thorns grew toward his skin, the sharp points grazing it.

Doto roared again, rage boiling in him. But he could do nothing. He couldn't hurt Clay, couldn't even bear to see him cringing and frightened like this. Maybe his father was right, after all. Maybe the fire bearer's magic had gotten inside him and made him weak. It was unfair. How could Clay best him like this? How could a puny, fragile fire bearer just refuse him like that and there be nothing he could do about it?

"Doto," Clay said in a frightened voice. "Please."

Doto's anger fell away from him as though it had never been. The stones toppled to their sides; the branches lifted; the brambles withered and died where they stood. "I'm sorry," he whispered. He stepped to Clay's side and put his arms around him. "I'm not him."

Clay clutched around his chest. "I know," he said.

A bead of blood welled at his cheek where a thorn tip had grazed it, and Doto licked it clean with a swipe of his rough tongue.

"I'm not a cage," he said.

"I know." Clay settled down to the ground, the places where the rocks had erupted already sprouting new, soft grass. He pulled Doto down with him and rested at his side once more. For a while he was quiet, and Doto wondered if the fire bearer would be afraid of him now, if he would cringe when he saw him, or not worship him with truth in his dance. The thought was intolerable.

"Your temple is a paradise," Clay said after a while. "Beautiful beyond description, just as you are. But could you remain here for your whole life?"

"No," Doto admitted grudgingly. The thought was not appealing. Here it was only him, and life was what happened when you went outside yourself. If he stayed here forever, stayed in any one place forever, he would become like Kwaee, never looking beyond the immediate world, ignorant, blind, somehow small. Kwaee never went outside himself.

A thought occurred to him. "We should go see Sarmu," he said.

Clay turned to look up at his chin. "The savanna god?"

"Yes. My father says the fire bearers sided with Ogya, and turned against the forest long ago. But I no longer believe all his stories. If there is something else to know about what happened, Sarmu may know it. He was born out of the war between Ogya and Kwaee. And I have heard he likes to talk."

"Heard? You've never met him?"

"Of course not. Sarmu is in the savanna. He would not come into the forest."

"And you have never left it?" Clay asked.

Uncomfortably, Doto answered, "No. The closest I have come to leaving the forest was when I went to retrieve you. It is not something a god likes to do, leave his own domain. The lesser gods, the animal gods, they may go anywhere, as do Mother Fam and Father Wem. But we do not." His ears folded back at a sudden wave of anxiety such as he had not felt since he was a cub and Kwaee was angry with him. "I do not like the idea of going. I do not know the savanna. I do not know how to navigate it."

Clay sat up. "But I do. If you can tell me how to find a god, then I can take you there. I can hunt, find food and water, and navigate."

Doto considered. To stay in the forest would be preferable, but if Kwaee was turned against Clay, and if he were keeping secrets Doto ought to know, then staying was not the best choice. All the same, leaving the shelter of the forest filled him with a creeping dread. "All right. I think I know how to find Sarmu, if you can help me get there."

"And then we will go see my father and advise him on what to do next," Clay said.

Doto hesitated at that. He did not want to agree to this. There was no reason why he ought not to. But he did not want to take Clay back to the fire bearers. What had they ever done for Clay? Caused him to injure his foot, made him useless. And he, Doto, had healed it, put his own strength into Clay. He had mated with the bearer. Clay was his, not theirs. He opened his mouth to refuse, and then saw the sad, hopeful look in the bearer's wide brown eyes. "All right," he said. "After that, I will take you back to your people."

Clay nestled back against him, and he was silent, stroking at the bearer's shoulder, but his thoughts were elsewhere. Clay could not live in the forest, not so long as Kwaee raged. And Doto could not stay outside it. That was what they would decide when Clay returned to his people. They would be apart once more. Doto thought about what Clay had said, that Doto had done everything Clay had prayed for. He thought then about another prayer that he had heard, the prayer from the aged fire bearer who had stood beneath them while they hid hanging from a tree branch above. *Return my son to me. Restore what is lost.* Doto tightened his grip about the fire bearer. Could his new feelings truly be nothing more than a clever trick of the enemy? If they were, he could do nothing to stop them. He was helpless before them. He could no more fight them than he could hurt Clay. Nor did he even wish to. All the same, he vowed to himself, no one would ever take his worshiper away from him. Clay was his, and always would be.

All through his temple, new bushes began to grow, thick and lush, leaves spreading, tiny white flowers blooming and wilting and dropping away. They left fat, dark purple berries behind them, glistening with juice, sweet as honey, and deadly poison.

⌒

The journey to the savanna's edge took several days, and was largely uneventful. Each night, while Clay slept, Doto kept watch, sending his senses out into the surrounding forest to feel for Kwaee's agents—baboons or leopards or sharp-eyed eagles. But he felt no creatures that moved with any apparent purpose. Why Kwaee stayed hidden away, even now, Doto did not have any idea. Surely he must have felt the dance again, felt the new saplings sprout around the temple when Clay danced. But if his father knew where they were, or even cared, he made no further attack against them. Doto led them straight north, toward the closest edge of the forest, far to the east of Clay's village.

If Clay was angry at Doto for roaring at him in the temple, he said nothing of it. In the afternoons, he would reach for Doto, or Doto for him, and they would collapse into a bed of leaves or a moss bank and mate again. Clay's initial, puzzling reluctance to mating seemed to have disappeared, and he moved against Doto with an enthusiasm that was both surprising and welcome. Their times together left bright explosions of flowers and pollen on the forest floor, and a giddy, bubbling emotion in Doto that he could not name, but that often made him smile inexplicably. Then he would remember where they were going, and his mood would sink all over again.

They ran with swiftness, and Doto was pleased to see that Clay was quickly building his endurance, requiring fewer rests. The bearer plainly loved to run, and if his gait was unusual and lopsided, he compensated for it with a sleek and easy grace that would have made any leopard proud.

Soon it was Doto holding their progress back, and then only because the trees were thinning. They were reaching the edge of the forest. His senses, usually sharp and resonant with the eyes and ears of the forest, dulled. Clay seemed to notice it too, as he began rubbing his ears and groping for the carved fetish about his neck. "I feel like I'm going blind and deaf," he complained.

"Yes," Doto said. "It is my power weakening. It is like this where the forest thins."

"Have I already grown so used to it?" Clay wondered aloud.

Doto shrugged, and they continued. Clay spent much of the time, with Doto's assistance, making preparations. They needed containers to hold water and food, and so Doto used his magic to create bowls and something called baskets out of shaped bark, wood, and leaves. They collected food as well, as Clay told Doto that it would be rare out on the savanna, and it would be best to be prepared. Within another day, they reached the beginning of the savanna.

To look at the forest, one might assume that it thinned out, blended with savanna, and eventually stretched into open plains, and one would not be wrong to assume it. But the forest had a border, a line that Doto had never crossed. Beyond it, he had no dominion. The world went dim and dull, his senses of life and energy cut off as surely as they had been with the stones of Abansin. Now he was approaching that border; he could feel it with a sense of mortal dread, and wondered if that was what beasts felt when they approached death.

He slowed to a stop, his tail rigid and bristling. He grasped at Clay's paw. There were few trees here, and the sun shone openly down on them. There was no cover, less greenery, the grass burned white by the sun. Ahead of them was a wall, a ripple in the air that rose up above the treetops. "Do you see it?" he asked Clay.

The bearer nodded up at him. "What is it?"

"The edge of the forest."

"It never looked like that before."

Doto tapped the carved leopard meaningfully.

"So if we go through that," Clay said, "It will be just like before, without the fetish? I spent my whole life that way. I can manage it." His brown eyes searched Doto's face. "But what about you?"

"I do not want to go. I have changed my mind. Let us stay here in the forest. We will find some other way to stop my father."

Clay shook his head. "No. I have to go. Come on. It will be fine." Doto shook his head and stepped backward, but Clay just pulled his paw free and bolted toward the border before Doto could stop him.

Hissing under his breath, he ran after, his fur on end. The world muted around him, life and color draining from it. He knew that he should be able to catch up to Clay, but the ability to move with lightning swiftness had fled him.

Clay reached the wall before him and pushed through it as though it were not there, but on the other side, he stumbled and fell onto his hands and knees, the sense of him in the forest vanishing from Doto's awareness. The sudden absence was startling and painful, a hollow that appeared in Doto's chest, and he knew that it was because a part of him had disappeared behind that wall. When he passed beyond it, would he wink out of existence?

He had no time to stop himself, though; his divine powers had all but fled him, and he careened through the border after Clay—Clay, who still had two feet, but now feet that each had flat nails on the five small toes, and smooth, brown, furless skin.

Doto passed through the border, and his world vanished.

For a while, he lay curled up on the hard, painful ground, bristles of stubby grass jabbing into his skin. He couldn't breathe. The air was hot, thick, and dead in his lungs. It had no scent or flavor.

"Doto?" Clay's voice seemed to come from a great distance. A paw rested on his shoulder and shook him. He opened his eyes. The harsh light of the savanna stung them. Above him was the shadow of Clay's figure against the stone blue sky. "It feels uncomfortable, doesn't it?"

Uncomfortable? Doto pawed at the ground, trying to push himself upright. The earth was rough against his fingers. He groped at Clay's arm, gripped it, and pulled himself to his feet, his weight heavy and unbalanced on his toes. His ears went back, his tail jerking as he tried to find his poise. Instead he stumbled and leaned on Clay's shoulder, who grunted with his weight, but held him up.

"I do not like this," he said. His voice sounded thin and weak to him. He wanted to call on his plants to support him, to catch him, but there was nothing. His senses ended at his toes and fingers.

"That was the hard part," Clay told him. "It will get better from here. Come on. I will help you."

Before him, the savanna burned, yellow and angry and hostile. Here, he knew, he was mortal. He might not die, but he could lie dying for an eternity, unable to return to his temple where he would be restored.

Over his shoulder was the forest, green and lush and dripping with life and death and magic. It glowed for him, ached for him, shivered without him. Kwaee no longer tended it, so what would happen to it in his absence? Would it go still and wrong like Abansin? His forest needed him. He needed it.

But Clay housed a part of him, a little wisp of his power. Clay walked a path to secrets from Doto's past, to soothing his father's anger and quelling the forest's rage against the fire bearers, who would surely retaliate against it if they could. Clay had danced for him, had given him the feather that still sprouted from his brow. Clay had worshiped him, had loved him. He needed Clay more.

He breathed hot, dry savanna air into his lungs, and leaned on Clay's shoulder. "Let's go."

About the Author

Ryan Campbell was raised in Arkansas in a family of nine, but eventually escaped to California to seek his fortune. Instead, he found a job at a university. In 2008, he married his husband David, and they live happily together in the San Francisco Bay Area. There, he tries to write the kinds of books that kept him both sane and strange growing up. He is the author of *Smiley and the Hero*, the *Fire Bearers* series, and numerous short stories.

About the Artist

Zhivago is a freelance fantasy artist born and raised in southern California, where she still lives with her boyfriend and two cats: Tequatchi and Kumatora. The oldest of five equally artistically-inclined sisters, she works in a wide variety of mediums and styles and is always on the prowl for new creative challenges. You can find more about her art and design work, including a schedule of upcoming conventions, at *www.fandomfashions.com*.

About the Publisher

Sofawolf Press was founded in 1999 to provide a venue to showcase great anthropomorphic storytelling and promote the genre to a wider audience.

Since the debut of their first publication, the short-story anthology *Anthrolations*, they have produced over 75 publications including: novels, shared-world and thematic anthologies, short story collections, graphic novels, artists' sketch books, and some things that defy categorization.

Their publications, and the talent featured within them, have been the recipients of numerous nominations and awards, including: 23 Annual Anthropomorphic Literature & Arts awards, one Russ Manning Promising Newcomer nomination for Teagan Gavet's work on the graphic novel *Nordguard: Across Thin Ice*, and both the 2012 Hugo Award for Best Graphic Story and the 2013 Mythopoeic Society Adult Literature award for Ursula Vernon's fantasy graphic novel *Digger*.

Visit their website at *www.sofawolf.com* for more information about their titles, submission guidelines, and upcoming events and releases.